Follow
the
Spinning Sun

Follow the Spinning Sun

A Novel

Leandro Thomas Gonzales

SUNSTONE PRESS

SANTA FE

Sunstone books may be purchased for educational, business, or sales promotional use.
For information please write: Special Markets Department, Sunstone Press,
P.O. Box 2321, Santa Fe, New Mexico 87504-2321.

Book and Cover design › Vicki Ahl
Body typeface › Arial
Printed on acid-free paper
∞

_____

Library of Congress Cataloging-in-Publication Data

Gonzales, Leandro Thomas.
  Follow the spinning sun : a novel / by Leandro Thomas Gonzales.
    p. cm.
  ISBN 978-0-86534-866-0 (softcover : alk. paper)
  1. Indians of North America–Fiction. 2. New Mexico–Fiction. I. Title.
  PS3607.O546F65 2012
  813'.6–dc23
                          2012022558

_____

WWW.SUNSTONEPRESS.COM
SUNSTONE PRESS / POST OFFICE BOX 2321 / SANTA FE, NM 87504-2321 /USA
(505) 988-4418 / ORDERS ONLY (800) 243-5644 / FAX (505) 988-1025

This book is dedicated to Lucille,
the love of my life since high school,
and to our two children, Darrell and Erika.

Acknowledgements

My thanks go out to:

My wife, Lucille, who with her limited eyesight, spent countless hours reading and editing all drafts. I would not have accomplished this work without her valuable feedback, encouragement, and moral support.

My children, Darrell and Erika, and also, author and songwriter, David Salazar, for reading my first draft and encouraging me to keep on writing.

Melody Groves, Rob Spiegel, and Kirk Hickman for teaching me the ropes of writing, editing, and getting published.

The staff of Sunstone Press for making *Follow the Spinning Sun* a reality.

My mother, who instilled my faith in God, and my father, who taught me how to work hard and persevere toward my goals.

Preface

This book is about the abandonment of an ancient village, Tyuoni, by the Anasazi (ancestral Puebloans). The spectacular Tyuoni ruins, along with the cliff dwellings, served as enough reason for the United States to establish the Bandelier National Monument in New Mexico.

I based this novel on the legend about the Great Migration, where the spinning sun led the Anasazi away from their ancestral homelands to new locations. I associated the role of the spinning sun to the cloud, in the Book of Exodus, that led the Jewish people out of Egypt. The legend intrigued me, because records of the spinning sun are found, not only on petroglyph etchings throughout the Americas, but also on ancient Buddhist temples in Asia, the place where the Great Migration is believed to have originated.

When one visits Bandelier National Monument, Chaco Cultural National Historical Park, Mesa Verde National Park, Canyon de Chelly National Monument, or any other Anasazi site, one cannot help but imagine what it must have been like to have lived in such an exciting community. We can envision the many festivities and societies taking place within the massive, complex, and elaborate structures. These people must have lived a good and secure life. Yet, they left everything behind and moved to other locations. I find it difficult to fathom how any new settlement could possibly approach the appeal of the places they left behind.

Some anthropologists have stated that a severe and prolonged drought led entire villages to pack up and leave. Others hypothesized that war would have been enough reason for them to have abandoned their villages. However, by considering the legend of the Great Migration, especially when coupled with the fact that religion was at the center of these peoples' lives, I propose that religion must have been the real reason. I wrote this novel to show how this could have been the case.

I could not write about the Anasazi without addressing the role that Chaco must have played amongst the myriad of villages in the Four Corners area comprising of vast sections of New Mexico, Arizona, Utah and Colorado. The impressive array of roads leading to Chaco has been compared to the "all roads lead to Rome" phenomena. I chose to portray Chaco as being the center for religious activity.

There have been many misconceptions about the religion of the Native American. What has been labeled as dance or art form is actually sacred prayer with Great Grandfather (God, the Almighty Creator) and with the gods (angels). The gods would prescribe how to heal the sick, answer prayers, or even how to look into the future through the use of intricately prepared rituals. Ceremonial dress and makeup, the words used in their prayers and songs, the various body movements of their prayer dances, and the symbols and figures used pertained to their religious beliefs, not art.

The impetus for this novel was my personal quest to better understand the Native American. I enjoyed my half-Apache grandfather's stories about his college baseball playing days. He was one of the first students to attend Saint Michael's Indian College in Santa Fe. He passed away when I was a teenager, which limited my opportunity to ask him more details about his experiences growing up, especially those pertaining to his Native American heritage. I patterned the love and attention he gave his grandchildren into the elderly protagonist's traits in this novel. Grandpa Thomas certainly wanted us to grow up to follow the path of life set forth by our Almighty Creator. My childhood memories, discussions with Native American friends and acquaintances, and literary research on the Anasazi were implemented in the development of this story.

It is of interest to note that the Los Alamos National Laboratory, the birthplace of the atomic bomb, sits on a mountaintop above Tyuoni. A portion of the land occupied by the Anasazi for hundreds of years has now been settled by several thousand scientists and engineers involved in nuclear weapons research and development. This ancient place, once home to a society based on religion, is now home to a most modern society based on the latest advances of science and technology.

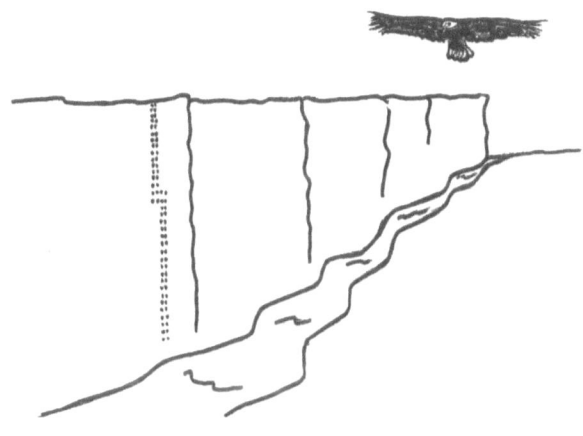

An Eagle's Feather

Jopin diverted his attention to the burning logs, to the occasional popping and snapping sounds that came from the fire, and to the reflection of the flames on the sacred images painted on the wall behind the elders. At times, the flickering firelight appeared to make the sacred images come to life and dance to the beat of distant drums, but not today. Even those favorite distractions of his failed to calm his troubled mind. His close friend, Chief Salamander, had betrayed him and proposed an event that could possibly destroy the lives of everyone in the village.

Chief Salamander proclaimed the time had come for the people of Tyuonyi to pack up and join the Great Migration, an event which was started by the ancestors many generations ago.

Everyone knew they would someday be called to finish the migration, so the proclamation wasn't that much of a surprise. Jopin certainly did not expect it to happen in his lifetime.

His chief's actions concerned him more than the evacuation. Chief Salamander had spoken with such authority, saying it was Great Grandfather's will. Thus, the elders would have no choice, but to obey. Instead of following the standard procedure of opening the meeting for discussion or debate, he tried to get the elders to start preparing the entire tribe for the move out of the village.

Two days had already passed and not one of the elders had been brave enough to take a stand or challenge their chief. Jopin would have ordinarily made a counterproposal designed to compel them to stop and think about the authenticity of the revelation or about the consequences of the evacuation. He would have led them to challenge the proposal, but this time Chief Salamander had ordered him to abstain from all discussions.

Why? This one command emotionally shook Jopin. Could it be that his services were no longer appreciated or needed? This thought kept nagging him as he sat there, witnessing Chief Salamander's performance.

Jopin attempted to read the faces of the elders to determine how all of them had managed to remain so devoid of emotion. He knew they would portray every passing moment of his silence as support for Chief Salamander, which in itself, added to his anxiety. Could he continue to let Chief Salamander get away with it? Like a mute with a lifetime of thoughts and emotions locked up inside of him, Jopin yearned to shout out everything or anything that could stop this madness from happening.

The smell of the burning logs reminded Jopin about the time when he first moved to the village of Tyuonyi and attended a Bear Clan meeting in the small, smoke-filled kiva. The clansmen asked him to participate in discussions pertaining to the selection of their new leader. This leader would also represent them in the village council of elders. Not knowing much about the clan or about village government, he asked some very interesting questions. "If this leader would be pressured to do something that could hurt his fellow clansmen or his family, what should he do? What should be the ideal qualities of a good elder?" His thought-provoking questions and ideas impressed his fellow clansmen, so they asked him, an inexperienced newcomer, to become their leader.

He became the youngest elder to ever serve in the village. Jopin joined the team of eight clan leaders and assisted the chief in managing the rules and laws established to govern the people of the Tyuonyi tribe. He lacked confidence at that time, so he turned to prayer, especially when dealing with major challenges. A more-experienced elder had told him about the Shrine of the Soaring Eagles, a sacred place high on the edge of a cliff, where answers to prayers were granted, but only after a difficult and dangerous climb. The cliff was about seventy-men high.

He reached for the eagle feather he had carried with him since that first climb many years ago and gently stroked it with his finger tips. The treasured feather gave him a sense of pride and satisfaction, and more importantly, hope when dealing with difficult situations.

Chiefs and elders had come and gone, but Jopin had somehow managed to remain on the council. The villagers never asked him to serve as their chief. However, the Bear Clan kept him as their leader. This made him, an eighty-year-old man, the oldest and longest serving elder of the village. Perhaps he never possessed the qualities required of a chief.

Memories came to him of days past when he and Bright-sunflower, his wife, walked or just relaxed on the banks of Frijoles Creek. His children laughed, bathed, chased fish, and played their favorite games in the clear water. They enjoyed everything about their homeland, the beautiful creek, the spectacular canyons, the majestic cliffs, and the tolerable weather, even during the cold of winter. Because of his deep love for his homeland and the good life which the village had provided his family, it would be difficult, if not impossible, to find a better place.

Once a large man, Jopin now stood somewhat thinner and short in stature, but rather distinguished looking with long, silvery hair tied back behind his ears and hanging down past his shoulders. He usually held his head up high as he sat on his designated bear rug, a position adjacent to Chief Salamander. Although known for sometimes having too much to say, Jopin remained focused, and thus, very successful in getting the chief and other elders to side with him on issues of importance.

The people awaited the new growth of vegetation and the appearance of newborn animals, the rebirth of life arriving after a long winter of sleep and death. The time had come to bless the corn, beans, chile, tomatoes, squash, and melon seeds before planting them into the moist ground. Some of the villagers discussed how they would prepare the soil for the new growing season. Others made a game out of predicting the words, prayers, and ceremonies the elders would use when asking the gods for the right mixture of rain and sunshine. The people expected the elders to emerge from the kiva with plans and preparations for the upcoming spring festivities and ceremonies. They were wrong.

Chief Salamander called a short break, so Jopin had an opportunity to have a private conversation with Elder Pine-needle. Jopin expressed his concerns about how Chief Salamander had managed to skillfully keep the elders under his control and about how he ordered Jopin to refrain from participating in the discussions.

"That doesn't make any sense. Why would he do such a thing? You worked hard to get the people to appoint him as our new chief, and you've always been his strongest ally, his most trusted friend. He designated you as his senior elder, so there must be some other reason for his actions."

"That's why I'm sharing this information with you. He may not want me to do anything to ruin his plans for the evacuation. Have you heard anything?"

Pine-needle waited a while before responding. "Just that people have complained about you having more power than he, our chief."

"What? That's not true. I've supported Chief Salamander in everything he has ever proposed. I ask a lot of questions, but that's how we sometimes uncover the real problem or hidden problems. This usually helps him. It's not to oppose him. He understands why I do what I do. Besides, this is the worst possible time for him to worry about such things. His latest actions make him appear quite childish and immature. We're talking about abandoning our village, and he's worried about his power?"

Pine-needle told Jopin about the scandal. "Heard you were being blamed for an old ruling, of twenty or more years ago, the one that prohibits the thieves and promiscuous women from residing within the Tyuonyi walls. They say the ruling was based on your personal prejudices and feelings, and not necessarily on something for the good of the people."

"That's ridiculous. All of the elders voted on it. The more I hear about such nonsense, the more I realize I no longer should be the senior elder. He could've talked to me about this. I'm very uneasy about his motives."

"I'm also beginning to worry, now that I've talked to you."

Chief Salamander called the meeting back to order. "Are there any questions or issues that have to be addressed? I would like for us to now have a quick vote and tomorrow, start working on the specifics of the move."

Jopin stood up. "I'm sorry Chief, but I must leave. I'm either coming down with an illness or getting sick to my stomach over this situation. Father Sun hasn't even started to spin, so why are we talking about leaving our homeland? I urge each of you elders to go home and pray for an answer. We must not make a mistake. Each and every one of us should question if Great Grandfather really expects us to leave this village where he brought our ancestors to live in, in the first place. My fellow elders, there has never been a more serious time when prayer is needed, than right now." Finally, having spoken what had been on his mind, he walked towards the ladder and proceeded to climb out of the chamber. "I must go."

Chief Salamander quickly glanced at Jopin and then made eye contact with the other elders. "Yes, I completely agree with Jopin. This will be the biggest, most important decision we will ever have to make. Please go home and take some time to pray for an answer. I, myself, spent every night in prayer while attending the All-chiefs' Pow-wow at Chaco. Every one of the chiefs in attendance decided the time had indeed come to evacuate. We each saw the sun spinning in our visions. I'm sure you will arrive at the same conclusion. We have no choice but to obey our Almighty Creator. Let's meet tomorrow morning and get this settled."

Jopin had already climbed out of the kiva when Chief Salamander yelled out, "Jopin, we pray you will get some rest tonight. You need to feel better to vote tomorrow. We should get this matter settled early in the morning."

Jopin smiled when he saw two rabbit pelts hanging from a pole near the entrance to his home. Deer-tracker must have come to visit his grandmother. The deerskins, which were used to cover the entrance, had been tied over to one side to allow fresh air to enter. He saw Bright-sunflower sitting on the floor next to a large willow basket full of roots and fresh picked greens. She was humming one of her favorite tunes, as she stirred a large pot of stew with a long wooden paddle. The heat from the burning coals radiated all the way to Jopin. He couldn't help but notice how beautiful she looked as she slaved in front of the hot fire. He stepped inside to give her a hug. "You've been cooking all day."

Bright-sunflower smiled as she turned to greet him. "I made a new pot of yucca and sunflower roots with rabbit, your favorite. Are you still fasting, or can you have some?"

"What would I do without my wonderful wife and also, without my grandson? I saw the pelts outside. You've been cooking all day, and it smells delicious, but I must continue to fast. I wish I could tell you about the mess we're in. We certainly need the gods to come down and help us get through this one. Why do things have to be so difficult?"

Bright-sunflower put her hands on top of Jopin's. "My dear husband, would you like to talk about it? Please let me help you. You don't have to disclose any council secrets, just share enough for us to talk. I've never seen you like this before. Something very serious must be happening. You haven't eaten anything for two days, and you toss and turn so much at night. You can't possibly be getting any rest."

"You help, just by understanding me. I've been lucky to have had you as my wife all these years, especially in difficult times. Please continue to believe in me and please pray for Tyuonyi."

"It must be very serious, if you're asking me to pray for our entire tribe. You have more than served your people. Why don't you let someone else take over? Chief Salamander has seven other elders to help him run the village. You don't have to put up with so much, not at your age. I'm sure they will understand. I would love for you to devote the rest of your life to us."

With words barely audible, "Chief Salamander wants me out of the way." He told her about the scandal and how Chief Salamander had asked him to refrain from participating in the discussions.

Bright-sunflower put her hands on his shoulders, putting her face next to his. "Well, that settles it. I received an answer to my prayers. You don't have to go back. You are mine and mine, alone." She started to chuckle. "That explains why you've been tossing and turning so much in your sleep. They aren't letting you talk."

"That's not funny." He then looked deep into her eyes, "I wish for nothing more than to stay home with you. However, I must first deal with this very important and grave challenge."

"No, my husband, they don't want to hear what you have to say. Stay home and talk to me. I'll listen to each and every word coming from your mouth. I appreciate you more than you will ever know."

"I do know, but you don't understand. I have to get us, and I mean everyone, through this one last crisis, now that I'm still the senior elder."

"No. Old people should stay home, where other people don't have to listen to them. Don't you see? Chief Salamander wants you to keep your mouth shut. I keep reminding you to stop giving advice and telling people what to do, but you don't listen. The other elders should run the council. You have already more than served the village. Let them handle whatever comes. You must let them take over."

"I will. I already asked my friends from the Bear Clan to find someone else. I feel so strong about what Chief Salamander wants, that—"

"Chief Salamander is a good man and also, your very good friend. Don't interfere. He's probably doing this for all of us."

"You're probably right, but this is something I can't ignore."

You don't have to do anything. If you had retired a long time ago, like I asked you to, you wouldn't even know about this crisis. Go visit Chief Salamander tonight and tell him today is your last day."

"I wish it were that simple. Believe me. I must participate in this ordeal. Tyuonyi needs a miracle. I better get back to my prayers."

She shook her head. "I'll go to bed and give you some privacy."

Alone, Jopin attempted to pray, but his emotions continued to interfere with his concentration. He finally joined Bright-sunflower and cuddled up to her.

He awoke early, before sunrise, and started to pray aloud. Bright-sunflower remained quiet under her fur blanket. Dressed in his ceremonial tunic, he placed his pipe, tobacco, and other sacred items into his large pouch. Then he grabbed his eagle feather and stepped out onto the plaza. He walked past the kiva, towards the village exit, and then proceeded on to the base of the cliff. The darkness prevented him from seeing the finger and toe holes carved into the face of the cliff, so he waited in the cold, for daylight.

He groaned as he pulled himself up to the first pair of holes, and then to the next, and to the next. After a short rest, he took a deep breath and conquered another set of holes. Each set became more difficult than the previous. It didn't take long before his strength had been exhausted, so he wedged himself into a vertical crevice. Dizzy, shaky, and becoming desperate, he barely managed to hang on. He should have known better than to think that at his age, he could still climb the cliff.

Jopin focused his attention on the canyon below, where the glittering sun reflected off the surface of the stream in those areas that weren't completely covered over by the tall pine trees. The deep canyon snaked its way towards his beloved village, bringing with it, sparkling water, all kinds of vegetation, and so much wildlife. What a fantastic view of his majestic homeland.

Raising his eyes to the skies above, he started to pray. "Almighty Great Grandfather, you placed your people here in this paradise where Mother Earth has provided our every need. You have given us so much vegetation and an abundance of food with so many animals: the bear, the deer, rabbits, squirrels, the birds, fish, reptiles, and the many insects. You placed all our brother creatures here to live alongside your people, for us to enjoy and eat. Our ancestors told stories about the lands they left behind. They never talked about leaving a place as beautiful as Tyuonyi. My heart is saddened."

He continued to thank his creator for sending Father Sun to cast his rays of sunshine upon him in the morning cold. Jopin attempted to loosen his grip, as his weak legs started to shake and slip out of the crevice. His fingers were bleeding. "Please send your gods from the mountaintop to help me. Tell them to give me the strength and determination I need to continue my climb to the top. May you accept my sacrifice and answer my question. Send me a sign. Speak and your servant will listen. I will do whatever you ask of me, but I need to hear it from you. Take me to the top, where I can get closer. I want to present my prayer to my brother eagles. They will spread their wings, fly up to the sky, and deliver my prayer to you."

Father Sun continued on his path across the sky, beating down and making it more uncomfortable. Jopin's hands had become numb. Weak from lack of food and sleep, he worried that he would start to lose consciousness.

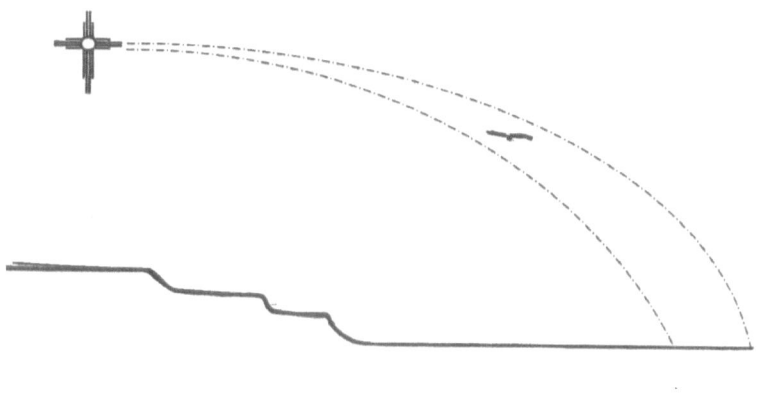

The Path of the Sun

Chief Salamander walked to the kiva in the early morning darkness, carrying a few burning ambers in a wide-handled clay pot. He swept aside the burnt coals out of the fire pit with a small flat rock, placed the hot burning ambers in their place, and then crisscrossed twigs and small logs on top of the flames. Jopin usually started the fire in the chamber, but Salamander couldn't sleep. He finally decided to get up and prepare for the council meeting. The details of evacuating the entire village were mind-boggling. He had intended to get the elders to concentrate on the migration instead of on the decision to evacuate. Everything would have been so much easier if Jopin hadn't made those remarks at the end of yesterday's meeting.

He thought about how Jopin had been such a good mentor and close friend, even treating him like one of his own sons. Jopin and Salamander's father had served together as elders under a previous chief. Salamander was only nineteen when Jopin introduced him to the people as a potential chief. Jopin spent a lot of time teaching him about the values of being a good leader to his people. Salamander had many fond memories of Jopin, but at that moment, he did not want Jopin to show up and ruin his plans.

Elder Cloud-burst started talking the moment he climbed down the ladder into the chamber. "Good morning. Didn't you get any sleep last night?"

"A little, why do you ask?"

"You've been here for a while. The fire has already burned the logs down to coals, and warmed the place."

Chief Salamander smiled as he leaned forward to add more logs to the fire. "I woke up early and didn't know if Jopin would be coming in today, so I decided to get the place ready. How about you? Were you able to sleep?"

"I thought a lot about what Jopin had to say, and I agree with him, but I don't want to argue with Great Grandfather. Carrying our sick and old ones out of this deep canyon will be very difficult. Many of them may not survive. Why would our creator put all of us through such a hardship? I want to hear what the other elders have to say. Like Jopin said, we don't want this to be the biggest mistake of our lives."

Elder Bobcat entered the chamber and spoke up, "Have you started the meeting without the rest of us? You're not supposed to be talking business without—"

"Now wait, just one moment. You've barely set foot on this chamber and you're already criticizing us?" They started to laugh. "No, we're just sharing a few thoughts until the others arrive."

"I came early today to ask Jopin some questions, since he's known for being wise and arriving at the best solution. Perhaps he knows something the rest of us don't. Isn't he usually the first one here?"

"Not today." Elder Cloud-burst interrupted. "Chief Salamander built the fire this morning. Jopin must still be sick. I wish I knew how to go about getting our creator to talk to me the way he talks to Jopin. Jopin certainly commands the honor and respect of his fellow elders." He turned to face Chief Salamander. "It was smart of you to appoint him as your senior elder. I was too emotional to relax and concentrate last night. Didn't the chiefs already pray at Chaco?"

The conversation had finally shifted from Jopin to Chief Salamander. "Thanks for asking. I'll talk about our prayers at Chaco during the meeting. We prayed together the entire time, even while traveling. Chief Brown-bear from Tsankawi, Chief Falling-water from Puye, and I prayed together on our five-day walk over there. We especially prayed on our way back, asking for guidance in doing the right thing and in getting our tribes ready for the evacuation."

The other elders climbed down the ladder and talked amongst themselves while waiting for the meeting to start. Elder Big-bear commented on the beautiful morning and on the warmth of the chamber. Elder Bobcat discussed the sleep he couldn't get. Elders Flying-falcon and Bear-claw were talking about how they may never get to see their sons again. Some of them discussed Jopin's health. Elder Little-raccoon asked Elder Pine-needle if he had thought about Jopin's comments.

"I sure did." Pine-needle had responded with a loud voice. "I'm curious if Chief Salamander understood what Jopin was trying to say."

Chief Salamander ignored him. However, he sure was aware of the many times Jopin's name had been mentioned. Jopin may not be attending, but he had certainly affected the meeting.

Elder Cloud-burst called out, "Should I go check on Jopin? He wasn't feeling very well yesterday?"

"Thanks for offering, but his grandson will soon come to deliver water. Why don't you ask Deer-tracker about his grandfather at that time? Tell him to let Jopin know we're praying for his health. Let's get started."

The elders formed a circle around Chief Salamander. He stepped into the sacred entrance to Mother Earth, a hole about knee deep, dug in the kiva's floor. He looked up at the sky through the opening on the ceiling, and started to pray. "Great Grandfather, we ask you to bless and guide us as we decide how to vote in this most important issue and start to prepare for our journey out of this deep canyon." He then lowered both arms, as if pointing to the dirt around him. "Mother Earth, we thank you for supplying us with everything we have needed here in Tyuonyi. We ask you to once again bless us with whatever we will need, as we emerge from here in search of our new homeland." He then asked them to pray for Elder Jopin's health.

He stepped out of the sacred hole and took his place in the circle of elders. They all sat down on the ground, their legs crossed in front of them. "I wish to continue talking about our pow-wow at Chaco, when Chief Spirit-dancer announced his Divine revelation. After much discussion and prayer, we decided each village would decide for itself if it would obey our Almighty's commandment. My friends, the time has come for us to decide if Tyuonyi will obey."

He held the sacred pipe with both hands and pointed it up, to the entrance on the kiva's ceiling, to the heavens above. "Behold the pipe-of-truth. I will soon be lighting the sacred tobacco and offer up our prayers for your people, especially for the people of Tyuonyi. Please guide us in our thoughts and actions." He lowered the pipe and held it out to the elders. "We will all smoke from this pipe today. We don't know why Great Grandfather created the Great Migration back then, and we don't know why he is asking us to join it again. But today, we must decide if we will choose to obey."

Chief Salamander grabbed a burning limb from the fire and lit the tobacco in the pipe. He inhaled four times and then passed the sacred pipe to Flying-falcon, the elder to his left. Elder Flying-falcon likewise pointed the sacred pipe up to the sky and recited the same prayer. "Behold the pipe-of-truth. I will smoke its sacred tobacco and offer it up for your people, especially for the people of Tyuonyi. Please guide me in my thoughts and actions." He took four puffs and then passed it to the elder on his left. Each took his turn reciting the prayer, taking four puffs, and passing it on to his left. The sacred pipe finally made its way back to Chief Salamander. By that time, the sweet-smelling smoke had infused the entire chamber and blessed everyone inside.

"My fellow elders, it is time to vote. Are you ready to say yes to Great Grandfather?"

Only a few of them answered, "Yes."

Chief Salamander looked around, as if questioning them. "What's the matter? I thought we would all be in agreement. We want to obey our creator, even if we don't like what he has asked of us." He held out both hands, with his elbows bent, wanting someone to say something.

After a short silence, Elder Little-raccoon spoke up. "Jopin isn't here."

"Do you mean to say you can't vote without Jopin? If present, my senior elder would support me, so we don't have to wait for him." Sensing their uneasiness, he continued. "Jopin said we must ask ourselves if Great Grandfather really wants us to leave the village he brought our ancestors to, in the first place. I fully agree with him. I, myself, spent every night in prayer while attending the All-chiefs' Pow-wow at Chaco. Jopin asked you to do the same. You must believe in your creator before you can commit to follow and obey him. So I ask again, are you ready to vote?"

After another long moment of silence, Elder Cloud-burst asked, "Can you tell us about your prayers at Chaco?"

"Yes, thanks for reminding me. I guess I should have followed the example of Chief Spirit-dancer. He had the medicine man from Chaco guide us in four days of prayer, day and night, kind of like in a cleansing ceremony. We fasted the entire time. He gave us sacred corn brew to drink and a special tobacco to smoke. In the end, we had committed ourselves to Great Grandfather, and finally, committed ourselves to obey his commandments." Chief Salamander stopped talking to get their feedback.

"Can you tell us exactly how you finally agreed to commit to obedience?" Elder Big-bear looked puzzled. "I mean, I prayed for advice last night, but I didn't receive an answer."

This was, exactly the question Chief Salamander had been waiting for. "Let me tell you about our visions. This, I believe, led to the obedience and commitment of each and every chief. We each had visions that convinced us to accept what we had to do. My vision took me to a sky covered with very dark clouds. They opened up on each side of Father Sun and created a long trail across the sky from the east to the west. All of the winged creatures flew along that trail, following Father Sun. The eagles flew closest to him, followed by the vultures, then the falcons, and finally, all the other birds, all following Father Sun along the path created by the opening of the clouds. I knew I must also travel along that same path."

The look on their faces said it all. They could have experienced the religious vision themselves. "I hope you now see. We are indeed being called to join the Great Migration. Let's vote."

Elder Big-bear turned to face the other elders as he addressed the chief. "I want to thank you for sharing such a personal experience with us. I now see why you're so committed to the evacuation. Why wasn't Medicine-maker invited to participate in our discussions?"

"I didn't think it was necessary to invite him. You as elders had already committed yourselves to enforcing Great Grandfather's commandments. Medicine-maker prays for help in healing the sick. We pray for help in leading his people to obedience. Talking about leading his people, can we do what we came here to do today? We need to start planning how to lead his people out of this canyon and on to their new homeland."

Most of them agreed, by nodding their heads. Elder Little-raccoon repeated his previous concern. "Jopin isn't here."

Chief Salamander quickly turned looking downward with a clenched jaw, as if he had been slapped, and then looked piercingly at Little-raccoon. "Do you have a different interpretation of my vision?"

"No. But, don't the rules say this vote must be unanimous?"

"Little-raccoon is correct about the rules. We need Jopin." Elder Flying-falcon then expressed his concern for Jopin. "I hope he recovers soon."

"Yes, I agree. But, Jopin may not be ill. I have good reason to believe Elder Jopin may have resigned."

The elders started to talk amongst themselves. Elder Bobcat asked Elder Bear-claw if he knew whether Jopin had resigned. "He didn't mention anything to me."

Elder Pine-needle whispered to Elder Cloud-burst. "Jopin said he was ill, not that he was resigning. Could he have resigned after yesterday's meeting?"

"This is the first time I've heard about any resignation." Elder Pine-needle spoke loud enough for everyone to hear.

Elder Flying-falcon looked puzzled at Chief Salamander. "Can you tell us why you believe Elder Jopin may have resigned? Either he did, or he didn't. Why haven't you told us?"

Chief Salamander knew he had said the wrong thing. Why did he have to lie about Jopin? "Let's come to order. No, not yet. Jopin was thinking about resigning a few days ago. I'm sure he intended to, but he got sick."

Elder Pine-needle faced Chief Salamander. "Does Elder Jopin want to resign because he doesn't agree with you? Perhaps he intended to resign before he knew about your proposal to evacuate, but now he can't. Could that be the reason why he's remained so quiet these past few days? It's not like him."

"Quiet, please. We can't answer any of these questions without Jopin. However, we can vote. Can we have a vote?"

None of the elders responded. "Very well then, let's adjourn. I'll go visit Jopin. Jopin and I will soon call another meeting, once he is well enough to come back."

"Wait." Elder Flying Falcon interrupted. "We can't adjourn. What do we tell the people about our plans for the spring festivities?"

"I'm sure there won't be any spring festivities, but you're right. We have to tell them something." He put his fist up to his chin. "I don't know. Tell them the truth. We didn't vote today, because Jopin became ill."

Elder Cloud-burst raised his right hand. "I suggest we tell them what I've been telling my friends and neighbors, to expect something very different this year."

Chief Salamander liked Elder Cloud-burst's suggestion. "That's what we should tell them." He then adjourned the meeting. "I'll go visit Jopin."

The Canteen

Deer-tracker ran to visit his grandparents. Still too young to join his father on hunting parties, the eleven-year-old would scout the area around Tyuonyi for small game. His parents called him, Deer-tracker, because he once got lost following a set of deer tracks leading away from the village. He could shoot an arrow through a rabbit or squirrel, and bring it home to his mother, or offer it to his grandparents. He once brought them a young turkey. Jopin told him it was the best meat he had ever tasted.

"Hi Grandma, what's a happening with Grandpa?"

"Your grandpa's a happening, that's what. Why have you come here so exhausted? Looks like you couldn't outrun that little rabbit or squirrel today. You can't even catch your breath. Yet, you find the strength to ask about your grandfather." She looked right at him and then continued. "Do you not care to know about what's a happening with me? What's so important about your grandpa? Do you love him more than me?"

"No, Grandma—"

"If you don't have enough love for both of us, then perhaps I should turn myself into a little bird and fly away. That way you won't have to share your love between your grandpa and your grandma anymore." The words were serious, but she revealed a big loving smile beneath those sparkling eyes of hers.

Deer-tracker didn't mind that she still treated him like a little boy, although he would soon be turning twelve. "I love you just as much as Grandpa. I just want to know what's been happening to him."

"I see. He left to his meeting early this morning, just like he has for the past three days. They should finish today, because they always finalize their plans on the fourth day."

Deer-tracker gently touched her forearm. "Grandpa's not there. When I delivered water to the kiva, Elder Cloud-burst instructed me to let Grandpa know they had prayed for him to recover from his illness. That's why I'm asking about him."

Bright-sunflower looked stunned. "I don't know about any illness. Your grandpa dressed in his ceremonial tunic and performed a hair-cleansing purification ceremony early this morning, before daybreak. I thought it was too cold for him to walk outside with his hair wet. But they usually have a fire in the kiva, so I knew he would be fine, once inside."

"He's not in the kiva."

"Let me think. He's been fasting for the past three days. Do you think he could have tripped and fallen on his way?"

"I don't think so. I would have seen him on my way here. I'll go ask around."

Bright-sunflower remained silent for a while. "Your grandfather didn't say anything about feeling sick. He was busy last night getting ready for what I thought, today's meeting. If he's not at the kiva, then where can he be? Perhaps he's visiting his cousin, Burnt-mountain."

"No. I was there earlier. Aunt Purple-lily had me taste her new stew. Uncle asked about Grandpa, so when Elder Cloud-burst told me Grandpa was sick, I started to worry."

Bright-sunflower laid her hand on her hip. "Could you do your grandmother a favor and walk through the village to see if you can find him? But don't let anyone know we're looking for him. I will search near the old cliff house. There's something strange about the way he looks at that place."

"Does Grandpa want to fix up great grandmother's old house?"

"No. I mean the cliff behind the house, not the house. My father died in that house. Jopin wouldn't think about living in a place where someone has died."

"What's so strange about the cliff?"

"I'm not sure. He studied the area, as if trying to figure out something. When I asked him what he was thinking about, he said he wished he were young again. He wanted to climb the finger-and-toe holes that were carved into the face of the cliff. I told him to get that idea out of his head. He's no longer a boy and much too old for such foolishness."

Deer-tracker grabbed her by the arm. "Let's go look for him at the cliff. If he isn't there, I will then search for him all over the village."

Deer-tracker and Bright-sunflower went outside. They briefly stopped to visually search for him on the plaza and beyond. Even the old men who usually stood on the roof tops of their residences, must have gone inside to escape the hot sun. The heat kept most everyone inside, except for some kids chasing a gourd ball. The dogs kept interfering with the game, but the kids didn't seem to mind. They didn't even notice Deer-tracker and his grandmother as they passed by their play area.

Deer-tracker and Bright-sunflower walked around the main kiva and headed towards the Tyuonyi exit. "This passageway is the only way out of the village. I'm sure the warrior guards would have seen Grandpa if he had gone through there."

"Please don't ask for him. We're just taking a walk."

The guards told them to enjoy their time away from the village. Deer-tracker and his grandmother walked through the exit, around the back of the village, and towards the cliff house.

Deer-tracker spotted Jopin right away. "Look; Grandpa's there on the cliff, about halfway up. Can you see him? He's not moving. Could something be wrong? He may be hurt. I better climb up there and see if he's all right."

"No, Deer-tracker. We shouldn't bother him. He may not want anyone to know what he's doing. Let's go someplace where we can observe him, someplace where he can't see us." She looked around and then pointed. "Under that tree." They scurried and squatted under a large cedar. She was relieved, but at the same time, confused with his actions. "I can't believe he still has the strength to do such things. What is he doing up there? It must have something to do with the ceremony he was preparing for this morning."

They watched for a very long time, but still, no movement. "There's something wrong with Grandpa. I better go check on him."

"No. Just wait a while."

"I should go get some help."

"No, Deer-tracker. We have to be sure about what is happening before we call anyone. I hope he hasn't fainted, or worse. It's too bad your father is out on a hunt."

"Papa won't return until another two or three days. They're hunting an elk herd they spotted moving into the burn area of the mesa above Water Canyon."

"Oh dear, what should we do?"

"I can climb up and act surprised to see him. If he's in trouble, I'll come back down and get some help."

"But your grandfather will not want to be bothered if this is part of a secret ceremony. He may even get mad at you. These ceremonies must be performed exactly as planned. He fainted last year when he became weak and quite ill."

"Grandma, he has not moved. Something is wrong. I will go get some medicine-water from mother and take it to him."

"Wait. Let's go back to the house. I also have some medicine-water. I don't want your mother asking what you need it for. He's probably weak, so I'll also get some jerky. If we meet anyone on the way to the village, please don't tell them anything about your grandpa."

The warrior guards greeted them as they approached the entrance. "That was a very short walk."

Bright-sunflower spoke rapidly as she hurried on past them. "We forgot something. We'll be right back."

They walked through the passageway, past the kiva, and on to the house. Bright-sunflower got some jerky. She grabbed the gourd-canteen and filled it with a new batch of medicine-water. "He didn't even take any water with him. Jopin will recognize his canteen. Just tell him you borrowed it." They hurried back out of the village and headed towards the cliff.

"Remember, you must respect the wishes of your grandfather. I will watch from here, under this tree, where he can't see me."

"I will do whatever Grandpa asks. I'm so worried about him. I better start climbing."

"Please be careful. Remember, your grandfather is too heavy for you. Please come down for help."

Deer-tracker looked at the small finger-and-toe holes and wondered how his grandfather could have managed to put his hands and feet into them. He then put his own fingers and toes into them and started to climb. He soon reached the area directly underneath his grandfather. Jopin's body appeared to protrude out above him, so Deer-tracker quickly moved over to his left to avoid being hit, if Jopin were to fall. Deer-tracker climbed up and positioned himself alongside the crevice. He could hear the birds chirping and the wind whizzing, but not a sound coming from Jopin. Deer-tracker stretched the upper part of his body towards the crevice to observe his grandfather.

Jopin had squeezed himself, sideways, into the narrow fissure. He held his hands up in front of his face, as if pushing the crack open. His forehead leaned against the back of his hands, eyes closed. His hero, the greatest elder of Tyuonyi, appeared very old and quite feeble.

Deer-tracker spoke quietly. "Grandpa, this is Deer-tracker. Are you all right? What's a, I mean, what are you doing here?"

Jopin quickly opened his eyes and looked directly at him. "Oh Deer-tracker, what are you doing here? Am I in your way? I might be able to move over a little to let you by."

"You're not in my way. The jog to the top is on this side, not the one you're on. I'm on my way to see how much snow might still remain up on top, but I don't really have to go. I can go back down."

"Wait. It's all right if you go past me. Please continue. How long will you be up there?"

"I'm just going up to look around. I'll soon come back down."

"Well, I might still be here."

"Grandpa, can I stay here and visit with you? I don't really have to go up."

"Are you sure you don't want to go play on top? You can't just stay here hanging on to the cliff. You'll get tired."

"You're right. I'll just go back down. I'm sorry I bothered you."

"You said you were going up. No, you did not bother me. You can go up or you can go back down. But if you go down, please don't tell anyone I'm here."

"Okay Grandpa. See you later. Are you going to be here very long?"

Jopin took a while to respond. "I don't know. No. Wait, I'm, ah, I'm confused."

"Grandpa, are you going up or are you going down? Do you need some help? How long have you been here?"

"I started to climb early this morning, but then I began to feel weak. I came to this area and decided to rest a while. I'm still here, because I'm too weak to continue."

"Are you sick? I have some medicine-water and jerky." Deer-tracker held out the canteen with his right hand while holding on to the cliff with his other hand.

"Thank you, but no. I'm not supposed to eat or drink anything, because I'm fasting. It's part of my sacrifice." Jopin looked surprised when he realized what Deer-tracker had offered him. "Why are you carrying medicine-water? Did you bring it up here for me?"

"I just happen to have it."

"Medicine-water and jerky, why?" Is that my canteen? What are you doing with my—" The markings on the canteen caught his attention. "I painted those images of the Great Migration and of the spinning sun, when I was just a little older than you. Why have you brought me these particular signs at this very moment?"

"I borrowed the canteen from Grandma. You weren't using it, so I asked her if I could borrow it."

Jopin focused directly into Deer-tracker's eyes. "You climbed up here to see if I was all right, didn't you? That's why you're here."

Deer-tracker turned away as if he were guilty.

"Why do you keep looking down below when I talk to you? What are you looking at? Oh dear, you climbed up here to help me. Who else knows I'm here?"

Deer-tracker looked trapped. "Just Grandma. Grandpa, I'm so sorry. I failed. Grandma told me not to let you know she was down there. She told me you were either in trouble or on a religious ceremony, not to bother you."

"Your grandmother was right. But no, you have not failed. I have. She didn't know anything about me wanting to climb here, because I've attempted to do something stupid. Your grandfather is much too old for such foolishness, even if I am on a special sacrifice."

"A sacrifice? Grandpa, are you going to jump?"

"No. My sacrifice consists of fasting, climbing up the cliff, and praying at the Shrine of the Soaring Eagles. All of these are part of my prayer quest."

"Why didn't you walk up the other side of the mountain, where the climb would have been much easier?"

"Because the gods will pay better attention to me if they know I'm serious. Dancing is a sacrifice when we do it for four days straight without taking a break. I decided to find favor with the gods by fasting and making the sacrifice of climbing up this cliff. It's very important that they answer my prayer."

"Grandma was right. She said I should not bother you, because you were probably performing a secret ceremony. I failed you. I failed Grandma. And I failed the gods."

"Your grandmother knows me too well, better than I know myself. People kept telling me how strong I looked for my age. Believing them, I planned to make it to the top, early enough to greet Father Sun as he came out from Mother Earth. And yet, you knew something was wrong. I wedged my feet into this crack and now, I'm stuck."

"Grandpa, I can help you. Let me climb a little further, and then you can hang on to my leg and raise yourself up."

"No, you're half my size. I'll knock you off the cliff and we'll both die. I have already lived my life, but you have your whole life ahead of you."

"You can hang on to me and let go whenever you want to. I won't hold you."

"Deer-tracker, you can't help me. Let me pull my foot out of here. I need to move my legs. Oh my, I'm so dizzy."

"Grandpa, don't move. You need to eat something to get your strength back. I'm sure the gods will understand you had no choice. You can always offer another sacrifice when you get to the top."

"The gods won't answer my prayer, if I give in to temptation. But I guess I have no choice. Give me some medicine-water." Jopin looked up to the sky. "Great Grandfather, please forgive me for breaking my sacrificial promise. Please tell your gods to have mercy on me."

Deer-tracker held on with his left hand and stretched out his right arm to pass the canteen over to Jopin. Jopin took a few gulps and then handed the canteen back to Deer-tracker. Deer-tracker then gave him some jerky.

Jopin held out a piece of jerky in front of him, as if talking to it. "Medicine-water and jerky. I prayed for Great Grandfather to send one of his gods from the mountaintop to come help me. Instead, he sent you from the canyon below, with nourishment from my wife. Let's see how long it takes me to get over my dizziness." He started to nibble on it.

Deer-tracker also bit on a piece of jerky. "When did you ask the gods to come help you?"

"I've been praying since this morning. But, I had just closed my eyes to visualize one of the mountain gods coming down to help me, when you appeared."

"Grandpa, when I saw your eyes closed, I thought you were, ah—"

"Dead? Ha, Ha. I was meditating. Well, it worked. I'm already feeling much better." Jopin wiggled his foot back and forth, in an attempt to pull it out of the crevice. "This jerky is good, exactly what I needed."

"Grandpa, take your time. We can still make it to the top before dark. Once on top, we can set up camp and start a fire. I will stay out of your way, so you can continue on your prayer quest."

Jopin managed to pull his foot out of the crevice. "That feels much better." He stretched out his arms and legs, and straightened his back. "I believe I'm now ready to continue." He looked up, stretched out his right arm, and started to feel around for a finger-and-toe hole.

"Wait, Grandpa, that path stops after a while. That's where most people would climb, but the real path is the jog over to this side of me. I'll step down so you can come over here."

"I had forgotten about the jog. But no, you need to go first. Why don't you climb a little further. I will follow you."

"Grandpa, I can help you get to the top by supporting you from the bottom."

"Deer-tracker, you have already helped me. I should now be able to make it the rest of the way on my own. The only thing wrong is that I should be the one protecting and providing for you. No, Deer-tracker, I will not put your life in further danger. Please go first and lead the way. I will follow."

Deer-tracker moved over to the other path of finger-and-toe holes, and started to climb. Jopin moaned as he pulled and lifted himself over, and slowly started to climb.

Deer-tracker reached the top and moved over to make room for Jopin. He grabbed his grandfather's arm to pull him over the edge, but Jopin refused his help. Jopin crawled over and then rolled on his back, gasping for air. "Thank you Deer-tracker, for helping this old man. And thank you, Great Grandfather for sending my grandson to help me. I need to rest a while."

"Grandpa, your fingers are bleeding. You better stay here until you're ready. I'll go get some firewood to keep us warm and prepare a place for us to spend the night." Deer-tracker walked away.

Sacred Campfire

Jopin layed on his back and took in the cool air as it swept across his tired body. Exhausted as he was, he could not rest. He had failed to keep his fasting promise, so the gods would surely be disappointed with him. His prayer would go unanswered. But, how else could he have been able to make it to the top? The proper thing to do now would be to completely devote himself to prayer and ask the gods for forgiveness. He had not planned to spend the night. And to make things more complicated, he now had to contend with his grandson. Young Deer-tracker would require so much attention. However, the only reason Jopin made it to the top was because of Deer-tracker. He couldn't possibly ask him to leave. Jopin decided he could still spend the night in prayer, after Deer-tracker would go to sleep. This thought brought Jopin some comfort. He finally dozed off.

Wham! Wham! Wham! Crack! Wham! Wham! Jopin awoke to pounding and smashing sounds. Wham! Wham! Crack! He stood up, noticed the sun was about to set into the western horizon, and staggered towards the noise. The many piñon, juniper and pine trees prevented him from seeing very far ahead, but he reasoned Deer-tracker must have been breaking logs to build a fire, or for shelter. The poundings grew louder and louder, and then, they stopped.

Jopin kept walking until he could see and observe Deer-tracker from a distance. Deer-tracker had already started a fire. A large pile of firewood, probably enough to last the entire night, could be seen near the fire. Jopin was amazed by all of the effort Deer-tracker had put into preparing a camp for them.

He approached Deer-tracker. "Why didn't you awaken me? I could've helped. There's a lot of firewood here. You've been very busy. I must have slept a long time."

"Grandpa, I started a fire so we can eat and stay warm. A squirrel ran in front of me. I hit him with a rock. I already skinned and cleaned him out. We can cook him, once the fire burns down a little."

"You'll never grow hungry, because you have such a good arm, just like your father. I'm glad my daughter married such a good man."

"We should soon have some fresh elk meat, when Papa returns from his trip."

"Yum, I love the taste of elk. Your father makes sure we always have a variety of meats to eat with the rest of our food. You're already showing the traits of a good hunter, just like your father. Did you thank Brother-squirrel for giving up his life for us? You must release his spirit."

"Yes. I released his spirit. I'm trying to become more grateful to Great Grandfather and his creatures. Sometimes I have so much fun that I forget to give thanks, but this time I did. I thanked my four-legged brother for giving his life for my grandpa, so you can regain your strength." He looked up at Jopin, as if seeking approval.

"Thank you." Jopin became uneasy about eating again, but he couldn't refuse his grandson's offering. "I especially want to thank you for everything you have done for me. I'm so lucky to have you for a grandson."

"Grandpa, you're a spiritual man. Now that we're together, can you teach me how to become more like you?"

Jopin put his hands on Deer-tracker's shoulders. "That's the best compliment anyone could give his grandfather, but I don't know if I'm worthy of such praise. And besides, what I teach you may not agree with what your mother and father would want."

"They told me I should talk to you about such things, because you know better. They said it's a grandparent's job to help teach us kids in the ways of the people, in the ways of the path commanded by Great Grandfather, the Great Spirit."

Jopin had to figure out what to do. His grandson had just asked him, a failure, to teach him about Great Grandfather and his gods. What should he do? "Well it looks like your parents have done a good job without me. It's up to them to make you into the person they want you to become. You're at the age that by the end of summer, you and other boys your age will move into your clan kivas. The clan elders will teach you these things. I wouldn't want to teach you something different than they would."

"Grandpa, I know I'll sleep in the kiva of the Cougar Clan until the time comes for me to marry. Our Cougar-elders will teach us the traditions, legends, songs, and prayers of the Cougar. But I want to become the type of person you are, even if you do belong to a different clan."

"I must not interfere with their work. However, I can probably answer whatever questions you may have. But first, I must help you set up camp."

"Grandpa, you can stay here near the fire. I'll go get some more firewood. I want us to stay warm throughout the night. You can cook Brother-squirrel, if you don't mind."

"I think you have enough firewood, but we don't have any corn leaves and animal furs to sleep on. We should collect some dry grass and leaves to protect us from the cold ground."

"Okay, but I have to build us a shelter first."

Jopin studied the sky. "It doesn't look like rain tonight, so we don't really need to build anything. We can sleep out in the open and enjoy seeing the moon and stars up above."

"But what if the clouds move in, and it starts to rain in the middle of the night?"

"Well, we can go under a big pine tree. Deer-tracker, it's not your responsibility to take care of your old grandpa. Would you build a shelter, if you were out here by yourself?"

"No, I would go further, to the area of the black bear, and sleep in one of the caves."

"You could get there, but those bears won't let you stay very long. They will chase you out like this." Jopin raised his arms, opened his hands wide, and started to chase Deer-tracker. They played around and gathered grass and leaves in the process, and soon delivered their first load of bedding material to the camp area. They kept going back for more grass and leaves until they had the right amount.

They then moved some large logs close to the fire to sit on. The darkness of night had come upon them. Jopin separated a few glowing coals from the burning fire and laid Brother-squirrel over them. Little flames reached out around the squirrel's body.

"Why is fire sacred, Grandpa?"

"I will answer in the way my father told me and in the way his father told him. I'm sure your father has already talked to you about fire. Hasn't he?

"Papa told me the legend about how fire was created, but we never talked about the bad part of fire. Everything exists because it was meant to be. Great Grandfather put everything into place for his people to live, like he wants us to live. He created Mother Earth, Father Sun, and all the stars above. Father Sun enters Mother Earth at night and impregnates her, so everything comes from Father Sun and Mother Earth. Father Sun warms everything above the ground, including the air and the clouds. This causes changes in temperature and weather. The rain and snows make it possible for things to grow. Why is Great Grandfather called the Almighty Creator?"

"You just answered your own question. He created everything. We're his people, so we have to do what he wants us to do."

"Papa says we're all relatives of everything on Mother Earth, so we have to take care of each other and of everything around us. But, I don't understand how some things exist for the good, like fire. We use fire to cook and to keep us warm, but at times it comes down from the sky in a violent bolt of thunder and lightning. It can start the forest on fire. Then everything is scorched, burned, or ruined. Why would Great Grandfather instruct Father Sun to do such a thing? Why does he allow bad things to happen? Is Great Grandfather mad at us when this happens?"

Jopin leaned back to give Deer-tracker a look of approval. "For a while there, you were teaching me about life. You've been taught well." He crossed his arms and paused for a while. "I don't really know the answer to your question. We don't know if Great Grandfather is punishing us or just using fire to purge the forest of its underbrush." He explained to Deer-tracker about how fire could be a form of purification. "A forest taken over by weeds and shrubs may not have enough moisture for the trees to continue to grow. So, getting rid of some of the undergrowth can help the trees grow big and healthy." Jopin agreed with Deer-tracker. Everything on Mother Earth must be in balance with everything else, including the animals and man. "Only our creator knows if he is purifying the earth or punishing it. It's a mystery. Perhaps that's why some call him the Great Mystery. Others call him the Great Spirit and of course, Almighty Creator. He has many names, but he is only one."

"Does purification make us stronger, like the trees of the forest? And, what if we have a very big fire? What happens when everything is burned and the only thing left are ashes? Our creator surely has to be mad at us or angry enough to make everything disappear. That's not purification, is it?

Jopin welcomed Deer-tracker's curiosity and interest in such things. "Yes, it could be. But it could also be punishment. He's the only one who knows. A forest doesn't stop to exist just because it has burned down. There's always new growth. We may not see it, but eventually, there will be something new growing. This is a little like us. No one can see us after we die, but our spirits might live on, up in the skies or wherever Great Grandfather may want us."

"I'm still confused about the difference between punishment and purification, but I have another question. Why do the elders call fire sacred? Is this campfire sacred?"

"Fire becomes sacred when used for prayer." Jopin separated out a few coals to the side and laid some sweet grass on them. He had Deer-tracker look at the smoke coming from the sweet grass. "It carries our prayers up to the skies, so this campfire has now become sacred, as well as the sweet grass and the smoke."

Jopin talked about the sacredness of tobacco. "We smoke it to open our minds, so we can better communicate with the Divine." He then told about how the sacred stones are heated with fire and then placed in the sacred chamber. "Water is poured over the hot stones to produce steam, which purifies those praying for forgiveness. We use fire, smoke, stones, water, fasting, and sacrifices to cleanse or purify ourselves from our wrongdoings, and to communicate with the gods."

"So I guess all fire can be sacred, whether it comes down from the sky, or if we start it ourselves?"

Jopin looked up, as if looking for the right answer. "When we do something wrong and get caught, we sometimes say we got burned. We learn our lesson and ask Great Grandfather to forgive us. We want to become more like what he would want us to be, so getting burned is a good and sacred thing."

Jopin took a long stick and used it to turn the squirrel over, so it could get cooked on the other side.

"Grandpa, is Brother-squirrel getting purified with our fire?" He laughed in a loud voice, and then quickly continued. "He may be getting burned, but I don't think he will be changing his ways."

Jopin laughed as he pushed the squirrel a little closer to the flames. "There's always a lesson to learn from nature and fire. Young people have a lot of energy, like this fire. We have to keep adding good dry wood to the fire for the flames to continue. They will not burn as well as they should, if we add wood that's green or wet. That would get us a bunch of smoke, instead of good healthy flames. Our bodies must be fed the right things, just like this fire. Eating the wrong foods or too much, can make us sick, even kill us. If we don't eat at all, we'll certainly die. Look at this fire. Coals have already begun to form and turn gray, just like your grandpa. As they burn themselves out, they'll soon become ashes and then dust. Everything turns to dust after it dies."

"Grandpa, I don't want you to die." He grabbed Jopin's forearm. "Do you know what kind of spirit we'll become after we die?"

"Our spirits live on, long after our bodies have died and decayed." He paused to think about what to tell Deer-tracker about his spirit. "When you live your life with good thoughts and do good deeds, you please Great Grandfather. Deer-tracker, you will continue to be a good spirit after you die, because you please your creator."

Deer-tracker smiled and then became serious, as he prepared to ask another question. "I've heard some of the elders refer to the spirits coming down from the mountaintops as mountain gods. Are mountain gods the same as mountain spirits?"

Jopin scratched his head above his right ear, before answering. "Ah, I don't think so. Great Grandfather created the gods to act as his messengers from heaven. He will allow a good spirit to live with him and his gods, and he might even allow a good spirit to come down and help someone in need. You know, like when we summon our ancestors to come down from the skies to help us. These good spirits can perform good deeds, like the gods. But, bad spirits also exist. Bad spirits can never be gods."

"Do we have to die in order to become like a god? It looks like our dinner is ready. Grandpa, why don't you take the first piece? It will make you stronger."

Jopin pulled a leg off the squirrel, held it up to thank the creator, and then took a bite. "Um, this is delicious. You have fed me twice today, first with jerky and now with delicious squirrel. I've really enjoyed our conversations tonight. There must be a reason why we have been placed here to spend this time together and talk about such things. Why did Great Grandfather send you, when I asked for one of his gods? Does he have big plans for little Deer-tracker? Who knows? Were you sent here for a special purpose or just to help your grandfather when he couldn't climb any further? We might have an answer by the time we get back to the village."

"Grandpa, I've heard you say Great Grandfather has a hand in everything. I came here, because he wanted me to come help you."

Jopin gently poked Deer-tracker in the chest to let him know he was happy with that answer. "You asked if we have to die in order to become like a god. Yes, I'm afraid so. Great Grandfather purifies our spirits to prepare us for his place in the skies, which is all pure. Ah, I just thought of something. Not everyone gets to go through the fire of purification."

"Grandpa, that would be great. Who wants to get burned?"

"That's not what I meant. I was referring to the very evil, those too evil to be purified. They will be burned completely to a crisp. Even their spirits might cease to exist.

Deer-tracker grabbed Jopin's arm and securely hung on to him.

Jopin continued. "But that won't happen to you. You try to please your creator, and you have a desire to go live with him. We all have faults and do things we shouldn't. Perhaps we have a problem with someone or with ourselves, thinking we may be better than our brother. Great Grandfather will command his fire-god to burn our faults away from us and prepare us to go live with him in the skies. I'm sure you will go live with Great Grandfather when you die."

"I don't want to die." Deer-tracker's voice was hardly audible.

Jopin gently lifted Deer-tracker's chin. "I want to tell you the legend about a boy, whom they called, Spirit-boy, who was taken up to the skies while still alive." He told him about how Spirit-boy lived many years ago in the area of Redondo Peak, a mountain to the West. Spirit-boy was known for being good-natured and for doing everything his parents ever asked of him. "The people would say he was sinless. He would climb the peak, every day after finishing his chores, offer sacrifices to the gods, and then come down exhausted, but still with enough energy to tell everyone about the gods. He started doing this since very young, so the people thought it was just a foolish childhood game. But, some of the people thought he was—"

"They thought he was crazy?"

Jopin nodded. "Even his father wondered about Spirit-boy. The father had asked the medicine man to go check on him, so the medicine man climbed the peak and observed Spirit-boy performing a prayer dance, from a distance. He came back and asked the father how the boy had learned the ceremonies. The father didn't know. The medicine man thought Spirit-boy could have been communicating with the gods, because he felt a strong presence there. He advised the father to give the boy a little more time. Perhaps it was a childhood game or perhaps, Spirit-boy was doing something sacred. Time would tell."

Deer-tracker pulled another piece of meat off the squirrel and moved closer to Jopin.

Jopin told how Spirit-boy grew older, but unlike his friends, was not attracted to girls or to the mischief boys like to create. "Spirit-boy became known as the poor kid with mental problems. He continued to climb this high peak every day to talk to the gods. The people did like him though, because he was such a good person, and quite entertaining. His face would light up and glow whenever he spoke about the gods."

Jopin noticed how he had captured Deer-tracker's complete attention, so he lowered his voice and started to speak slower, in an attempt to cause Deer-tracker to become sleepy. He told about how one day, Spirit-boy's mother looked up and noticed snow on the peak. "She sent Spirit-boy's older sister to take him some warm clothing, and to bring him back. The sister went straight to the area. No Spirit-boy. He might have already gone home, but something was wrong. There in the snow was an impression of Spirit-boy's body. The snow had covered everything except the area where he had lain on the ground with his arms held out. No footsteps could be seen leading away. Steam rose from within that area. She panicked, dropped Spirit-boy's clothing and ran."

"Did his sister know that Great Grandfather had taken him?"

Jopin laughed. "You don't even know if that's what happened." He cleared his throat and continued the story. "The sister had told her parents what she had seen. They all climbed the mountain and saw for themselves. They searched around the ceremonial area, but nothing. There was no way to track him, because the snow had continued to fall, covering all tracks. It soon became too dark, so they went back down." Jopin lowered his face to portray sadness. Deer-tracker opened his mouth, but remained silent.

"The frustrated father went straight to the medicine man's home to ask for help. They waited for morning before going back up. They had no trouble finding the ceremonial area, although the snow had grown to about knee deep. It looked like Spirit-boy had lain there on his back the entire night, with his arms stretched out. There was deep snow everywhere, except where vapor rose from within Spirit-boy's silhouette. Everything should have been buried in snow. Even the flakes that were still falling melted in that area. A very distinct glow appeared. The people later said it was the same glow Spirit-boy had when he would tell his friends about the gods. The medicine man said that, even though Spirit-boy's body was no longer there, his spirit still melted the snow as it fell.

"Wow, Grandpa. Was his spirit really in the snow? That must be how Spirit-boy got his name."

"I don't know. Spirit-boy was never found. The medicine man spent two more days on top of the mountain, until the glow finally subsided. He walked back down and proclaimed the gods had found favor with Spirit-boy, and Great Grandfather had taken him up to live with him in the skies." Jopin pointed up towards the dusty trail of stars leading from one end of the sky to the other. "Look, we can still see his afterglow, the path he took on his way to go live with Great Grandfather."

Deer-tracker jumped up. "That's the most beautiful story I've ever heard. I wonder why no one ever told me the legend of Spirit-boy. I've heard about White-buffalo-woman, Spider-woman, Blood-clot-boy, and others, but never about Spirit-boy. Why Grandpa? Every boy and girl should know this beautiful story. Is this legend not as well known?"

The question surprised Jopin. "The legend of Spirit-boy is very well known, probably one of the most popular legends of all. People from all over the land make annual visits to the sacred place on top of Redondo Peak. But, the legend of Spirit-boy must not be shared with young children. Missing children were found dead on top of hills, lying on their backs with their hands held straight out to their sides. They starved themselves, waiting for Great Grandfather to come take them away. If Great Grandfather took them, he only took their spirits, because their bodies were left behind. Young children are not mature enough to hear this legend. So Deer-tracker, please promise not to tell this legend to any child."

"I promise. I don't want some little kid to die because of me." Deer-tracker stood up on his feet. "Grandpa, this is the best night of my life. Do you have another legend to tell me? You said Great Grandfather may have sent me here for a special purpose. Do you know what it might be? The more we talk, the more questions I have. I'm learning so much from you and we're having so much fun. Grandpa, you have made me the luckiest boy on all of Mother Earth."

Not knowing how to handle his grandson's excitement, Jopin pressed the tips of his fingers against his forehead and smiled.

Darkness

Chief Salamander had wanted Jopin to stay away, but now he needed Jopin to return to the Kiva and help him convince the elders to vote for the evacuation. But Jopin obviously opposed the migration. Salamander should have known better than to think he could have done it without his senior elder's help. If only he had confided in Jopin and asked for his advice. Instead, he had pushed him away, letting him know his services were no longer needed. Once Salamander's strongest supporter, Jopin would now probably distrust and seriously question anything Salamander would now ask of him. These were some of the thoughts getting tangled up in Salamander's mind as he walked to Jopin's house.

He took a deep breath before calling out, "Jopin, I've come to see how you are feeling? May I come in?" He waited a while before calling again. Still no answer. "Jopin, I know you may be mad at me, but we need to talk. Bright-Sunflower, can you hear me?" He was determined to see Jopin, so he bravely moved the door covering over to one side. "Hello. Jopin I need to talk to you. How are you feeling?" He stared into a silent, empty room.

Salamander stepped inside to adjust his eyes to the darkness. No one was home. A bed, consisting of an elk skin on top of dried grass and corn leaves lay on the floor alongside one of the walls. A blanket of sewn-together rabbit furs covered the elk skin. A small, sun-god kachina stood on top of a log protruding out of the wall. A deer skin hung on the wall over their bed. Another hung on the opposite wall. He wondered why they would have covered the sacred paintings with these skins, but then remembered how Jopin had expressed concern about how the plaster had started to fall off the walls. Salamander quickly looked at the floors. The bear skin had also been moved from its usual place to cover cracks in the floor. Salamander shook his head, disappointed, because he had not followed through with his offer to help Jopin replaster the walls and floors. This was more than three seasons ago.

As in Salamander's home, a corner of the room served as the cooking area. A hole directly above allowed the smoke to escape out of the room. The area smelled like old fire. The coals had completely burned themselves out. A cooking pot, with stew, sat on a flat rock at the edge of the cooking area. They had been gone for some time, because the stew had already solidified. A single small bowl remained on the floor, so only one of them must have eaten. Memories of the many meals they had shared together, in that very spot, came to mind. This was where Jopin had taught him about village government. "The secret to good leadership is to let the elders help you make the decisions. It's important to always have a discussion session, before calling for the vote, in order to bring out the truth, hidden intentions, or other problems." Jopin had also told him the people would support him if he had their best intentions at heart, if he supported them.

Jopin's advice had been well accepted, but for some reason, Salamander had insisted on doing it his way. He had intentionally violated Jopin's trust, because he wanted to have full control of this most important situation and show how he was the person in charge, not Jopin. His people needed to know they would follow a strong leader taking them out of their homeland, into the unknown to a place that will become their new home.

But, Chief Salamander had tried to force the vote on his elders, without showing much concern for their thoughts or their feelings. He had certainly demonstrated his lack of leadership ability by failing to gain their support. How could he possibly obtain the people's support and confidence, when he couldn't even earn his elder's support?

Chief Salamander would have to convince the entire tribe to pack their belongings, but only those things they were capable of carrying on their backs, and abandon their homeland. Why should they leave everything behind and follow their chief to who knows where? He needed Jopin more than ever. Salamander's pride had led him to mistreat the one elder he respected the most. However, he still did not want Jopin to have control over the village, especially over the evacuation.

Still determined, Chief Salamander decided to go look for Jopin at Medicine-maker's home. One of those special herbal remedies may be what Jopin would have needed to get his health back. The sooner Jopin could recover from his illness, the quicker he could help Salamander get the elders to support him on the evacuation.

Chief Salamander walked in the direction of the village's exit, to Medicine-maker's home. Thunder-head and his two friends approached him. Chief Salamander became a little nervous, because these three individuals always managed to complain about whatever occurred in the village. Fat-man and Little-boy had a habit of whispering their thoughts into Thunder-head's ear, causing Thunder-head to open his mouth and criticize their chief. Thunder-head wanted to know when the announcement would be made about the spring festivities. Chief Salamander remembered what Elder Cloud-burst had mentioned. "We still haven't finalized our plans, but we'll let you know as soon as we do. You should expect something very different this year."

"Why won't you tell us the truth?" Thunder-head had a way of challenging or putting down Chief Salamander. "You always have everything finalized on the fourth day."

He tried to tell them as little as possible. "Jopin became ill, so we didn't have a chance to finalize our plans."

"So you're no different than all of the other chiefs we've had?"

"What are you trying to get at, Thunder-head?" Salamander made sure to look at each of the other two. "Are you speaking for yourself or someone else?"

"You're letting Jopin run the village, just like all the other chiefs have done, before you. Perhaps Jopin should be our chief."

"Perhaps so, but this is no different than you. You allow Fat-man or Little-boy to tell you what to say. Why don't you talk to the rest of the villagers after your two friends tell you what to tell them? Perhaps you can get them to make Jopin our chief. I certainly wouldn't mind. Jopin is a good man."

Thunder-head quickly replied. "I will. I want my chief to be a true chief, not a puppet of Jopin's." Thunder-head had a devilish, little smirk on his face.

"As you say. If you'll excuse me, I've got some work to do." Salamander started to walk away.

"Wait. You did meet this morning, didn't you?"

"You already know we did. We'll meet again, once Jopin recovers from his illness."

Fat-man stepped forward with a wicked smile, and then cleared his throat. "I'm sure you know about the curse, Chief. Something really bad happens every time the elders take more than four days to make a decision."

Surprised, not only by the statement, but because Fat-man had actually spoken, Chief Salamander decided to respond. "You have too much time to think about such things. This always gets the three of you in trouble. If you believe something bad will happen, it will happen to you, because you believe as you do. You better change your attitude. I must go."

The men felt successful. They had managed to irritate their chief, so they wished him well as he walked away.

Chief Salamander hurried on to Medicine-maker's place, thinking about the three troublemakers. Little-boy hadn't spoken a word, but Salamander knew Little-boy was as much to blame as the other two. They weren't worth worrying about, but Salamander knew they would cause more problems. Salamander smiled as he thought about how Fat-man had eaten himself into his name, but Little-boy, the tallest, skinniest man of the tribe, had managed to keep his childhood name. The three of them were known for having quick tempers, especially when teased about their names. Although Salamander had no use for their opinions, he couldn't stop thinking about the curse. Salamander quickened his pace to avoid any other confrontations.

"Medicine-maker, are you home?"

"Well, yes Chief, what a pleasant surprise. Please come inside, but be careful. Watch your step. I wouldn't want to have to explain why my chief fell at my house. What brings you here?"

Chief Salamander glanced around for Jopin, as he stepped in. "I'm concerned about Jopin. He felt ill yesterday and didn't attend today's meeting. Has he come to see you?"

"No, he hasn't. Did he say he was coming to see me? I spent most of the morning searching for fresh herbs, now that the snow has melted. Perhaps he came when I was gone."

Salamander looked around. "It looks like you have gathered enough to last you a year." The place was packed with all kinds of plants. The fragrance of boiling herbs filled the air. Bowls with special medicinal plants took up most of the floor area, and dried plants hung from long poles leaning up against the walls. Medicine-maker would have trouble walking around in his own home.

"Now you know why I prefer to heal people at either their place or in the kiva." Medicine-maker laughed. "There's not much room here for anyone."

Chief Salamander smiled. "I'll go see if Jopin is at his daughter's."

"I can tell you're truly concerned about his health. I'll pray for him to get well. Will he be playing a special role in this year's spring festivities?"

This question caught Salamander by surprise. "Yes, all elders must be present when deciding on the ceremonies. We need Jopin to hurry and recover from his illness."

"I'll ask the gods to send me a special cure for him and then I'll go visit him."

"Thanks, Medicine-maker. I better go. Oh, by the way, would you be interested in leading the elders in a special prayer quest? We're having trouble coming to a consensus on a certain issue. Perhaps you can help us."

"I would be happy to help. Just let me know when."

"I'd like to try one more thing, before I call on you. I'll let you know. Thanks for everything."

Salamander walked out, but soon encountered a group of chattering women. They swarmed towards him and quickly gathered around. All of them seemed to talk at the same time, almost as if competing for his attention. Whispering-rain spoke out in a loud voice. "They tell us you're the best chief Tyuonyi has ever had." Excited, another one put her hand on Chief Salamander's arm. "Chief, we're so lucky to have such a young, strong, and smart man to protect us and to be our leader." An older woman in the back raised her voice. "Just tell us what you want us to do and we'll do it. We're ready to support you with whatever you may need." He felt a hand on his back. It was a little uncomfortable, but he welcomed the positive support, compared to what he had been experiencing in the council meetings. It felt good to finally be appreciated.

Chief Salamander's father interrupted. "I don't mean to pull you away from your friends, but could you stop by when you're done?"

Salamander held up a finger and nodded.

"Chief, we know you have to go see your father, but can you first tell us about the preparations for the spring festival?"

This one question was enough to stop him from feeling so good about himself. "Excuse me, but I've got to hurry and talk to my father. You'll soon be hearing about the festivities."

He scampered towards his father. "Thanks for saving me from those women. Is there anything I can do for you?"

"Just a word of advice, Son." He had that concerned look on his face, like in the old days, when Salamander knew he would be getting a lecture after doing something wrong. "What I just witnessed back there, doesn't look right. You have worked very hard to build up your reputation. Don't ruin it. You don't want people to start talking about your having a roving eye. You have to be aware of how others see you. That's all."

"You don't have to worry about me. I love Little-acorn. I would never do anything to hurt her or our marriage."

Chief Salamander asked his father if he had seen Jopin. He hadn't, so Salamander explained that Jopin was ill and he was on his way to Brilliant-pebbles' home to see if Jopin might be there.

"Brilliant-pebbles, how are you?"

"I'm well, Chief Salamander. What brings you here?"

"I'm looking for Jopin. Have you seen him?"

"No. I went to check on Mother, but she wasn't home. She usually comes to visit when Father attends his council meetings. But you're here, so there must not have been a meeting today. That must be why she didn't come to visit today. They must be together. Well that explains it. They probably went for a walk."

"You're probably right. Please ask him to come see me, if you do see him. Thanks and oh, tell Great-hawk I'm so grateful for all he does for his people. I heard they're hunting elk."

"Yes, they're excited about the possibility of bringing us some delicious elk meat."

Chief Salamander had experienced a most difficult and trying day, so he decided to go home, where he could finally get a moment of peace. Little-acorn wasn't there. She wouldn't have expected him to be home so early, so she must have gone to visit her sister.

He couldn't stop wondering about the whereabouts of Jopin. But then, he started to worry about how difficult it would be to evacuate the entire village out of this steep canyon. Chief Salamander decided to walk out of the village and follow the creek upstream to determine what kind of problems would be encountered along that path.

He walked north, paying special attention to difficult or challenging areas. The narrow path would only allow one person at a time. They would have to carry the sick and infirm on elk skins tied to two long poles, where a carrier would have to walk, single file, behind his partner. The only place wide enough to gather and set up camp, on the first day, would be an area, just a little ways north of the village. This place would be closer to Tyuoni than what he would want, but at least, they would be out of the village. It could also serve as a staging area to get everyone ready to start the treacherous climb on the following day.

Salamander paid special attention to those areas having loose rocks and to those which were quite steep and dangerous. He surprised a buck that jumped out of the bushes, and squirrels chattered to warn of a possible intruder, but Salamander was focused on the terrain. The trail was much worse and thus, the exodus would be more challenging than what he had envisioned.

He hadn't taken in the beauty of the canyon or listened to the soothing sound of the water cascading down from one rock to another, until he approached the top. Salamander sat on a rock and looked down at the beautiful canyon. The cool breeze felt so good, but sadness had overcome him. He would miss his beloved homeland. Salamander remembered the fun times he had experienced growing up, playing, hunting, and fishing with his friends and relatives. All of his male friends had moved out to other villages to marry. He wondered if they would ever meet again, perhaps by chance, some time in the future. Little-acorn would probably never see the relatives she left behind at Chaco. Chief Spirit-dancer didn't say where he intended to take the Chaco tribe. He just mentioned they would be following the spinning sun out of there.

Darkness set in, but Salamander still needed to sort out his thoughts before heading back home. Jopin had once advised him to walk in his people's moccasins in order to determine how they would accept a controversial ruling. What would it take for Salamander to gain their trust, especially now that he would be asking them to follow him out of their beloved homeland? They would certainly encounter challenging and difficult times, which would be quite different than what they had been used to. This beautiful canyon had supplied them with everything they ever needed and more. They weren't used to going thirsty or hungry, and they certainly weren't used to hot and harsh climates. Would they stick with him when times got tough, seeming impossible? Only if they saw him as an honest leader who always did what was best for them.

Thoughts such as these haunted him. The current situation with his elders had revealed a big weakness in his leadership. Perhaps he wasn't qualified to be a chief. The longer he sat there, the more concerned, frustrated, and disillusioned he became.

The moon traveled a good distance across the sky and sank into the horizon before he realized he had to get home. Little-acorn would be worried. He slowly but carefully walked back in the dark, using the noise of the falling water as his guide. His eyes had started to adjust to the darkness, by the time he finally reached the village.

He quietly entered his home, attempting not to wake Little-acorn. But, she had been quietly waiting for him in the dark, sitting up on the bed with her legs crossed, tears running down her cheeks.

"Little-acorn, are you still awake? I walked out of the village, all the way to the mouth of the canyon. The time got away from me, and before I knew it, half of the night had passed by. I'm so sorry for worrying you."

"Did you expect to sneak in here while I was asleep? I'm not blind. I know exactly what you've been up to. Who is she?"

"No. It's nothing like that. I walked upstream and stopped to think on a rock. The night slipped away before I realized how late it was."

"The night always slips away when you're with a woman. Isn't that the same direction where the promiscuous women live?"

"Yes. They live in that direction, but I wasn't there. I was way north of there, at the top of the canyon."

"On a rock with her?"

"I was there by myself. Why don't you believe me?"

"Because I'm tired of you coming home in the middle of the night. This time, you made it home, right before sunrise. I think it's time for you to take me back home to live with my relatives in Chaco."

Salamander tried to hug her. "Don't think like that."

She pulled back. "Don't touch me. I'm tired of your lies. You don't fool me. Get away from me."

"Little-acorn, you must believe me. I don't—"

"You listen. I'm not blind. I saw you today with all those women. I've never seen you with such a big grin on your face. You usually have a mad face when you look at me."

"Oh, I see. You think I was with those women today. I can explain. They came to talk to me, because they wanted to know about our plans for the spring festival."

"So you talked to them about the festival? You surely don't talk to me about it."

"I didn't. I told them they would have to wait."

"You don't have to tell lies anymore. I saw you with my very own eyes. Besides, people have been talking about how you visit the promiscuous women. I used to make excuses for you, but not anymore. I would tell them you had business there. I was fooling myself. I now know the truth. I'm the biggest fool in Tyuoni."

"I go there to visit Wild-flower. Why have you told them I have business there? I've been visiting her since—"

"So have all of the other men."

"I can't talk to you. Listen, I can understand why you doubt me, but it's not like that. Even my father talked to me about those women today."

"What did he tell you?"

"He told me these women could ruin my reputation, and that I've worked too hard to build up my good name in the village. He didn't think I should be seen talking to them."

"You see, even your father knows about you. Many people know."

"He saw me talking to those women today, so he warned me not to let myself get in that position again. There's nothing going on."

"So I should be happy, because I'm the only one who knows the truth?"

"I haven't done anything wrong. Father was only trying to protect me from getting into trouble."

"Who is he to give you advice? You learned from him. You're just like him."

"That's unfair. You know better than to accuse me of being like my father. I had a terrible day, so I had to take a walk. You don't know what I've been going through. I sat on a rock all night long and now this. I can't handle it. I'm going back outside."

"Go. You want to get away from me. Go back to Wild-flower. You're a cheater and you know it. It runs in your family. Take me back to Chaco, tomorrow."

It was easy to lose his temper when it came to being compared to his father's past. It seemed so unfair to be blamed for something his father had done. But that was years ago, before Little-acorn even knew his father. Salamander wanted to say something in return to get even, but all he could think about was how she did not appreciate him. He had worked so hard to be a good chief to the village, but she didn't care. She wanted his complete attention, on top of all these accusations. Selfish. All she had managed to do was criticize him for every single thing he said or did. His temper was ready to get out of control, but then he noticed how she stood with her legs wide apart, balancing her big stomach. He realized she hadn't always been like that, not until the pregnancy. "You can't walk all that distance. You're pregnant."

"You finally noticed? What do you care? I'll probably lose the baby anyway, because I'm so unappreciated. You've humiliated me."

Salamander froze. All this time, he had worried about how the old and weak ones would handle the difficult journey out of the canyon. He hadn't even considered what it would do to Little-acorn. She could lose the baby.

She lowered her voice and spoke slowly but firmly. "Just look at you. Your face shows your guilt."

"I'm not guilty of what you think. I suddenly realized how pregnant you are."

"Well surprise, surprise, but how can that be? You look at other women, because I am pregnant. I'm no longer appealing to you. You're just like your father. Why didn't you tell me about him, before you brought me here? Take me back to Chaco."

"I can't. It wouldn't do any good for you to go there. I mean—"

"You're now making up stories about my home? I'm sick of you. Get away from me. I'll get home on my own. I don't need you."

Salamander tried to hug her, but she lifted her arm in anger. He quickly moved back. "You need to calm down. I can't talk to you about anything right now. Nothing is how you see it. You need to relax, for the baby's sake. We'll talk tomorrow. I'll try to explain."

"Get out of here. You're disgusting."

He took one last look at her and then slowly walked out into the darkness.

The Least of Everyone

Jopin waited for the right opportunity to get away from Deer-tracker. He needed to spend some personal time with the gods. Although he had purified himself prior to his prayer quest, he hadn't been completely honest with his chief nor with his wife, or even with himself. By confessing his sins and failures, Jopin would attempt to find favor with the gods. Asking for forgiveness and mercy would be the first step, because he had to be as pure as possible before stepping onto the sacred grounds of the Shrine of the Soaring Eagles.

The night had brought a cold chill with it, but the warmth of the fire seemed to create a soothing, relaxing, and comforting atmosphere. Deer-tracker sat next to him, looking out into the darkness, eyes wide open. He wouldn't be falling asleep for some time, so Jopin searched the skies for the right combination of stars to appear. They would signify the appropriate time for him to leave Deer-tracker and continue on his prayer quest.

"Grandpa, I meant what I said. I want to be just like you when I grow up."

"No, Deer-tracker, we already talked about this. I couldn't even make it to the top of the cliff without your help. Besides, this foolish old man shouldn't even expect to talk to the gods, because he lied to Chief Salamander and to the other elders. I couldn't accept what they wanted me to do, so I told them I was feeling ill. I couldn't get myself to vote. Instead of telling them the truth, I pretended to be sick so I could have enough time to come ask the gods for the right answer. You don't want to become dishonest like me."

"Grandpa, they may have already voted without you, since you didn't attend the meeting."

"No, they must wait for me. This situation requires a unanimous vote."

"Is that why we're here, on top of this mountain?"

"I'm not supposed to talk about it. What we discuss in the main kiva is sacred and very secret."

"You see, that's why I want to be like you. Everyone knows you're the greatest of the elders. They say you always know how to arrive at the right decision."

"This time I don't know. The answer the gods will give me might not be what I would want. I need the wisdom and the courage to do what is right, what Great Grandfather wants me to do."

"Do you have any advice for me, so I can become great like you?"

Jopin gently grabbed Deer-tracker's arm. "Listen, a dishonest person is not great. You also need to learn that it's wrong to want to be great. You may want to remember the old proverb: If you have more than your brother, you're not taking good enough care of him. Likewise, I say to you, if you desire to be the greatest, you must learn how to become a servant to the least of your brothers. Deer-tracker, it's not how we see ourselves but rather, how our creator sees us. Great Grandfather sees deep within our hearts. He placed us here on Mother Earth to love and serve our brothers and sisters. Just as you thanked Brother-squirrel for giving up his life for us, we must likewise give our lives for our brothers and sisters."

Deer-tracker stood back and frowned at Jopin. "You said you weren't going to jump off the cliff. Now you say we have to give up our lives for our brothers. I don't want to be here if you're going to sacrifice yourself for the rest of us."

"No, Deer-tracker, being a servant to your people is a sacrifice in itself. I'm not going to jump. Your grandfather would become known as the mad elder who lost his mind and jumped to his death."

"Grandpa, I understand that in the old days, a young boy or girl would be sacrificed. Perhaps I'm here with you, because Great Grandfather wants you to sacrifice me. I'm willing to be sacrificed, if that's what Great Grandfather wants."

Jopin quickly looked up at the stars and then at Deer-tracker. "That won't be necessary. Don't even think like that. We would end up with the same result. The people would say the god of darkness possessed the old elder's mind and made him murder his own grandson." Jopin laughed in a wild manner. "They would say I went crazy."

Deer-tracker joined in with his own little nervous laugh. "Our ancestors were insane? I thought sacrifice was a sacred practice."

Jopin stopped laughing. Deer-tracker had made an important statement. "In the old days, long before the days of your grandfather and long before the days of my grandfather's grandfather, the people would offer up their one most precious possession to the Almighty Creator. A young son or daughter would be sacrificed in exchange for an answer to their prayers. Perhaps it hadn't rained for a long time, so no grass, no shrubs, no berries and soon, no animals. That meant no food. The elders would then decide the gods were disappointed or angry at them. So in exchange for rain, they would sacrifice the most beautiful young person in the village. The victim would have been required to be pure, almost sinless, to be pleasing to the gods. So yes, this was indeed, a most sacred offering."

Deer-tracker stood there with his mouth open, which interrupted Jopin's thoughts for a while. "Sometimes the elders would wait a very long time for an answer and still, no rain. What should they do, sacrifice another precious child? It always came down to this question: Did they perform the sacrifice because Great Grandfather wanted them to do it, or did they fool themselves into thinking he wanted them to do it? What if they were wrong? They would have taken a precious life and ruined any special plans which Great Grandfather may have had for this special child. Life is most precious. I believe we're making a most serious and critical mistake, when we speak for Great Grandfather in such matters."

"But Grandpa, you and Grandma keep talking about sacrifice?"

"We mean personal sacrifice and hardships, not taking someone's life. Your grandmother knew I might be on a special sacrifice, which required secrecy and time alone. The sacrifice I'm on, the answer I need, is for the good of the entire village. We must do what is right. The only one who knows the correct answer, is Great Grandfather."

"How do you get Great Grandfather to talk to you? Could you teach me how to talk with him? I wish so much to hear his voice."

Jopin put his arm around Deer-tracker and then cleared his throat. "Well, you heard his voice, right after being born, when your skull was still soft. Great Grandfather welcomed you into his world and told you about his love, and about the special purpose he had for you. This happens every time a newborn appears to be happily carrying on a conversation with someone, even though he is all by himself. Parents worry that evil spirits or the god of darkness might attempt to communicate with their babies, so they don't take them out of their home for at least forty days. Their skulls would have hardened enough by that time to protect them from these evil spirits."

"Grandpa, when I first saw you at the cliff, you said you were making a sacrifice to the gods. Now you say you must talk to Great Grandfather. Why would you make a sacrifice to the gods if you really want to talk to Great Grandfather?"

"It makes me happy to know you're interested in such matters. Brother-eagle, more than any other animal, can fly the highest, closer to the gods. I will visit the Shrine of the Soaring Eagles to ask Brother-eagle to deliver my prayer to them. The gods will present my request to Great Grandfather. Because they serve as his special messengers, they will then deliver his answer to me and hopefully, tell me what to do."

Deer-tracker raised his head, opened his mouth, and looked up above Jopin's head. He had an idea. "Grandpa, isn't there a way to soften your skull so you can listen to Great Grandfather again and hear his answer? It might have been easier for you to have softened your skull than for you to have climbed the cliff."

Jopin couldn't tell if Deer-tracker was serious, but he laughed, anyway. "No, that's not possible. My skull is old and very hard. The only way to communicate with Great Grandfather is through fasting, making sacrifices, and praying."

Deer-tracker looked like he was ready to ask another question. "There are many elders. Why are you the only one on a sacrifice, asking for an answer? Don't they talk to the gods? Shouldn't they be up here with you? What can I do to help?"

"Those are a lot of questions. The other elders have already decided to support Chief Salamander, but I have not been able to reach a decision. Nothing has turned out as planned. You had to help me get up the cliff. I broke my fast promise, and I'm not at the Shrine of the Soaring Eagles. You, my little grandson, have already helped me. It's now all up to me."

"You're not a failure, Grandpa. Great Grandfather created all of us with problems and faults, and he loves us just the way we are. Doesn't he already know you were weak and couldn't make it to the top? You had no choice, but to break your fast promise. You can still offer your prayers at the Shrine of the Soaring Eagles."

Jopin put both hands on Deer-tracker's shoulders. "Thank you. I'll pray there tomorrow morning, at daybreak. The senior elder should agree with his chief and with the other elders on this most important issue. I failed them, as well as Great Grandfather. How can Chief Salamander expect the entire village to follow and obey his orders, if his senior elder refuses to support him?"

"What does Chief Salamander want us to do?"

"Sorry, can't tell you. I shouldn't have allowed you to get involved in this situation, but I'm now very confused. I feel like I should talk to you, yet I can't." Jopin searched the skies. The stars hadn't moved very far across the sky, but he felt they had a message for him. He could help his special grandson prepare for his life. "You're wondering what you should become when you grow up. Perhaps you should just concentrate on becoming a good citizen of your village."

"What kind of citizen?"

"Like your father. He serves his fellow brothers and sisters by working hard to bring them meat to eat. You have inherited his good arm and hunting instincts. You could certainly become a good hunter like him, unless you're thinking of something else. It's important to find out what Great Grandfather wants you to become."

"How, Grandpa? How do I find out? "

"You might find out this summer. Your parents say you're ready to go on your vision quest. The gods will speak to your heart at that time."

"I know I'll go on a vision quest, but I don't know what to expect. I'm a little scared about what might happen."

"It's normal to be worried and scared. You will first go through a purification ceremony early in the morning, and then you'll be sent out alone, far into the woods, where you'll remain without food or water for as long as it takes your mind to be ready. Great Grandfather will present you with your very own vision and with your own spirit guide, a person or an animal who will become your spiritual helper for life. I can't tell you what to expect, because it will be your very own personal experience between you, Great Grandfather, and your spirit guide. This will be the most important experience of your life. You'll find out if you have any special gifts or powers, like the power of leadership or the gift of healing."

"Leadership? That would be nice. How can a chief be a servant to his people, when the people are the ones whom serve the chief?"

This question reminded Jopin about the legend of Chief Ene-wetok. He grabbed a long stick, poked the fire, and started to tell Deer-tracker the story. "Someone had intentionally been destroying the personal property of some of the villagers, the kind of trouble youngsters get into to get attention. In order to embarrass the youngsters, Chief Ene-wetok proclaimed the perpetrators, when caught, would be tied to a tree in the center of the village and whipped, where everyone could see them."

Jopin paused to remember the details of the legend. "When the perpetrator was caught and delivered to the chief, it turned out to be Chief Ene-wetok's very own elderly father. Chief Ene-wetok thought about how his father had been acting more and more like a mischievous boy, and not like the wise old man who had brought him up. The old man couldn't remember his own son's name, half the time. However, the chief announced there was no excuse for all the damage and distress his father had caused. The punishment would be delivered as proclaimed. Chief Ene-wetok ordered one of his warriors to tie the old man to a tree and whip him with a long thin branch from a willow tree. The old man was tied to a tree but, just as the warrior was about to carry out his orders, Chief Ene-wetok stood up and gently put his arms around his father. He covered the old man's back with his, and then nodded for the lashings to begin."

"Wow Grandpa, what a sad legend. Is that how a good leader becomes the least of everyone?"

"Yes. A chief does not ask for the position, nor does he compete for it, because he doesn't want to be great. Rather, he takes the position, because people want to reward him for being the least of everyone. As you just learned from the legend, being great means being the least. A chief must be fair, honest, strong and compassionate. Yet, he must enforce the laws of the village, or else his people will not follow his direction. He sets the example for his people to follow."

Deer-tracker looked confused, so Jopin decided to tell a different version of the legend. "This time, the perpetrator was not the chief's father, but rather some other old man from the village." Jopin told about how Chief Ene-wetok stood up to take the place of the old man. But when he signaled for the whipping to start, the old man's son came forward and announced it was his duty to take his father's place, not Chief Ene-wetok's. Jopin made sure Deer-tracker was listening before continuing. "A chief must not only serve his people, but also model the behavior expected of the rest of the villagers."

"Grandpa, both versions of the legend were very good. It takes a very special person to have a high position in the village. Perhaps I should become a hunter like my papa, so I won't have to be the least of everyone."

Jopin started to chuckle. "Are you not aware of the number of times your father and his hunting party have not had enough meat for everyone in the village? At times like these, they are the only ones who do not take any meat home to their families. And, when they do bring enough, they always give the choice pieces of meat to everyone else and kept the least favorable for themselves. Great Grandfather put your father on this earth to feed the rest of us, even if he and his family have to go without. I'm very proud of Great-hawk. My daughter couldn't have married a better man. He's certainly, the least of everyone."

Deer-tracker portrayed a proud look on his face. "Papa said he was going to visit the Shrine of the Twin Lions. Is this like the Shrine of the Soaring Eagles? Would papa be making a sacrifice?"

"Yes, I believe he would. The Shrine of the Twin Lions is up there, past the west ridge, and then a long ways south. Most hunters make at least one sacrificial trip in their lifetime to the Shrine of the Twin Lions."

"Why do some people pray at the Shrine of the Twin Lions and others at the Shrine of the Soaring Eagles?"

"We make a sacrificial trip to the Shrine of the Soaring Eagles to ask Brother-eagle to deliver our prayers to the gods for us. It's a little different when a hunter visits the Shrine of the Twin Lions. There, they ask the twin lions to teach them the hunting ways of the lion."

"Papa told me there was a place where two lions are carved from stone. Is this the same place as the Shrine of the Twin Lions? Who carved them?"

Jopin decided to tell Deer-tracker about the legend of Lion-hunter. "This happened a long time ago, before Tyuonyi, when only some of the cliff houses existed. It was the father, mother, and their young baby boy, not even old enough to start walking. They called him Baby-rabbit, because he crawled around with his behind up in the air, like a little bunny tail. They had been playing and bathing in the creek, but the sun was hot, so they rested in the shade of the trees, where they fell asleep. The mother heard her baby cry out, as if something had happened. She stood up to help him, but Baby-rabbit was gone. In panic, she woke the father. They heard Baby-rabbit cry out again, so they ran in that direction. The cry seemed to have come from above the canyon. The father started to climb and froze when he saw a large lion carrying his baby in its jaws."

Deer-tracker covered his mouth and yelled out, "No!"

Jopin continued. "The father yelled and threw stones at the lion, but it was too quick for him. It just kept climbing, running faster, and getting further away. It jumped over the ridge and disappeared. Some of the neighbors heard the commotion and came to help. They climbed the ridge and searched for Baby-rabbit, but nothing. The search continued for three or four days, but the lion couldn't be tracked. They finally gave up. The lion had probably taken Baby-rabbit to feed to her cubs."

"Grandpa, this is a very sad legend."

Jopin nodded. "The parents had to face the fact that Baby-rabbit was gone, and they would never see their son again. Devastated, they were unable to eat and sleep, so they lost a lot of weight. They even started to argue and fight, blaming each other for the tragedy. More importantly though, they blamed themselves. If only they had not fallen asleep. If only they had taken better care of their baby. The father continued to climb the canyon to search for his son, each time going further away from the area. Sometimes, he wouldn't return for two or three days. At first, he hoped for a miracle. Later, he would have been happy, just to find Baby-rabbit's bones. He then feared lions might eat bones as well as meat. He finally stopped climbing the canyon. The father hated the area, never wanting to ever go up that ridge again."

Deer-tracker tapped Jopin on his arm. "That's not a legend. It's a sad story about a little boy who was eaten by a lion."

Jopin laughed. "There's more to the story. You have to be patient and listen." Jopin cleared his throat. "On the following year, a hunting party came to visit Baby-rabbit's father and mother. They did not want to raise false hope, but they had seen some tracks, possibly the footprints of a small child, mixed in with lion tracks. They took the father to the area, but the tracks were old and thus, too hard to distinguish. They could've been the tracks of a small child or of some other animal. It gave the parents hope that their baby might still be alive. Once again, the father started to search the area, but there weren't any tracks to follow."

Deer-tracker smiled. "I'm glad there's more to the legend."

"Then again on the following year, in the distant north, the same hunting team discovered a small human footprint amongst the lion tracks. This time the tracks were fresh. The hunters followed them, but the lions became aware they were being followed. They started to run. One of the hunters climbed a tree, hoping to get a glimpse of the lions. He saw five or six lions running amongst the brush. It looked like two mother lions and their cubs. He also saw a small, naked boy running with the lions."

By this time, Deer-tracker had sat up straight, anxiously waiting to hear what happened. Jopin told about how, once again, the hunting party came to visit the boy's parents. "Both parents started to cry. This had to be their Baby-rabbit. The hunters took them to the area. The footprints were still quite visible, but the lions and the boy once again, had moved out of the area. The entire village got together and organized a massive search party, but the lions and the boy were nowhere to be found. The parents were sad, but at least they had a new hope that Little-boy could still be alive. The snows and the cold of winter came, making it difficult for the people to conduct a thorough search for Baby-rabbit."

Deer-tracker couldn't wait to hear the end of the story. "Grandpa, how did they find him?"

Jopin motioned for him to wait. "They never did," he announced, as he looked into Deer-tracker's eyes.

Deer-tracker lowered his head, but Jopin immediately continued, "Be patient; there's more. Early one morning at daybreak, his parents were awakened by the growling of lions."

"Grandpa, you said they never found him."

"You have to be patient." Jopin told about how the parents peeked out the door and saw Baby-rabbit standing in the middle of the field, naked. He looked cold, confused, scared, and troubled. They feared he might run from them, so they slowly and carefully approached him. He would not face them, but instead kept looking out into the distance, beyond the creek. Two lions stood there, staring back at Baby-rabbit. His mother started sobbing, causing Baby-rabbit to be afraid of her, so she tried to control herself, not wanting to lose him again."

"Grandpa, they did find him."

Jopin laughed. "They did not. He found them."

Deer-tracker didn't think his grandfather was funny. "Did Baby-rabbit ever recognize his own mother?"

"He had probably not seen a human since taken away as a baby. His mother gently spoke to him, hoping he would remember her. She told him how much she loved him and how happy she was to see him. She held out her arms to invite him to come to her, but Baby-rabbit just stood there, confused. He couldn't understand what she was saying, since he had never learned to speak. He just studied her. She started to sing softly to him, like when he was a baby. He seemed to like the sound. She asked the father to go back to the house and bring out the gourd-rattle Baby-rabbit played with, when he was a baby. The father came back gently shaking the rattle. Baby-rabbit became interested in the sounds coming from it."

Jopin explained how the parents had slowly walked back towards the house, gently shaking the rattle and singing to him. Baby-rabbit kept looking back across the creek, as he cautiously followed them to their house. "Once inside, they showed him several things to get him interested, one of which was a little doll he had played with as a baby. He didn't show any signs of remembering it. Baby-rabbit was shivering, so they carefully wrapped a fur blanket around his shoulders. Looking at them suspiciously, he did allow them to cover him. He seemed to like the warmth and softness of the furs. His mother wished she could grab and hug him, but she feared it would scare him away. They placed some cooked squash and corn in front of him and motioned for him to eat, but he just looked at the food. They put some in their own mouths to show him what to do. He approached the food, not liking it at first, but eventually he did eat all of it. Anyway Deer-tracker, that's the story of Baby-rabbit."

But this ending wasn't acceptable to Deer-tracker. He wanted to know what happened to Baby-rabbit. "Did he grow up with his human parents? Did he learn how to speak? Was he wild?"

Jopin looked up at the sky to study the position of the stars. Morning wouldn't come for some time, so he patiently answered. He told about how Baby-rabbit had learned how to become human: how to talk, eat, dress, and act. He had to learn how to become part of this new family. "Still loyal to his lion family, his twin lion-sisters would occasionally come to visit. They would wait in the field for Baby-rabbit to come out and join them. The three of them would go up the canyon where they ran around and had fun. The lions taught him how to stock, hunt, and capture his prey. They even taught him how to patiently wait for an animal to come near, before pouncing on it. He learned how to kill a skunk when it first stuck its head out of its burrow."

"Oh, Grandpa, why would anyone want to kill a skunk? That's disgusting!"

"Because skunk meat tastes very good, especially if it doesn't have the smell. And besides, their fur is used to ward off evil spirits during religious ceremonies. The lions taught him how to kill it in its own home, where it won't spray. If you make sure not to burst the stink sac while cleaning out brother-skunk, you'll have a good meal. Why did you bring me squirrel instead of skunk?"

Deer-tracker laughed, but he still wanted to know what the lions had taught Baby-rabbit. Jopin described how Baby-rabbit could dive to the ground, land on his two hands, place his feet right behind his hands, and then leap forward to capture his prey. "Baby-rabbit could grab a deer by its neck and then stab it with his knife. He became known as the best hunter ever. His hunting friends tried to learn how to do this, but they never could master his technique. The name, Baby-rabbit, no longer suited him, so they started calling him Lion-hunter. That became his new name."

"Does the Shrine of the Twin Lions have anything to do with his lion sisters?"

"Yes. I almost forgot why I even told you the legend. One night, while in his sleep, the spirits of his twin sisters appeared to Lion-hunter. One of them had become very ill and died. This caused the other sister to go into shock, and her heart stopped beating as well. They were born together and they died together. Lion-hunter became very sad, for he loved his sisters so much. He claimed he had lived, because his sisters didn't let his lion-mother eat him. Their spirits told him they would now be available to help him or any other hunter. All they had to do was summon them. Lion-hunter climbed the mountain and went to the lion's den where they first took him. He found two large rocks and used the hard, shiny black stone to carve and shape them into the image of his lion-sisters. It took him four full moon cycles to carve those big rocks into a memorial for his sisters. This place is now called the Shrine of the Twin Lions. Every hunter makes at least one trip in his life to the shrine to ask the lion-sisters for help and to seek their advice and knowledge of hunting."

"Papa never told me about Lion-hunter."

"Oh no. I ruined the surprise your father had for you. He probably intended to tell you the story about Baby-rabbit when he took you to the Shrine of the Twin

Lions. I'll have to explain to him about how I never planned to tell you the story. It just happened."

Deer-tracker revealed a proud smile. "I now understand about being the least of everyone. The farmers sacrifice and work hard to supply everyone in the village with corn, squash, and beans. The potters sacrifice and work hard to supply bowls and dishes to the villagers. Likewise, the weavers sacrifice to supply weavings for everyone." He started to mention the medicine man, but then he stopped. "What about our medicine man? It must be quite an honor to cure someone. How does one become a medicine man?"

"It would be almost impossible for you to become a medicine man. Medicine-maker would have to train you, but he already has a son of his own. They usually train their own children, and pass down their special powers and healing secrets to them."

Jopin explained how it would take most of Deer-tracker's life to learn the trade. Deer-tracker would have to learn all of the ceremonies, chants, songs and dances, and also, how to identify and prepare countless medicinal plants. And then, he would have to learn the secret and sacred names of each and every part of the body, plus the many prayers required during healing rituals. Deer-tracker would have to learn how to make his sacred medicine rattles, drums and medicine bags.

"The medicine man possesses special powers, like no other. However, they say his life is tougher than everyone else's. He's required to be pure, because the healing of any one individual depends on his ability to communicate with Great Grandfather and the gods. The gods instruct him what to do in order to conduct a curing. The medicine man can't even think of the person being treated as being unworthy, even if that person were a thief, a promiscuous person, a murderer, or someone evil. It would be a major mistake for the medicine man to believe he were better than this bad or evil person."

"That's not fair. It wouldn't be the medicine man's fault if the person were a thief, or worse."

Jopin explained how that judgment, in itself, could keep Great Grandfather's gods from giving him the knowledge and power required for a healing. "A medicine man can never brag about the good he has done. He must be the most humble person in the village, the least of everyone, especially less than the person being healed."

"That doesn't seem fair. I don't know if I would be capable of becoming a medicine man." Deer-tracker leaned back to look at Jopin. "Grandpa, are the gods physically present when they talk to us? Can we see and touch them, or are they like a spirit? Papa says spirits are like smoke. You see them, but you can't touch or grab them."

"I've never been able to touch a god. They appear to me as a dream." Jopin had spoken softly, as if telling a secret. "However, when White-buffalo-woman appeared to our ancestors a long time ago, she handed them the sacred pipe and taught them how to prepare the red-willow bark tobacco for use in their prayers. The gods appear to me in a vision after I summon them with my sacred pipe."

"What does Great Grandfather look like? Is he big and strong? Does he look wise? Does he smile a lot, or does he look angry?"

Jopin was overwhelmed with so many questions. "I don't know. I have never heard of anyone who has ever seen him. They say he created us in his image, so I assume he must look like us. But, I have never heard of anyone who has actually seen his face or any part of him. Some refer to him as Pure Bright Light. He is magnificent and majestic. We'll get to see him face-to-face when we die, depending on whether we have obeyed his commandments or not. We can't see him, but for some reason, he does allow us to see his gods through our visions."

"It's interesting that he uses his gods to talk to us. Do we only get to talk to him during the forty days after we're born, when our skulls are soft?"

"No, Deer-tracker, communication does not stop at birth. It continues throughout our entire lives. He talks to us during our vision quest, and also during our prayer quests. He prepares us as we go through life, by giving us the right spiritual gift at just the right time."

"Like what, Grandpa?"

"Like today. We've had a lot of discussion about Great Grandfather and his gods, so knowledge has come to you tonight through me, your grandfather. If you think of it, you have already been given a lot of knowledge. This will continue as you mature and go through different experiences. You will soon go on your very own vision quest, where you will be presented with your very own spirit guide. Deer-tracker, Great Grandfather has prepared you well for your age. You know what is right, what is wrong, and what pleases Great Grandfather. Your understanding of such things will make you a very wise man. He might be giving you all of this wisdom to prepare you to become a councilor to your people. Remember when you asked if our Almighty Creator could be angry enough to burn down the forest or even an entire village?"

"Yes. I was wondering about the sacredness of fire."

"Not everyone realizes Great Grandfather is all powerful and mighty. Some think of him as being completely merciful, always ready to forgive, but as you made me realize, he can easily eliminate us. You may become one of our great thinkers."

"I was wondering about the sacredness of fire. Perhaps I should have wondered about the sacredness of life."

Jopin felt so proud of his grandson. Deer-tracker had helped him forget about his failures, and about how he had disappointed the gods. His family was certainly much more important than how Chief Salamander had treated him.

Jopin's stubbornness had brought him to this place on top of the cliff, and now he was spending time alone with his grandson. Teaching Deer-tracker about Great Grandfather had brought Jopin, not only satisfaction, but hope for the future. The quietness of the night, the relaxing atmosphere, and the love he received from Deer-tracker had given him the opportunity to examine his true feelings. Was he upset because of the pending migration or because of the way Chief Salamander had betrayed him. His family was certainly much more important than the migration.

Deer-tracker leaned on Jopin's shoulder, so Jopin raised his arm and hugged him, allowing Deer-tracker to snuggle up against Jopin. It felt good to just enjoy his grandson in the quietness of the night. At that moment, Jopin didn't care if he would ever make it to the Shrine of the Soaring Eagles.

The logs had burned themselves down to coals. Jopin looked into the fire and noticed how the flames had slowly diminished to a red glow. Could this be a sign for him to give up his quest? Yes, all the signs and events had indicated he should stop worrying about the evacuation. His pride and stubbornness had caused his attempts to fail.

Jopin decided he would walk back down to the village in the morning and tell Chief Salamander the truth about his illness. It was time for him to devote more attention to his wife and family. Another member of the Bear Clan could take his position. Jopin felt relieved, because the future of Tyuoni was no longer his responsibility. Bright-sunflower had advised him to let Chief Salamander and the other elders decide what to do about the migration, but he needed time away to appreciate her wisdom and advice. He could hardly wait to go back home to Bright-sunflower. His prayer quest was over.

Sins of the Village

The night had grown quiet, except for the hooting of an owl and an occasional rustle or cracking of twigs, the sounds of wildlife walking nearby. Jopin and Deer-tracker had stopped talking. Deer-tracker's eyes were still open, looking out into the darkness. He looked content, but tired. Time for prayer had finally come, but Jopin no longer cared. He still intended to devote some personal time with the gods to confess his sins, but not until the morning, right before heading back down the mountain.

Jopin felt relieved that the decision to evacuate the entire village no longer depended on him. He ignored the owl hooting. The flickering of the campfire reflecting off Deer-tracker's forehead, cheeks and nose, put Jopin into a trance. His mind wandered back to the time, early in his marriage, when he first became a father.

He visualized his newborn son sleeping next to Bright-sunflower. Jopin couldn't control his excitement, for he now had a son to hold, love, play with, and enjoy. He would have to teach his son the right way of life, the path set forth by Great Grandfather, and the customs and traditions of the Tyuonyi tribe. Jopin wanted his son to have a good, satisfying life. Bright-sunflower had brought him so much love and happiness. He could see how young and beautiful she looked, sitting on the floor with her legs crossed, naked from the waist up. Her breasts had grown big and full, like ripe delicious melons ready for savoring. Great Grandfather had filled them with milk for their baby to drink, so he could be nourished. Jopin told her how she had made him the happiest man in the world. Jopin would now have to be sure to follow Great Grandfather's example and help his son grow and become the person the Almighty would want him to be. That moment truly became the beginning of his conversion. He now had to be a good role model, because his baby would study and copy his every action, emotion, and more importantly of all, his bad habits. From that moment forward, Jopin had intentionally attempted to set a good example for his son.

"Grandpa, Grandpa, what's wrong. Are you feeling sick again?"

"No, I'm not sick, just remembering the time when I first became a father to your Uncle Double-eagle."

"What was Uncle like, as a baby?"

"Just like when you were a baby. You can't imagine the love one feels, the love one has to offer, until you become a parent. Your uncle had those precious little strawberry lips of his. He and your grandma were the most beautiful creatures in the whole world. This truly was the most wonderful thing that had ever happened to me."

Deer-tracker looked confused. "What about my mother, when she was born? Did you feel as much love for her as you did for Uncle?"

The question surprised Jopin. He quickly put his thoughts together and then answered. "Your uncle was very special, but not any more than your mother. I, once again, went through the same happiness a second time. She had those big beautiful eyes and all that black hair. Her eyes sparked like bright pebbles shining in clear shallow water, so we named her Brilliant-pebbles. She was so precious and beautiful. The love and emotions I felt for her and for your grandmother were exactly the same as those I felt for your uncle. As a matter of fact, I had the same loving emotions for each and every one of our children." Jopin stopped and then continued. "This happiness happened again, when my grandson was born."

This pleased Deer-tracker.

"My only regret, we only had one daughter. That makes your mother very special. I get to see her every day though. All of the boys, your uncles, had to move away to distant villages to live with their wives, but we were blessed when you were born."

Jopin felt good about how he had answered. "Deer-tracker, it's late. You should get some sleep."

"Grandpa, I will stay awake and keep the fire going so you can stay warm while you sleep. I'll serve you by keeping you comfortable."

"Thanks, but I'm not sleepy. And besides, I won't let you serve me. I should serve you. You would have to stay up all night if you were to serve me."

Excited, Deer-tracker jumped up and started talking. "Do you mean it Grandpa? I can stay up all night with you? We can both stay up. I've learned so much, but there's so much more I've been wondering about. You said you would not teach me, but you would answer my questions."

Jopin knew he had spoken the wrong words. He wanted to object, but the thought came back to him that, perhaps the gods wanted him to teach Deer-tracker about such things. After all, Deer-tracker did appear to him as an answer to his prayer for help. Jopin would gladly devote whatever time would be required for his grandson. Deer-tracker was indeed, much more important than any migration, and besides, his prayer quest was over.

"The longer I continue talking to you, the more trouble I get into with your mama and papa. How will I ever face your father after you tell him about the things we discussed tonight?"

Deer-tracker's big smile showed he was not giving this a second thought.

Jopin knew he had to be firm with Deer-tracker. "We can continue to talk some more, but I must have some personal time to pray early in the morning. This I have to do by myself." He looked up to see how far the moon had traveled across the sky, but then, he realized he no longer cared. Jopin could quietly ask the gods for forgiveness while talking to his grandson and then, just take a little personal time to perform a prayer dance in private.

"Okay Grandpa, I won't bother you."

Jopin noticed how Deer-tracker became deep in thought. "You're not bothering. What's wrong?"

Deer-tracker blurted out, "We have a good chief, don't we? Is Chief Salamander a servant to his people?"

Jopin had expected Deer-tracker to continue asking about the gods, not Chief Salamander. "Yes, he's responsible for all of us. He tries to do what's right for Tyuonyi. Why do you ask?"

"Why isn't he up here, instead of you, or why isn't he here with you? Doesn't he want to know what the gods want us to do?"

This question made Jopin think about how Chief Salamander had attempted to force the elders to support the evacuation and worse, prohibit him from the discussions. This behavior had led to Jopin's almost impossible sacrifice of climbing the cliff, while fasting. Chief Salamander's actions had pressured Jopin to behave dishonestly and hide his intentions from Bright-sunflower.

Jopin wanted to tell Deer-tracker his true feelings about Chief Salamander, but he couldn't even tell him about his decision to discontinue his prayer quest. "I must pray to the gods in my own way. Chief Salamander already had his time before the gods. He did attend the Chiefs' Pow-Wow at Chaco, and he does have his elders to help him with important decisions. Chief Salamander has been good for the village. I'm here because I need to be here, without Chief Salamander."

Once again, Jopin had failed to tell the whole truth. How could he talk to Deer-tracker without telling him everything?

Deer-tracker positioned himself to ask another question. "How did Chief Salamander get his name? When I ask some of the older people, they get this dumb look on their faces and never answer. Have I been asking something I shouldn't?"

"What do you mean, this dumb look? It's okay to ask. They probably don't answer you because they don't want to, or because they don't know what to say. Maybe it's because Salamander is his nickname, not the name given to him at birth. His real name is Large-red-mushroom. You know those big, colorful mushrooms? They're poisonous, but they can be used for some medications, if prepared correctly. And, they're used in some very important ceremonies."

"But, they act like I said something wrong or that I shouldn't have asked that question." Deer-tracker swung his palms out and shrugged his shoulders in defeat.

Jopin wondered if he should tell Deer-tracker the truth. "Do you know about the game kids sometimes play on each other, when they go swimming? They wait for everyone to remove their clothing and jump into the water, and then they yell out, 'salamander, salamander.' This causes everyone to run out of the water covering their bum-holes with their hands. That's how Chief Salamander got his name."

Deer-tracker looked puzzled. "Chief Salamander liked to play that game?"

"His pretty mother, when she and others were swimming in the creek. Snowflake was very young at the time, just a little older than what you are today.

All of a sudden, she yelled out 'salamander, salamander.' Everyone ran out of the water, screaming and laughing, covering their bum-holes, everyone, except Snowflake. She was hysterical, crying out and screaming very loud. She said a salamander had attacked her."

"Is it true that a salamander can do that? I thought it was just a joke people played on each other."

"I don't know. I think someone made up the story a long time ago. But, a lot of people do believe a salamander can do bad things, through the use of black medicine. Her parents took her to the medicine man. He made her a special drink, but it didn't work. Her stomach started to grow. It grew bigger and bigger with each new moon until finally, she delivered a healthy baby boy, instead of having a ball of salamanders, as the story goes. Poor little Large-red-mushroom. People started calling him Son-of-salamander, even as a little baby. And then, as he got older, they just called him Salamander."

"Is he half salamander and half man?"

"No, he's all man. Snowflake refused to admit her baby had a human father. She would say her baby somehow came out human. Not even her parents knew who the father was. Snowflake brought shame to the family, so they disowned her, forcing her and her baby out of their home. The good elder, Gray-wolf, and his joyful wife, Singing-bluebird, were childless, so they invited her and her baby to come live with them. They had so much compassion for Snowflake."

"It sure was nice of them to take her in."

Jopin nodded. "But, as the baby grew, he started to look and act like the good elder who was helping to raise him. People started to wonder if Elder Gray-wolf might be Large-red-mushroom's true father."

"But Elder Gray-wolf was married." Deer-tracker had a surprised, but confused look on his face.

"Yes, Singing-bluebird became suspicious and confronted him. Elder Gray-wolf denied it, but deep in her heart, she knew he was Large-red-mushroom's father. She had noticed, not so much all the love and affection he gave Large-red-mushroom, but the way he looked at Snowflake.

Singing-bluebird had been betrayed. She grew jealous and bitter, unable to accept what her unfaithful husband had done to her. And worse, she didn't like what Elder Gray-wolf had done to young Snowflake."

Deer-tracker had been listening with a perplexed look. "Where is Singing-bluebird? I've never seen her."

Jopin motioned for him to wait. "Singing-bluebird first accused him of seducing Snowflake. She then accused him of forcing himself on her, since Snowflake was so young. He never answered her. Instead, he said the only honorable thing for him to do, would be to take Snowflake as his second wife. This was the last time his joyful wife ever smiled again. She climbed to the top of the cliff and jumped to her death, right over there." Jopin used the long stick he had been using to stoke the fire, to point in the direction where Singing-bluebird had jumped off the cliff.

Deer-tracker quickly leaned back in disbelief. "That's another sad story. That's why Chief Salamander's mother is so much younger than his father. I never knew Mr. Gray-wolf was once an elder? Grandpa, why did you refer to him as the good elder? Isn't he responsible for his wife's death and also, for Snowflake's sin?"

"Yes, he's very much responsible. I'm sorry I referred to him as the good elder. I did it on purpose. Deer-tracker, it's important for you to respect your elders, but always listen and watch closely. Just because someone holds a high position in the village does not mean he is a good person. Elder Gray-wolf proved he wasn't really a servant to his people. He only cared about himself. He seduced Snowflake or forced himself on her when she was only a child. This betrayal drove Singing-bluebird to her death. Chief Straight-arrow proclaimed Gray-wolf was no longer worthy to serve as an elder in the council. I referred to him as the good elder to get a reaction out of you. Some people aren't always what they appear to be."

Deer-tracker looked serious. "The title of elder is one of respect, but the name Gray isn't."

"I don't understand what you're telling me."

"Doesn't the color gray indicate he might be a shadowy figure?"

Jopin opened his eyes and then started to laugh. "Well in his case, you might be right. However, Gray-wolf has been a good father to Salamander and, as far as I know, a good husband to Snowflake. It looks like he might have learned his lesson and changed his ways."

Deer-tracker laughed out. "You mean, he got burned?"

"I believe so. He certainly has paid for his sins." Jopin smiled back at his grandson.

Deer-tracker looked perplexed again. "How could Chief Salamander bring a wife to come live here in Tyuoni? Isn't a man supposed to leave his mother and father, and go live at his wife's village? And, isn't Chief Salamander's wife not fulfilling her duties of caring for her own mother and father? Did she leave them behind to come live here in Tyuonyi?"

"You're very observant. Great Grandfather commands us to leave our mothers and fathers, and go live with our wives." He paused to think but then became sad, thinking about how Deer-tracker would soon be at the age when he would be leaving Tyuonyi in search of a wife." Jopin continued. "The situation with Chief Salamander just happened. Neither he nor Little-acorn intended to break Great Grandfather's commandment. He had vowed to remain single to help his mother take care of his aging father. The people saw him as a caring and giving person, so they asked him to serve as their chief. He met Little-acorn while attending a Chiefs' Pow-Wow at Chaco. Little-acorn's parents had both died, so he brought her back here with him. He asked the elders for permission to continue residing here in Tyuonyi, so Little-acorn could help care for his parents."

"Interesting. That was nice of Little-acorn to care for Chief Salamander's parents. Is that why Honey-bee also lives here?"

"Yes, Little-acorn wouldn't think of leaving her little sister behind."

"Grandpa, how did you get your name?"

Jopin laughed. My parents named me Jumping-bullfrog. I couldn't pronounce jumping, so they started calling me Jopin, the way I pronounced it as a child."

Deer-tracker smiled. "It's interesting that both you and Chief Salamander have names coming from animals that live both in, and out of water."

"I never thought of that. It's one more thing I've learned from my grandson tonight."

Jopin had a way of bringing out the best in Deer-tracker, who was always ready and eager to learn. "I have another question. You said we must be worthy enough for the gods to talk to us. Do you mean we must be the least of our brothers, if we want the gods to answer our questions?"

Deer-tracker had once again surprised Jopin with such a thought-provoking question. Jopin took a deep breath before answering. "I said we must be worthy, because if we don't make time for Great Grandfather, then why should he want to talk to us? We all make mistakes and do things we shouldn't. Fasting, sacrifice, cleansing, and prayer can make us worthy again. You first asked about fire. Great Grandfather can either allow us to go live with him up in the skies, or he can get rid of us, perhaps with fire, as we previously discussed. It all depends on how we have lived our lives. Have we been good, bad, or evil? If we've been very bad or evil, and have refused to go through a conversion, then we won't be worthy to be in his presence."

"Grandpa, since Great Grandfather can get rid of us through fire, is it possible for him to burn up our entire village? What if there were a lot of evil people living in our village? Could Tyuonyi be punished and burned to the ground if it were evil?"

Jopin leaned back to look at Deer-tracker. "That's a terrible thought. I don't know. I guess it's possible. Tyuonyi could be destroyed if its people were really bad and evil. But this isn't the case. I hope you don't think the people in our village are evil. We have ordered some of the residents out of the village. I've always thought of it as the council not wanting them to have a negative influence on the good people of Tyuonyi, especially on the children. But you might be right. An entire village could be punished or destroyed if its people were bad or evil. Can my young grandson be teaching his old grandfather, Tyuoni's senior elder, another lesson?"

"Grandpa, is that why the promiscuous women live in those cliff-houses outside of Tyuonyi, because the elders have ordered them out of the village?"

"Yes, that's the situation with the promiscuous women and also, with the thieves. How do you know about the promiscuous women? I guess you aren't too young to know about them."

"Everyone knows about them. But, I didn't know they weren't allowed to live in the village. I thought they lived there, because they wanted to. Their houses are so much bigger and fancier than ours."

Jopin couldn't believe what he had just heard. "Deer-tracker, have you been in those houses?" Jopin leaned back to study Deer-tracker's response.

"No, but I have walked by there. The older boys say these women have so much more than the rest of us that live in the village. I've seen Chief Salamander and Elder Big-bear there."

"You have?" This is the kind of information he did not expect to hear from his pre-teen grandson.

"Yes. The council must have business there, as well as here in Tyuonyi."

"Well I guess so. Only they know their business. Deer-tracker, I want you to stay away from that place. The gods wouldn't want you to visit those women. Don't even walk close to those houses, because they will call you over and offer you something to eat or drink. They might even fool you into assisting them with something. Please walk on the other side of the stream if you have to go in that direction."

Deer-tracker nodded his head. "OK, Grandpa." He then acted shy, as if not knowing whether it would be proper to ask.

"What is it? It's OK to ask."

"The boys bring them the shiny, broad-leafed, clump bush. They say these women get happy and offer them special treats to eat in exchange for this plant. Sometimes, the women even kiss them, because they're so excited. I took a bite of this bush and it tasted terrible. What do these women do with that plant?"

"Deer-tracker, I'm saddened to know about boys spending time with these women, but it doesn't surprise me. These women have ulterior motives. They promise to have sex with them in exchange for certain things or favors, a serious mistake for everyone involved. They take advantage of these boys. The boys and women are deceiving each other. There is no sacrifice here, only self-fulfillment. This is a grave action against the Almighty. Sex happens because of the love between a husband and his wife. This love brings children into the world. Love is good and sex from love is good, but sex without love is wrong. You asked what these women do with the shiny, broad-leaf, clump bush. Well you can't eat it, because it will make you very sick. However, they do boil it into a brew." Jopin swallowed hard. "It kills the babies growing inside of them. They use it to kill our Almighty's most precious little ones."

Deer-tracker looked shocked. "That's very bad. Why do these women kill their babies?"

"They don't want to have children. Their sex doesn't come from love, so they don't want to take care of babies they won't love. They use sex as a means to obtain special favors from boys and men. They can't continue living the way they do if they have to care for an innocent baby. Babies grow and need good parents to care for them."

Deer-tracker hung down his head. "I understand, but why do they have so much more than the rest of us in the village?"

"Because they only care about themselves. Men fix up their dwellings and present them with beads, furs, rugs, baskets, food, meat, pelts, and who knows what else. These men will do whatever these women ask of them. The women have an abundance of possessions. It makes them feel important. But, Great Grandfather has commanded that no one should have more than anyone else. These women don't intend to be the least of their brothers and sisters."

"Grandpa, many of the men that visit these women are married with children. This is also wrong, isn't it?"

Jopin raised his voice. "Yes, this is very wrong. You said many? It disturbs me that you used the word, many. Deer-tracker, I don't want to know who these men are. It makes me very sad to know about them. They know their babies will be killed, yet they continue to visit these women?"

Deer-tracker hurried on to the next question. "They say Wild-flower is the ugliest and oldest of the promiscuous women, but many of the men would rather go with her than with the younger, prettier ones. Why? They say she's so crooked and bent over, she can't even stand up straight. What makes a man desire the worst one there?"

"My grandson, I don't know how to answer your question. Um, let's see. I just want you to remember to walk on the other side of the stream, when you have to go in that direction."

Deer-tracker nodded his head. "OK, Grandpa."

"I said this for a couple of reasons. First, these women know how to persuade the weak, especially the inexperienced boys and young men who tend to be vulnerable. Boys look for adventure. They're too trusting, and they don't know how to avoid being trapped. Second, some men and boys, who see themselves as strong in their morals and values, think they have no reason to worry. But even the strong have fallen. Black medicine can make anyone fall. It's well known that Wild-flower uses evil techniques to get her men. And who knows, some of the other promiscuous women may also be witches. Wild-flower may have taught them her ways. There have been instances where good husbands and fathers, those having the strongest, most solid morals, have left their families to go with a disgusting and immoral woman, because of black medicine. Deer-tracker, I would be very sad, if I were to see you with an old ugly, hunched witch, who is old enough to be your grandmother."

Deer-tracker shook his head. "No, Grandpa, I wouldn't."

"Yes, you would. And, no one would be able to help you, except for the medicine man. But his help would come way after you would have already gone with her and sinned against your family and against Great Grandfather."

"Grandpa, how can I protect myself?"

"By walking on the other side of the river and keeping your distance. You must also know how these people perform their evil work. Not all witches are women. We know about Wild-flower, but some of your neighbors might also practice black medicine. No one knows who they are, so always be nice and courteous to everyone. You don't want to give them a reason to harm you, so be extra careful. They can put something in your food or drink. Or, they can harm you, if they have something personal of yours, like a strand of hair, or a sample of your urine or spit. These simple little things are all they need to cast a spell on you."

"Grandpa, there's no way I would give them a sample of my urine or spit. They will never get that from me."

"Grandson, you don't understand. You don't have to give it to them. They can get it without you even knowing how or when. A strand of hair may snag off when you brush up against a tree. They might watch from a distance, waiting for you to go behind a large boulder or bush to urinate. All they need is some of the mud left after you walk away. You would probably never know when or how they obtained a part of you. Deer-tracker, do you hear that owl? It could very well be a witch, who is watching us."

Deer-tracker nestled against Jopin's arm and peeped out into the darkness. "Grandpa, that owl has been hooting all night. I feel helpless. Is there anything we can do to avoid being trapped by these witches?"

"I didn't mean to scare you. I just want you to be very careful. Always be alert and aware of your surroundings. Trust your gut instincts and always carry your medicine bag with you, to ward off evil. Never underestimate the power of the god of darkness."

"The god of darkness is real? I thought it was just a story adults told children to scare them into behaving. They say he will carry us off into the darkness and eat us. Has anyone ever seen the god of darkness?"

"I don't know. The legend has been handed down to us from our ancestors. The god of darkness supposedly walks around in the dark carrying a torch, pretending to help us find our way. The torch gets our attention and helps him gain our trust. As he moves closer, the torch may illuminate his body and more importantly, the blood on his face. They say we should never look into his eyes, because they will draw us into them, into death."

"Grandpa, isn't that like what you told me about the promiscuous women and witches? You told me to be very careful and avoid them in every way possible."

"Yes, that's exactly right. Great Grandfather will take us to live with him if we've been good and obeyed his commandments. We will then live with him forever in happiness. The very bad and evil people will eventually be eaten by the god of darkness."

Jopin was very disturbed with what Deer-tracker had been telling him. Jopin had decided to abandon his prayer quest and let Chief Salamander and the elders decide what to do about the migration. But his young grandson had just revealed some very disturbing information, especially about the chief and some of the elders. How could the gods be talking to Chief Salamander if he has been visiting the promiscuous women? That might explain why he had been underhanded in keeping Jopin from participating in council business.

Once again, Jopin felt compelled to do something, so he nervously pointed up to the sky. "The morning star has been up for some time now, and the sky will soon begin to gain its color. I must leave right now, if I am to greet Father Sun at the Shrine of the Soaring Eagles." He leaned forward and put his face in front of Deer-tracker. "I will need some privacy. Please don't follow me. Could you go back down and tell your grandma I will soon be home? And don't worry. I'll take the long way down. I now know better than to go down the cliff. You won't have to come rescue me again."

"Okay. I'm so grateful for all you have taught me. Thanks for spending the whole night with me and for making me feel so special. You better hurry, Grandpa. The gods are waiting for you."

They hugged, and then Jopin picked up a long, narrow stick and walked away.

A Gift from Above

The moon had disappeared behind the mountains, so it became difficult for Jopin to see. He waved a stick in front of him to keep from running into something, and he walked with his feet close to the ground to avoid any tripping hazards. It was probably too early and dangerous to be walking, but he felt an urgency to continue on his prayer quest. He had decided to forego his journey, but he now felt more determined than ever to arrive at the truth.

Some of the things Deer-tracker had told him were very disturbing. Many of the men and older boys had been seen visiting the promiscuous women. Worse, Chief Salamander and Elder Big-bear were among those men. Jopin couldn't help but feel sorry for Little-acorn. Why would Chief Salamander want any of these other women, especially when he had such a loving, wonderful wife at home? Instead of setting a good example for the boys, Chief Salamander had been showing them how to cheat and break Great Grandfather's rules.

Jopin knew he had no right to judge his chief, but the future of every man, woman, and child was at stake. Chief Salamander had been determined to evacuate Tyuoni, regardless of what his elders thought. Elder Pine-needle had told Jopin about how he had been blamed for banning the promiscuous women from residing within the Tyuoni walls. That might explain why Chief Salamander had estranged him. But, why would Chief Salamander make the entire tribe pay for something Jopin had done? It didn't make any sense.

Jopin once again, was on his way to visit the Shrine of the Soaring Eagles to pray and ask the gods for guidance and forgiveness. He felt good about having had the opportunity to teach Deer-tracker in the ways of the Almighty. But who was Jopin to judge? He, the longest residing elder, couldn't even fulfill his own promise of sacrifice and prayer.

Jopin looked up and started to pray out loud. "Great Grandfather, please forgive me for my failures, for my many weakness, and for not wanting to vote for the evacuation. Last night I had realized how wrong I had been and thus, was ready to accept what Chief Salamander wanted me to do. But now, I question his motives more than ever. Please answer my questions and tell me what to do."

Jopin felt ashamed, because he had lied to Chief Salamander, Bright-sunflower, his grandson, and even to himself. Who was he to believe he should be the one receiving a message from the gods? "I'm not worthy to be in the presence of your gods, but please accept me with all of my failures and faults. It is for the good of the village, not for me."

Jopin knew he had to pray for forgiveness and mercy, but instead, he kept thinking about the wrongdoings of Chief Salamander. His prayer quest would certainly fail, as long as he saw himself as being better than the chief. This attitude would certainly cause Jopin to fail. In the end, he would have to give in to Chief Salamander and accept the inevitable. The entire village would be moving out of their beautiful homeland.

Would Chief Salamander lead them to a harsh and barren land, or to another place, like Tyuoni? Jopin called out, "Chief Salamander, I feel like I don't have the right to challenge you, but I must. What if Wild-flower has a spell on you, just because she and her friends aren't welcome in our village? What if she wants all of us to leave the village, out of revenge? Then everyone will suffer, because of your sins."

Realizing he had no right to judge anyone, he stepped back to analyze what might be happening. He, the senior elder of Tyuoni, didn't like how Chief Salamander had treated him, so he took it upon himself to go on a prayer quest and challenge his chief. His prayer quest had been a complete disaster, perhaps because Jopin had lied to everyone. Although he had prepared for his prayer quest with purification and cleansing, he hadn't cleansed himself of his lies. Jopin now approached the Shrine of the Soaring Eagles, stained and shameful, crying for forgiveness. His entire quest had been one big joke and a waste of time. The gods would be disappointed in him. What should he do?

He noticed a taint of orange color in the eastern horizon. Father Sun would soon show his face, so Jopin quickened his pace and started to hurry. He covered a lot of distance, although he could only see a few feet in front of him.

The entire mesa started to light up at once. Jopin, realizing he couldn't make it on time, started to run. He tripped and found himself face down on the ground. Jopin lifted his head off the ground and cried out to Great Grandfather. "Almighty Creator, I'm so ashamed of myself. I haven't been able to do anything right. Why am I such a failure? What else can I do? Should I jump off the cliff and sacrifice myself for the good of the village?" He remembered how he had just explained to Deer-tracker how he would become known as the crazy old man, the elder who jumped to his death.

Jopin's tears flowed down his cheeks, as thoughts of self-pity cluttered his mind. "I'm the worst of your creatures, therefore not worthy to walk in the presence of your gods. That must be why I couldn't make it to the top of the mountain without the help of my grandson. I couldn't keep my promise of fasting, of sacrifice, nor of prayer. I'm not worthy to greet Father Sun, so I might as well not even continue on to the Shrine of the Soaring Eagles."

Jopin felt like such a fool. He would now go back down and confess to Chief Salamander, and ask for forgiveness. Chief Salamander would probably proclaim Jopin as no longer deserving to serve on the village council. "Perhaps he could use this old man to help get the village ready for the great evacuation. He would love to see me, as the village monitor, telling everyone to pack up and prepare for the Great Migration out of Tyuonyi." Chief Salamander had won.

Jopin stood up and wiped the tears off his face. Defeated, he decided to start walking back towards the village. He took a deep breath and looked around. The beauty of the morning light caught his attention. The backlit sky brought out the silhouette of the trees and distant mountains. He slowly turned to enjoy all of the majestic scenery, and spotted an old dead tree, which appeared to have many birds on it. What would all those birds be doing on that bare tree? They were so silent. Had he walked into a place of black medicine? He kept his eyes focused on the old tree, as he carefully moved in closer. Those weren't birds, but feathers, many feathers of all sizes, tied to a dried-up cedar tree.

Jopin raised both arms, and started to bounce and sing. "I'm at the Shrine of the Soaring Eagles! I'm at the Shrine of the Soaring Eagles! I'm at the Shrine of the Soaring Eagles." His heart pounded with joy. Realizing he was standing on sacred ground, Jopin suddenly stepped back experiencing his surroundings, and then started to chant and dance around the old tree.

Light coming from Father Sun illuminated the great eagle, a gigantic rock protruding out the top of the cliff. Jopin stopped to admire the amazing sight, a natural rock formation created by the Almighty, himself. It resembled a giant eagle with its head and beak overlooking the canyon below. Jopin stood on what would be the right wing of the giant bird. "Oh great eagle, won't you break lose from this cliff and fly me to greet Father Sun, now that he's rising up to the sky? I will beg him not to lead us out of our father's homeland, out of our beautiful canyon. Your people have been good and obeyed the commandments of the Almighty."

Jopin stopped abruptly, for he now knew his statement might not be true. He could no longer ignore the sins of the village. He had been fooling himself into thinking he lived in a perfect village, probably because he had participated in the council and helped shape Tyuoni into the village he thought it was.

Jopin had come to the shrine as a complete failure, so he knew he wasn't worthy enough to represent the wishes of the village. "Giant eagle, it is better for you to remain here and continue serving all of your people. I will attach my prayer feather to this sacred cedar tree and await your reply." He reached into his leather pouch and took out the eagle feather he had carried with him since a young man.

He didn't have any trouble climbing the cliff that first time, as a young man. Jopin had spotted the mother eagle sitting on her eggs. His intent was to sneak up on her from behind and take one of her feathers. She slowly turned to watch him as he approached her large nest. At first, Jopin thought she would let him put his hands on her. She looked so calm and relaxed. However, she flew up in a panic when she saw his hand reach out to grab her. A large feather fell from one of her wings and landed at his feet. She flew to the top of a tall pine tree and watched him pick it up. Jopin knew this was her gift to him.

Jopin held the feather up to the sky and offered it for the people of Tyuoni. He then tied the feather to one of the branches with a thin strip of leather he had made from the skin of a squirrel. "Giant eagle, please take my prayer offering high up into the sky and deliver it to Father Sun. Ask Father Sun if he can take my prayer even higher, to the Almighty Creator. Great Grandfather is awaiting my petition."

Jopin walked to the area directly behind the giant eagle's head. He used his long stick to draw a line on the dirt, from what would be the back of the eagle's neck, to the eagle's tail. He then walked over to what would be the eagle's left wing, and drew a line from that wing to the other, making a giant cross on the ground. He twirled the stick, back and forth, to make a shallow hole at the end of each line, and then again at the center where the two lines met. He removed some sacred tobacco from his leather pouch and sprinkled a little into each hole, starting with the one on the east. He offered a tobacco prayer up for everything on Mother Earth and all brother-creatures that reside in that direction. He repeated his tobacco offering for the other directions and then for the underworld. He took out his prayer pipe and held it high above his head pointing it up towards the skies. "Great Grandfather, behold the sacred pipe. I will soon light the sacred tobacco in this pipe and offer it up to you for your people and creatures, especially for the people of Tyuonyi. I'm begging you not to direct Father-sun to lead us out of this beautiful canyon. However, I'll do whatever you ask, whatever may be your will. You know what is best for us."

He held his pipe out in front of him, and looked directly into Father Sun. "Father Sun, please accept my prayer from Brother-eagle, and deliver it up to Great Grandfather. I know you will do exactly what Great Grandfather asks of you." He prayed in this position for a very long time. But then, he sensed a presence, as if being watched. Something was wrong. He quickly turned to his left and looked towards a noise. Deer-tracker dove to the ground to hide from his grandfather. Jopin faced Deer-tracker, but he couldn't see. Father Sun had blinded his vision. Jopin yelled out, "I know someone is there. Who are you? What do you want with me? What kind of person are you to interfere with sacred prayer?"

Deer-tracker knew he was in trouble. "It is me, Deer-tracker, your grandson."

Jopin yelled out "What? Deer-tracker, you promised not to follow me. You promised. Get out of here. I don't want to see you, and I don't want to hear your excuses. Get away from me."

Deer-tracker stood up and sadly started to walk away.

Jopin twisted his body, as if being tormented. "Wait, I do want to talk to you. You knew how important this prayer quest was to me and worse, you promised.

Why have you betrayed me? It hurts so much that you have disappointed me. I devoted the entire night to you. Why did you disobey me? Why did you follow me?"

"I did not follow you, Grandpa, and I did not betray you, not on purpose. I walked back to the edge of the cliff to go back down, when this deer family came to me. The little one came really close, but then kept getting away when I tried to touch him. I followed him until he came to you. I stopped when I saw you, but he continued to walk right to you."

Jopin stuttered, "What, what deer? Deer-tracker, are you making up a story? Uh, are you making this up to get out of trouble? Don't try to fool your grandfather. I want the truth."

Deer-tracker pointed at the deer, "Right there Grandfather, next to your leg. Can't you see him?"

Jopin looked around, but he still couldn't see, because of the sun.

Deer-tracker cried out, "Grandpa, can't you see? What happened to your eyes? Are you all right? Grandpa, you're blind. Let me help you."

"I can't see, because I was looking at Father Sun in prayer. I will be blinded for a while, but I should soon be fine. What's this story you're telling me about a deer?"

"Grandpa, he's sniffing your leg. Don't you feel him?"

Jopin reached down and touched the little fawn on its shoulder. The fawn allowed himself to be petted, but held his head down, as if a servant to Jopin. Jopin didn't know why this baby deer came to him.

He continued to pet the young deer, as he squatted down in an attempt to communicate face-to-face, with the fawn. Jopin held up the fawn's head and asked, "Baby deer, what do you want with me? Who sent you? Where's your mama?" The fawn once again held his head down, but kept looking up at Jopin.

"Grandpa, his mother and sister are over there." Deer-tracker pointed to a clump of shrub oak trees. "I wonder if they sent the baby deer to you. Do you want me to chase them away, so you can finish your prayer quest? I too will go, so you can be alone."

Jopin petted both sides of the deer's belly and then stood up. "No, I want to tell you about it. I had a vision of a small spotted deer, just like this one. This happened when I offered up my prayer pipe to Father Sun. I don't understand. Could this little fawn be the answer to my prayer?"

"Grandpa, he keeps putting his nose up close to your knee. You must have something there that smells good to him. He looks very sad."

Jopin once again squatted down and held up the fawn's head to let him know everything would be all right. He placed his hands on the area above the fawn's eyes and explored the top of its head with his fingertips.

"Grandpa, are you looking for antler stubs?"

"No, I'm trying to determine if there's a hole on top of his head. The vision I had was of a spotted fawn with a hole on top of his head. Light from a big star entered this hole on his head."

"Did you say a hole? Does he have a hole in his head? What does this mean?"

"I don't know. There's no hole." Jopin continued to explore the fawn's head.

"Grandpa, he has his nose up against your knee again."

"Well, maybe we should call him, Knee-nose."

Deer-tracker chuckled. "Knee-nose is a very fitting name for our little brother-deer. Look Grandpa, his mother and sister have started to leave. Look at how they look at Knee-nose as they walk away. Brother Knee-nose and his mother are looking right into each other's eyes. This is spooky. I think she's telling Knee-nose to remain with you."

Jopin scratched his head and then wiped his eyes, in an attempt to see Knee-nose's mother." Very interesting. Could this be the answer to my prayer? I'll have to discuss what has happened with Chief Salamander and the elders. They'll help me make sense of brother Knee-nose and of this entire prayer quest of mine. I can't figure out what any of this means, so I need their help. Deer-tracker, we better start working our way back down to the village. You can go the long way with me, or you can take the finger and toe ladder down the cliff, the way we came up. It's up to you."

"Grandpa, I want to go with you. I'm sorry I interrupted your vision. What about Knee-nose? Do we just leave him here?" Deer-tracker carefully approached his grandfather.

"Knee-nose belongs here in the woods where he can do whatever he wants. Why would he want to come with us?" Jopin put his hand on top of Deer-tracker's head. "I sure was disappointed in you. I already felt betrayed by Chief Salamander, so I'm glad you didn't come here on purpose."

"What did Chief Salamander do to you?"

"I'm sorry, I can't talk about it."

Deer-tracker looked disappointed, but it didn't stop him from asking another question. "Grandpa, could you show me the Shrine of the Soaring Eagles before we go?"

Jopin pointed out how the giant rock resembled a great eagle. Deer-tracker noticed the cross drawn on the ground, so Jopin explained how he had conducted the ceremony. He also showed Deer-tracker the dead cedar tree with many prayer-feather-offerings tied to it. "A wise eagle gave me her feather when I was a very young man. I've now returned it to her, so that my prayer can be answered." Jopin then pointed out several eagle nests nearby. "Something mystical draws so many eagles to this sacred area."

"This is their home. Perhaps, this may also be their sacred area."

"Yes, I suppose so."

They started walking back to the village, expecting Knee-nose to remain behind. However, Knee-nose wanted to join them. Jopin bent down to face the fawn. "Knee-nose, we must go to our village. You better go back to your mother. You belong with her, not with us." He gave Knee-nose a little slap on his back. "Go, good-bye."

Knee-nose jumped away, but then turned around and came right back. They decided to ignore him and start walking away, but Knee-nose continued to walk alongside. Jopin decided to once again, have a talk with Knee-nose, "Don't you understand? You don't belong with us. You're a deer. You need to stay here." He looked around searching for Knee-nose's mother. "There she is, hiding behind the brush. Come. Let's go to your mother."

The mother deer approached them as they brought her little baby back to her. Knee-nose's twin sister came running to meet her brother. The mother quickly separated them by getting in between the two fawns. She approached Knee-nose and placed her nose up against Knee-nose's cheek. Knee-nose then sadly lowered his head to the ground as his mother and sister walked away. Jopin and Deer-tracker remained speechless.

"What are they doing? Did she tell him she no longer wanted him? What does all of this mean?"

"I don't know. Perhaps they're telling Knee-nose to go with us. But, that can't be. What would we have to do with a baby fawn? Let's ignore him and act like he's not here."

They once again, started to walk back to Tyuonyi. Knee-nose quietly followed, but at a distance. Deer-tracker couldn't control his excitement and looked back over his shoulder. All of a sudden, Knee-nose ran past them, waited for them to catch up, and then started running again. Knee-nose had begun to feel more comfortable with Jopin and Deer-tracker. He let Deer-tracker pet him at times, but only when Jopin would tell Knee-nose to allow it.

Knee-nose finally settled down and started to walk alongside Jopin, as if he had always been the family pet. Jopin felt good, because the gods had sent Knee-nose to him. He was relieved he had finally received an answer to his quest, although he didn't know what it meant.

They heard the children laughing and playing in the stream, so they knew they would soon approach the village. Jopin reminded Deer-tracker that his prayer quest was to address a secret village council concern and thus, use good judgment when it came to explaining what had happened up on the mountain. "You can tell them you accompanied me on a prayer quest, but you don't know what the quest was about."

Deer-tracker stopped walking. "I really don't know, Grandpa."

Jopin smiled. "Thanks for saving my life. I would still be stuck up there on that cliff if it were not for my brave grandson. You're my hero!"

"Oh Grandpa, I just delivered some medicine-water and jerky from Grandma. This has been the best experience of my life. I'm so lucky to be your grandson. Thanks for teaching me so much about Great Grandfather, as well as some of the other things that will help me go through life."

"Arf, arf, arf, ruff, ruff, woof, yip, yip, arf, yap, bow wow, ruff, ruff." All of the dogs from the village must have sensed Knee-nose, for they barked unceasingly. "Quick Deer-tracker, get on the other side of Knee-nose. We have to protect him." Knee-nose pressed his body against Jopin's leg, afraid to move. Deer-tracker quickly bent forward to pick up some rocks to throw and scare the dogs. He yelled for the dogs to stay back. They kept their distance but continued to bark.

The warrior guards came running, but stopped abruptly, when they saw Knee-nose. "What do we have here, Elder Jopin? Who's your friend? Is this little guy a deer or a dog? He looks like a deer but acts like a puppy." The guards found the little fawn amusing. Knee-nose studied the guards' actions and expressions. The dogs continued to bark, but kept their distance.

"My dear friends, I want you to meet Knee-nose. This little brother-deer is my friend. Do you know if Chief Salamander is home? I would like for him to meet Knee-nose."

Warrior Quick-foot moved in closer. "Knee-nose must be a very important deer, because not all guests of Tyuonyi have an audience with the chief. Chief Salamander has not left the village today, so he should be home." He motioned for them to continue.

Knee-nose appeared a little shy from all of the attention. The dogs began to quiet down as the three of them slowly walked through the narrow entrance to the village. They entered the open area and walked past the main kiva. "I have to talk to Chief Salamander in private. Can you stop at your grandma's and let her know I'll soon be home? Tell her about Knee-nose. Perhaps she can figure out how we can feed him." Jopin gave Deer-tracker a hug and then motioned for him to go on his way.

"Okay, Grandpa. Thanks for everything. Bye."

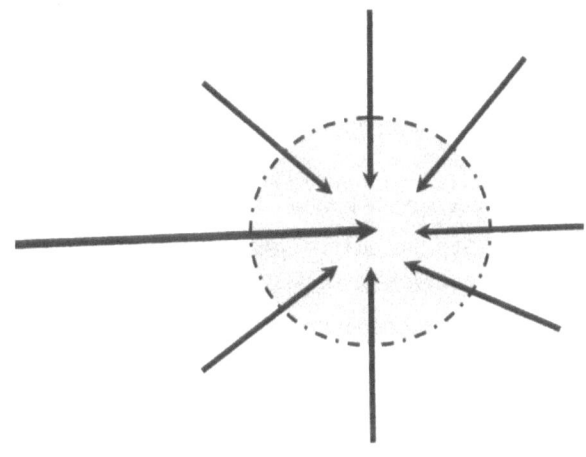

Confession

Jopin was about to request permission to enter, but he hesitated. Chief Salamander might not want to see him. Jopin had attempted to sabotage Salamander's plans by walking out of the council meeting, so anything could have happened. Chief Salamander might have removed Jopin of his elder responsibilities. If so, the decision would have already been made.

Jopin yelled out, "Hello, this is Jopin. Chief Salamander, are you home? I have someone I would like you to meet."

"Jopin, I'm so happy you're walking around. Please come inside out of the sun."

"Chief, could you come outside? It may not be appropriate for my friend to come into your house."

"What are you talking about? Everyone's welcome in my home." He peaked outside. "Oh, I see. What are you doing with the fawn? Where did you find him? Is his mother dead?"

"No, I didn't find him. His mother came and left him with me. My little brother deer is so important, he's been given a name. This is Knee-nose."

"Hello, Knee-nose. This is very interesting, Jopin. What are you doing with this little creature and what concern is this of mine? How are you feeling? The council didn't vote on the tribe's evacuation, because you weren't present. I now have to call another meeting."

His words were businesslike, but he had the look of relief on his face. Knee-nose's eyes were fixed on Chief Salamander, as if he were studying Salamander's every word and action.

"That's why I've come to talk to you, Chief. Yes, this little deer very much concerns you and perhaps the elders. He's a very special little brother-deer of ours. We need to talk. Is there a place where we can have some privacy?"

"It's going to be hard to have a private meeting anywhere out here. The two of you have already attracted so much attention. Look, they're coming to see your little friend, because he's gotten their attention. You better come inside. Can you hold on to him to keep him under control? If so, please come in."

Jopin and Knee-nose quickly followed Chief Salamander inside. Salamander motioned for Jopin to sit on the bear rug. Jopin sat and then gently tugged on Knee-nose's legs, until Knee-nose settled down next to Jopin. "Where is Little-acorn? Isn't she home today?"

"She's visiting her sister." Chief Salamander looked nervous. "We may not have to explain anything to her, if we hurry. How long have you had this little spotted deer, excuse me, I mean Knee-nose?"

"Since this morning."

"Since this morning? I can't believe how well behaved he is. It takes a long time to train an animal to act like this." Knee-nose continued to sit, quietly, next to Jopin.

"Well how old do you think Knee-nose is?"

"He's just a baby, not more than one moon's time. There's no way—" Salamander stopped talking. "Oh, I see. Knee-nose can't possibly be old enough to be trained. But, he's so well behaved. Also, isn't it still too early, I mean, isn't it too early in the season for deer to be having babies?" Salamander rubbed his chin and then continued. "I'm beginning to agree with you. This is a very special deer. And you said this little critter may have some pertinent information?"

"Yes. Chief, I have a confession to make. This has been the most difficult decision I've ever had to make. I couldn't face what was happening. I wasn't really sick, I couldn't stomach the vote."

Salamander looked deep into Jopin's eyes. "Why are you wearing your ceremonial tunic, and how did you get it so soiled? Did you have an accident?"

Jopin wondered why Chief Salamander ignored his confession. "No. I'll soon tell you about my experience, but I must first apologize."

"No need to apologize. I'm the one who owes you an apology for treating you the way I did. Jopin, I need your support now, more than ever. This is the most important decision each and every one of us will ever have to make. I myself have not slept since the Chiefs' Pow-Wow at Chaco. Puye just decided to evacuate, but they're waiting for us to make our decision, before they go public. I need your help in getting the elders to decide how to vote."

Jopin welcomed Salamander's new attitude, but he wasn't ready to support Chief Salamander. "We need to talk, and then you can tell me what the next step should be. I was not ready to decide what was right for the village, so I went on a prayer quest. I needed to ask the gods what to do, not what I want, not what we want, and not what the Chief-of-chiefs at Chaco wants."

"So what did the gods tell you?"

"I'm not sure. I received a sign, but I'm confused. I need you to help me figure out what it means."

"Sure, but would you rather talk to the elders?"

Jopin felt uncomfortable, thinking Chief Salamander must have detected his uneasiness. "You tell me. My prayer quest gave me a vision of a young spotted deer with a hole on the top of its head. There was a bright star giving off light which entered the hole, in such a way that the fawn appeared to be communicating with the gods. The strange thing though, right after I had my vision, this mother deer brought her little spotted baby to me. I don't understand the meaning of this, but I do know there is something very special about Knee-nose. Look at him. He follows me around and obeys me, as if I were in control of his destiny. You should have seen the look as their eyes met, and then his mother walked away, leaving him behind to stay with me."

Chief Salamander's eyes searched around, as if deciding what to do next. He then turned to look at Knee-nose, "Is there a hole in his head?"

"No. I couldn't feel one. He lets me touch him and do whatever I want with him, but only me. Deer-tracker was with me, but Knee-nose won't let Deer-tracker touch him, unless I tell him to."

Chief Salamander leaned back, as if disappointed in Jopin. "What? Your grandson was with you? Why Jopin? This is secret council business."

"No. Deer-tracker stumbled upon my prayer quest, right in the middle of my vision. He followed the deer family: the mother deer, Knee-nose, and his twin, straight to me, where I was performing my prayer ceremony. They interrupted my vision. All of a sudden, this little spotted fawn was leaning against my leg. Look at him. I don't think it's a coincidence. Knee-nose looks like the fawn in my vision. As for my grandson, he knows I was on a prayer quest, but he doesn't know why I was there."

Chief Salamander scratched his cheek. "I believe the entire council of elders needs to listen to your story. We must determine the meaning of your vision and the significance of little Knee-nose. Light coming from the bright star might be the voice of Great Grandfather. We must determine what your vision has to do with our decision to evacuate. Why have the gods sent you Knee-nose? He can't even speak. Can you meet with us again? We'll need to know every little detail. Could you be ready to meet this evening?"

"I've been gone since yesterday, so I would like Bright-sunflower to know I'm all right."

"It will take a while to round up the rest of the elders. I'll invite Medicine-maker, so he can help us determine the meaning of all of this. Someone will come get you." Chief Salamander put his hand on Jopin's shoulder. "I'm glad you went to the gods for help in this very important decision. Thank you. Please give my love to Bright-sunflower."

"I surely will. And please give my love to Little-acorn." Jopin got up and walked out. Knee-nose followed right behind. Chief Salamander stood at the doorway, smiling, as he watched Jopin and Knee-nose walk away.

"Bright-sunflower, I have a very special new friend I would like for you to meet."

"I've been waiting for you. So this is Knee-nose. Oh, you're a darling. Deer-tracker told me all about you. You're a precious little baby. I have a bowl of mixed-greens paste for you." Jopin stood there, expecting a hug and a kiss, but Bright-sunflower's attention went to Knee-nose.

"Mixed-greens paste, what is mixed-greens paste? I've never heard of it."

"That's because you're not a deer. We don't have any milk to give Knee-nose, so Deer-tracker and I went out near the stream and found some fresh grass and other greenery. We picked whatever might taste good to a deer. We don't know if Knee-nose can eat solid food yet, so I ground it up and mixed it with water."

"Oh, thanks for being so thoughtful and going through all that trouble. Let's see if Knee-nose will eat it." Jopin held up the bowl for Knee-nose to smell it. Knee-nose studied it, but he didn't know what to do with it. Jopin dipped his finger in the bowl and rubbed some of the paste on Knee-nose's lips. Knee-nose licked it off his lips and teeth. Jopin took a bigger amount and shoved it into Knee-nose's mouth. This time Knee-nose chewed on it and eventually swallowed the mixed-greens paste. He appeared to have liked the taste.

Bright-sunflower gently touched Jopin's arm to get his attention. "I've been so worried about you. You're finally back home, and safe. I made a stew from sunflower and yucca roots, with jerky bits. Ready to have some? You better eat before Chief Salamander comes for you." She leaned over and gave Jopin a hug. "Knee-nose is so cute and special. I forgot to welcome you back. It doesn't mean I haven't been worried about you. Are you all right?"

"I'm fine, hungry, but not starving. Deer-tracker took good care of me. He saved my life. Thanks for sending him to search for me. How did you know Chief Salamander would be coming for me?"

"I just know. I know Chief Salamander and I know you. Have you forgotten? I've been the senior elder's wife for many, many moons."

"I hope you don't think we've had too many moons together. This stew is delicious. Thanks also for taking care of Knee-nose, and for being so understanding."

"You're welcome. Deer-tracker also liked the stew."

"Oh good, I'm glad you fed him. We hadn't eaten since last night. You know, we have a real hero in the family. I'm talking about Deer-tracker. He helped me climb to the top of the cliff, and then he killed a squirrel to feed me. He even helped me understand a lot of things about life and about our village. I can't believe how wise he is. He'll someday become very important to our village, or to whatever village he marries into. And thanks again for sending him to me with jerky and medicine-water. You know me better than I know myself. You warned me not to even consider climbing that cliff, but I was stubborn. Now I have to face the truth. I'm too old for such nonsense."

Bright-sunflower accepted his compliments with a smile. "Jopin, you're still the strong, handsome man I married. But you must realize you no longer have the strength you once had. And besides, you hadn't eaten or drunk anything for three days."

Jopin looked at her with acceptance, agreeing with what she had told him. By this time Knee-nose had learned how to eat out of a bowl. Jopin happily ate his stew, as well.

Deer-tracker called from outside, "Grandpa and Grandma, I've come to visit. Mom and some of our friends want to see Knee-nose."

Brilliant-pebbles walked through the door opening and hugged her parents, but her eyes were focused on Knee-nose. "Oh my, he's so precious."

Someone spoke from outside. "You mean he's in the house?"

Jopin and Bright-sunflower looked at each other and chuckled. Bright-sunflower raised her voice. "Well of course, he's in the house. He's our very special guest. He's family." She pulled the door covering open to welcome them. "Oh my, we have a lot of people here."

"Yes, Grandma, they all want to see Knee-nose." Deer-tracker must have told everyone about Knee-nose.

Bright-sunflower asked Jopin to bring Knee-nose outside. "We don't have enough room for all of Knee-nose's visitors."

Jopin walked outside. Knee-nose slowly followed behind. They all exclaimed, "Oh," at the same time. Knee-nose instantly won everyone's heart. They made various remarks about him. "He's beautiful. He's perfect. Look at his perfectly shaped little head. Oh, those large charcoal black eyes. Look at all of those perfectly placed spots. He's so well behaved. He's so pure."

Knee-nose had command of all their affection. Sensing their good will, he held up his head and lifted his little tail as high as possible. He then slowly blinked his eyes and started to prance around, all the time staying close to Jopin. This drew more words of praise and affection from the crowd. Even the dogs bowed their heads to him. There was something very special about Knee-nose.

One of the neighbors asked, "Where did you find him?"

"I didn't. He found us. Deer-tracker and I were on top of the mountain when Knee-nose and his family came to visit. His mother brought him over to me and motioned for him to stay with us."

"His mother? Things like this don't happen, unless there's an important reason. She brought him over to you and walked away? Did she think you could take better care of him than she could? What a tremendous sacrifice for her to give up her baby. Could the gods be sending you a message? Jopin, what's the meaning of this?"

"I don't know. I just returned from Chief Salamander's house. He wants the council of elders to review what might be happening. We'll soon meet to determine answers to such questions."

Chief Salamander had difficulty clearing a path to Jopin's home, because the crowd had become so large. "Jopin, do you think you can find time to break away from your friends? The others are on their way to the kiva."

"Yes, I think we better get this over with and get some answers. I wonder if Knee-nose will stay here with Bright-sunflower and Deer-tracker."

"He probably needs to come with us, since he's the reason we're meeting. Do you think we can carry him into the kiva?"

Knee-nose had figured out the chief was there because of him. He walked over to Jopin and leaned up against his leg. The crowd parted for them to walk through. Knee-nose followed closely behind Jopin and Chief Salamander. Jopin bent forward to lift Knee-nose, but Chief Salamander stopped him. "Please allow me to carry Knee-nose into the kiva. Do you think Knee-nose will let me?"

"I don't know. Perhaps he will, if I also hold on to him."

Chief Salamander attempted to pick up Knee-nose, but Knee-nose moved over just far enough out of the chief's reach. Jopin knelt down, gently caressed Knee-nose's head, and looked right into his eyes. "Chief Salamander is a friend. He won't harm you."

Chief Salamander gently laid his hands on Knee-nose. This time Knee-nose allowed the chief to lift him off the ground. Chief Salamander held Knee-nose up with one arm and petted him with his other. Knee-nose's eyes were fixed on Jopin as Chief Salamander carried him up the short ladder, through the kiva entrance, and then down the long ladder into the chamber. Jopin followed. Chief Salamander set Knee-nose down. Knee-nose immediately moved over and leaned against Jopin's leg.

The other elders were already standing at their regular positions. Elder Big-bear yelled out, "What do we have here, Jopin? Have you been hiding your little secret from us for these past nine moons? You go away sick and return with a little baby." Everyone laughed, including Jopin.

Elder Little-raccoon approached Jopin. "Are there anymore out there? I would love to have a little deer like that of my own."

Chief Salamander motioned for him to return to his position. "Elder Jopin needs our help in the interpretation of a vision. We would also like to know why this very special little creature was delivered to him. Let me introduce you to our little brother-deer, who came to Jopin during a special prayer quest. He is so important, he's been given a name. This is Knee-nose. Perhaps we should get started."

Elder Bobcat yelled out, "Knee-nose, what kind of a name is Knee-nose?"

Jopin smiled and then replied, "Just look at him, and you will get your answer. He likes to keep his nose next to my knee."

The elders started talking amongst themselves and became so amused with the little fawn that they forgot they were at a formal meeting. Once again, Chief Salamander raised his voice. "Can we please have some order, so we can get started? Please, we must get to business. I invited Medicine-maker to help us. Medicine-maker, please sit here, next to me."

Jopin moved over to make room for Medicine-maker, but Chief Salamander asked him to take a position opposite him. "Medicine maker and I must be able to see you as you explain your vision."

Medicine-maker and Chief Salamander stood in the direction, where Father Sun rises out of Mother Earth. Jopin and Knee-nose stood opposite them, where Father Sun enters back into Mother Earth at the end of the day. The rest of the elders completed the circle with Medicine-maker, Jopin and Chief Salamander.

Chief Salamander raised his hand to call the meeting to order. "Medicine-maker knows we're having difficulty reaching a very important decision, but I did not tell him about our issue." Some of the elders looked at each other, as if questioning their chief's decision to keep Medicine-maker in the dark.

Chief Salamander started by offering a prayer. He performed a blessing of the sacred pipe ceremony, all the time, holding the pipe up to Great Grandfather. He took four puffs of the sacred tobacco and then walked around the circle of elders, as if following the path of the sun. He entered the circle and approached Jopin. "Behold the sacred pipe. This pipe of truth was presented to us by White-buffalo-woman. Take it and smoke from it. Its sacred smoke will fill this chamber and rise thru the opening above, bringing peace to everything living on earth, below the earth and also, to those living in the skies above. We offer up this prayer for all of the peoples of the world, the two-legged, the four-legged, for those living underground, and for the winged that fly above."

Jopin held up the sacred pipe above his head, as he offered it up to Great

Grandfather, the Great Spirit, and asked for help in interpreting his vision. He took four puffs and then passed it to the elder on his left.

Each elder prayed over the sacred pipe, taking four puffs from it, until the pipe made its way back to Jopin. Chief Salamander nodded to Medicine-maker. Medicine-maker moved over to the center and asked Jopin and Knee-nose to join him. He took some sacred corn pollen from a pouch and drew a wide circle of pollen around Jopin and Knee-nose. He took the pipe from Jopin and leaned forward to face Knee-nose. He inhaled and then blew smoke on Knee-nose's face. "Knee-nose, behold the sacred smoke of truth, the smoke which Great Grandfather sent us by way of White-buffalo-woman. We must find out why the gods have sent you to Jopin." Knee-nose stood still and allowed the medicine man to blow smoke on his face, not once, but on four different occasions.

Elder Big-bear yelled out, "Knee-nose must certainly be a messenger from Great Grandfather."

Chief Salamander motioned for him to be quiet. Medicine-maker finished his prayers, moved back out of the circle of pollen, and then nodded for Chief Salamander to start.

Chief Salamander asked everyone to be seated. "We're now ready to hear about Jopin's vision and about how Knee-nose came to him. Jopin, please tell us about your prayer quest and vision. Do not leave anything out, because it might be vital to the interpretation. Tell us every single detail, for you know as well as the rest of us, the sacred stones, this sacred chamber, everything around us, and the sacred pipe, all of these will hear you, so you must tell the truth."

"I will tell you about how Knee-nose's mother brought him over to me. But first, I have a confession to make." Although Jopin mostly faced the chief, he managed to look around at the elders to let them know he was talking to them, as well. "I haven't been completely honest with you. This vote has been hard to stomach and certainly the most difficult decision I've ever had to make. I couldn't face what had been happening, why we had to have this vote. I felt I wasn't worthy to make such an important decision for our people, so I decided to go ask the gods. What do they want us to do, not what I want, not what we want, and not what the Chief-of-chiefs at Chaco wants? What do the gods want Tyuoni to do? I fasted for three days, performed a purification cleansing of the hair ceremony on the morning of the fourth day, and then set out on my prayer quest. That was yesterday, the day of the vote." Jopin made sure to face Chief Salamander. "Your senior elder was too sick to vote, but not too sick to climb the cliff and visit the Shrine of the Soaring Eagles."

He took a deep breath, looked around, and then continued. "But this old man soon discovered he was too old and weak to make it to the top. I was stuck up there, halfway up that cliff for most of the day." Jopin told them about how his grandson had come to his rescue. Tears ran down his cheeks when he explained how he had to break his fast-promise and thus, become unworthy to stand in the presence of the gods. His prayer quest would be a failure.

The elders listened to Jopin's every word. Some of them appeared to understand why he had to lie and go on his prayer quest. Others hid their feelings and continued to look at him with questioning faces.

Jopin told them about Deer-tracker's thirst for knowledge and understanding, especially of Great Grandfather and the gods. He explained that even though he had proven to no longer be worthy to communicate with the gods, he could still guide his grandson in the path of life set forth by the Almighty. They were surprised it had taken the entire night to answer his grandson's questions.

The elders wanted to know what kinds of things interested Deer-tracker.

"The first thing Deer-tracker asked about was fire, specifically if fire could be a form of punishment coming down from our creator. Deer-tracker even wanted to know if an entire village would be punished or burned to the ground if a lot of people in the village were evil or very bad."

Elder Pine-needle asked why Deer-tracker would think of such a question.

"I'm not sure. Maybe, it's because some of the elders visit the promiscuous women."

Several of the elders displayed startled faces and then, silence. Others expressed surprise and disappointment.

Jopin continued to discuss his grandson's questions and his answers to these questions. Deer-tracker's thirst for knowledge and his depth and maturity of his understanding, impressed the elders.

Elder Cloud-burst spoke up. "Can you summarize your grandson's questions? Why are we even having this discussion? What does he have to do with Knee-nose and this vision of yours?"

"I still haven't told you about my vision, but the gods might have sent my grandson to help me. If it hadn't been for him, I would still be stuck up there on that cliff, and never would have made it to the Shrine of the Soaring Eagles. But, let me try to summarize. Deer-tracker has a thirst for Great Grandfather, so I couldn't refuse to answer his questions. I should have continued on my prayer quest, but his yearning for sacred knowledge was too great to ignore. I had already broken my fast-promise and failed on my quest, so I had decided to devote my attention to him. More than anything, he wishes to communicate with Great Grandfather. Deer-tracker said he wanted to be just like me, even though I let him know I had become a failure." Jopin worried about how the elders would react to his grandson's admiration for him, but he felt he had to address it.

Sure enough, some of them looked disgruntled and were restless. Elder Bobcat asked, "Did your grandson have an opinion about your being a failure?"

"Yes, he told me Great Grandfather loves and understand everything about me, because he created me, and since he knows everything, he already knew why I couldn't make it to the top of the cliff. Deer-tracker said I had to break my fast-promise to restore my strength and continue on my prayer quest. My grandson doesn't see me as a failure. He thinks I had attempted the impossible." Jopin smiled. "Deer-tracker told me it would probably have been easier for me to have softened the bones of my skull, so the gods could communicate with me, than to climb that cliff."

The elders laughed and then quieted down. Elder Pine-needle commented on how Deer-tracker's knowledge and depth of understanding impressed him.

Jopin talked about the frustration he had experienced walking to the Shrine of the Soaring Eagles in the dark, and about his surprise when he came upon the dry cedar tree with the many feather-prayer offerings tied to it. It was time to tell them about his vision.

"I was holding my prayer pipe high in front of me, facing Father Sun, when the vision of a small, spotted fawn floating in the sky, came to me. There were stars all around him. The light from the brightest star entered a hole on top of the fawn's head. I didn't see anything else, because I was interrupted." He looked down and pointed at Knee-nose. "This little fawn had leaned against my leg. His mother stood at a distance and motioned for him to stay with me. She then turned and walked away, leaving Knee-nose with me. Knee-nose has remained by my side, since early this morning."

Elder Bobcat yelled out, "Knee-nose certainly must be a messenger from the gods. But, what's his message? Jopin, you probably know better than any of us. What do you think?"

"I don't know. My vision didn't last long enough for me to make any sense out of it, because Knee-nose interrupted me. My grandson then came along, so I don't know. I never went back into my vision."

Elder Bear-claw raised his hand and pointed a finger towards the sky. "Could your vision have been nothing more than a premonition of this little fawn coming to visit you?"

"Yes, it could have been, but what's the meaning of the hole on top of his head, and why the stars?"

Elder Bear-claw started to say something, but then stopped to gather his thoughts. "You had just explained to Deer-tracker about how Great Grandfather communicates with newborns through the soft bones on top of their skulls. Could this vision of a newborn fawn with a hole in his head, be nothing more than a dream, an extension of your discussions with Deer-tracker?"

"Perhaps, but I don't think so. We did stay up the entire night, so it's possible I could've been half asleep while standing and holding up my prayer pipe. But I was wide awake."

Medicine-maker walked into the circle of corn pollen. "Jopin, I need to share something with you. At Chief Salamander's request, I offered up prayers for you to get well. Like you, I held my prayer pipe up high above my head. A vision of a small spotted deer with starlight entering the top of its head was also given to me."

Stunned, Jopin didn't know what to think. "What are you saying, that we both had the same vision? How could it be?" The room became very quiet.

"It means you had a true vision and not an ordinary dream or premonition. Knee-nose is no ordinary spotted fawn, but rather, a messenger from the gods."

Elder Cloud-burst stood up and pointed at Knee-nose. "How could he be a messenger, if he can't even speak? He can't tell us what these sacred messages are or what these visions mean." Chief Salamander gave him a look of disapproval, so he sat back down.

Medicine-maker then stood up to get their attention. "That's a very good observation, but I haven't told you the rest of my vision." He turned to face Jopin again. "It includes you. I saw Knee-nose with a hole on his head and then you appeared. You were floating in the sky and you also, had a hole on top of your head." He waited for the elders to quiet down. "I thought I knew what it meant, that perhaps the gods were instructing me to somehow use a small deer to heal you." He looked around to address the elders. "But that can't be because Jopin wasn't sick, as he just confessed. So, my vision must have pertained to Jopin's prayer quest, and not to his health." He stopped to make sure they had all heard. "This is a different question, so we must be very careful about how to interpret these visions. The things I saw in my vision were Knee-nose and Jopin, both with holes in their heads. Light from a bright star entered these holes."

The chamber became deathly silent. Most of the elders had lowered their heads to keep from being called on. Chief Salamander finally asked, "What do these visions mean? Does anyone know why the gods have sent us Knee-nose?"

The elders continued to keep their heads lowered, so Jopin finally spoke up. "Chief Salamander, I believe we're all in agreement as to what must happen. Knee-nose and I should have holes cut in our skulls in order for the gods to communicate with us."

Chief Salamander narrowed his gaze, right at Jopin. "What are you saying? We always open our meetings up for discussion, before deciding what has to get done. You are out of order."

Jopin thought about how Chief Salamander had been out of order when he barred Jopin from participating in the discussions. Jopin slightly lifted an arm and opened his mouth to object but then, he chose to remain quiet.

Chief Salamander tried to explain. "We must talk about all issues involved, before we decide what action to take. We haven't even decided what these visions mean, so it's too early to talk about what we should do."

"We don't have to discuss anything. Isn't it obvious? Medicine-maker's vision told us what he must do to both Knee-nose and me."

The elders shook their heads, confused, but their expressions indicated they agreed with Jopin.

Chief Salamander stood up. "I don't like this. We can't cut a hole in your head. That would certainly kill you. Our people stopped having human sacrifices a long, long time ago. I won't allow it."

Jopin didn't even request permission to speak. "Then how else will we receive this most important message from the gods?"

Salamander quickly snapped back. "From a dead man? There's something wrong with your logic. Knee-nose can't talk, so how can he possibly deliver an answer from the gods? What makes us think a dead Jopin can speak any better than a deer who can't speak?" He kept his eyes fixed on Jopin.

"I want to communicate with Great Grandfather and his gods. What if you cut this hole in my head, and I live just long enough, to tell you what the gods told me. My wish would have been granted, and you would know what to do about the evacuation. I'm already an old man who will soon join my ancestors anyway. And who knows, the hole may heal, and I might be around for many more moons."

"No, Jopin."

"What if Knee-nose was sent by the gods to offer himself up as a sacrifice? Can't we cut a hole in his skull to learn how to do it on mine? We would then, have only one sacrifice. We all agree Knee-nose was sent here for a special purpose. I hate to do this to him, but first, we need to learn how to cut holes in skulls. He will sacrifice himself for me, so I can survive the ordeal and bring you a gift, an answer from the Almighty."

"No." Chief Salamander was losing his temper.

"We may both survive. It's important to know what the gods want."

"Jopin, you're out of order. The only one, who has spoken here, is you. What do the rest of you think? We will address this very important issue like everything else. We must first have the issue discussed, an action proposed, and then a vote." Chief Salamander paused a while to think, and then softly spoke. "Puye already decided. Why can't we do the same? If we vote as they did, we won't have to sacrifice anyone, not even Knee-nose."

Most of the elders accepted the chief's proposal, but not Jopin. "The gods sent us Knee-nose for a reason. We must do the right thing. What if Puye made the wrong decision? We, at Tyuonyi, should do what the gods want."

There was silence, once again, in the chamber. Elder Bobcat asked for permission to speak. "Chief, you're looking for a vote about Tyuoni, but I don't think you'll get one tonight. We now have more questions than ever about this whole situation."

Chief Salamander took time to determine what to do, and then addressed Jopin. "The gods felt compelled to send you little Knee-nose, along with a vision about a hole in his head. I will allow a hole to be cut into Knee-nose's skull, but let me make it clear. I will never allow this to happen to you. We won't go back in time." He scratched his chin. "There was an ancient ceremony which involved cutting holes in the heads of men, in an attempt to communicate with Great Grandfather. The ceremony was discontinued, because all these men died. No one knows if communication was achieved or not. Our ancestors learned it was a mistake to cut holes in the skulls of men. I will not allow human sacrifices in this village. I ask each and every one of you to look at Knee-nose. It's a shame to sacrifice such a beautiful and pure little creature. However, you all need proof that this is a bad idea. Do you really want to do this to little Knee-nose? Medicine-maker, do you have any suggestions?"

"I don't know what this vote is about, but it must be something very important, especially since you're talking about cutting holes in Knee-nose and Jopin. You may be overreacting to this issue. What could be so serious that you're considering the sacrifice of our new beautiful and loving, baby brother-deer? I can't even imagine what it could be." He paused and then continued. "Also, why are you considering the sacrifice of our most respected senior elder? What's going on? I don't understand." He cleared his throat. "I don't think I really want to know."

"Medicine-maker, even though you've been blind about this situation, we can't tell you what this is about. I still think it's better if you don't know. Your statements and the questions you just asked are exactly what we should be asking ourselves. Your participation tonight, in this most important matter, has been invaluable. We thank you for your assistance. I request that you continue to help us. However, we need your independent guidance. You will soon know all of the details. Because of your knowledge and experience in healing, can you cut a hole in Knee-nose's head? This is a very serious and pressing matter. Could you do this tomorrow?"

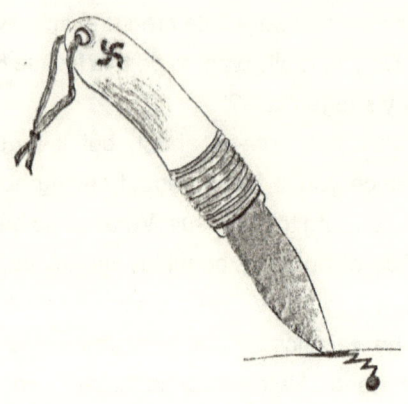

Playing with Innocence

Jopin yelled into the doorway of his house "Knee-nose and I are home. The meeting's over."

"Your meetings usually last till late into the night, so I wasn't expecting you yet. I prepared a place for Knee-nose to sleep, right next to us. Do you think this old bear skin will do?" Bright-sunflower tried to get Knee-nose's attention, but he refused to look at her. She put her hands on her hips. "What happened to poor Knee-nose? He isn't the same happy and proud young deer who left here earlier. What happened at the meeting?"

"My sweet Bright-sunflower, we need to talk."

"You better believe we need to talk. What happened to Knee-nose? Just look at him. His disposition is shattered." She leaned down and started to brush his fur with her hands. "Did those mean old men make fun of you?"

"No. It's worse than that. Medicine-maker, the village, medicine man, will cut a hole on the top of Knee-nose's head tomorrow. He will do this in order to—"

"What? That's the most ridiculous thing I've ever heard. Why didn't you object and say something?"

"We haven't had a chance to talk. I need to tell you about my vision and the part Knee-nose had to do with my prayer quest."

"Jopin, you better not tell me that cutting a hole in Knee-nose's head was your idea. I'm so mad, I can't—"

"You're so mad that you're not allowing yourself to listen to what I have to say. Please give me a chance to speak. Have a drink of water and take a few deep breaths. You need to hear what I have to say." Jopin handed his canteen to Bright-sunflower and motioned for her to drink. He started talking as she started to swallow. "I had to go on a prayer quest, because Chief Salamander wants us to make the biggest decision we have ever had to make. It's something that will affect each and every one of us, the entire village. Everyone's life will change. I couldn't make such a decision without contacting the gods for advice.

I wanted our decision and our actions to be what the gods want, not what Chief Salamander and his fellow chiefs that met at Chaco want. So, I decided to go on a prayer quest. The gods gave me a vision of a small fawn, as I prayed at the Shrine of the Soaring Eagles. The fawn floated in the heavens with stars all around him. Light from the brightest star was entering a hole on top of his head. I had this vision at the same time Knee-nose's mother brought him over to me. Knee-nose leaned up against my leg and interrupted my vision."

"Jopin, a vision doesn't mean you have to make it happen. You don't have to cut a hole on Knee-nose's head, just because you had this dream. I should've been at the council meeting. This is absurd." She lifted up her hands and clasped them together ready to wring someone's neck. "I will not allow this to happen to Knee-nose. You will take Knee-nose back to his mother tomorrow, before sunrise. I should've known something was wrong when you took Knee-nose with you to the council meeting. I knew you were up to no good, ever since you became interested in climbing that cliff. You got stuck there, because you shouldn't have gone there in the first place. Don't you see what's happening?"

"I only wanted to do the right thing, but there's more. You need to hear the rest. I had mentioned to Chief Salamander and the elders how I wasn't feeling well, so—"

"So you lied? I knew you had lied to them. You weren't sick, you lied. You're always preaching about how one must always tell the truth. What could be so important, that you had to lie?"

"You're getting excited again. Let me continue. Tonight, I confessed to Chief Salamander and to the rest of the council. I told them the idea of voting on this decision made me sick to the point I couldn't get myself to vote, so I had to go ask the gods."

"Why didn't you just tell them the truth? You weren't really sick. You lied to them again tonight, and you're lying to yourself right now. You've always preached that one should always tell the truth, no matter what."

"Please let me finish. Chief Salamander had asked Medicine-maker, the medicine man, to pray for me, because he was concerned about my health."

"Huh? Nothing's wrong with your health, perhaps with your head. Why do you have to tell me who Medicine-maker is? I already know he's the medicine man. Tell me what I want to hear, not what I already know. I don't care about Medicine-maker. I care about Knee-nose."

"I'm telling you about Medicine-maker, because we had similar visions. It was about a small, spotted fawn with a hole on top of its head, with starlight entering through this hole on his head."

"Jopin, did he tell you about his vision, after you told him about your vision? Perhaps he just wanted to get some attention, just like you. After all, you're the one who came to them with the beautiful, small, spotted fawn."

"Yes, it happened after I shared my vision, but Medicine-maker can't act like that. He must remain unbiased and pure, so the gods can instruct him on how to cure others."

"He doesn't appear very pure to me."

Jopin couldn't believe she was saying such things, but he continued anyway. "And, there's more to his vision. Knee-nose wasn't the only one with a hole on top of his head. Medicine-maker also saw a man floating in the sky with a hole on his head, with starlight entering the hole. That man was me."

Bright-sunflower swung her head up, opened her eyes wide, and held her mouth open. "What? I've heard enough! I'm going with you to take Knee-nose back to his mother tonight. Perhaps we should leave you up there with him. No one is going to cut a hole on my husband's head."

"Not tonight. I still haven't slept from last night. Besides, the night is very dark. Can't we get up early and take him back, before anyone else gets up?"

"No, we must take care of this matter tonight." She reached down to tug on Knee-nose, but he squatted down, putting all four legs under his body. She attempted to pull his front legs out, but he refused to budge. Bright-sunflower attempted to lift him off the ground. Knee-nose refused to straighten out his legs. She leaned back to look at him. He then took his front legs out from under his body and held them out in front of him. Gently, he put his head down to the ground. His eyes stared up at her and slowly started to tear up.

Bright-sunflower immediately turned her back to him as she gasped and wiped her own tears.

Jopin gently touched her shoulder. "Look at him. He understands every word we have spoken. He's deeply saddened, yet he doesn't want us to spare him from what will happen to him tomorrow. There's something very mystical and sacred about Knee-nose, too much to be a coincidence. He interrupted my vision. Then his mother brought him and nudged him towards me. You should have seen the look in their eyes, as they said good-bye to each other. It was heart breaking. He has been by my side since that moment. I took him back to his mother and she pushed him back to me, as if he had to follow her orders. He willingly came with us, along the path down the mountain, into our village, and here to our home. Now, he's willingly offering himself up as a sacrifice to our village. It's difficult to understand."

Bright-sunflower kept her eyes fixed on Knee-nose. "He knows what you elders plan to do to him tomorrow, because he came back from the meeting looking beaten and in despair. Yes, he knows exactly what's happening." She sat down in front of Knee-nose, gently lifted his head, and looked into his eyes. "Knee-nose, it doesn't have to be like this. We can take you back to your mama, tonight. You don't have to stay here and allow these men to hurt you. Come. Let us take you back up the mountain."

Knee-nose looked directly back into her eyes. Tears broke loose and ran down his cheeks. He then backed up a few steps away from her, and lowered his head onto the ground.

Bright-sunflower leaned forward and whispered, "You must obey us. Come on Knee-nose. Let us take you back to your mother. I'm sure she's worried about you."

Knee-nose clearly understood her, but his actions let her know he would not be going back.

Bright-sunflower gave Jopin a hopeless stare, and then started to cry. "Why are you going to sacrifice this most innocent, new brother of ours?"

"Because the gods sent him. Just look at him. He has freely offered himself up for us." Jopin lowered his voice. "Chief Salamander doesn't consider it a sacrificial offering. And, Medicine-maker doesn't want to kill him. As for me, Chief

Salamander said he would not allow a hole to be cut into my head. He doesn't believe in human sacrifice."

Bright-sunflower looked startled. "Human sacrifice? Jopin, are they also talking about cutting a hole in your head? The more we talk, the more disturbing this gets. What's going on? Why won't you let me know what this is all about? You're very mistaken if you think I'm going to agree to any of this. You may be crazy, but I'm not. What ever happened to the wise man I married? There's something wrong with your logic. What happened to you up on that cliff? Did you lose your mind?"

"I don't know. The more I address this most important issue, the more confused I get. After talking to Deer-tracker, I had decided to break my oath and share this problem with you, but now I can't. You've become too involved and emotional about Knee-nose." Jopin felt hopeless.

"Yes, I'm very involved in this situation, but what about you? Don't you see yourself as too emotional and irrational? Who tried to climb that cliff after fasting for three whole days, and at your age? Who has the problem, here? I want to help. What's the real issue? Why won't you tell me what's happening?"

Jopin slowly lowered his head as he started to speak. "Chief Salamander invited Medicine-maker to join us at the meeting tonight. I thought Salamander would have told him what this was about, but he didn't. He wanted Medicine-maker to remain impartial and independent. You can't ignore the fact that Medicine-maker had the same vision as I did, except that I also appeared in his vision."

"These visions can mean anything. It doesn't mean they have to cut holes into your heads. Medicine-maker will kill you. I guess he intends to kill Knee-nose first and then you."

"This isn't about killing. It's about preparing us to better communicate with Great Grandfather, like when he communicates with a newborn, while the skull is still soft."

"A hole is quite different from a baby's soft skull. Besides, Knee-nose can't speak, even if Great Grandfather does tell him what he wants. How will Knee-nose tell the elders what our creator has told him? This plan is preposterous. It's obvious that Chief Salamander and Medicine-maker intend to cut a hole in Knee-nose's head first, to practice and learn how to cut a hole in your head. I can't believe this is happening. What has everyone been drinking?"

"Everything you say sounds very reasonable, but Chief Salamander made it clear. He will not allow anyone to cut a hole in my skull. This is true. We don't know what we will gain by cutting a hole in Knee-nose's skull. Perhaps our creator will reveal something to us or give us an important message, with Medicine-maker's help."

Bright-sunflower remained quiet for a while, as if trying to figure out how to respond. "I don't know how you elders could possibly receive this very important message. Knee-nose can't speak, even worse, Knee-nose may die."

"I don't know. Medicine-maker speaks to all kinds of animals and objects during his ceremonies."

"If true, he wouldn't have to do anything to Knee-nose. We might be the dumb ones for believing he has such powers. But, for your sake, I hope you're right."

Knee-nose had been observing and studying them. Jopin felt defeated, and Bright-sunflower was overwhelmed. They soon stopped talking, sat next to him, and started to pet and brush his fur. It was time to give Knee-nose some attention. However, Bright-sunflower still had a lot on her mind. She cleared her throat, as to get Jopin's attention. "There's a rumor that the people of Puye will be leaving."

"Leaving, what do you mean, leaving?"

"I mean, leaving. Everyone in the village will pack up and evacuate, for good."

Jopin carefully asked, "Where will they go?"

"I don't know, but I think you do."

"Why would I know? I'm no longer from Puye. I grew up there and some of my family still lives there, but I'm not involved in Puye's affairs."

"But you're involved in Tyuonyi's. This is what this crisis is about, isn't it? Does Chief Salamander want Tyuonyi to evacuate, as well?"

"Bright-sunflower, you know I'm under oath. I can't share secret council matters with anyone, not even you. Why do you keep testing me?"

"I just want to let you know I understand how much pressure you must be under. This big decision is about evacuating Tyuonyi. Isn't it? My poor husband, I understand what you've been going through. No one should have to make such a decision. Perhaps this has something to do with the Great Migration, where Father Sun directs his people to go where he wants them to go. Is this the case with Puye?"

"I can't say. You know more about what Puye is doing than I do. What do you think?"

"It's just a rumor going around, mostly among the women. But it does make me wonder if this may be what has been going on with you and the council. This is very serious business."

"I can't talk to you about council business. My reputation will be ruined if word gets out about information I shared with you. Please, can we change the subject?"

"What are you going to do about Knee-nose?"

"I don't think it's up to me, nor you. The gods sent him to us for a very important reason. It may not be right for us to interfere with their plans. I'm very tired. Can't keep this up much longer. Knee-nose is very much aware of his surroundings. It wouldn't upset me if he were gone by morning." Jopin walked over to the entrance and pulled the deerskin to one side. "Look, Knee-nose. This is the way out. You are free to leave. I'm going to get some sleep."

"You go ahead and get some sleep. I'll stay up with Knee-nose. I might be the only friend he has left." Jopin gave her a frustrated look.

Knee-nose squatted down on his four legs and allowed Bright-sunflower to pet him. Jopin started to snore. She also, soon fell asleep, right next to Knee-nose. Knee-nose watched the coals glow until they faded off into darkness. The only one awake was Knee-nose.

"Jopin, it is I." Medicine-maker called from outside. "We'll meet at the sacred rock in front of the main kiva. Let me know when you and Knee-nose are ready."

"I didn't know it was so late. We were still sleeping. Give me some time to get ready." He looked over at Knee-nose to see if he had remained with them. "We'll be there soon." Bright-sunflower had a blank look on her face.

"I also have to get a few things ready, so take your time."

"Okay, we'll be there soon."

Bright-sunflower started to cry as she hugged Knee-nose. Knee-nose pulled away from her and started walking towards the door.

"Wait Knee-nose, we don't have to be there until we're ready. I mean, it looks like you're ready, but I'm not. Let me wash my face and comb my hair. I'm sure Bright-sunflower wants to clean you up a little."

Bright-sunflower took out her sweet-smelling oil and started to rub it on his body, sobbing as she applied it. Knee-nose appeared to appreciate the love and attention she gave him.

"Don't put any on top of his head."

She instantly gave Jopin a hopeless stare. She applied a little on his head, and then continued to rub some on the rest of his body. "I'm sorry I fell asleep on you," she told Knee-nose. She then snapped at Jopin. "I hope you all know what you're doing."

Jopin finished getting himself ready, stopped to look at Bright-sunflower, and then said, "It's time."

"I'm not going to give you anything to eat. I don't think we should eat at a moment like this."

"I'm not hungry. I wouldn't be able to eat. Come, Knee-nose." He exited the room. Knee-nose followed. Jopin paused outside for a second. Bright-sunflower was sobbing. Tears formed on Jopin's eyes as well. He and Knee-nose then walked to the kiva.

An eerie, silent crowd awaited them. Word about the event must have circulated throughout the village. Everyone was there, except for Bright-sunflower.

Chief Salamander greeted them. "Good morning Jopin and Knee-nose." He moved in close to Jopin. "We can stop this craziness right now, if you wish."

Jopin felt relieved. "I agree with you, Chief Salamander. This is wrong. I'll take Knee-nose back to his mother." He bent forward to lift Knee-nose, but Knee-nose escaped his grasp. Jopin tried again, but Knee-nose refused to let Jopin get near him. Instead, Knee-nose started walking towards Medicine-maker.

Jopin stood up and turned to face Chief Salamander. "Bright-sunflower and I talked about taking him back to his mother last night and he acted the same way. This is really strange. The gods must be directing him."

"I guess so." Chief Salamander scratched his left cheek. "But I doubt if this will tell us anything. Knee-nose can't talk, so even if he does survive, we still won't know what this is all about. What could the gods possibly tell us through Knee-nose?"

"I don't know. Perhaps Medicine-maker has it figured out. I better go and support Knee-nose."

Bright-sunflower showed up and walked directly to the chief. "Chief Salamander, can you stop this madness?"

"I tried, but Knee-nose acted like he had no choice, but to go through with this. Never, in my life, have I known of an animal who acts like Knee-nose. There is something very sacred and mystical about our little brother deer."

"Then why are you going to sacrifice something so sacred?"

"I just talked to your husband and informed him we could stop this from happening, but Knee-nose let us know we had no say. He dodged Jopin's grasp and headed towards Medicine-maker. I don't understand. It's almost as if it's out of our hands. I feel as helpless as you do."

Medicine-maker already had a fire burning near the sacred rock. He squatted down to greet Knee-nose, as he addressed the public. "I smoked the sacred pipe this morning, and now I know what I must do."

Everyone remained speechless, silently looking at Knee-nose, except for the three of them. Fat-man and Little-boy had been talking to Thunder-head.

"Shouldn't you be doing this at the sacrificial rock?"

"That's a very good question, Thunder-head. This isn't a sacrifice, but rather a procedure prescribed by the gods. Knee-nose is sacred, so it is right and proper for Knee-nose to be here on this sacred rock. We expect Knee-nose to live. This is being done to help us answer a very important question."

"What's this about an important question? I don't know about any question?"

"I don't either. I'm only doing this at the request of Chief Salamander, for the council of elders. I myself, don't know what this is about."

"That's ridiculous," Fat-man cried out. "How can you answer something, if you don't even know the question? How can you—"

Chief Salamander spoke up. "Let me explain. I decided it would be better if Medicine-maker doesn't know what we're attempting to accomplish. Right now, he is the only one who isn't emotionally involved, so it is better for him not to know."

Little-boy decided to say something. "And you expect to receive an answer from an innocent baby deer, who can't even speak?"

"Another good observation. I also, don't understand. I tried to stop this act, this very morning, but Knee-nose let us know he had to have this done to him. So, I guess, he is speaking to us, in his own way. Two people had the same prayer vision of a small, spotted fawn with light coming from a bright star which entered a hole on top of its head. Medicine-maker first told me about this vision. Then, later in the morning, Jopin came to me with the same vision as Medicine-maker's. The strange thing though, Jopin came to me with this beautiful, innocent, little fawn. Knee-nose's mother delivered him to Jopin. I'm disturbed by this, most complicated situation. Twice, I have tried to stop this from happening, but Knee-nose appears to demand it. I don't understand." The people listened intently to Chief Salamander.

Medicine-maker shook his rattle and started to chant. He removed several sacred items from his bag, placed them around Knee-nose, sprinkled sacred tobacco on Knee-nose's back, and then used corn pollen to make a large circle around Knee-nose. Medicine-maker filled his prayer pipe with tobacco, lifted it high up above his head and praised the gods for bringing Tyuonyi this most precious and sinless, brother deer to the people. "Great Grandfather, you have asked me to cut a hole in Knee-nose's head. Please guide my hands as I follow your instructions." He reached into his bag and removed a beautiful white knife, holding it up, for the people to see it. "This is the knife I will use. I made it a very long time ago, when studying to become a medicine man. The gods told me not to use it, but rather, to save it for a very special purpose. The time has come for me to now use this knife. I made the blade from the hard, white stone found in the area of the Thundering Falls. The rock there is pure, like Knee-nose. The handle came from a deer antler, perhaps, from one of Knee-nose's ancestors. I carved the symbol of the sun on one side of the handle, and the spinning sun on the other side."

Some of the council members appeared stunned. They looked at each other in amazement when Medicine-maker talked about the carvings on the knife and the materials used to make it.

Medicine-maker explained how he would first cut into Knee-nose's scalp, but not completely detach it. He intended to place it back in place to cover the hole. He then signaled for the drummers and prayer dancers to start. Medicine-maker offered up his prayer pipe for all creatures living to the north, south, east and west, and then for all creatures living above, and below, in the underworld. He blessed Knee-nose by blowing smoke on his face. Knee-nose bowed his head and slowly lowered his eyelids, accepting the blessing.

Medicine-maker asked Elders Cloud-burst and Flying-falcon to enter the circle to help Jopin hold down Knee-nose. He looked into Knee-nose's eyes and said, "I'm sorry. This will hurt." He then signaled for the three men to hold on to Knee-nose as he started to cut. Knee-nose twitched as the knife cut into his scalp. A few drops of blood started to flow. Jopin began to massage Knee-nose and whispered into his ear. "I will be here with you. Everything will be fine." The men held on tight to Knee-nose, expecting him to try to get away, but Knee-nose didn't even move. Medicine-maker started to use a sawing motion to cut away at the scalp. Knee-nose continued to let him, but his body began to shake. His eyes slowly started to lose the life in them. However, he still stood up on his own.

The people expressed awe and reverence for the way Knee-nose allowed himself to be cut. Some of them whispered how they would not have been able to handle the pain.

Medicine-maker finally finished cutting and pulled the scalp away from the skull. He folded it aside to lay it back into place, after the hole would be cut into his skull. He knelt down to look into Knee-nose's eyes. "We have completed the first part of the process. I will allow you to rest a while, before we start cutting into your skull."

Medicine-maker joined Jopin in massaging Knee-nose. He asked for someone to bring him some water. Deer-tracker ran off to fetch it and quickly returned, passing the canteen over to Medicine-maker. Jopin noticed that once again, Deer-tracker was using his canteen. Medicine-maker took the canteen and sprinkled water on Knee-nose. "Perhaps this will refresh you a little." The elders rubbed water on Knee-nose's fur.

The crowd started to take turns coming in close to see Knee-nose and observe his exposed skull. Bright-sunflower backed off to avoid seeing him. However, Knee-nose must have sensed her apprehension. He turned his head in her direction, in an attempt to see her.

Medicine-maker raised his knife up in the air to address the crowd. "I am now ready to cut the hole in Knee-nose's skull. The point of my knife will be used to drill four holes in the skull, like at the corners of a square. I will then cut the skull in a line from one hole to the next until I can remove the square-shaped piece of skull."

He pressed the point of his knife on Knee-nose's skull and started to rotate his wrist, to the right and then to the left, to the right and then to the left. He continued doing this for some time, but the process wasn't working. Disappointed, he pulled his knife away to assess the problem. A small indentation could barely be seen on Knee-nose's skull. He then applied more pressure with his knife, rotating the blade to the right and then to the left, to the right and to the left, to the right and then to the left. Knee-nose kept lowering his head to get away from the force of the knife, until his chin came into contact with the sacred rock. Although in pain, he continued to allow Medicine-maker to continue working on his head. Medicine-maker finally stopped. "I thought his skull would be soft, being that he is just a baby." He reached into his bag and pulled out his knife-making equipment. "Please pour some more water on Knee-nose to refresh him. I must make a sharper point on my knife."

Medicine-maker used the tip of an antler to chip off pieces of stone from the blade. He soon had a very slender and narrow, sharp point. "I think this will work better." The men once again, held on to Knee-nose. Medicine-maker pressed his now more-pointed, narrow blade onto the area of the skull where he had been working. He rotated his wrist to the right and then to the left. "This point is working much better." He continued and then stopped to evaluate the progress. "I have to make sure I don't cut into the sheath that separates the brain from the skull." He quickly completed all four holes and then addressed Knee-nose. "We have completed the second part of the process. I can't believe how well you have handled all of this. It must have been very painful. You should rest a while, before we start to remove bone." He then motioned for the men to pour some more water on Knee-nose.

Medicine-maker soon announced it was time to continue. He placed the blade, almost horizontal to the skull, in line with the first two holes drilled, and started to saw. Progress was poor, so he increased the force and speed of his strokes, faster and faster. Still, not much progress. He lifted his knife from the handle, carefully stuck its point into a hole, and started to saw, using very short strokes. "I have to make sure not to puncture his brain." This process worked better. He finally completed the cut between the first two holes. "Let's pour some more water on Knee-nose."

By this time, Knee-nose had plastered his head onto the sacred rock. He showed little response to anything being done to him. Jopin massaged both sides of Knee-nose's head, "I wonder what you're thinking. Are you communicating with the gods, or are you in too much pain? Speak to me, Knee-nose."

No reaction, whatsoever.

Medicine-maker looked over to Jopin. "It doesn't look promising." He then leaned forward to whisper into Knee-nose's ear. "I'm sorry it has taken so long. I'll hurry and try to get you through this." He started cutting between the second and third holes, applying more force and sawing faster. Success. He finally started to cut into the fourth hole, faster and faster.

Knee-nose began to jerk. "Please hold him down. I just have a little further to go before I complete the last cut." Knee-nose jerked again and attempted to raise himself up on his feet. "Please hold him down." His feet started kicking and his entire body began to tremble. Knee-nose had gone into convulsions. "Pour some water on him. Someone, please give him some water." The water didn't help. Knee-nose continued to shake and kick.

The shaking and kicking finally subsided. Knee-nose's tongue hung out of his mouth.

Feast Day

Not knowing what to say or do, the elders just stood around Knee-nose's lifeless body. Likewise, the villagers remained deathly quiet. Many of them looked shocked. Some were overwhelmed with sorrow. Nothing but silence. Medicine-maker faintly spoke out, "I pierced his brain. He jerked up at the time when I was cutting, and I pierced his brain."

Chief Salamander stepped forward and held his own knife up in the air. "Will the fire chief please add some more wood to the fire? Knee-nose has sacrificed himself for us. We must now offer Knee-nose up to our Almighty Great Grandfather. The sacred fire and sacred stone have now taken on the properties of a sacrificial altar. Medicine-maker, please open him up. I need to get to his heart." Jopin quickly turned to look at Bright-sunflower. She had an empty, blank stare about her. He could sense the deep, deep sorrow in her heart.

Medicine-maker stabbed his knife deep into Knee-nose's chest cavity, pulled hard on his knife to split the chest all the way to the throat, and then pulled the ribs apart to expose the heart. Medicine-maker quickly stepped back and shouted, "His heart is still pumping. He must have been in shock. He is still alive."

It was too late to save Knee-nose, so Chief Salamander raised his voice to make a statement. "Offering a beating heart to Great Grandfather is of the highest honor. This is another sign indicating the sacredness of Knee-nose, a sacrifice for Tyuonyi, and a true offering to Great Grandfather."

Chief Salamander asked Medicine-maker to hold Knee-nose's chest open, so he could reach in and cut out the heart. Medicine-maker would collect the precious blood for the ceremony and then, cut Knee-nose in half. The two halves would be laid out on each side of the path the villagers would walk through on their way to offer up Knee-nose to their Almighty Creator.

Chief Salamander cut out Knee-nose's heart, while Medicine-maker captured the blood in a medium sized bowl. Elder Flying-falcon quickly cut Knee-nose in half, and laid out the two halves, as instructed. Chief Salamander approached the sacred fire by walking between the two halves of Knee-nose, holding Knee-nose's beating heart high above his head. "Great Grandfather, we offer you this most precious gift. We know you will find it most pleasing, for it is from our most pure and beloved, Knee-nose. Please accept this offering in appreciation for everything you have given us. You gave us this most beautiful, pure, and sacred brother-deer to come and teach us how to sacrifice ourselves for each other. We now offer him back to you. We release his soul, so he can go live with you and become a most gracious and loyal servant of yours."

Chief Salamander cast Knee-nose's heart deep into the fire. The impact caused sparks and ashes to fly up, out of the burning ambers and then, a little whirlwind of smoke emerged. It settled on the ground in front of Chief Salamander, spinned its way around the chief, and continued to swirl down the path, between Knee-nose's body parts, on to Jopin. The elders moved away but Jopin remained stationary. It swirled around Jopin, slowly rising up in a spiral pattern around him, until it dissipated on top of Jopin's head. The council members looked at each other in amazement, not believing what they had just witnessed.

Bright-sunflower stared right into Chief Salamander's eyes, as if asking, begging.

Chief Salamander acknowledged Bright-sunflower by looking right back at her, but he ignored her silent demand. Instead, he ordered everyone in the village to come pay homage to Knee-nose. He yelled out, "Knee-nose has completed his duties, here in this world, and will now be given new duties helping the Divine up in the skies. He will join Great Grandfather today. I proclaim this special day, the Knee-nose Feast Day. We must turn this sadness into joy. Why have the drummers and prayer dancers stopped? From now on, Knee-nose will be our very own intercessor with our Almighty Great Grandfather. This is a great blessing for each and every one of us. Let's start this most important feast day with his offering. Please accept this blessing by approaching the altar and offering Knee-nose up to Great Grandfather. If you wish, you can then return to this side and drink some of his life-giving blood, so Knee-nose can continue to live on, in each and every one of us."

Bright-sunflower joined Jopin, letting him know she was ready to accept the blessing and offer Knee-nose up to Great Grandfather. The villagers started to line up behind Jopin and Bright-sunflower.

Chief Salamander, once again, addressed the crowd. "We can do certain things today, other than the fire offering, to honor Knee-nose. Jopin, would you and Bright-sunflower like to prepare Knee-nose for consumption? If you agree, I will ask some of the young men to bring you some firewood for the outdoor baking ovens. We need volunteers to help with the cutting and, ugh—"

Bright-sunflower shook her head, letting Jopin know it was not acceptable. Jopin raised his hand to get the chief's attention. "I don't think this is a good idea. Knee-nose was like a family member of ours. We couldn't."

"Of course you can't. How could I be so insensitive? You've already, more than honored Tyuonyi by bringing us the sacred offering. Do I have a volunteer to cook our offering?"

Elder Pine-needle got the look of approval from his wife, so he raised his hand. "Chief, Whispering-wind and I would like to prepare Knee-nose for Elder Jopin and Bright-sunflower. We will do this with all of the love and respect they would want us to give Knee-nose."

"Thank you, Elder Pine-needle and Whispering-wind. You honor the village by being such good friends to Jopin and Bright-sunflower. The Honor Guard will escort Knee-nose to your place and remain with him throughout the rest of the day. Please let me know if there is anything you may need. I'll have some firewood delivered to your place."

Chief Salamander asked the rest of them to go back to their homes and prepare whatever food they may have to share, but not until after Knee-nose's fire offering. The hunting party had not returned, so they would have to prepare a feast with whatever food they had on hand. Some of them would bring stew, others corn, sunflower root, beans, bread, fish, rabbit, and drink. He asked the flute players to join the drummers and prayer dancers. "This is a most joyful event in honor of our sacred fawn."

He asked the Deer Clan to lead the people in prayers to be offered up for Knee-nose. The drummers, flute players, prayer singers, and prayer dancers would all join in the prayers to Great Grandfather and his gods, for the rest of the day. "This is the feast day of Knee-nose! Let's start by offering up Knee-nose to the sacred fire."

The villagers lined up behind Jopin and Bright-sunflower, awaiting their turn to honor Knee-nose at the fire offering. They walked the path between Knee-nose's halves, approached the sacred fire, solemnly offered him up to the Creator, and then sipped from the bowl of his blood.

Most of the people returned to their residences to determine what to prepare for the feast. The members of the Deer Clan joined the drummer and prayer dancers to teach them the songs of the Deer Clan.

Jopin and Bright-sunflower walked back to their home, not speaking a word to each other. Bright-sunflower started to look through her cooking pots and utensils. Jopin was curious. "Are you looking for something to make for the feast?"

"No, I'm wondering if I have something big enough to cook you in, when it's your turn."

"Look, I don't know what's going to happen. Chief Salamander said he would not allow human sacrifice. He allowed it to happen to Knee-nose, but he made it clear it would never happen to me."

"We'll see. It's not what the chief says that matters. It looks like you have already volunteered. Why do you desire to be the next sacrifice, the next victim? Are you starving for so much attention that you're willing to give up your life? What about your family? Will you achieve satisfaction from all those people looking at you, while a hole is cut into your head, while Medicine-maker kills you? It's obvious, you don't care about yourself. Don't you care about your wife? I'm old and need your help. Why don't you want to take care of me? What's wrong with you?"

"I do care about you, but I don't know what to say. You have seen with your own eyes. This whole situation is being driven by the Divine, not me. There has never been a deer like Knee-nose. He never fought us, not even when Medicine-maker cut into his head. It must have been very painful, yet he allowed it."

"And what about you? Do you also want to experience this pain?"

"Of course not. I'm sure Knee-nose didn't want it done to him, either." Jopin put both hands on her shoulders. "Your parents named you Bright-sunflower, because they wanted you to follow Great Grandfather, like when a sunflower turns to face the sun as it travels across the sky. We have to be willing to follow his commandments, no matter what he asks of us. I didn't ask for Knee-nose to come to me, and I didn't ask for his whirlwind of smoke to come to me from the sacred fire. It came on its own and danced around me. Something very sacred is happening. I must obey Great Grandfather. You also must obey him."

She pushed his hands away from her and stood back. "You have lost your mind. What makes you think you're following the wishes of the Almighty? Why don't you go visit Chief Salamander and make plans for your death. I'll start planning your funeral. No, wait. I'm sorry. That's wrong. You won't have a funeral. We will have to cook and eat you, just like Knee-nose. You'll get all the attention you've been longing for."

Jopin tried to put his arms around Bright-sunflower, but she shrugged away from him. "Why don't you go visit the chief and his sick followers?"

"I don't want to see them at this moment. I'll go dig up some sunflower roots so you can have something to bring to the feast."

"You don't have to do anything for me. Deer-tracker must have known, because he brought me a whole basketful, and some yucca root. I'll make a stew with jerky pieces. You could go fetch me some water from the river, if you like."

"I would be happy to do that. You will also need some firewood."

"Just go."

Jopin grabbed the large, water pot and walked out on to the plaza. The drummers, flute players and prayer dancers were offering up prayers for Knee-nose. He noticed a fire had already been started in the oven for Pine-needle and Whispering-wind. The older boys were delivering firewood to all ovens. He wouldn't have to collect firewood after all. Little things like these were what made Salamander such a good chief, he thought. Medicine-maker, Elder Cloud-burst and Elder Flying-falcon were having a conversation with Chief Salamander. Jopin chose to ignore them, so he focused his attention on the prayer dancers. He continued to walk towards the exit. They stopped talking when they saw him, so he assumed they were probably talking about him.

The warrior guards at the exit joked around, warning him the stream might be dry, because everyone in the village had taken water out of it. Jopin walked down to the bank, filled his pot, and headed back. The guards let him know he had been very lucky, because the others had left him some water.

Just as Jopin had suspected, the men had been talking to Chief Salamander about him. Elder Cloud-burst had wanted to know if Jopin would be next. Chief Salamander replied, "Absolutely not. Knee-nose died. This is exactly what I was afraid would happen. And, what did it tell us? Nothing. I will not allow anything like this to ever happen again, especially to Jopin."

Elder Flying-falcon had his opinion. "We all saw how the smoke whirlwind swirled around Jopin and climbed to the top of his head. What do you think it meant? Was this how Knee-nose delivered his message? I think Jopin knows something, but he has chosen to keep it to himself."

"Your guess is as good as mine. Perhaps it was nothing more than a whirlwind."

"I don't know. It looked like more than just a coincidental whirlwind to me. I think Knee-nose was letting us know Jopin would be next, and also, that Jopin would be all right. What do you think, Medicine-maker? You're trained to interpret such signs."

Chief Salamander interrupted. "Medicine-maker will say nothing. He's too closely associated with this situation to have a voice in this matter. Don't answer."

Medicine-maker looked at Chief Salamander and then at the other two, but remained silent.

"Then how are we going to come to a vote?"

"What do you mean, Flying-falcon? I'll just pressure Jopin to make a decision. He's the only one who has been reluctant to vote."

"But, this whole situation with Knee-nose will now make it much more difficult, if not impossible. The elders will not come to a consensus, unless Jopin agrees to—"

"Agrees to what, agrees to be killed, or agrees to evacuate Tyuoni?"

"I think he will agree to have a hole cut into his head, before he will agree to evacuate."

Chief Salamander sternly stared into their faces. "Knee-nose couldn't speak, because he was a deer. He is now a dead deer. Jopin won't talk because he also, will be dead. There must be a better way for us to settle this."

Elder Cloud-burst straightened up and then lowered his head a little. "Chief, I hate to bring you bad news, but there are rumors going around about Puye. Some of the villagers already know they will be evacuating. Because of everything that has happened here with Knee-nose, they may not accept any decision we make, unless Jopin publicly agrees with it."

"Are you saying they will only do what Jopin decides?"

"I am afraid it won't take long for them to figure out why Jopin went on his prayer quest. He needed Divine intervention to help him decide what to do about our evacuation. And now, it's obvious that Jopin's question has not been answered. The only answer they might accept might be the one coming from Jopin, after a hole is cut into his head."

"That's ridiculous. You're implying that I've lost control of the village. I've already lost control of the council."

"Jopin has control of everything."

"Medicine-maker, why have you been so quiet? What do you have to say?"

"Chief, I've been listening to this very interesting discussion. I have to agree with Elder Cloud-burst. I myself was asked about the rumor, even before you invited me to join you at the council meeting. I denied knowing anything about the migration, because I didn't know. However, because of everything that has taken place, I now believe this must be the case. Puye has decided to evacuate, and a lot has happened here at Tyuonyi with Knee-nose. The people will soon demand to know the truth. This is their beloved homeland. They will want to know if you will order them to leave."

"Perhaps we should make the announcement this afternoon, when we all get together to share our meal. I can inform them that Tyuonyi, like Puye, will obey Father Sun's orders to move out of this area."

"I don't belong to your council, and I don't know all the details of what has happened, however, the people won't believe Father Sun has really spoken. Knee-nose was sent to Tyuonyi to help answer that question, but that question has not yet been answered. Either Father Sun needs to start spinning, or I have to cut a hole in Jopin's head."

"No, I won't permit this to happen. There must be another way. Bright-sunflower is begging me not to allow such a thing. We already made one sacrifice. Knee-nose showed us how bad of an idea it was. Jopin would surely die if we were to do the same thing to him. I shouldn't have allowed you to cut into Knee-nose."

Elder Cloud-burst seemed confused. "What if Knee-nose was sent to us, so we could learn how to do it right, so we wouldn't make the same mistake with Jopin? Medicine-maker, do you think you could cut a hole in Jopin's head without killing—?"

"Don't answer that, Medicine-maker. Elder Cloud-burst, you are speaking out of order. You have no right to ask."

"Chief, please let me answer him. Besides, you will have to know how to answer when others ask you this same question."

Chief Salamander did not respond.

"I deeply regret what I did to Knee-nose, especially for the heartache I brought to Jopin and Bright-sunflower. It's too bad, because I was almost finished. If only he hadn't jumped into my knife. This won't happen with Jopin, because things will be different. We couldn't give Knee-nose anything to relax him or to kill the pain, because he was a deer. Deer don't drink our sacred corn brew, and they don't smoke special tobaccos, like when we set a broken leg on someone. That's why he jumped. He didn't have anything to deaden the pain."

"I'm sorry, but I don't agree with what you're saying. Knee-nose might have jumped into your knife, because you poked his brain. Could that have caused him to go into convulsions?"

"You might be right. I had made a very sharp point on my knife to drill into his hard skull. I should've rounded the sharp tip, before I started to saw in between the holes. That way, I could have avoided piercing his brain. On Jopin, I could drill all of the small holes first, with the sharp point, and then round or break the point off, before cutting between the holes."

"You can still puncture his brain while drilling with that very sharp point. No matter what all of you believe could be done, I won't allow it. This conversation is over."

"Here's the water. Would you like for me to build a fire for you to cook the stew."

"Yes, but first I need some water to rinse the roots. I had enough to wash the dirt off of them, and I already cut them up, so they just need to be rinsed."

"Could I rinse them for you?"

"Why are you being so nice? Do you want me to remember how good of a husband you used to be?"

"I'm not going anywhere."

"Yes, you are. You will be joining Knee-nose. We both know it will be happening very soon."

"Do you know something I don't? Chief Salamander was very definite about not allowing anything to happen to me. He was even against it happening to Knee-nose."

Chief Salamander is a good man. He gave in to what you elders wanted to do to Knee-nose, and he will give in to what the people will want to do to you."

"The people don't have anything to do with this. This is council business. Everything is done in secret."

"This matter is no longer a secret, because your private concerns are out. They know about Puye and they witnessed what happened to Knee-nose. But of more importance, they know that a hole has to be cut into your head."

"No, you're the only one who knows about the evacuation. I shouldn't have told you anything, because you have now decided what will happen. You're imagination is worse than the truth. You're not supposed to know anything about this. I have broken my vow of silence."

"Your wife is the only one who never knows anything. The entire village has been talking about this for the last two days. I'm married to the senior elder, so I'm the last one to know about anything. Why are you doing this?"

"Are you saying that some of the elders have spoken to their wives about the evacuation?"

"Yes. The wives know about Puye and they know you were against us moving out of Tyuoni. They know the gods sent you Knee-nose to help you make a decision, so everything now depends on you. You're known as the elder who always gets to the core of an issue in order to make the right decision. You have dug your own grave, and I don't know how to help you."

"I didn't know some of the elders were breaking their vows of silence. I just have this feeling that the chiefs at Chaco made the wrong decision. What if everyone moves out of Tyuonyi just because an influential chief got this big idea? I've heard that the Chiefs' Pow-wows at Chaco have become one great party, where they drink too strong of a corn brew and smoke too potent of a tobacco mix."

"You elders and the chief are the only ones who talk about what happens at the pow-wows. Why are you judging the chiefs? You also used to drink strong corn brew and smoke the potent tobacco when you were Chief Salamander's age. Jopin, are you jealous because you're not the chief who gets to attend the pow-wows? So what if we have to move out of Tyuonyi? I'm sure we can find another nice place where we can live. Tyuonyi isn't everything. What's so important to make you risk your life and bring hardship to your family?"

Jopin had to think before answering. "I take my job seriously, and want to do what is right for the village. It's not about what we want. It's about what Great Grandfather wants. You don't mind moving out of Tyuonyi, because of what you fear might happen to me. There have been several times when you wished we lived in Puye instead of here."

"That's because of the bad things that have happened here. Yes, I have some sad memories, and have even threatened to grow wings and fly away like a little bird, but I wasn't serious. However, this discussion is not about me. It's about you. What makes you think you are the one who should speak for the Creator? It looks like your pride has taken over your life. Sometimes I wonder if you're not just trying to prove Chief Salamander wrong. What has he done to you? Chief Salamander is a good person."

"It is not about problems between me and him, and it is not about me wanting to be great or admired. The council, as one, is supposed to carry out our creator's wishes. We each search our souls and hearts individually and then gather together as a group to come to a decision. I search my soul and then decide. I didn't chase after a mother deer to take her baby away from her. She delivered Knee-nose to me and now, all this has happened. I don't know what any of this means. Great Grandfather might be trying to tell me what to do, but I don't understand. I'm blind and clueless."

"You're not blind to what Medicine-maker wants to do to you. However, you're very blind to what your wife needs. Where is your responsibility as my husband?"

Jopin didn't know how to respond. Bright-sunflower turned her head away in despair, not knowing what else she could possibly tell her husband. She finally spoke. "Time is passing, and we haven't even started to cook the stew."

Jopin went outside to get some firewood. He needed to think about the things on Bright-sunflower's mind and heart.

The drummers, flute players and prayer dancers had been performing nonstop, since early in the morning. Many of the villagers had joined the dancers to pray for Knee-nose. The commotion and excitement intensified as the people started to deliver their cooked and baked goods to the gathering place in front of the main kiva. The people waited for Pine-needle and Whispering-wind to bring the main offering, so there was time for visiting and praying. They talked about the food, the weather, and about their families. The rumor about the evacuation of Puye, started to be discussed. This led to the possibility of Knee-nose and Jopin having something to do with an evacuation of Tyuonyi. Could Chief Salamander and his elders be preparing to order them to leave Tyuonyi?

The commotion quieted down when Jopin and Bright-sunflower walked towards the crowd to deliver their stew. The silence made Bright-sunflower feel uneasy, so she tightened her grip on Jopin's arm. "It was very nice and considerate for Pine-needle to prepare Knee-nose for us. Do you think we could leave our stew here and go help them?"

Jopin knew about these tense feelings of hers. He put the stew down and smiled. "Lets go see if they could use our help."

She embraced his arm with both of her hands, as they walked over to offer their assistance. Jopin called out, "Hello, can you two use the help of a couple of sentimental old goats?"

"Well of course we can, please come inside. You're always welcome. Is the whole village out there, just waiting for us? The meat is already cooked, but Knee-nose was so small that we decided to shred him. It would be a shame if not everyone would get at least a little piece of him. We're almost finished, except for putting the meat into these serving bowls. Would you like to fill them?"

"I'd be honored." Bright-sunflower handed Jopin a bowl. He held it as she scooped shredded pieces into it. Jopin thanked them again, telling them they would not have been able to cut him up and prepare him.

"It was difficult for us too," replied Whispering-wind. "Even though we barely knew him, it was almost as if he had become one of us."

Bright-sunflower started to cry. "Jopin brought him down from the mountain into our home, and in just a very short time his love touched each and every one of us. But look at him now." She wiped her tears, as she pointed to one of the serving dishes.

Jopin broke in to the conversation. "There never has been, nor will there ever be, another Knee-nose. Tyuonyi now has a feast day in his honor. I think the entire village is waiting for us."

They each grabbed a bowl and walked out, but the plaza was so full of people, the crowd had to separate themselves to create a path for the four of them to walk through.

Chief Salamander greeted them. "It's good that the four of you have gotten together. Is there more to bring, or should we get started?"

Whispering-wind replied, "We had to shred Knee-nose, because he was so small. We want each person to have at least one little piece of him. This is all we have."

Chief Salamander motioned for them to place the bowls on a special rug they had set up and adorned with flowers, leaves, herbs, a small bowl of corn pollen, and some tobacco. He then held his hand up, asking everyone to stop talking. It was time for the blessing. He started by thanking Great Grandfather for everything, for Father Sun and Mother Earth, for the stars and the skies, for all the plants and animals, and for all the peoples of the earth. "We have been blessed with all these gifts, especially with Knee-nose, who was sent to the people of Tyuonyi to teach us how to love, how to serve, and how to sacrifice. There is no greater love a person can give, than to lay down his life for his brother."

Chief Salamander used three fingers to sprinkle corn pollen on the four bowls holding Knee-nose. "This sacred corn pollen will make Knee-nose fertile, so he can, in turn, make us fertile. We must take what Knee-nose has given us and share it with everyone we meet on our life journey." It was time to eat. He reminded them that Knee-nose was small and thus, to serve just a very small portion so everyone could have at least a piece of him. "Remember, your brother-fawn was small but his gifts are very big. Just a tiny piece of Knee-nose can change our lives. He will certainly continue to live in each and every one of us."

Broken-feather wanted to say something. "Chief, I've heard that Puye is evacuating. Do you know anything about this? Why would they do such a thing?"

"I'm Chief of Tyuonyi, not of Puye. I can't speak for Puye."

"Will you be ordering Tyuonyi to also evacuate?"

"Why are you asking me such questions? Today is the feast day of

Knee-nose. We celebrate his life, because today he journeys up into the skies to join Great Grandfather and the gods. This isn't the proper time to talk about evacuations at this most sacred event."

"I believe it is proper. If Knee-nose was sent to us by the gods to bring us the answer to such a question, then it is very proper for us to do so in his honor."

Elder Cloud-burst and Medicine-maker had warned Chief Salamander about not being prepared to answer such questions. The crowd was intently waiting for him to say something. He couldn't afford to lose control of the situation. "The food is getting cold. Please, let's start the feast. "

Fat-man stepped forward. "Chief, Broken-feather has asked a very proper question. We all loved Knee-nose. If he were sent here to teach us how to live, love, and serve each other, like you just mentioned, then why did he have to die? Why was he sacrificed, just a day after he was sent to teach us these things? It doesn't make any sense."

The crowd got very noisy. "Yes, that's right. What's going on? Why did you sacrifice little Knee-nose? Why do you want us to leave beautiful Tyuonyi? It's obvious that Jopin doesn't agree with you. That's why the gods sent Knee-nose to Jopin, to show us you're wrong."

Although he had been warned, the people's unrest caught Chief Salamander by surprise. He raised his hands high above his head. "Please calm down. I agree with you. I'm also greatly troubled by what has happened. Let me assure you, Knee-nose did not die in vain. Sometimes the answers don't come until later. In time, we'll all understand why these events have happened. What we do know is that Knee-nose was a very special and blessed brother-fawn, sent to us from above. This is a day of celebration. Please join us in the feast."

Thunder-head decided to help Fat-man. "No, we need to know. Knee-nose died because of a vision given to both Jopin and Medicine-maker. You say he did not die in vain, but rather, for a special purpose. What special purpose? Why did he have to die?"

"I never heard of any vision." A woman's voice called out from behind the crowd. "Why haven't we been told about this vision? Smoking those strange tobacco-mixes and drinking strong corn brew will give you all kinds of weird visions. Is that why you had to kill Knee-nose, because of a vision? Did killing a weak little baby deer make you feel big and strong?"

"I'm insulted by that remark. Listen, I really don't know the answer to your questions. We elders will be meeting again to determine what all of this means. Please, let's get started. The food is getting cold."

Broken-feather once again spoke out. "When will you have this meeting? Chief, can you report back to us, once you determine what the council has decided?"

Chief Salamander looked over to get the attention of his elders. "We're meeting tonight, immediately after this feast. I'll have the drummers call you, when I'm ready to make the announcement, probably tomorrow morning. In honor of Knee-nose, let us all partake of this most sacred meal."

The people grumbled, as they formed a line to serve themselves. The drummers and prayer dancers once again started to perform their prayers. The festivities continued until late in the evening, until the people finally started to return to their dwellings. The fires burned themselves down.

The council members gathered in the main kiva. Chief Salamander usually opened his meetings with a prayer, but not this time. He let them know how disappointed and upset he was. Word had leaked out to the people, putting the entire decision about the evacuation into jeopardy. "A vote will have to be made tonight, so we can report to the people in the morning."

"We don't have to vote. The village already knows about Puye evacuating." Elder Big-bear had a habit of saying what the chief would want to hear. "All we have to do is announce that all villages are evacuating, starting with Chaco. It is what the gods have commanded, so Tyuonyi must also obey the gods. This is part of Great Grandfather's plan. We must continue on with the Great Migration, as prescribed to us since the beginning of time."

Chief Salamander revealed a slight grin. "I wish, if only it were so simple. That's what I was thinking, before Jopin decided to go on his prayer quest, and before Knee-nose was sent to us by the gods. And now, because some of you couldn't keep your vow of secrecy, the people know about the evacuation. They believe the gods are somehow involved through Jopin and Knee-nose. As Broken-feather tried to tell me, Knee-nose was sent to us to bring out the truth." His face turned red. "Is Broken-feather calling me a liar, because someone couldn't keep his mouth shut? The people won't listen to me anymore, only to Jopin."

He had just scolded his elders, but he also had talked to Little-acorn about everything that had been happening since his trip to Chaco. He had no choice, because she was ready to start walking back to her homeland. She now understood the pressure he had been under. However, she was still hurt with how he had let himself be manipulated by all those women.

Jopin's heart sank. "You're over-reacting Chief. I've never intended to control your tribe. In every situation, all I've ever wanted was to know how to vote, in order to support you. It's not about you or me, it's about doing the right thing."

"I know, Jopin. It's the people that I'm concerned about. They saw the whirlwind of smoke rise up to your head, where it dissipated." He looked around the chamber for a moment, studying their eyes. "They want to know what the spirit of Knee-nose told Jopin. I'm afraid that the only way to get through this situation is for Jopin to completely agree with the decision of the council. What do you think, Jopin? Did the spirit of Knee-nose speak to you?"

"I don't know; however I did receive a deep feeling of peace. Knee-nose may have been telling me everything would be all right. I didn't receive any other message."

"I'm afraid to ask, but I must. Did Knee-nose let you know everything would be all right with the evacuation, or that you would survive if a hole were cut in your head?"

"I'm not sure. I'm very confused. My intent was to go ask the gods for an answer. They sent me Knee-nose. I never even imagined we would cut a hole in his head, because of my vision. Medicine-maker's vision made me think of cutting the hole. Knee-nose is now dead and we're talking about cutting a hole in my head as well. I was willing to do this, as a sacrifice for my people, but now, I realize this would happen at the expense of Bright-sunflower and my family. That may be too much of a sacrifice. I can't hurt my family."

"I don't expect you to. For everyone's information, I have not changed my position. Human sacrifices at Tyuonyi will never be allowed. Jopin, we need to know where you stand. Will you vote to tell the people they must leave Tyuonyi and continue on with the Great Migration? Do you agree with this decision?"

"Yes, Chief Salamander, I am now in agreement with the decision to evacuate."

Chief Salamander reacted as if he couldn't believe what he had just heard. "Great. I didn't know this would be so simple. Is there anyone here who does not agree with this decision?"

None of the elders spoke up.

"Very well, then. Tomorrow, I'll gather the people to make my announcement. I want you, Jopin, to stand next to me. This has been a very long day. Let's return to our families."

Elder Cloud-burst had a concern. "The people will want to know the specifics of the evacuation. Where are we going? When are we leaving, and how? There are still a lot of details that need to get worked out. Don't we have to know the answers to such questions before tomorrow?"

"We can meet again tomorrow afternoon to discuss such issues. I'll announce that several more meetings might be required to work out the details, but in the meantime, I'll get them to start thinking about what they will need to take with them. There are but a few items a person can carry, but isn't this the purpose of the Great Migration? Great Grandfather wants us to live by faith. He will take care of our every need, if we obey his commandments and have faith in Him."

Jopin raised his hand. "They'll want to know what to do with the old and the sick. Do we carry them out of this place or do we leave them behind? One of the reasons I decided to go on my prayer quest was because I couldn't face the consequences of such a decision. Are you prepared to answer these questions tomorrow?"

"No, I'm not. Perhaps we should let each family decide what to do about their sick and aging parents. Those are the type of decisions we elders should never be responsible for making. The villagers will, hopefully, give us more time to work out the details of the move. We're all tired. I'll call a meeting tomorrow morning and let everyone know what has been decided. This meeting is over. See you in the morning."

"Jopin stopped to listen, before entering his home. It was dark inside, so he quietly walked in, removed his clothing, and then carefully lay down next to his wife, trying not to wake her.

"It must be a miracle. The meeting is over?" Bright-sunflower spoke in a loud, excited voice.

Jopin rolled off the bed laughing wholeheartedly. "Ah ha ha. Ah ha ha. I expected you to be asleep, ah ha ha, you scared me." It felt good to finally just be able to laugh, especially after everything he had been through.

Bright-sunflower joined Jopin on the floor and laughed along with him. "It's good to see you acting so silly. Are you OK?"

"They say we start to act like youngsters again, as we get older."

"Yes, I know. It seems like only yesterday when my young Jopin decided to climb the cliff."

"The nightmare is over. We were all in agreement, so Chief Salamander let us come home early."

"The nightmare isn't over. I couldn't sleep, thinking about everything that has happened. I'm worried about you. Will you be next?"

"What do you mean, next? No, we agreed to announce the evacuation in the morning. Like I mentioned before, Chief Salamander will not allow anything to happen to me. He just wanted to make sure we were all in agreement with the evacuation. I'll join him tomorrow when he makes the announcement."

"Are you in agreement with that decision?"

"Yes, Salamander knows I'm ready to support him in this most important decision."

"Thank you, Great Grandfather. I might get some sleep tonight, after all. Please hold me. I was so afraid this would be our last night together. How could I possibly live without you?"

"You're very important to me. I love you so much. We may not know where we'll be living tomorrow, but everything will be all right."

Bright-sunflower fell asleep in the arms of her husband. Jopin remained awake, pondering his decision to evacuate Tyuonyi. Would he ever see his boys again? What about his sisters and relatives who live in neighboring villages? Where will Puye go? Where is Tyuonyi going? They won't be able to grow crops this year, because they'll be on the move. It's final. They really are going to continue on with the Great Migration. How will they store up food to last them through the winter? What will Chief Salamander decide about the old and the sick?"

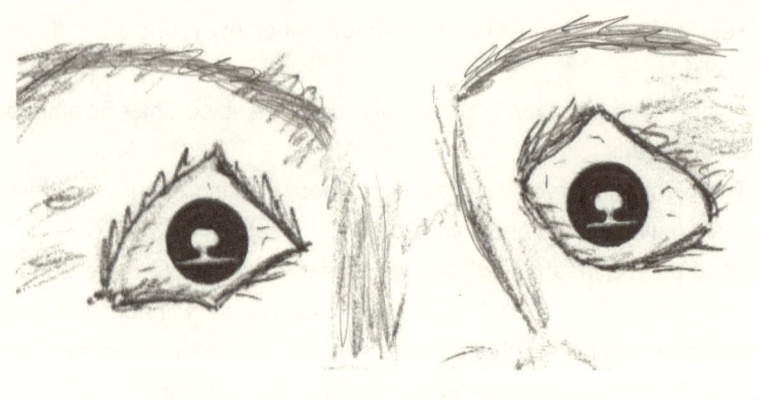

Eyes Open to the Future

Bright-sunflower tenderly pushed and pulled on her husband's arm, "Jopin, Jopin, wake up. Most of the village is up and you're still sleeping. I'm so happy you finally got some rest. You must have really been exhausted."

"Yes, my energy was drained. These last few days have been very trying. Has Chief Salamander called for me?"

"Not yet, but you better have some dried fruit and jerky. It won't be long before he does send someone to come get you. There's a lot of commotion out there."

"They all want to know if Chief Salamander will call for an evacuation. He wants to make the announcement to the entire village this morning. Both of us should be there, so you also have to get ready."

"I'm ready." She grabbed Jopin's forearm. "I still worry someone will demand a hole must be cut into your head, just like they did for Knee-nose."

"That won't happen. Chief Salamander was very clear about that. He won't allow anything bad to happen."

"What if the people refuse to leave? Will Salamander give in to their pressure?"

"No, he understands that not everyone will want to leave, and some may even stay behind. It will be their decision. As you previously mentioned, he is a very good chief. Um, listen, the drums. Chief Salamander is calling. I'll eat something on the way."

Chief Salamander greeted the villagers as they approached the meeting area. They briefly talked to their chief, and then joined others to partake in various conversations.

"Good morning Jopin. Did you get much rest last night?"

"Yes. I finally got a full night's sleep. How about you? Were you able to sleep?"

"I couldn't. I kept thinking about the old and the sick. I still don't know what to say if they ask me about them. Every time, just when I was about to fall asleep, I started to worry that Thunder-head would contradict everything I had to say. He's such a pain in the ass."

"You'll do fine. This is not the first time Thunder-head has challenged you. You always know how to handle him and his friends."

"I was also thinking about you, Jopin. You were fully justified in going on your prayer quest. This has been the most difficult decision we've ever had to make. Bright-sunflower, you're married to a very good person."

"Yes I know, but I'm relying on you to protect my man. You know what I mean."

Chief Salamander stared back into her eyes for a while. "I know exactly what you mean. Don't worry. We won't let anything happen to him."

"Chief, we will walk around and talk to the people until you're ready."

"Okay. It shouldn't take much longer. Most of the villagers are already here."

They made their rounds to the various groups of people. Jopin mentioned how it would be a good day, because the people appeared to be extra respectful and friendly today. Bright-sunflower couldn't help but wonder if the respect existed because of the Knee-nose experience, or because of what they thought would be happening to Jopin?

Chief Salamander ordered the drummers to announce the beginning of the meeting by beating rapidly on their drums. As the people moved in closer, he raised his hands high above his head with his palms facing out towards them. This caused the drums and the people to immediately stop and become silent. He raised his eyes up to the sky, asking Great Grandfather to guide his words. He then lowered his arms, looked directly into the faces of his people, and opened his mouth, but nothing came out. He was afraid of how they would accept what he would be telling them. He took a deep breath to silence his nerves and then tried again. "I want to thank everyone for coming. As you know, we've been more than blessed by Great Grandfather, our Almighty Creator. According to legend, he ordered Father Sun to lead our ancestors across a vast, dry, and rugged land to this beautiful place, where they settled and built our village. Since then, he has provided us with everything we could possibly want here in Tyuonyi."

Thunder-head interrupted. "When are you going to tell us about the evacuation?"

Salamander chose to ignore him. "I recently attended the All-chiefs' Pow-Wow meeting at Chaco. Chief Spirit-dancer, our chief-of-chiefs, announced he had received a Divine revelation indicating it was once again time for us to continue on the Great Migration. After much discussion and prayer, we decided each village would have to decide for themselves if they would obey Great Grandfather's commandment or not. I recently received word from the Puye Council. They have already decided to evacuate, as well as Amoxiumka and Nonyishagi. By now, all of you have probably heard that for the last few days, the elders have been meeting in prayer to discuss and decide what we should do here in Tyuoni. Last night, we finally decided Tyuonyi would also obey our Great Grandfather's commandment and evacuate."

He gave them a moment to let his words sink in. "I want to make it clear. It was our choice to obey Great Grandfather. Chief Spirit-dancer did not order us to evacuate. The decision last night was made of our own free will. Tyuonyi will evacuate and follow Father Sun, as he guides us to our new homeland."

He paused again to give them time to think about what he had just told them, especially about it being their free will. "Great Grandfather does not force anyone to follow his commandments. Likewise, the council will give each and every one of you the freedom to obey or not to obey Great Grandfather. No one will force you to join the rest of us. However, if you decide to remain behind, there will be no support from your fellow tribesmen. Are there any questions?"

Little-boy yelled out. "Chief Salamander, when will this evacuation take place?"

"In four days. Today is this first day. We will go back to our homes and decide what we must take with us and what we will have to leave behind. On the second and third days, we will prepare ourselves for the migration by gathering and packing those things we may need on our journey. We will depart on the fourth day. Winter is over, and most of our stored food and supplies have been used up, so spring is an ideal time for us to start on our migration. Great Grandfather will provide us with the food and water we need, as we need it, and when we need it."

Another person spoke out. "Chief, my mother is old and frail. What should I do about her?"

This was exactly the type of question he had been afraid of. "Like I mentioned, each of us has to go back and prepare for the journey. You have three days to build whatever may be necessary to carry her out of here."

"But Mother is too old and feeble to make the trip. She will surely die. I can't imagine putting her through such an ordeal."

"We completely understand. That's exactly why this decision has been so difficult to make. We have to decide what to do about our loved ones, especially those who are old and sick. We'll have to decide whether to carry them out with us or leave them behind. Some of you may decide to remain with them until they're called to their final resting place by Great Grandfather. We'll mark a trail for you to follow and join us at a later time."

Thunder-head asked, "Chief, did Chief Spirit-dancer really receive a Divine revelation? Could he have been mistaken?"

Chief Salamander tried to act unaffected by this question. "He was sincere. He really believed his revelation was real. A revelation that brings hardship to the people is very difficult to propose. He prepared with many days of prayer and fasting, before he told us about it. The other chiefs and I, who attended the Pow-Wow at Chaco, believe he had genuine intentions."

Fat-man spoke up. "I've heard that the All-chiefs Pow-Wows have become nothing more than one big party, where the chiefs drink strong, corn brew and smoke potent tobacco. Could Chief Spirit-dancer have smoked and drunk too much, when he received his so-called, Divine revelation? I don't believe him. Why would Great Grandfather make us go through such hardship?"

"I don't know where you get your information, but you're wrong. Your attitude always gets you in trouble. I assure you, Chief Spirit-dancer is a most respectable man. He doesn't abuse his power as chief-of-chiefs."

Thunder-head decided to help Fat-man. "What about you, Chief Salamander? I know things about you that you would not want your people to know. Do you abuse your power? Are you covering up for Chief Spirit-dancer? What are you trying to do to us? After all, we are your people."

Chief Salamander wondered how these accusations had affected Little-acorn, but he chose not to answer. "Thunder-head, the council voted to evacuate. It is their responsibility to decide for the village, not yours. You now have to decide for yourself if you will join us or stay behind. And by the way, Puye and some of the other villages have also decided, or will soon be deciding whether to evacuate. How can the whole world be wrong and you, Thunder-head, be the only person who is right?"

"But Chief, I believe I'm right, because this time I have seen with my own eyes and heard with my own ears."

"What are you talking about? The decision for Tyuonyi to evacuate belongs to the elders. The decision for you to evacuate belongs to you. Your decision does not belong to me or to the council. You act like you will choose to remain. It is your right to make that decision. I must honor it."

"I'm talking about Knee-nose. His spirit whirled past you and rose up to Jopin's head where it dissipated. Knee-nose was telling us he gave up his life, so Jopin could live."

"You're exactly right. Knee-nose died as a result of the hole in his head. He let us know Jopin would also die, if we were to cut a hole in his head. Knee-nose saved Jopin's life by showing us what happens when we cut holes in peoples' heads."

"Yes, Chief, I agree. Knee-nose sacrificed himself, so Medicine-maker could learn what he did wrong on Knee-nose and thus, learn what he should do right on Jopin. Jopin went on a prayer quest to learn the truth. I've heard that he and Medicine-maker had the same vision of Knee-nose, but Medicine-maker's vision indicated a hole in Jopin's head, as well. This part of the vision has not yet happened. I want to know what the gods will tell Jopin through a hole in his head."

"There's not going to be any hole cut in Jopin's head. Jopin voted last night for Tyuonyi to evacuate. Isn't that so, Jopin?"

"Yes, that's right. It's time for Tyuonyi to evacuate. I was a little skeptical, like some of you, refusing to believe we had to leave this beautiful and most sacred land. However, because of what happened to Knee-nose, I have now accepted that no matter what, we must obey our creator's commands."

"But what if Great Grandfather wants you to have a hole cut in your head? Would you then obey Him?"

"You know I would, but this isn't the case. Knee-nose sacrificed himself, so I wouldn't have to. Knee-nose wants me to remain in this world and take care of my wife and family."

"Jopin, you know very well that Great Grandfather asked you to have a hole cut in your head, but you're afraid. Medicine-maker is our medicine man, not Chief Salamander. He's the person who is supposed to get the official messages from the Almighty, not Chief Salamander, and not Chief Spirit-dancer. Isn't that right, Medicine-maker?"

Medicine-maker responded. "I don't know what you're trying to prove. Yes, I'm the person with the most training to receive messages from the Almighty Creator. But, any of us can do the same thing. My job is to communicate with Great Grandfather and his gods. I receive their guidance and direction on how to perform a healing. It is Chief Salamander and the elders who obey Great Grandfather's guidance in making decisions which may affect the village."

Chief Salamander quickly raised his palm up towards Thunder-head. "I'm telling you again, Thunder-head, you're out of order. I will not allow any more sacrifices in this village. Knee-nose was the first, and he will be the last. Those of you, who will join us on the evacuation, should go home and begin preparing for the move. The rest of you can join Thunder-head, and do as you wish."

Chief Salamander was relieved when Honey-bee asked to speak. Anyone would be better than Thunder-head. "Chief Salamander, how can we join you if we're not satisfied with the implications of what has happened here with Knee-nose and everything else?"

This question stunned Chief Salamander. Why would she, of all people, ask such a question? He was prepared to fight with Thunder-head, not his wife's sister. He's always considered her a true sister. Could she be mad at him, because of Little-acorn? "What do you mean, Honey-bee? Why aren't you satisfied?"

"From what I understand, Jopin went on a prayer quest, because he wanted our Almighty Creator to tell him what to do about the evacuation. Instead, the Almighty sent him Knee-nose, along with a vision of a fawn with a hole in his head. You cut a hole in Knee-nose's head, in accordance to Great Grandfather's commands, and Knee-nose died. Now, as far as I understand, Great Grandfather also presented Medicine-maker with the same vision. They say this vision consisted of a hole in Jopin's head, as well. Aren't we disobeying Great Grandfather, if we refuse to cut a hole in Jopin's head?"

Chief Salamander quickly responded, although he didn't really know what to say. "No, we're not. We don't really know if Great Grandfather asked us to cut a hole in Knee-nose. We just did, and it turned out to be a big mistake. It was just a vision, not a commandment."

"But then, how do we know if Chief Spirit-dancer had a Divine revelation, or just a vision? Medicine-maker and Jopin had the same vision, so it must have been a commandment from Great Grandfather. I believe the Almighty Creator will talk to Jopin through a hole in his head, as both Medicine-maker and Jopin were instructed in their visions."

The crowd went out of control. "Yes, we want to know what Great Grandfather really wants. We won't leave Tyuonyi until Jopin tells us what Great Grandfather and the gods have told him. Salamander, we no longer want you as our chief. We demand the truth. Jopin needs to have a hole cut into his head. We won't evacuate, unless—"

"No, you will kill him. Jopin is no good to us if he is dead. I will not allow it."

Thunder-head stood up on the sacred rock and yelled out. "Medicine-maker, do you think you can cut a hole in Jopin's head, without killing him?"

Chief Salamander started to lose his temper. "Thunder-head, get off the sacred rock. You know better than that. You're being disrespectful of the gods, and your request of Jopin is ridiculous and insensitive." Thunder-head quickly stepped off the sacred rock not realizing what he had done. Chief Salamander stopped scolding him and turned to Medicine-maker. "You don't have to answer him. Please don't answer."

"I must answer him, Chief." He turned to face Thunder-head. "Yes, I think it is possible. Knee-nose died, because he jumped up into the sharp point of my knife. It penetrated his brain. I think I can first use the sharp point of my knife to make three or four holes in Jopin's skull, making sure not to penetrate the membrane protecting his brain. I can then break the point off my knife and finish the job. I won't penetrate his brain if I don't have a sharp point. Jopin will live if I'm extra careful. The mistakes I made on Knee-nose taught me what not to do on Jopin."

Medicine-maker's comments shocked Chief Salamander. "What are you saying? No, this will never happen. This meeting is over. We will meet here on day four to start out on our Great Migration. Go back to your homes and decide what you will be carrying with you."

The crowd booed at Chief Salamander. "Never. We will not go. You will be going alone, Chief, you and your elders. We want Medicine-maker to speak. Yes, we want Medicine-maker. Medicine-maker, can you please do what has to be done? We won't leave until Jopin tells us what Great Grandfather tells him what has to be done. We won't leave. We want Medicine-maker to heal this village from its crooked chief."

Medicine-maker became very uneasy. He raised his hands and held them there until the crowd quieted down. "I have the greatest respect for Chief Salamander. He is not crooked. He's a good man. I refuse to side with you against Chief Salamander. However, I do agree with what you're saying. When I received my vision, I thought Jopin was sick. I didn't understand why the fawn was in my vision, but now I do. Knee-nose was sent to us, so I could learn how to cut a hole, without killing Jopin. I'm now ready to do this, but only if Jopin is willing and Chief Salamander agrees."

Bright-sunflower cried out, "No! I will not allow this to happen. Isn't it easier for us to evacuate than for his death to be forever on your conscience?"

Medicine-maker addressed her concern. "Bright-sunflower, Jopin will not die. I have treated others before with breaks in their skulls, and they lived a normal, full life. I will not allow him to die."

Chief Salamander tried, once again to gain control. "I will not allow something like this to happen to Jopin. Medicine-maker, I order you to abide by what the elders have decided."

"Chief, you're asking me to decide between the council and my Creator. I must obey my Creator, and so must Jopin."

"That's not fair, Medicine-maker. You don't know for sure if this is what Great Grandfather wants. It's not right for you to pressure Jopin to agree to such a thing. You must stop."

Jopin spoke out, while looking at Bright-sunflower. "You know, I once thought I should have a hole cut into my head, like Knee-nose. However, I had not considered what this would do to my wife, or to the rest of my family. I'm not willing to put them through such hardship. It's better for all of us, if we continue on our Great Migration, as commanded by Great Grandfather. Our people have participated on the Great Migration since the beginning of time. This has always been part of His plan for us. It's our destiny."

Medicine-maker responded, "We don't know if this is the proper time for us to join the migration or not, but we both received the same vision. You knew at the time what this was all about, but I did not. I thought you were ill. Our visions must have come from the Divine. I have no choice but to wonder if the decision made at Chaco was wrong."

The crowd broke out into a loud uproar. "Yes, Jopin, that's why you went on your prayer quest. We need you, Jopin. It is up to you. We will not leave until Great Grandfather tells you what to do. Jopin, we need you to do this for us. Bright-sunflower, Jopin will be all right. Great Grandfather loves him. He won't let anything bad happen to him. Chief Salamander, we're not going anywhere unless—"

"Unless you kill him? Absolutely not."

Jopin grabbed Bright-sunflower by her arms and looked directly into her eyes. "You know what I must do."

"There must be another way. No." Bright-sunflower clenched her hands around Jopin's.

"Bright-sunflower, I created this mess, so it is up to me to solve it. I have faith that Medicine-maker knows what he's doing. I must obey my Creator's commands. It's important that you understand." Even though she held on to him as tightly as she could, he broke loose and walked over to Medicine-maker. "Let's hurry and get started. We must do this."

The crowd started to cheer and applaud. Chief Salamander once again motioned for the drummers to bring the crowd to order. The people finally quieted down. He asked for someone to bring him some water. Deer-tracker volunteered and approached the chief with Jopin's canteen. Chief Salamander cusped his hands together and asked Deer-tracker to pour water on them. Deer-tracker looked at his grandfather for approval. Jopin motioned for Deer-tracker to comply. Deer-tracker poured water on Chief Salamander's hands, as Chief Salamander spoke. "You, the people of Tyuonyi are doing this, not I. I wash my hands of this act." He paused to make sure the people would listen to what he had to say. "Jopin's blood rests on your hands, not mine. As for me, I will join the prayer dancers and offer up my sacrifice in prayer for Jopin's health, especially for his life. I pray you all know what you are doing."

Jopin fixed his attention on the canteen. It reminded him once again, of the day he painted the symbols of the spinning sun and of the Great Migration. He thought about how Deer-tracker used his canteen to save his life on the cliff. This canteen was later used to refresh Knee-nose right before his death. And now, this same canteen was being used to wash Chief Salamander from any responsibility of what would soon be happening to him. If only he had known then what would be happening now. He had painted those symbols many, many moons ago while preparing himself for manhood, just like Medicine-maker had also carved those same symbols on his special knife, while preparing for his journey of healing.

Chief Salamander ordered the drummers and singers to start the healing chant. He walked over to them and started his prayer dance. Bright-sunflower was moved by his actions, so she also walked towards the chief and joined him in the prayer dance. Deer-tracker rushed over to join Bright-sunflower, but she sent him back. "Deer-tracker, you need to comfort your grandfather. Please take him some water and give him your support. You're good for him. Please stand by his side."

"Okay." Deer-tracker ran back, with Jopin's canteen in hand, to join Medicine-maker.

Brilliant-pebbles approached Jopin, "Father, are you sure you should do this? There's got to be another way. Don't you want to think about it a little longer?"

"My little Brilliant-pebbles, you know how much I love you. I also love your mother. It's not what I want, but what Great Grandfather wants. It's out of my hands. What you can do is pray for me and console your mother."

"I will Daddy, but I don't want you to do this. I love you very much."

Jopin gently held both of her hands, kissed her on the forehead, and then pushed her away. Brilliant-pebbles let go and then slowly walked away from her father, towards the prayer dancers. She looked back at Jopin and then rushed to join her mother. She had to go pray for her papa.

Chief Salamander led them in a circle around Jopin. The others joined Chief Salamander, making the line so long, it circled around all of the kivas and sacred areas of the plaza. The entire village had joined Chief Salamander in his prayer dance, except for those who were too old, crippled or incapable of dancing.

Medicine-maker told Jopin, "The entire village is praying for you, so Great Grandfather will surely take care of you today." He reached into his bag, took out his sacred pipe and special healing tobacco-mix, and held them high above his head, offering them up to Great Grandfather, the Great Healer. He lit his pipe, took four large puffs from it, and then handed it over to Jopin. "Smoke the sacred healing pipe until all of the tobacco is used up. The smoke from this special tobacco will get your mind ready to receive Great Grandfather. I have to go gather a few things and will return shortly."

"No need to hurry, I'll be right here waiting for you." Jopin started to puff on the pipe as Medicine-maker ran off. Deer-tracker asked his grandfather if he could do anything for him.

"Just take care of your grandmother. I plan to be here, but if not, please take care of her."

"You know I will Grandpa, but right now, I'll take care of you, so you can take care of Grandma yourself." Jopin looked into his grandson's face and smiled. He knew he was doing what was right, for everyone in the village.

Medicine-maker went to his house and put some corn pollen, herbs and other sacred objects into his bag. He grabbed the bowl of special drink he had brewed from ground-up corn, and quickly returned to Jopin.

"Jopin, please drink all of this. It will prepare your body to handle the pain. I should have had you drink this before smoking the special tobacco, but I didn't know we were going to do this today. Did you smoke all of the tobacco?"

Jopin looked up at him, as if he hadn't understood what Medicine-maker had asked. "Yes, I smoked all of it. Here is your pipe. I already feel dizzy."

"Good, the tobacco will open your mind to the gods. You must drink all of this brew, before I begin to cut. It will help you handle the pain. Knee-nose wouldn't have jumped up into my knife, if he could've taken these things. You will do just fine, Jopin."

"Medicine-Maker, I want to, I mean, I want to thank you before you start. What I want to do is take care of Bright-sunflower, as she grows old." Jopin had started to lose control of his speech and had begun to slur his words.

Medicine-maker knew the tobacco had started to work. "Jopin, you will be taking care of Bright-sunflower for a very long time. The Almighty Creator certainly has a hand in your future. Just look at everything that has happened here. Jopin, you have a very good and holy family. Even your grandson Deer-tracker is focused on Great Grandfather. Jopin, you need to keep drinking the brew."

Jopin cusped his hands to Deer-tracker's ear and whispered, "I've been drinking the corn brew, but I think Medicine-maker has been drinking more of it than me. He keeps calling and repeating my name. Has he forgotten that I'm here?"

Deer-tracker smiled. Medicine-maker looked surprised but pleased that the corn brew was taking effect.

Jopin kept sipping while Medicine-maker shook his rattle and prayed over him. Medicine-maker blessed him with smoke, corn pollen, tobacco, and other sacred herbs and objects. He finally finished his prayers and asked Jopin how he was feeling.

Although he could barely open his eyes, Jopin nodded. "I'm good"

It was time to start.

"Jopin, please open your mouth and bite down on this stick. This will help you control the pain. Please let me know, in some way, if you want me to stop."

Jopin took the stick between his teeth and nodded, signaling he was ready. He bit down hard as Medicine-maker cut into his scalp and folded the skin back, exposing the skull.

Medicine-maker told Jopin and Deer-tracker he would now use the sharp point of his knife to drill four small holes forming the corners of a square. Then he would break the point off his knife to avoid puncturing his brain, when it was time to start sawing in-between the holes.

Although sedated, the affects of the drink were not enough. The pain became unbearable, especially when magnified by the scraping and grinding sounds against his skull. Jopin bit down harder on the stick and tried to project his mind away from the pain, to prayer and to the beating of the drums.

Medicine-maker stopped drilling and asked, "Jopin, is this too painful? Are you all right?"

Jopin slurred out, "Yes, I'm fine. Why do you ask?"

"You keep moving your head up and down. Is the pain too much for you to bear?"

Jopin spoke out in a raspy voice. "I'm trying to think of something other than the pain. I'm praying to the beat of the drums."

Medicine-maker had to think about what Jopin had told him. Then he smiled, because he finally understood. "It's very good for you to pray, Jopin, but can you pray without dancing? I'm afraid to puncture your brain, like I did to Knee-nose. Don't move your head up and down in prayer."

"Okay, I'll try."

Medicine-maker continued to work on Jopin's skull. Deer-tracker wet a softly knitted yucca cloth with water from the canteen and wiped Jopin's forehead. Jopin tried to concentrate on prayer and meditation. He knew he needed to focus his attention on something other than what Medicine-maker was doing to him.

He felt a light pressure against the side of his leg. Could this be Knee-nose? Of course not. Knee-nose was dead. But yes, Knee-nose was here. He looked right into Jopin's eyes and then moved over and leaned up against Jopin's leg. Jopin now knew everything would go as planned. The special healing tobacco mix and drink had started to numb his pain, as Medicine-maker drilled the holes into his skull. He soon fell into a very deep trance. "Great Grandfather, I am now ready to continue on my quest. I don't want to leave this beautiful place. Please let me know what will be happening to my homeland, the place I love so much."

Jopin received a vision like no other. Adolph Hitler had greeted his troops with a speech about how he planned to conquer the world. He told them Germany was working on the development of the atomic bomb. His troops became excited, because this new bomb would make Germany the most powerful nation in the world. He also told them about his plans to create a super race, which would populate his new super kingdom. Jopin had never seen anyone that looked and dressed like these solders, nor had he ever seen a human race other than his own. He certainly had no idea as to what an atomic bomb might be. Seeing the great numbers of soldiers marching past Hitler and saluting him in a highly regimented manner, Jopin concluded that Hitler must be Great Grandfather, especially since all the other gods were praising and worshipping him.

Jopin was in awe. But then, he spotted the swastika on Hitler arm, as his soldiers marched past him. This god couldn't be Great Grandfather, but rather, Father Sun telling Jopin it was time to evacuate and follow the spinning sun. But, why did he look so mad? Jopin had always imagined Father Sun to be a happy, caring, and peaceful god, always ready to keep Mother Earth warm, pregnant and vibrant with all of her vegetation and living creatures. Could Father Sun be mad at Jopin? Perhaps he was mad at the people of Tyuonyi.

Jopin started to receive another vision. Albert Einstein was telling President Harry S. Truman that Germany was developing the atomic bomb. Einstein tried to convince the president to also get the United States involved in the development of the bomb, or else. Jopin found Einstein quite friendly, but rather funny looking with wild hair. And, Jopin became intrigued with the eyeglasses over President Truman's eyes. He wondered if Einstein might be a spiritual-medicine god, giving advice to this other very important god. Once again, he was in complete amazement, and surprised by the size of President Truman's dwelling in Washington, DC. He reasoned that surely, this god must be Great Grandfather. His house was so extraordinarily monumental, perhaps bigger than the entire village of Tyuonyi.

Jopin then received a vision of many people working on the Manhattan Project. They were busy building roads, houses, utility projects, and the Los Alamos Scientific Laboratory, the birthplace of the atomic bomb. The complexity and diversity of projects overpowered his ability to understand what they could possibly be doing. Jopin had never seen nor imagined anything, like horses, automobiles, heavy equipment, airplanes, and the construction of rows and rows of buildings. There wasn't much he could comprehend here. However, he did recognize his homeland as the place where these people were so actively working. These must be the mountain gods that take care of Tyuoni, he thought. Some of them dressed in white, long-sleeved uniforms, and wore full-face helmets, as they poured molten plutonium and molten explosive materials into special shaped bowls. Jopin couldn't see their faces, so he thought they must be gods with no faces. Some of the others, those with faces, fabricated the other components that would be assembled into the bomb: detonators, batteries, and shells. The assembly technicians carefully placed white explosives around the yellow nuclear components, and then put shells around the assemblies. It looked like these gods had built a very big, shiny egg. He wondered what kind of a bird would hatch from this egg.

The mountain gods loaded the giant egg on to the Enola Gay. Jopin was frightened by the noise it made, when it started its engines and then, amazed when he saw it fly high up into the sky, way above the clouds. The B-29 bomber flew over Hiroshima, Japan, where it dropped the bomb. Jopin watched the giant egg fall slowly through the clouds, down to the earth below, where it exploded into a tremendous, thundering blast.

In his final vision, Jopin found himself right in the middle of ground zero, Hiroshima. There was nothing but utter destruction, smoldering ruin, and death. This vision left him with extreme sadness, a very deep void in his heart. Everything slowly started to fade away, leaving Jopin in complete darkness. Afraid to move, he looked around, but couldn't see anything. Finally, a small flickering light appeared in the distance. It started to move and dance around in a nonroutine fashion, coming closer and closer. It was a torch. Someone was coming to help Jopin get out of here.

"Jopin, don't be afraid. I've come to help you. My torch will allow you to see and help guide your steps over the dead, so you can find your way out of here. I'll help you get home."

"Thank you, I'm so afraid. This is horrible! What happened? Who are you?"

"Don't you recognize me? You've been searching for me all of your life. Weren't you looking for me when you set out yesterday morning on your prayer quest? Jopin my son, I'm here, your Almighty Creator, the one you've been yearning to be with. Come, hold my hand, and I'll lead you home."

Jopin wanted to fall to his knees to adore Great Grandfather, but he was afraid to kneel on one of the dead. He slightly bent his knees and lifted both arms up in adoration. "Oh, Great Grandfather, my Creator, I've wanted to be with you all of my life. I'm so grateful you've come for me. Please take me out of here."

"Whatever you ask of me, my son. You've been a good and faithful servant. Let me take you home with me."

Excited, Jopin finally stood before Great Grandfather. He would finally get to see his creator. But, as he looked up, he saw the blood on the creature's face. Jopin quickly turned his face away and screamed out loud, "Get away from me, you liar. You're not Great Grandfather. You're the god of darkness, the god of death. Get away from me."

"Don't be afraid my son, I'm here to help you. I can get you whatever you want. You're a better man than Chief Salamander. He goes with the promiscuous women, and then lies about it to his wife and to all of you. He has lost all credibility with his people, but they have a strong belief in you. They are ready to follow you, not him. I can make you Chief of Tyuonyi, the most beautiful village in the world, or I can make you Chief of Chaco. I can make you into the greatest, most popular chief ever. All you have to do is come with me. Let my light guide you out of here. I will take care of you and make you great."

"Get away from me, you liar. I order you in the name of the Almighty Great Grandfather. Get away from me!"

The torch instantly blew out. Once again, Jopin stood in total darkness, looking around, but seeing nothing. He was scared, and afraid that all of a sudden, he would be looking directly into those eyes, the eyes belonging to the god of darkness.

But then a comforting light appeared, round like the sun, but not blinding. It was pure and soothing. Jopin knew about this light.

"Jopin, my son, I'm so proud of you. Are you ready to come with me?"

Jopin fell on his knees, and put his forehead to the ground. "Yes, my Almighty Creator, I am. I'm so happy and honored to be in your presence. I've been waiting for this moment, all of my life. Was that really the god of darkness?"

"Yes, it was. Each of you must make the choice whether you go with him or come live with me. I never force any of my children to choose me, so I'm very happy with the choice you just made. The only thing left for you to do now, is walk into my light. Remember, it is your will to come to me."

"Great Grandfather, I want to come live with you more than anything in the world, but I have unfinished business. I promised Bright-sunflower I would be around to take care of her, so I can't leave her, not at this time. And the people from the village are waiting for me to tell them it is, indeed, time for them to follow Father Sun and join the Great Migration."

"I understand. It is up to you. You're free to go back to your loved ones. I'll be waiting for you when the time is right."

"Thank you. Great Grandfather, my grandson wanted to know if you would destroy an entire village if it were evil. Would you?"

"Yes I would, if it were all evil. But let me explain. Just like you explained to Deer-tracker, fire can take on the form of purification. Let's look at you. You too will have to go through the purification process, before I will allow you to walk all of the way through my light."

"Great Grandfather, are you saying I'm evil? I've tried so hard to do everything you ever commanded of me, and cleansed myself of my wrong doings through sacrifice, prayer, and ceremony. What else must I do to earn your approval?"

"You don't have to do anything else. I'm not saying that you are evil. Like you just mentioned, you have obeyed my commandments and lived in accordance to my will. And, you just chose not to go with the god of darkness. You chose me, so I am very pleased. You have done everything required, so it is now up to me. I will purge you of your problems and purify you, so you can get ready to come all the way through the light and live with me."

"But Great Grandfather, why are you going to punish me with fire? Why will you allow the fire to hurt me?"

"My son, I'm going to purify you with the fire of my love. You will be happier than what you could ever possibly imagine."

"Great Grandfather, I thought you loved me, just the way I am. How can I prove myself to you?"

"You don't understand, do you? Take a look at yourself. Just take a look."

Jopin felt confused, but he looked down at his body, anyway. Shocked by what he saw, he asked, "Is this really me?" His body was so heavily soiled and stained from all of his sins and faults that he couldn't recognize himself. He fell to the ground and cried out, "My Creator, I'm not worthy to be in your presence. Why would you want me? I'm so ashamed."

"My son, I know everything you've ever done, and I still love you, exactly the way you are. You are my creation. I would like to explain something about the god of darkness. I once loved him exactly the way I love you. I was so proud of my very special creation. A very bright and distinct glow emitted from the god of darkness, because he had so much love coming from him. It was brighter than all of the other gods', so he knew he was gifted and thus very special. Some of the other gods began to take orders and direction from him, because he was so bright and smart. They called him the god of light. He did a lot of good, helping them accomplish the things I wanted. However, he soon felt he deserved to be their leader, because he believed himself to be better than them. As he gained more and more power over the other gods, he decided they should do what he wanted and not what I, their creator had asked of them. He told them they no longer needed me. I talked to him about it, but he refused to listen. His glow decreased as his love for power increased. I had to cast him out into the darkness, where he belonged. He now uses a torch light as bait to attract and capture innocent souls. That's why he came to you with a torch. The god of darkness thinks its flickering light will make up for the glow he lost. He wanted you to think he was me."

"Great Grandfather, I never knew he was also one of your children. I've never been so scared in my life. Why do you allow him to do such things?"

"Each and every one of my children comes to me by choice. Once they make that choice, I make sure they will be happy with me forever. He promises glamour and greatness to everyone, but what they really get is darkness and death. I will never allow another power hungry soul to be in the presence of my other beloved children, whom have chosen to come live with me. That's why I allow him to go around offering temptations of grandeur. If someone has aspirations of being great, he does not belong here with me. That is why you, my son, will go through a purification process the next time you come to me. I'm so proud of you, and I have so much love to give you. You have followed my commandments, offered sacrifices, and purified yourself of your wrong doings. And, you just offered up your life for your people, so I'm very pleased with you; however, you still must go through the purification process."

"But Great Grandfather, you just mentioned that you love me for who I am."

"Yes, I have an equal love for all of my children. I want you to be happy for eternity. We still need to work on a few things to prepare you to travel all the way through the light. Even the god of darkness knew you considered yourself to be better than Chief Salamander, so he used this weakness of yours to draw you to him. You taught your grandson how to be the least of everyone. However, you don't think of yourself as being less than others."

Jopin thought about how critical he had been about Chief Salamander.

"You think you know better than he, your chief. Let's look at the evacuation that has been so heavy on your heart. You don't want to evacuate, because you love beautiful Tyuonyi and everything you have worked so hard to establish in the village. Yet, you look down on Chief Salamander, because he visits the promiscuous women. This may be the case. Yes, he is very fond of a particular woman. His heart goes out to all of these people, as well as to the old and the sick. Chief Salamander worries he may not be able to carry all of them out of Tyuonyi. He doesn't want to leave anyone behind. It's important for you to see the good in your brothers and sisters, not only the bad. Yes, he has faults, just like all of your other fellow brethren. You and Chief Salamander, each have your own particular problems, but that doesn't mean any one child of mine is any better than another. The purification process will be different for each of you, because you're each unique. I love each and every one of my children."

"Oh, my Great Grandfather, I'm so ashamed of myself. This is a very big problem I have. I had no idea I was doing this. Please forgive me."

"You're forgiven, my son. All of my children come to me with problems they don't even realize they have. But once they enter my light, I reveal every fault, plus every hurt or wrong they ever did to anyone, even those they have long forgotten. My light will help you realize what must happen in order to purge you of your weaknesses and tendencies. Such traits will not be appropriate on this side, where only pure souls are allowed. The law about being the least of your brothers will still pertain to all, even more so, when you come live with me. I'm honored to receive you, exactly as you are. But, I will make sure you will always remain extremely happy and satisfied with me, forever."

"Holy Great Grandfather, did I hurt your feelings when I said I wanted to go back and take care of Bright-sunflower, before coming back to you?"

"No, my son, I understand. Go back and take care of your family. You will soon return here, where I'll be waiting for you with open arms."

"Great-grandfather, may I ask you one more question, before I go back?"

"Yes, my son. What is your question?"

"My grandson, Deer-tracker, wanted to know if you only talk to us right after we're born, when the bones of our skulls are soft. I told him you also talk to us at various times of our lives. Why don't you talk to us more often? I had to go through so much, just to come and be here in your presence."

"I'm so glad you asked me that question. It is true that I first talk to each of my children right after they are born. But I talk to you, to each and everyone of my children, all of the time. The problem is that you're not listening. Newborn babies listen, because they're totally dependent on their mother and father, and on me, their creator. It's not that their skulls are soft. It's that they are completely receptive to my voice. Their brains aren't cluttered up with all kinds of information, and their hearts aren't full of earthly desires, so these little ones of mine are eager and willing to listen to what I have to tell them. My older children, on the other hand, have too much on their minds, so they don't listen. They have learned how to do things on their own, so they think they no longer need me. Their hard skulls aren't the problem, it's their hard heads. They don't think they need me, anymore, even you, Jopin. You couldn't hear my voice during your prayer quest. You were too busy trying to figure out Chief Salamander's actions and motives. Most of my children are too involved and emotional, when managing their own lives. So Jopin, your answer to Deer-tracker was mostly right. You listen to me through the use of sacred ceremony, such as vision quests. And, I have sent my gods to teach you how to pray and use sacred materials in ceremonies. However, my children still continue to be too busy with everything, and not include me. Much too often, you only listen to my voice when you're totally dependant on me, right after being born, or when you're close to death, like in your situation right now. You—"

That statement, about being close to death, startled Jopin. He stopped listening to what Great-grandfather was telling him, and started to fight for his life. Jopin was now coming out of his vision.

Knee-nose, once again, came in close and rubbed his nose against Jopin's leg. Knee-nose ran off and jumped over a star, and then returned to Jopin. He then ran and jumped over two more stars, and returned back to make sure Jopin was still looking at him. Knee-nose then took one very long and high leap over the brightest star. It was the sun. The sun was spinning.

Of Gods or Men

Deer-tracker grabbed Medicine-maker's hand. "Grandpa isn't breathing! Please help him. What can I do? Grandpa, wake up. Medicine-maker—"

"Why didn't you say something? Here, let's lay him down, so I can massage his heart. Jopin, can you hear me? Pour some water on his chest. I didn't know he was getting weaker."

Deer-tracker poured water on his grandfather's face as well. Medicine-maker pushed on Jopin's chest and shook his arms. Jopin showed no response.

"Grandpa, are you all right? Please say something."

Medicine-maker continued to massage Jopin's heart. "Jopin you can't leave us now, everything is done. Can you hear me?" Jopin produced a very weak moan, as he tried to open his eyes.

Medicine-maker gave out a sigh of relief. "I think your grandfather will be fine. He was just in a very, deep sleep. Jopin, we have finished. Everything has gone as planned. Can you hear me?"

Jopin tried to speak, but he couldn't.

Medicine-maker stood up and held his arms up in praise. "Thank you, Great Grandfather." He then asked Deer-tracker to go get his grandmother and Chief Salamander. "I think the affects of the special brew and tobacco are beginning to wear off. Your grandfather is beginning to wake up. Tell them he is going to be all right. Could you also bring some more water on your way back?"

Deer-tracker ran to catch up with the dancers. "Grandma, please hurry. Grandpa is waking up. Medicine-maker has finished and he wants you and Chief Salamander to be there when he comes out of his sleep."

Bright-sunflower looked like she couldn't believe him. "Jopin is all right? Are you sure?" Deer-tracker nodded his head and gave her a very big smile. "Thank you, Almighty Great Grandfather, for answering my prayer, for listening to all of our prayers." She grabbed Deer-tracker by his shoulders. "I was afraid you were coming to tell me your grandpa was gone, just like Knee-nose. This is good news."

"Yes, Grandpa is waking up. Chief Salamander, please go with Grandma. Grandpa tried to talk, but he was still groggy. I have to go get some more water. Hurry. Grandpa would want you there when he opens his eyes."

They hurried over to see Jopin. When they saw them leave, the drummers and prayer dancers stopped performing, and then slowly followed behind. They remained at a distance to give Bright-sunflower some privacy.

Bright-sunflower froze when she saw Jopin's limp body propped up against the sacred rock. His upper body was wet. She could see where the blood had clumped his hair together. His eyes were swollen beyond belief with what Medicine-maker had done to him. A huge bulge could be seen on top of his head, where she had expected to see a big hole. Medicine-maker had somehow plugged the hole and then covered it with Jopin's scalp.

Brilliant-pebbles stood frozen, afraid to come any closer. She didn't know if she would be able to control her emotions.

Medicine-maker had been waiting for them. "Everything went as planned. Jopin is a very strong man. Bright-sunflower, please talk to him. Let him know you're here and that everything is all right."

She gently held one of Jopin's hands and tried to get his attention. "Jopin this is Bright-sunflower. Can you hear me? Jopin, you made it. I'm so happy. Can you hear me?"

Jopin could barely open his eyes. The sun was too bright, but its rays wrapped around a figure with a familiar voice. It was Bright-sunflower. Tears ran down his cheeks, as he smiled at her. Jopin tried to talk, but he was still too weak. He moaned and then pointed to his throat. Deer-tracker arrived, just in time to hand his grandmother the canteen. Jopin could barely see. However, when he was handed the canteen to sip, he recognized the images he had painted a long time ago. Chief Salamander held up Jopin's head, so Bright-sunflower could press the canteen up against his mouth. The water flowed past his lips, but Jopin did manage to get in a few sips. Once again, he tried to speak. This time his voice emerged in a weak, raspy whisper. "The gods have spoken. It is time." He then became very excited and tried to move, but his face became distorted. His tears once again, flowed down his cheeks. They couldn't tell if he was crying from the pain, because he had made it, or because he was so happy to have talked to the gods.

Chief Salamander moved in closer. "Jopin, this is Salamander. Don't try to talk. You don't have to say anything right now. I'm very happy you made it and that you got to see the gods. Rest and get your strength back. You can tell us later what the gods asked you to do. They will be speaking to us through you. Jopin, you're now sacred, yourself, and it is an honor to be in your presence. I'll make sure someone will always be here to take care of you. Get some rest and then let us know when you are ready to talk. It's important for you to get your strength back." He then ordered his warrior guards to bring some furs for Jopin to lie on. He also asked them to figure out how to protect his body from the hot sun.

Bright-sunflower sobbed as she massaged Jopin's hands, arms, neck and face, while thanking Great Grandfather for allowing her to still have her husband. The warrior guards delivered some furs for Jopin to lie on. Two of them held out a blanket between them to shade the sun away from his body. Jopin closed his eyes and fell asleep.

The villagers never left his side, even though Jopin slept through most of the afternoon. They were so excited and happy for him. Yet they all remained very quiet, and allowed him to sleep. Not only did they want to be in his presence, they wanted to be sure to hear about the gods when he would wake up.

Jopin opened his eyes and started talking. "Bright-sunflower, are you all right? I've been so worried about you. Please forgive me for breaking lose from your hold on me, and for offering myself up to Medicine-maker. You see, I felt responsible for bringing Knee-nose here and creating all this doubt and unrest. They became disrespectful and refused to obey Chief Salamander, because of me. Can't you see? I had no choice but to do it."

"Yes, I do understand. Don't worry about me. You're the one who's been through so much. I'm very happy I still have the love of my life with me. I was so afraid you would die, just like Knee-nose. Poor Knee-nose, he really did give up his life for you. I was hurt with you for not thinking about me, but I now understand. Could I do anything to make you feel better? I love you so much."

"I love you too. Thanks for supporting me, no matter how foolish I've been. Where is Brilliant-pebbles? She's afraid to see me like this, isn't she? You can tell her I'm all right."

Brilliant-pebbles had remained at a distance, afraid of what she might see, for she had imagined blood and brains protruding out of a large hole on top of her father's head. She moved in closer. "I'm here Papa. I'm so happy you made it." She burst out crying, as he hugged and pulled her in close to his heart.

"My daughter, I told you everything would be fine. I guess you're still my little baby girl."

"Are you in a lot of pain?"

"Not too much. You and your mother are taking away my pain."

"I was so worried about you. I still have my daddy. This is the happiest day of my life."

"Thanks for your prayers and also, to my grandson. Where is Deer-tracker? I must thank him."

"He's someplace here. He moved back so that the rest of us could see you."

"He's truly the least of his brothers. You must be very proud of him."

"I am, Papa. Thanks for giving him so much attention and teaching him so many things."

"He's very important to me. But, don't worry about me. Everything is going to be fine. I'm now ready to talk about the gods. Please call the chief."

"I'm here, Jopin. As a matter of fact, everyone is here. They have all been praying for you and now, they're here supporting you. I'm sure their prayers will help you to recover. How do you feel?"

Jopin looked around and smiled, trying to focus on the crowd standing around him. "You're all so quiet. I thought I was here all alone."

Medicine-maker broke into the conversation, "Jopin, I want you to know it was a success. I cut a hole in your skull, about the size of this small stone." He held out a stone to show Jopin. "I did not penetrate your brain, not even the membrane covering your brain, so you should start to feel better, as soon as your wound heals. The pieces of bone fit too loosely into place, so I mixed some of your blood with clay and filled in the gaps with it. I used some of the good, pure clay we use to make ceremonial bowls. It should harden up, just like your skull. I then laid your scalp back over the hole and used your hair to tie it into place, so your skin can grow back together. You can't comb your hair for a while. It will take some time. How do you feel?"

"I have a pounding headache, as if someone hit me on my head with a big rock. But, I think I will survive."

"You have already survived. I'll make you a special batch of medicine-water to help you relax. It will numb your pain."

"I want to thank you, Medicine-maker, and also my grandson, for everything. Chief, I'm now ready to tell you about my visit with the gods. I had several visions, so I guess I'll tell you about them in the order they came to me. I need Deer-tracker to be here, close to me."

"I'm here." Deer-tracker approached Jopin and gently gave him a hug. "How are you feeling, Grandpa?"

"I'm so lucky to be your grandfather. Sit here with me." Deer-tracker sat between Jopin and Bright-sunflower. They continued to hug, as Chief Salamander and the council members surrounded Jopin and his family. The people crowded in behind.

Jopin spoke out as loud as he could. "I first want to let you all know Knee-nose was with me throughout the surgery. He stood next to me, letting me know everything would go fine." Jopin paused to make sure Bright-sunflower had heard what he had just said about Knee-nose. "I prayed to Great Grandfather, before Medicine-maker started to work on me, and asked him to show me what would happen to our beautiful Tyuonyi.

My first vision came to me when Medicine-maker started to drill into my skull. There were so many things I saw and heard, so I might have a difficult time explaining everything to you. It is very hard to understand. The first thing you should know is that there are many gods, too many to count. I thought I first saw Great Grandfather early in my vision, but I was wrong. A large number of other gods danced in prayer in front of this very important god, praising and singing out loud to him. They repeated words of praise, over and over again, so I memorized them, even though I don't understand what they meant. It sounded something like,

'Hail Hitler, hail Hitler, hail Hitler.' The important god stood on top of something, like a rock or log, so the other gods could see him as they danced past him. They all sang these words of praise to him, so I was sure he had to be, none other than Great Grandfather. If not, then why would all these gods, be praising him? However, it took some time before I realized he was not Great Grandfather."

Jopin had trouble remembering exactly what had happened. It was difficult to put into words the many indescribable things he had seen and heard. "This one god, standing higher than the rest, lifted his arm and pointed over the mountains, I think, motioning for us to evacuate in that direction. This god must be Father Sun."

Chief Salamander wrinkled his forehead. "Jopin, it could have been Great Grandfather who told you to evacuate, but you think this god was Father Sun? Why? Can you tell us anything else about this god?"

"This god was finely dressed, unlike anyone. His skin color was light, and he had short black hair, and a short mustache. I can't describe his clothes, because only a god could look and dress like that. Oh, and what's more important, he had the symbol of the spinning sun on his arm. I saw it when he raised his arm, as if instructing me to go over the mountains. I'm not sure, but I thought he was telling me to evacuate, just like you've been telling us, Chief. The only thing that bothers me is that he looked very mad and angry."

"What do you mean, mad and angry? Was he mad at you?"

"It surely looked like he was, but I had other visions that made me think he may have been mad at Tyuonyi."

"What are you saying? Perhaps you should just tell us every detail, like when you return from a vision quest. We'll try to help you determine the meaning of this vision."

"Okay, but I saw so many things. I don't know how to describe everything. I don't even know where to begin. There aren't any words to describe the things I saw with my eyes and felt with my senses, but I will do my best."

"Why don't you just continue to tell us about your visions? You don't have to try to make sense of it, just tell us what you saw."

"I had another vision of two gods talking to each other. One of them was strange-looking with wild hair, and the other was very important-looking, with these shiny things around his eyes. This strange-looking god with wild hair appeared to be advising the important-looking god, the one who had those shiny things over his eyes. The important-looking god's home was big and majestic.

However, I don't think my vision had anything to do with his huge and beautiful home."

"What were those things on his eyes?"

"I don't know. It might be better to explain how I felt, and not what I saw, because I can't answer."

Chief Salamander always preferred to deal with visions, not feelings, but he had no choice. "What did your feelings tell you about these gods?"

"I'm not sure. At first, I thought the god with the wild hair, could be a spiritual-medicine god giving advice to Great Grandfather. This god had a home, much bigger and more impressive than all of Tyuonyi, so I thought he must be Great Grandfather. Anyway, that's what my feelings told me, but later, I did meet the one and only true Great Grandfather. I don't really know who this god might be. Perhaps I should tell you about another vision."

"Tell us everything. I want to know, especially about Great Grandfather, but we also need to know about the other gods. Things about the other gods might help explain things about this god."

"I then had a vision of many gods building all kinds of things on the side of the mountain, up above us, where the aspen trees surround the pond, not too far from here. They may have been mountain gods, but they looked and dressed very different than the mountain gods we are familiar with. They had different skin colors, some white with yellow hair, others brown with brown or black hair, and a few had black skin with very curly black hair. Some of them had eyes, like the color of the blue sky, and others had green eyes, like the leaves of the willow tree. A few of these gods rode on the backs of big four-legged animals. Others rode on giant animals that were not made of skin and flesh, and sent out puffs of smoke. These animals had no legs, but they moved around eating dirt and pushing big rocks out of their way. It looked like these gods were busy building very large and strange things."

Most of the people had blank looks on their faces, so Jopin knew he had some further explaining to do. But the villagers weren't the only ones who were confused. Chief Salamander stood there with his mouth open, wondering what to ask next. "This is quite interesting. You called them mountain gods, but you described them as looking very different than what you expected. I've never heard of mountain gods riding giant animals. Can you tell us more about these animals?"

"I don't know if I can explain these creatures to you, except for one of them.

This animal was big, like an elk, but without antlers. A god jumped on it, and the animal took off running, carrying the god on its back, like when a dog carries things tied to his back. But, some of the very large, the giant animals, were grey, green, or bright yellow in color. They didn't run; they rolled. I believe they were animals, because the gods would also ride on them, as they knocked down trees, and moved dirt and large rocks, big like the boulders we see between us and the cliff houses. It is hard to explain these animals."

"Jopin, could this be witchcraft, like when a witch rides on the wing of an owl? Perhaps you saw witches on the mountain, not gods."

"I don't think so. I didn't get the feeling of black magic." Jopin then realized he had received a very wicked vision. "Well, not until the torch, but I'll tell you about it later."

"Please tell us everything you know about these mountain gods."

"I did get a bad feeling from two, very different gods, who had bodies, but no faces. They made a giant, shiny egg, put it into the belly of a giant bird who took it up into the sky, and then, boom."

"Wait, Jopin, please slow down. What are you saying? This doesn't make any sense. Are you saying these gods, with no faces, could have been witches?"

"I don't know. If I had to call them anything, it would be the gods-of-wrath, because I think they might want to destroy Tyuonyi."

"What. This is very serious. You must explain why you think this may happen."

Jopin nodded. "These two gods were as white as snow. They had fat arms, fat legs, and fat heads, but their faces were missing. I can't explain. Perhaps I can draw them here in the sand." He picked up a stick and started to sketch. "The two gods faced each other. One of them poured something hot into a big bowl and the other poured something hot into a smaller bowl. Each bowl had a strange symbol on it, something like this." He drew the symbol, HE, on the big bowl and Pu, on the smaller one. "The smaller bowl was filled with something yellow, and the large bowl with something white. These gods-of-wrath took the white stuff out of its bowl and put it around the yellow stuff. They made a big giant egg." Jopin looked around to make sure they had heard him. He then became more dramatic and started to move his arms around. "They dropped the egg on Tyuonyi. Boom."

"Jopin, Jopin, please slow down. Why do you keep saying this word, boom? What does this word mean? I've never heard of boom. What are you saying?

Nothing makes any sense. I'm beginning to wonder if witches got into your vision."

"No, Chief, they were not witches. I think Great Grandfather may be mad at the people of Tyuonyi for all of the bad things we are doing. He might be warning us about how he will order the gods-of-wrath to drop this giant egg on us, as punishment."

Chief Salamander motioned for him to stop, but Jopin kept talking. "Let me continue, even if it doesn't make any sense."

Chief Salamander did not respond, but rather, just remained listening.

"You see, the gods-of-wrath made this giant egg and put it into the belly of a gigantic, shiny bird that roared like a lion, but flew with its wings spread out, like an eagle in flight. This big lion-eagle flew way up into the sky, higher than the mountains and higher than the clouds. It dropped the giant egg while still in the air. The giant egg fell slowly through the clouds and landed on Tyuoni, where it turned into a huge ball of fire, bigger than the village and higher than the mountaintops. It made a very large noise, boom." Jopin had tears running down his cheeks.

Bright-sunflower took the canteen from Deer-tracker and handed it over to Jopin. Jopin had been through so much. But, when he looked at his canteen, he realized the answer to his quest had always been there painted on his canteen. He took a sip and then continued. "All of a sudden, I stood right here in this spot, the place where the giant egg had been dropped. There was nothing left, nothing except burned ruin, the smell of smoke and worse, the smell of death. It was very, very sad."

Jopin took another sip. He looked at his chief and then at the people. All of them were deathly quiet, waiting for him to continue. He faced Deer-tracker before he continued to speak. "My young grandson, Deer-tracker, once asked me if Great Grandfather would destroy an entire village if it were evil. I wasn't really sure how to answer him, so I told him I guess so, if it were really evil. I believe these gods-of-wrath were sent to inform us that this could very well happen, here in Tyuonyi."

Sighs of surprise and disbelief could be heard. "Up to now, I was having visions of many gods. I saw them walking, talking and doing whatever they were doing. But, something very significant happened to me after the giant egg fell on Tyuonyi. All of a sudden, I became part of the vision. I stood right here in the middle of this most horrific tragedy. It was worse than anything I could ever imagine. There was nothing left, except dead people." Jopin paused. "This is the time when I was approached by the god of darkness. He knew my name. He knew about Chief Salamander, and he knew about all of you here in the village. It is very hard for me to talk about this." Jopin had to clear his throat. "Everything turned dark after the big ball of fire. I thought I had died, along with the rest of you in the village. I then saw this very small light flickering in the distance. What could it be? The light started to move and dance around, moving all over as it came closer and closer. I recognized it as being a torch, but I didn't think it could really be the god of darkness. I wanted it to be my creator, coming to take me home with him. But no, it was the god of darkness."

Bright-sunflower tightly held one of Jopin's hands. He looked into her eyes and continued. "The god of darkness told me not to be afraid, because he had come to help me. His torch would allow me to see, so I could step over the dead and find my way out of there. I asked him who he was, and he replied, 'Don't you recognize me? You've been searching for me, and now you don't know who I am? I'm your creator, Great Grandfather, and I've come to help you. Come, hold my hand, and I will lead you home.'"

Bright-sunflower suddenly pulled her hand away from Jopin, as she anxiously put her fingers over her lips. Jopin kindly smiled at her; took ahold of her hand again; and then gently squeezed it. He turned to address the people. "I was so excited. I praised him and let him know how much I've wanted to go with him, more than anything, not realizing I had fooled myself into believing he really was Great Grandfather. But I was wrong. He turned away from me, and I noticed the blood on his face. I quickly turned my face away from him and yelled out loud, 'Get away from me, you liar. You're not my creator. You're the god of darkness, the god of death. Get away from me.'"

The people shivered at Jopin's words and nervously turned their faces away, afraid of what he might say or do. Jopin looked over at Chief Salamander, then at the people, and then started talking louder, in a more confident voice. "The god of darkness told me I was a better man than Chief Salamander. He told me Chief Salamander had lost all credibility with his people, but that the people of Tyuonyi believed in me. He could make me chief of Tyuonyi, the most beautiful village in the world. Or, if I wanted, he could make me chief of Chaco. He said he could make me the greatest and most popular chief ever." Jopin stopped talking to make sure everyone was listening. "But, I knew what he was trying to do. I yelled at him again, 'Get away from me. You're not my creator. You're not Great

Grandfather. You're the god of liars, the god of death.' I ordered him to get away from me, in the name of my true creator, Great Grandfather." Jopin looked up recalling the event, creating much suspense. "The god of darkness disappeared."

The crowd started to clap and cheer, which made Jopin feel a little awkward and embarrassed.

Chief Salamander started talking. "Jopin, you had me worried for a while. I thought I was no longer your chief. However, I want you and everyone to know, I would be honored to have you as my chief."

"Well, thank you, but I'm more than satisfied being your servant. We couldn't ask for a better chief than you, no matter what the god of liars says. Here is the best part." Jopin pulled Deer-tracker a little closer to him. "I finally got to meet Great Grandfather. He appeared as a big comforting light, round like the sun, but not blinding, and so pure and comforting. It's the most wonderful feeling anyone could possibly ever imagine. I can't describe the love I felt while in his presence. Great Grandfather called me his son and told me he was very proud of me. He asked if I was ready to go live with him. I instantly replied that I was."

"I asked if that really was the god of darkness. He said it was. Great Grandfather then explained how each of us will have to make the choice of whether to go with the god of darkness or with him. He made it clear that the choice is ours. Great Grandfather never forces anyone to go with him. He then informed me that, since I chose to go with him, the only thing left was for me to walk into his light."

Jopin stopped talking for a while to make sure Bright-sunflower was listening. The people were wondering if he had walked into the light. If he did go in, then what was he doing back here with them? "I approached the light, but I couldn't get myself to enter. I wanted to step in, more than anything in the world, but I couldn't, for a few reasons. It's hard to explain, because his light is so pure, soothing, and as inviting as can be. I had promised Bright-sunflower I would be around to take care of her, so I knew I had to return back here to Tyuonyi and also, to tell all of you it is time for us to evacuate and join the Great Migration." He had to swallow, before continuing. "Great Grandfather graciously allowed me to come back."

Chief Salamander patted Jopin on his shoulder. "I'm so happy to have you back." The crowd cheered, for they also were happy to have him back.

Deer-tracker reached over and tugged on Medicine-maker's arm. "Would Grandpa have died if he had walked into the light? We're lucky Great Grandfather let him return back to us."

Medicine-maker nodded, letting Deer-tracker know he agreed, and then he started to explain to Jopin what Deer-tracker had just told him. "We almost lost you, probably when you were ready to step into the light. Great Grandfather must have let you come back for a very important reason."

Chief Salamander stood at attention, as if he were ready to hear about the evacuation, but Jopin decided to ignore his wishes for the moment. Jopin had an important message, not only for Medicine-maker, but for everyone. "Great Grandfather wants me to give all of you a message. He doesn't only talk to us right after we are born, when the bones of our skulls are soft, he talks to us all the time. As we grow older, we become too busy to listen to him. The hard bones of our skulls aren't the reason why we don't hear him. The true reason is that we're too involved with our lives, and too busy being entertained by all of our thoughts, emotions, and problems. As we grow older, we learn to think and solve our own problems. And, the more we think for ourselves, the less we think we need him, so we stop asking for his guidance and direction. We don't make time for him."

Medicine-maker looked confused and ready to challenge Jopin. "Are you saying I didn't have to cut into your head?"

"I'm afraid not. Great Grandfather has given us other methods, but I failed to prepare myself for his voice. Great Grandfather said he had to send his gods to teach us how to pray and conduct our sacred ceremonies, because our minds had become too cluttered to hear him. Our prayer-ceremonies are extremely important. We just have to learn how to ask, and then prepare ourselves to listen to his voice."

"But Jopin, you did go on your prayer quest to ask for an answer. Isn't that exactly what the gods taught us? Isn't this how we prepare ourselves to listen to his voice? I don't understand."

"Yes, you're right, but I made a huge mistake. Even if I was fasting and performing sacrifices, I wasn't ready to hear his voice. You see, I thought I already knew the answer. The gods were to inform me about how Chief Salamander was wrong, and it would be possible for us to continue to live in this beautiful village. I had to have this hole cut into my head, because of my stubbornness."

They silently listened as Jopin told them about his failures on the cliff. Jopin then extended his arm to Medicine-maker. "I'm so glad you knew what you were doing. Bright-sunflower and I want to thank you and Deer-tracker, for doing such a fine job on me. And of course, we thank Great Grandfather for allowing me to come back to deliver this most important message."

Deer-tracker expressed a proud smile. Medicine-maker slightly bowed his head. "The thanks should go to Great Grandfather's gods, because they are the ones who told me what to do."

Jopin had more to tell them, so he continued talking. "Great Grandfather said most of us only listen to his voice, right after we are born and then again, when we're close to death. So yes, I was close to death, but this was when I finally got to be with Great Grandfather. I must now go through a lot of cleansing and purification, before I go back and stand in front of Great Grandfather's light again."

Jopin looked up to the stars, as if reciting a prayer. "I must tell you, Knee-nose appeared to me once again, when I was awakening, after Medicine-maker had finished working on me. I saw Knee-nose jump over four stars. The last one, the brightest, was the sun. It was spinning. So we were right about Knee-nose. He certainly was a messenger from Great Grandfather. Our creator has spoken through him."

Chief Salamander chimed in. "Great Grandfather must have known we wouldn't evacuate, unless he would allow you to come back to tell us these things. We will now follow Great Grandfather's wishes, because of Knee-nose's and your sacrifices. You've been through so much for us. Thank you, Jopin." Chief Salamander then asked Jopin if he had a chance to peek into the light. "Perhaps there is something else you can tell us about the other side."

Jopin smiled, and then became serious. "No, I could not see past the light. However, Great Grandfather let me know it wouldn't be that simple. We don't just step through the light and go live with him. If we choose to go live with our creator, I think each of us will be purified and purged of our bad tendencies and habits, before he will allow us to travel all the way to the place where there is nothing, but purity."

The people were focused on Jopin, perplexed about what he had just told them. They had always believed that if they lived a good life, performed good deeds, and made sure to go through regular cleansing ceremonies, Great Grandfather would welcome them with open arms. They deserved to go live with him in the skies. But now, Jopin had told them they would have to be purified, perhaps with fire. They all seemed to question his statements, but no one spoke out. Their silence let Jopin know something was wrong.

"Let me try to explain. I was hurt and discouraged, and didn't know what to think. Great Grandfather had just welcomed me as his most beloved son. But then, he let me know I would have to go through a purification process. The light would purge me of my problems, bad habits and offenses. I was very disappointed, because Great Grandfather did not really want me, as I was. It's difficult to express my sadness and discouragement. I have tried to live a good life and do everything right, so I felt I deserved to go live with my beloved Creator."

Jopin told them the story about the god of darkness. "I didn't know he was once, one of Great Grandfather's most beautiful gods, who lived with him up in the skies. The other gods called him the god-of-light, because he was so bright. But, being special made him think he was better than the other gods, and he soon wanted them to obey and honor him, instead of their creator. Great Grandfather finally had to cast him out into darkness. You see, Great Grandfather does not want us in paradise, as we are, because we might start acting like the god of darkness did. The commandment about being the least of your brothers, still holds, even more so, when we go live with him."

Medicine-maker asked, "Are you saying that Great Grandfather allows the god of darkness to bring evil to the world? That doesn't make any sense, does it? Why won't Great Grandfather just destroy the god of darkness, like he might destroy Tyuonyi?"

"I don't think he is going to destroy Tyuoni. It was only a vision. He might have allowed me to witness the destruction of Tyuonyi to show me what could come from evil. If we choose evil, we choose death. If I had chosen to believe the promises of the god of darkness, he would have grabbed me by my hand and never let go. I knew why he had that blood on his face. He is a liar and a thief who will say or do whatever it takes to steal away our souls. The god of darkness exists, so we can have the choice: death or everlasting life. Great Grandfather gives us that choice."

"That's why the chiefs decided to give each village the choice of whether to evacuate or not. We want everyone to have a free choice—" Chief Salamander had started to talk about the evacuation, but Jopin interrupted.

"Chief, I would like to tell you something else about the light. I'm almost finished" Chief Salamander nodded for Jopin to continue. "I only stood at the edge of the light, but it illuminated my life in such a way that I could see each and every bad thought, vice, and wrongdoing throughout my life, even all the hurt and pain I have caused my family and friends. Many of these things, I had long forgotten, especially those I had failed to cleanse myself of. With so many blemishes and dirt on my body, I knew I wasn't worthy to enter to the other side, where everything is pure. Yet, he still wanted me to join him. Of course, he wouldn't allow me, or anyone, to contaminate his purity. That's why he makes us walk, all the way through his light. We can't go live with him, unless we are pure. That's the only way for us to remain perfectly and completely happy with him, forever in the skies."

For a moment, there was an atmosphere of peace among the villagers. They didn't really say anything. However, by their smiles of acceptance, their gestures and attentiveness, and by their comradeship, something very special had happened.

Chief Salamander knew it was time to address the people. "Great Grandfather has spoken to us through Jopin. It is now up to us to ponder his words in our hearts. Jopin, the entire village has spent the day here in your support, first in prayer and dance, and now in full attention, listening to your every word. No one has had a bite to eat since this morning, not even the children. Should we stop for now and continue in the morning?"

"Chief, I thought I had finished, but I would like just a little more time, to talk about the big message I received from the gods." Jopin paused as if trying to decide how to say it. "Great Grandfather loves us exactly for who we are. It's important for us to know he has an equal amount of love for each and every one of us. Therefore, we should not enter paradise thinking we are greater than anyone else or more deserving. However, when we do enter his light, he will purge such traits and tendencies from us, before we're allowed to pass all of the way through the light. We will enter a place of purity, where fights, arguments, jealousy, and disappointments can't be found, no more tears or sadness, only joy and happiness. We should not fear his purification. Great Grandfather will purify us with the fire of his love, so we can become completely satisfied and happier than we could ever possibly imagine. I can hardly wait until I get to stand in front of Great Grandfather again. I will work harder at learning how to listen to his voice. Great Grandfather is talking to us. We all need to learn how to silence our hearts, open our minds, and listen."

Jopin stopped talking, but the people still held on to every word that had come from his mouth. This man, with a hole in his head, had stood in the presence of Great Grandfather and returned back to them. This was surely a most sacred moment. No one wanted to break the peace and quiet that had filled the air. But, the most precious silence was finally broken by the hoot of an owl, out at a distance.

Chief Salamander spoke out. "This has been a most beautiful, memorable and sacred day. Please, let us all thank Great Grandfather and all of his gods for taking care of Jopin and allowing him to return to us with his message. And thanks to Medicine-maker and Deer-tracker. Jopin is still here among us. And of course, we want to thank you, Jopin, for sacrificing yourself for your people. There can be no greater gift, than what you have done for your brothers and sisters. The gods have spoken to us through you. I guess we all know we must evacuate Tyuonyi and get on with the Great Migration. I had said we would leave on the fourth day, but I would like for Jopin to go home tonight to rest and regain some of his strength. We will count tomorrow as day one, instead of today. We have to decide what to take with us and what to leave behind. On the second and third days, we will prepare ourselves for the evacuation by packing those things we may need on the journey. We will leave on the morning of the fourth day. I will send some of my warriors ahead to prepare a camp for us for that evening. Let us all go back to our dwellings to eat, rest and give thanks to Great Grandfather. We will meet every morning to discuss our various situations and prepare for our evacuation. The drums will announce the beginning of each of these meetings. Good night."

Chief Salamander leaned forward to talk to Jopin. "I will have my warrior guards carry you back to your house."

"Chief, I think I can walk." Jopin held on to the sacred rock as he tried to get up.

Chief Salamander quickly grabbed him by one of his arms. "You shouldn't do this. Let me help you."

Medicine-maker quickly moved in to help. Jopin gave them a nod of gratitude as they steadied him up on his feet. Jopin insisted he could walk on his own, but Bright-sunflower, Brilliant-pebbles, and Deer-tracker stepped forward to take over and support him. They wanted to be the ones who would take Jopin back home, assisting him as if they would never let him go.

"Jopin, are you sure you don't want my warrior guards to carry you home?"

Brilliant-pebbles answered for Jopin. "My family and I will do it. We'll be taking care of him from now on."

"Okay. It looks like you and your mother have claimed ownership. I can't blame you. Take good care of him."

Jopin grabbed ahold of the two women of his life. "You two sure know how to spoil a man."

"We're taking you home, but I don't want you, my charming and unselfish husband, to say a single word about the evacuation. You have already gone through too much. It is now our turn to take care of you. You will eat, rest, and gain your strength back."

They slowly walked Jopin home, where they planned to take care of him and give thanks for one another, but more importantly, to thank Great Grandfather. There was so much happiness and gratitude in their hearts.

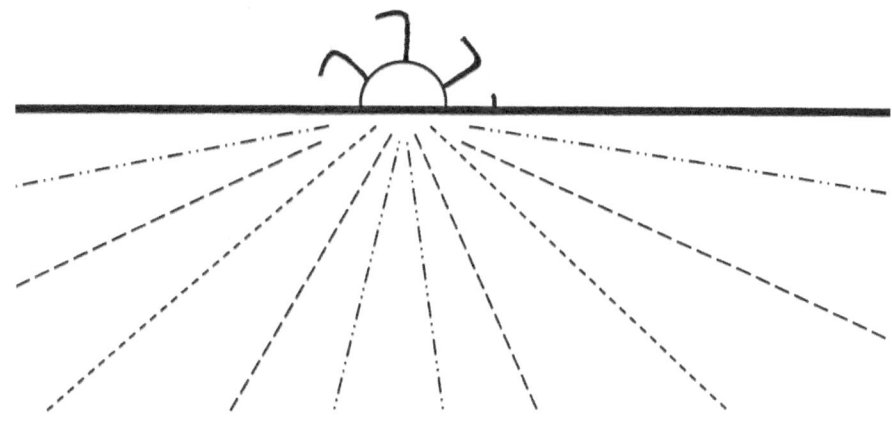

Realization Sets In

The morning sun had risen, yet the village remained quiet. Jopin had been awake for some time, but he hadn't attempted to get up. Rather, he just lay there thinking about everything that had happened over the last few days. He hesitated to move or to make a sound, wondering if Bright-sunflower might still be sleeping, lying besides him. She's so quiet, he thought. He couldn't hear her breathing, so he wondered if she might have gone to visit Brilliant-pebbles and Deer-tracker. He started to turn on his back. "Oh, what a headache."

Bright-sunflower quickly came to his side. "Jopin, are you hurting? I've been so worried about you. You slept through most of the morning. Can I get you something?"

"No, I don't need anything, thank you. I'm all right. I just have this splitting headache."

"Why haven't you said anything?"

"I thought you might still be sleeping, so I tried not to move. But, you have been on my mind. I owe you an apology. I didn't mean to go against your wishes. When the people ganged up against Chief Salamander, I felt like it was all my fault, so I decided to give in to them. This excruciating pain might keep us from getting ready for the move. Who knows how long it will take for it to go away? We have so much work to do."

"No, Jopin, what you have to do right now is rest. You don't have to do anything. I need to apologize. I acted selfish, only thinking about myself." Bright-sunflower told him how she couldn't blame him for climbing the cliff and going on his prayer quest, not even for having that hole cut into his head. She could now see how the evacuation had been such an important decision, a burden, weighing heavily on his shoulders for quite some time. "I wanted you to be around for me, but you acted as if you cared more about stupid council business than about your wife and family. I couldn't understand why you didn't even care about your own life. How could I have lived without my special husband? But, I had a lot of time to think last night, as I lay there next to you. By putting myself in your moccasins, I started to think about the many things you must have been so worried about, those concerns that were too heavy for you to carry all by yourself.

Jopin interrupted, trying to stop her, but she continued. "I couldn't get any sleep at all. The reality of the move has set in, and I am now worried about everything. My poor Jopin, you suffered all by yourself. You knew that once we moved out of this valley, we probably would never see our boys again. Didn't you? This is probably the one thing that would concern you and me the most. I was so busy worrying about losing you, I couldn't think about the other things we will actually lose, because of the move. We may never see many of our families and friends again. And what about the old and the sick who are in no condition to walk out of here? Almost all of us older ones, are stricken with arthritis. I now understand the tremendous pressure you must have been under, why you had to go to Great Grandfather for guidance. You should know by now that I'm always ready for you to talk to me about anything. Your wife is one of the few people you can depend on. I don't care if it is secret council business or not. I'm your wife. I also know how to keep a secret. This has been a tremendous burden for you. Where will our boys be going? I cried all night, because we may never see them again. What about our grandchildren?"

Jopin had also been worried about these things, but as Great Grandfather had pointed out, he had been more concerned about having to leave the place he had worked so hard to create. There were so many things he had done wrong in his life. He could start by being a better husband. Jopin reached out and gently ran his fingers on her cheeks. "We don't even know where we'll be going. I assume we'll go over the mountain and keep on going, until Father Sun tells us when to stop. It's been very difficult for me to accept this move. I had to have this hole cut into my head to knock me to my senses and finally, to accept the inevitable. Yes, I have thought about the boys and their families. Double-eagle lives the closest to us, in Tsankawi, but it would still take us a whole day to go tell him and his family goodbye, plus another day's travel to return. Besides, we don't have time to go visit anyone. We only have time to pack and get ready for the move. It's impossible for me to make the trip now, that I'm in this condition. My head better start to heal, if we expect to be ready in time to join the rest of the villagers. As for the other two boys, they live too far away. We can't even consider going to see them. It would take four or five days to make it to Amoxiumka and back. I don't know why Great Grandfather only gave us the one daughter. We wouldn't be worrying about where our children would be moving to, if he had given us all girls. They would all be going with us. Let's pray that Father Sun will lead all tribes to a common area, where someday, we can once again be united."

"Why can't Chief Salamander give us until the end of summer to get ready? By then, we could visit all of our families and say our good-byes. Perhaps they might want to come with us instead of with their own tribes."

"They must have discussed such things at Chaco. I imagine it would create nothing but confusion, or even chaos, if we had more than four days to prepare for the move. Can you imagine everyone, from every village, traveling to see their families at the same time? What if the sons want to go with their parents, and their wives refuse to leave their mothers? Our sons don't need those kinds of problems. I'm sure Chief Salamander and the other chiefs considered all of these situations. The important thing though, we shouldn't be surprised this is happening. We have all known about the Great Migration. It has always been part of our destiny. Our ancestors talked about it and told us it should, someday continue. We must obey and follow Great Grandfather's plan. I just didn't expect it to happen in our lifetime."

"Will we have enough time to get ready in four days?"

"I assume so, ah wait. I think someone is coming to visit."

"Jopin, are you awake? How are you feeling? May I come in?"

"Medicine-maker, please come inside. I slept late, so I haven't even had time to get out of bed. It is good to see you."

Medicine-maker carefully walked in. He was carrying something that looked like a basket made of fur. "Good morning Bright-sunflower. Jopin, I came to see how you're feeling. Were you able to get any sleep last night?"

Bright-sunflower didn't let Jopin respond. "Jopin was exhausted. He got in a full night's sleep, but he moaned most of the time."

"I bet he did. Jopin, I brought a few things to make you feel better and to help you heal. Let me look at your head. Does it hurt?"

Jopin leaned forward to show him the top of his head. "It feels like someone split my head open. I had a very sharp pain last night, but today, it is beginning to feel like a dull pain. How is it supposed to feel?"

"I don't know. I've never cut a hole in someone's head before, but I have helped heal broken bones. The idea is to put the bones back into place and bind them together to keep them from moving. They then grow back together and mend themselves. I didn't have to bind your head, because that part of your head doesn't move. I planned to put the piece of bone I had removed from your skull, back into place, so it could heal. But, it was quite a bit smaller than the hole it came out of. The bones won't grow together if they don't touch each other, so I had to come up with a solution. All I could think of was the legend of Blood Clot Boy. As I mentioned before, I mixed some of your blood with ceremonial clay, and used it to hold the bone into place. That's what's keeping the bone from moving around in the hole. It's important for you not to hit it or bump it into anything. I got up early this morning and made you this headdress. There are several layers of padding and shielding to protect your head, in case you do get hit. We'll soon be traveling through the forest, and I was afraid you might hit your head against a branch or something hard." Medicine-maker removed a canteen and a small bowl from inside the basket, and handed the headdress to Jopin.

Jopin received the headdress and studied how it was made, before putting it on. "I like how you covered it with Raccoon skin. It fits. Thanks for thinking of me. I will wear it, but I may appear rather distinguished looking in this headdress. I hope I won't be mistaken for a great chief or some other important person. What if I meet someone on the way, and they challenge me to a fight for my position? What should I do? They might want my very distinguished looking headdress?"

Medicine-maker started to laugh. "Don't fight, just hand it over to them. I can always make you another one." The three of them joked around. After all, Jopin was alive and on his way to recovery.

"You don't have to worry about me. I'll soon heal and be back to normal in no time. You have a couple more things with you. Is all of that for me?"

"I brought you some medicine-water, and a salve made from special weeds mixed in with intestine fat. The medicine-water in this gourd was made from herbs known for deadening pain. Drink this at morning, noon and night. Here, take a few swallows of it right away." He handed the gourd over to Jopin. "You need to start feeling better, because we're leaving in just a few days. You will heal faster if the pain mellows. I want you to gently rub this salve over your wound." He motioned for Bright-sunflower to pay attention, because she would probably be the person applying it. "This will keep any infection away and help you heal faster. Don't eat this one. It's not good for your insides. You must keep the wound clean, so keep putting this salve on it. Try not to bump it into anything. Please wear this headdress at all times."

"I will wear it, even if it means drawing a lot of attention to me." Jopin smiled. "I hope Chief Salamander won't think I now want to take his position as chief."

Chief Salamander called out from the doorway. "What? Jopin, is that you, who's saying those things? Did I hear you say you want to replace me?"

Jopin and Medicine-maker were too busy laughing, so Bright-sunflower let him in. "Please come in. The boys are having some fun."

"Chief, I want you to see my new—" Jopin suddenly stopped talking, because of pain. Medicine-maker looked concerned, but Jopin motioned he was all right. "Pain from laughter is good."

But Chief Salamander didn't help. "Jopin, it is I who should wear that distinguished looking headdress, not you. I will fight you for it." He raised his fists as if wanting to start a fight. They all burst out in laughter, including Bright-sunflower. Jopin was hurting, but he chuckled anyway, knowing he must look like quite a sight.

Medicine-maker stood up to leave. "Where are you going?"

"It's getting crowded in here. I just wanted to check on your progress. And besides, Chief Salamander is in a fighting mood. I don't want to fight him for my position in this room." They all laughed as Medicine-maker walked out.

"Is there anything I can do for you?" Chief Salamander was now serious.

"No, thanks. I believe it's now up to me. Medicine-maker brought me some medicine-water and a special salve to help me heal faster, and this headdress."

Chief Salamander smiled. "What about the headdress. Will it keep your head warm as the hole heals?"

"I don't know about it keeping my head warm. He built a shield into it to protect my head if it gets bumped when under tree branches. He was worried I might run into something."

"I'm glad he's taking care of you. I intentionally waited until now, before coming to visit, so you could get the rest you so much deserve. I also wanted to give your family and friends time to visit with you."

"That's very considerate of you Chief, but Medicine-maker is the only one who has come to visit."

Bright-sunflower spoke out. "That's not true, Jopin. A lot of people have come to see you. Brilliant-pebbles and Deer-tracker came, first thing this morning. I think she worried all night about you. Just hearing you snore, made her so happy. She said to tell you she loves you very much, and she wants you to rest and recover. Deer-tracker wondered what he could do to help. Jopin, that boy worships you."

"What? Where was I? Did I sleep through all of this? We truly are blessed with a beautiful daughter and a wonderful grandson."

"You were in a very deep slumber. Most of our neighbors also stopped by to see how you were doing. There were so many well-wishers. I decided to go greet them outside. That way, they wouldn't wake you."

"What? I didn't hear a sound. I never heard anyone talking."

"That's what we wanted. They were all very quiet and considerate of your condition. They all wish you well and want you to have a speedy recovery."

"I'm humbled. It was very nice of them."

"I'm just so happy I still have my husband." She reached over and pulled back the rabbit fur cover, so she could sit next to him. "You're still here with us."

Chief Salamander decided to tell Jopin about his morning. "There were so many people coming to ask about you, I began to feel guilty, because I hadn't come to see you, myself. But you needed to get some rest and sleep. It's no secret that you sacrificed yourself to help me get out of a mess. You didn't have to, but you did. Jopin, I don't blame you if you're mad at me, or if you're disillusioned with my leadership. Yet, you still offered up yourself to save me. I want to personally thank you for your sacrifice. I'm forever indebted to you, and to you too, Bright-sunflower. Things got out of control. The villagers were about to scalp me. You sacrificed yourself for me and for your people, just like Knee-nose. You're truly a favorite son of Great Grandfather and a servant to your people. I'm sure he has a very special place awaiting you in the skies."

"I have to correct so many things in my life, before I go back to see our creator. Chief, I've been thinking. Last night, you told me I should tell you everything about my vision. There is this one thing I would like to talk about, something I can't get out of my mind. You can't imagine the feeling I had, while standing in front of Great Grandfather. This majestic, most wonderful, pure light filled me with a sacredness that is indescribable. This was undeniably, the most wonderful feeling in the whole wide world, nothing equal to it. The problem is, I didn't get this kind of feeling with his gods, not even close in comparison. I thought there was sacredness there, when I first saw them, but after being in the presence of Great Grandfather, I now know I had fooled myself. Perhaps, they weren't gods at all. What if my visions were of strange looking people in a future time, instead of gods?"

"Jopin, you did convey the feeling of sacredness when you told us about the gods. Are you saying you could have been mistaken? Exactly what are you trying to say?"

"I'm not sure. I did have a vision of these other gods, but something tells me they were just people like us, not gods. But the visions were very strange, so I don't know. The feelings I got from them, just weren't the same as with Great Grandfather. Great Grandfather is so much greater and holier than all of his gods. But this morning, when I woke up, I kept thinking I had made a mistake. Could they have been people living here, in our homeland, in some future time? Before I started having my visions, I had prayed to Great Grandfather, asking him what would happen to this land that I love so much. I didn't want to leave this place. Perhaps he was just answering my question."

"I don't know what to say. It is difficult to understand. What about Father Sun, what kind of a feeling did you get with Father Sun?"

"That is mostly, why I'm so confused. I got the feeling that Father Sun was mad, as if he wanted or demanded something of me, of everyone. He looked angry and appeared greedy. This is not what I would expect from one of Great Grandfather's gods. Didn't Great Grandfather throw out the god of darkness from the skies, because he became greedy and self-centered? I'm confused.

Was Father Sun mad at me, or was he just a mad man? I woke up this morning wondering, if I may have misinterpreted my visions."

"Perhaps you did, but that's why we had you share your visions with us, so that we could help you determine their true meanings. I talked to a lot of people this morning. They all believe that the gods are mad at the people of Tyuonyi for the way we have been living. You helped all of us realize we have not lived according to Great Grandfather's rules. Your vision convinced them it was time to evacuate. But, I just thought of something. Who ever heard of people with yellow hair and blue eyes? And who ever heard of people with no faces? They must be gods."

Chief Salamander started to laugh, as if trying to convince Jopin. Jopin just looked back at him with a half-hearted smile. Chief Salamander stopped laughing and asked, "What about the evacuation? Do you still believe Great Grandfather wants us to continue on with the Great Migration?"

"Yes, I believe the Great Migration has always been part of Great Grandfather's plan for his people, ever since the beginning of time. This might be his way of keeping us humble. I now know that my pride got in the way of the move. I had devoted my entire life to improving this village, so I felt proud of my many contributions and accomplishments. But, after being in Great Grandfather's presence, I know we are nothing without him. Being proud is wrong. I believe he will send us on the Great Migration, so we can once again, learn how to depend on him and only him. We have done these great things for Tyuonyi with him working through us. He is the one who has allowed us to do great works. I became so self-absorbed that I forgot he is the Almighty Creator. I'm just one of his servants."

"So am I, Jopin. You have just taught me another lesson. It's tough to be a leader, because pride sets in. I agree with you about the Great Migration. We all have to get rid of the pride that has taken over our lives. Do you have any advice about the Migration? Is there anything I should do to get our people ready?"

"No, I can't think about anything right now. I'm just glad you are the one in charge and not me. You have the toughest job of all. I would not want to walk in your moccasins, even if I am the one wearing this fancy headdress."

Chief Salamander laughed and then acted like he was getting ready to leave. "I'll soon get the drums to announce our first day's meeting. We probably don't have to meet, because most of the village has already come to talk to me. They're worried about only having four days to prepare for the move. They would like to visit and say goodbye to their sons and families that live in the other villages. They want to do this, before we move out of here. I feel badly, because I had to say no to all of them. That would create too much chaos and confusion. The Chief-of-chiefs at Chaco warned us, to not give in to their demands. These will be the longest four days of my life."

Jopin faced Bright-sunflower, as he told Chief Salamander how he understood and agreed with his position. "Is there anything I have to do or bring to the meeting?"

"No, you've already done enough. Just bring your headdress. Perhaps they will see it and think you're now their new chief. They certainly need a new chief, right now."

"No, they don't. Don't even think about it." Bright-sunflower nodded to let him know she agreed with her husband.

"The only thing that would make me delay our evacuation date by a day or two would be your health, Jopin. I don't want to bring you any more pain than what you have already endured."

"Chief, I've only been awake for a short while and yes, I am in pain. I believe Great Grandfather will give me the strength to walk out of here on day four."

"Okay Jopin. I better get back to business. I'll give you enough time for you to eat and get ready, before I call a meeting."

"Bye, Chief." Bright-sunflower squeezed Chief Salamander's arm as he walked out, her way of saying thanks. She then fed Jopin, applied the special salve on Jopin's wound, and then helped him freshen up for the meeting.

The drums had been beating for a while, indicating the meeting was about to begin. Many of the villagers, anxious to learn more about the evacuation, had already been waiting at the gathering place. Some of them worked their way to the area in front of the main kiva. Others procrastinated, because they did not want to hear anything about having to leave their homes. It was too painful to think they may never see their loved ones again. Those with health problems appeared worse, walking slower, or appearing more crippled than ever. Jopin and Bright-sunflower walked slowly, but carefully towards Chief Salamander. They held their heads up high, as if telling everyone they were ready. The people became excited when they saw them, and started to clap. All of their eyes focused on Jopin's headdress. Even the procrastinators became excited at the sight of Jopin and

Bright-sunflower. If Jopin was ready, after everything he had gone through, then perhaps they should also decide to be ready, as well.

Chief Salamander signaled the drummers to stop. He opened the meeting with a prayer, and announced that Tyuonyi would be evacuated, in order to please Great Grandfather. He then asked for Divine guidance in preparing the village for the move, especially since there will be many hardships and illnesses that will have to be addressed and dealt with. "Great Grandfather will give you the answers and the strength you need. Jopin sought Great Grandfather's guidance, and now he is ready to accept what he must do. We have accepted what Jopin has shared with us, so thank you, Jopin, for sacrificing yourself for us." Chief Salamander gestured towards Jopin in recognition and respect.

Jopin nodded, as the crowd cheered and clapped. They finally quieted down.

"We must now learn from Jopin's example and sacrifice ourselves for each other. Some of our brothers aren't strong enough to walk out of here on their own. The move will be very difficult on them. We must work together and help those who aren't as healthy or as strong as we are. I've asked my warrior guards to prepare a place where we can camp at the end of the first day. They will also have some food and water ready for us, so we can regain our strength for the following day's journey. I'm sure there are other ways we can help each other. Are any of you having trouble deciding what to do? Would any of you like to say anything?"

Wildcat-man raised his hand. "My Uncle Tsetse-fly is too old and weak to travel. He probably can't make the trip, even if we carry him out of here. We have no choice, but to remain behind to take care of him until the time comes, when Great Grandfather calls him home.

"I fully understand your situation. You want to be with your uncle, especially during his final moments. The warrior guards will mark a trail, so you can join us later. Does anyone else have something to say?"

Leaping-cougar spoke out. "Both my wife and I are crippled to the extent where we can barely walk. We don't want to be a burden to the rest of you. We would slow you down too much, so we will stay behind and help Wildcat-man care for Tsetse-fly. We're not sure what we will do. There aren't too many choices for us, with our health the way it is."

"I learned a lesson from Jopin this morning. He believes that Great Grandfather is sending us on this Great Migration to keep us humble. We need our creator, and we need each other. We must help our brothers and sisters in need. That is how Great Grandfather wants it. We will be honored to help you out of here."

"We'll see. If we do stay, we can help those left behind. This will also make Great Grandfather happy. Won't it?"

"I guess so, but remember, we're still a village. No matter where we may be, we will still exist as one big family, one that must continue to feed and take care of each other."

Thunder-head stepped forward. "Chief, as you know, my family doesn't agree with you and Jopin. We'll stay behind, here in Tyuonyi, where we have plenty of water to drink and food to eat. There is no better place than right here. Who knows where you might be going? I'm sure you will encounter many problems and difficulties on your journey. And besides, who in his right mind believes Great Grandfather will send his gods-of-wrath to destroy us?"

"You have expressed your beliefs, and I respect them. Like I stated previously, we will not force anyone to leave. Each and every one of us must make his own decision to either obey Great Grandfather or to choose another alternative. Are you speaking for yourself and your family, or for Fat-man and Little-boy?"

Thunder-head was so angry, he just stared right back at Chief Salamander.

Chief Salamander continued. "No one knows for sure if Great Grandfather will order the destruction of Tyuonyi. It comes down to this. Do we want to please Great Grandfather or not? I myself do not want to test our Almighty Creator."

"Chief, if that were the case, then what about the thieves and promiscuous women, who live outside of the village? Will they remain behind, because they're not good enough to join the rest of us? Are they cursed, because they don't act and think, like the people of Tyuonyi?"

"You were here yesterday, Thunder-head, and you heard Jopin's report with your very own ears. Bad habits such as pride and our thinking that we're better than the least of our brothers and sisters, offend Great Grandfather. Our creator won't allow any of us to enter his home, until he has purged us of all of our faults. As far as I know, we don't allow these people, who have refused to change their ways, to live within the Tyuonyi walls, because we can't have them around our young ones, influencing their behaviors. I want to make it clear. These thieves and promiscuous women still remain citizens of Tyuonyi, just like the Eagle Clan people who live high up in the big cave. So yes, Thunder-head, you're right. I appreciate your insight. We can't be so proud as not to welcome these brothers and sisters of ours, to join us on our migration. They belong to Great Grandfather, just like we do. I told Little-acorn this morning that I would go visit these people about this very matter, but time got away from me. I'll go visit Wild-flower, right after this meeting."

"I bet you will," he snapped in a strifeful manner. Thunder-head looked around to see if anyone would act on his hostility, but even Fat-man and Little-boy looked away. However, he still wanted to discredit his chief. "You know you have been too proud to allow these people to live next to you within these walls of Tyuonyi. You're guiltier than the rest of us."

"Perhaps so, Thunder-head, I admit it. I'm guilty. I also know how much you enjoy giving me a hard time. I know you so well, that I predict you and your family will join us, when we leave this village on the fourth day."

Thunder-head started to laugh. Some of the villagers could be heard chuckling.

"Wild-flower, this is Chief Salamander. May I come in? I would like to speak with you."

"Yes, please come inside, so we can be alone." She had been waiting for him, so she started talking as Chief Salamander put his arm around her. "I was wondering when you would finally make time to come see me. What took you so long?"

"I intended to come visit you first thing this morning, but I–" He stopped talking when he realized what she had said. "You were waiting for me? How did you know? Were you there? I thought I heard the cry of an owl. Was that you?"

"I wasn't the one hooting, but yes, I was there. My spirit was under one of his wings." Wild-flower crossed her arms and stared at him. "Thanks for coming to inform me, but I already know about the evacuation. What were you planning to do with me and the others who live here?" She had expected Salamander to come and talk to her early in the morning, but she now knew she wasn't important enough. "It took you so long to get here. I was getting ready to cast a spell on you."

Chief Salamander tried to change her attitude, by showing her that big smile of his. It's always worked before. "If you were there last night, then you heard it with your very own ears. By the way, what's all this talk, about you casting a spell on me? I'm too strong for that. Medicine-maker fixed this pouch especially for me, to protect me from such things. And besides, you already know everything. As you heard, Great Grandfather will not allow any of us to enter into his home in the skies, as long as we try to have more or attempt to be greater than the rest. You can't have more power than anyone else, especially me, your chief."

"Don't be so sure, and please stop smiling."

"Why do you continue to cast curses on your brothers? You know that the bad we wish on others, always comes back to us, four times worse. Just look at yourself. You're already hunched over and disfigured. It's difficult for you to even walk. How could you even consider doing more evil, knowing you will only hurt yourself in the process? It hurts me to see you like this. I know that, deep inside, you're still a very good person."

"You only say those good things about me, because you know I'm mad at you. You can't sweet talk me, you and that sweet smile of yours. You know what I look like, and I know what I look like. But, the men who come calling at my door think I'm beautiful. I love the way they look at me."

Chief Salamander leaned forward to look directly into her eyes. He wanted her to know he was aware of her wicked behavior. "This is only, because you have them under your spell. You know, I've been thinking a lot about what Jopin told us yesterday. When he stood in front of Great Grandfather, the pure light revealed every little fault and blemish he had. We can't hide from the light of truth. According to Jopin, all of us will all have to stand in front of that light in the end. That must be how the god of darkness got his name. He hides out in the dark to keep away from the light of truth. Jopin almost believed his lies, because the god of darkness told him what Jopin wanted to hear. That little flicker of light from the torch was enough to make Jopin believe it was Great Grandfather. Wild-flower, it's never too late to purify yourself, before you find yourself standing out in the light. I wish all of you could live with the rest of us. We're all sons and daughters of the Almighty Creator."

"What? Why do you look down on me and the others living here? Look at yourself. You might be the chief, but you also have many faults, just like the rest of us. Why do you allow yourself to live in Tyuonyi, knowing you're blemished, perhaps worse than some of us who live here?"

"That's a very good question and, an important observation. Yes, I know I have faults. We all do. But I make it a habit to go through purification ceremonies. Isn't that what Great Grandfather has instructed us to do? He loves us for who we are. All he asks is for us to love him enough to admit our faults, and go through regular purifications. I know he sees the good in all of us."

"And, he also sees a lot of bad." She put her arms on Salamander's shoulders. "That's the one thing I love about you. You accept me, just the way I am, and you're always very honest with me. Come to think of it, that's the one thing I don't like about you. You tell me the truth. The men, who come here, tell me what I want to hear, but they don't know any better. You're just like your mother. Gosh do I miss her."

"Are you talking about my birth mother or about Singing-bluebird, your sister?"

"You know very well, I'm talking about my sister. Why would I miss Snowflake? She isn't dead. Your other mother, Singing-bluebird, is the one who is dead. She loved you so much. As far as she was concerned, you were her one and only, true son. She even loved Snowflake as her daughter. If I had only known. Singing-bluebird was very sad on that day, when she came to talk to me. She didn't tell me what she had planned to do, but she made me promise I would take care of you and Snowflake, if anything were ever to happen to her. I should've known something bad was about to happen, especially when she made me promise not to ever cast a curse on your father. I assumed she was probably sad, because they were having marital problems. I didn't know she was on her way to jump off the cliff. I should have gone with her. All the signs were there, but I was too blind to see them. I hate myself for not realizing what she had planned to do. I was too busy planning my next conquest. I could have stopped her."

Chief Salamander put his arms around her and pulled her up to his chest. "I don't have a lot of memories of her, because I was so young at the time. However, the ones I do have are very special. She was so good to me."

"Of course she was. You were the answer to her prayers. She asked Great Grandfather for children and he sent her you and Snowflake. She loved both of you so much. I still remember when the two of you came to live with her. Singing-bluebird couldn't stop talking about you." Wild-flower paused for a while. "Since we're talking about coming clean, I do have a confession to make. I broke my promise to my sister about not casting a spell on your father. He hurt my sister.

She's dead because of him, so I had him become impotent. I couldn't stand for him to continue having fun, knowing that Singing-bluebird was dead, because of him. I was so mad at him. That's why you don't have any brothers and sisters."

Surprised and shocked, Chief Salamander started stuttering. "I, I don't know what to think about what I just heard. What have you done? You also hurt my mother."

"I might have helped her. Your father couldn't do her wrong, the way he did my sister. You may be mad at me. I deserve it. There are a lot of things you don't know about me. Perhaps you don't want me to go before Great Grandfather's light, after all. Singing-bluebird devoted herself to one man, and look at what happened to her. I on the other hand, have devoted myself to all men. I might be all decrepit, but I'm still alive."

Chief Salamander was very disappointed with what she had told him, but he had come to visit her for a purpose. "What you have done to Father, is not for me to judge. If Great Grandfather is willing to take you, as you are, then why should I judge you, or anyone else? I do appreciate the fact that you've been so good to my family, and to mother. By the way, Little-acorn instructed me to tell you hello for her."

"I meant to ask you for that pretty wife of yours. I trust she's doing fine?"

"Yes, she is doing fine, thank you. The baby should be here soon. But, like the rest of the village, she's very worried about the journey out of this canyon. Can you tell the rest of the people, here, about the move? We will leave in three days. The beating of the drums will announce the next meeting. I'll expect all of you to be there."

"Don't be so sure. A lot of the people here are mad at you for not allowing them to live with their families and friends in the village."

He gently grabbed one of her hands. "You understand why that hasn't been possible. It's nothing personal, so just explain to them it's for the sake and welfare of the children."

"You want me to do your dirty work? No, you go talk to them yourself."

"Wild-flower, I can't. I don't have the time. Please do this for me."

"No, something as important as this has to come from the chief. Come on. Let's go see if we can round them up. You owe it to all of them."

"Okay, I guess this is something I must do."

They walked outside and called into each of the homes. Wild-flower announced that Chief Salamander wanted to talk to them. They gathered under a large tree near the creek. He told them about the decision to evacuate Tyuonyi in order to join the Great Migration. Realizing some of these people may have abandoned their religious beliefs long ago, he told them the whole story, starting with the Chiefs' Pow-Wow at Chaco, and ending with Jopin's visions. Some of them were skeptical, but they listened intently, granting him the respect and attention expected towards a leader. They wanted him to tell them everything they might need to know. He felt their uneasiness, so he apologized about not allowing them to live within the Tyuonyi walls. He explained how it had become necessary, to protect the children. He stressed how they were all brothers and sisters, and then, he invited them to join Tyuonyi for the meeting on the following day. When asked if the villagers would welcome them, he told them about how he had just returned from the first meeting. "The people asked me to come and invite you to attend."

Chief Salamander felt he had done his duty. They were definitely welcome, and he had invited them to join in on the discussions and participate on the specifics of the evacuation. He had encouraged them, once again, to attend the next meeting, and he thanked them for their time. However, he wasn't sure if he had convinced them. They said they would discuss the matter amongst themselves and decide whether or not to attend.

Chief Salamander left the area and continued to travel further away from the village. He felt relieved and happy, because these people, whom he had banned from residing in Tyuonyi, had actually welcomed him and treated him so well. The attentiveness and respect they had given him had been unexpected.

He now had to go inform the members of the Eagle Clan about the evacuation. The Eagle Clan also lived away from Tyuoni, but by choice. Chief Salamander expected it would be much easier talking to them, so he was excited, as he approached the area where they lived. He looked up and saw their huge cave, high above the tall trees. Salamander started to climb up the long row of ladders. Finally, reaching the top, he pulled himself over the edge and stood up on the floor of the cave. After dusting himself off, he walked past their kiva, towards the dwellings, where he was greeted by Friend-of-eagle, the leader of the Eagle Clan.

"Chief Salamander, what a pleasant surprise. What brings you to this place? Have you finally come to your senses and now realize this is where you belong?

After all, this is where the mountain gods reside. Come live with us, where you can always be among them."

"Once again, Friend-of-eagle, you're always most welcoming and yes, you're so right about this place. As many times as I've come up here, your home always takes my breath away. You truly do live close to the skies, where the gods reside. If only you didn't have to carry your food and water all the way up here."

"Chief, that's why we have our young ones. They don't seem to mind having to climb up and down those ladders. And, as far as the rest of us are concerned, the exercise keeps us strong."

"What about the sick and the old ones? Do they ever make it down?"

Friend-of-eagle started to laugh, "If they do, they never make it back up again. That's why you have old man, Tsetse-fly, living in your village. You know the story. The poor man dreamed about taking a bath in the creek one more time, before his death. And, he got his wish. He managed to make it down and get into the water, but he couldn't make it back up again. Now you have to take care of him in the village. I don't mean to laugh, but that's exactly what happened." He continued to chuckle.

Chief Salamander joined in on the laughter and then suddenly became serious. "I need to talk to you. I meant to come see you first thing this morning, but a lot of things have been happening. I've been too busy to come see you, until now."

"I can tell this is going to be a serious matter. Come. Let's go into my humble home. Are you hurt, because I haven't made it to any of your meetings? Your council meetings never pertained to my clan, only to things within the Tyuonyi walls." He continued to talk, as they walked into the house. "Here, please sit on my favorite bear rug. Two-sparrows-singing, can you get Chief Salamander something to drink?"

Two-sparrows-singing approached Salamander with open arms. "It's so good to see you, Chief Salamander. What a pleasant surprise. How are you, and Little-acorn? What makes such an important man climb up here to see us? Is Little-acorn ready to have her baby? I've been told that she looks so pretty and happy, now that she's pregnant."

Chief Salamander started to answer, as he hugged her. "It's also good to see you. Little-acorn is doing fine, thank you. She told me to be sure to send you her love. I think I saw your kids playing near the kiva. They look healthy and appear to be growing so fast. Little Black-hawk is so big, I hardly recognized him."

Friend-of-eagle broke into the conversation. "I've heard a lot of drums lately. Something must have happened. You came to talk to me, because something is wrong, didn't you?"

Two-sparrows-singing offered their canteen to Chief Salamander. "Here, please have a drink of water before the two of you get to business. I'm sure the climb up here has made you thirsty."

"You're so kind. Thank you. I do need a drink." He took the canteen from her hands, but before taking a drink, he studied the etchings carved on the gourd. "Who made this beautiful canteen?"

"I did, a very long time ago, when I was but a young man. I'm glad you like it. Please, have a drink. I don't want my chief to faint from dehydration." He jokingly added, "I wouldn't want to have to carry you down the long row of ladders."

"That's terrible. What an awful way to treat our chief." Two-sparrows-singing gave her husband a look of disapproval.

Chief Salamander started to laugh. "Don't worry, I don't mind. Being family and a friend, is much more important to me than being anyone's chief. But your husband is right. I better drink before I start to get dizzy and light-headed." He took a few gulps. "Very refreshing, thank you. Friend-of-eagle, you carved some of the same symbols on your canteen that Jopin carved on his. Look, you included the spinning sun and the symbol of the Great Migration, among your other etchings."

"I guess we all did, didn't we? Our clan leaders would instruct us to carve those symbols which would make Great Grandfather happy. I have a strange feeling you're trying to tell me something."

"Yes, you're very intuitive. The reason you've been hearing drums lately, is because the time has come for us to continue on with the Great Migration. Tyuonyi will evacuate in three days. I have come to inform you that your clan needs to decide if your people will join us or not. I know this is a very short notice, but—"

"What? The drums have been beating for a few days, and you finally decided it was time for you to come and tell us about it? No, Chief Salamander, we will not join you on your journey. We'll stay right here, close to the mountain gods, where they have graciously taken care of our every need. They and Great Grandfather will certainly continue to take care of us, just like they always have.

I'm very disappointed it took you so long to come and let us know what has been happening. Are you sure you consider us your family and friends?"

Salamander knew he had upset his close friend. He hadn't meant for it to come out so direct. "Of course I do. I too am sorry, but it hasn't been that long, although a lot has been going on. We didn't know about the evacuation until late last night. I meant to come see you first thing this morning, but the people haven't given me a moment to myself. There are so many details involved. We have to get the entire village ready to evacuate."

"But you just agreed. The drums have been beating for the past few days. Haven't they been beating because of the evacuation? Why didn't you send one of your messengers to come talk to me? You could have sent someone."

"No, I could not. This is something I had to personally do myself, because there are too many things to discuss with you. I had to do this myself. Please let me explain. I sent one of my messengers to invite you to the council meeting. Didn't he tell you it was very important for you attend?"

"Yes, he did, but like I said before, your meetings hardly ever have anything to do with us, and it appears I'm right, once again. This evacuation has nothing to do with me, nor does it have anything to do with the members of my clan." He looked at his wife who had intentionally remained silent.

"Friend-of-eagle, don't do this. Please listen. The Great Migration has everything to do with you. Let me tell you about how Jopin—"

"Jopin," he interrupted. "Jopin is nothing more than a spoiled old man who has always had too much to say about the affairs of your village. Why do you allow him to make all of your important decisions? We have too many sick people living up here who can't possibly make it down those ladders. Do you want me to throw them over the edge? That will get them down there, so they can join you on your Great Migration. If they don't die from the fall, they surely will die from your trip out of this canyon. Old man Jopin has lost his mind. We have several old people here who have lost their minds as well. Perhaps we can send all of them out of here with Jopin."

"Friend-of-eagle, I haven't had time to come see you. I've been dealing with people just like you, ever since last night when the decision was made to evacuate and join the Great Migration. You must listen. Let me tell you about the things that happened these past few days. Please give me the courtesy of hearing me out." Friend-of-eagle listened intently, allowing him to continue.

Chief Salamander started by telling about the Chiefs' Pow-Wow at Chaco. He mentioned, "Jopin had been against the evacuation, just like you are right now, but Jopin took matters into his own hands and went on a prayer quest." He told them about the things that happened on Jopin's prayer quest, about Knee-nose, about how the village rebelled against the decision to evacuate, and finally, about the hole cut into Jopin's head. He became very emotional and excited as he spoke about the various gods in Jopin's visions.

Friend-of-eagle became noticeably uneasy and anxious, when he heard about the destruction of the village.

"Is there anything wrong? The vision of the gods-of-wrath and the destruction of the village, may sound pretty crazy, but this is the vision the gods gave Jopin."

"No, Chief, it's not that I don't believe you. A vision is a vision. This vision reminded me about this recurring dream I've been having. I approach this wise old eagle, but he turns his head away, as if he's mad at me, and then I wake up. It's interesting how Jopin's vision is similar to my dream. His vision is about a giant lion-eagle, who is so mad at the village. It flies high above the clouds and drops a large egg on it, destroying everything. Excuse me for interrupting you. Did Jopin have any other visions?"

"I'm glad you interrupted me, because it's very difficult to interpret dreams and visions. That's why we have the council of elders review them. In Jopin's case, the entire village was there when he woke from his deep sleep, after the hole was cut into his head. He then told us about his visions. You might be right. His visions may somehow be related to your dream. But to answer your question, yes, he had two other visions. The god of darkness came to take him away, but Jopin recognized his lies and yelled for him to get away from him." Chief Salamander took in a deep breath and then continued. Tears came to his eyes, even before telling about the next vision. "This is the best part. Great Grandfather appeared to Jopin." Chief Salamander was visibly in awe, as he recounted the vision about the pure light, and especially how all of Jopin's faults became visible in the light. He told them about Jopin's conversation with Great Grandfather, just as if he had been there himself.

Friend-of-eagle couldn't control his emotions anymore. "That's why the large eagle in my dream is mad at me. Living up here has turned me into a proud man, thinking that I have it better than the rest of you living down, below in

Tyuonyi. That's why I haven't come to your meetings. I have been too important to climb down those ladders. Yes, Friend-of-eagle was too proud to come to your meetings. And it isn't just me. We have become a stiffed-necked people living up here, where we can look down on everyone. Chief, please forgive me. I even rubbed it in your face just a few minutes ago, when I first greeted you." Friend-of-eagle raised his eyes up towards the skies, as if in prayer. "Great Grandfather, please forgive me. I haven't been living, as the least of your people.

"As Jopin mentioned, Great Grandfather is always ready to forgive everyone, no matter what. But you should know. It isn't just you who feels this way. These visions of Jopin's have touched everyone, revealing faults and weaknesses in each and every one of us. We're all guilty of pride and not living in accordance to our creator's commands. I guess I don't have to tell you that Jopin is now willing to evacuate Tyuonyi and obey Great Grandfather." Chief Salamander then informed him, once again, that all of these events just came to a peak last night. Thus, he hadn't had any time to come talk to them or to anyone else. "Just like Great Grandfather gave Jopin the choice to step into the light or not, everyone will likewise have to choose whether to join the Great Migration. Why don't you think about the things we've discussed today? We had our first meeting this morning. There was a lot of concern and discussion about what to do with the old and the sick of the village. You and your people may want to attend the meeting tomorrow, so you can see for yourselves what this evacuation involves. Please invite anyone whom you may want to come and participate in the discussions. There are so many problems to address."

Friend-of-eagle looked relieved. "Thanks for explaining everything. I can see why you haven't had time to come see us, until now. I'll talk to my people, and hopefully, some of us will attend your meeting tomorrow."

On With the Migration

The drums continued to call the people to gather in front of the main kiva. Chief Salamander was busy talking to the people who had arrived early; however, his eyes kept looking away from them, towards the Tyuonyi entrance. Curious as to who would be showing up, he anticipated that several of the thieves and promiscuous women would come. He wondered if Friend-of-eagle had convinced some of the other members of the Eagle Clan to attend. Little-acorn walked over to greet Wild-flower and her friends, as they approached the gathering place. The villagers followed her example, also hugging and greeting these people, doing their best to welcome them to the village. Chief Salamander excused himself from the small talk and joined his wife in welcoming his exiled brothers and sisters. The drums stopped beating, but Chief Salamander instructed them to continue. "Not everyone is here yet." He nervously looked around, searching for Friend-of-eagle. The mood was like a feast day, where everyone portrayed an atmosphere of happiness, understanding and brotherhood.

The drums continued to beat for a very long time. This gave the people time for some intense conversation. They all made sure to personally visit with Jopin and Bright-sunflower, and with their chief. Some of them asked Chief Salamander if the Eagle Clan would attend.

"I'm hoping they will."

It didn't look like they would be showing up, so Chief Salamander decided to start the meeting. He motioned for the drummers to stop. "I'm so happy and honored that you have all taken the time to come to this meeting. This evacuation will be very tough for all of us, but as we can all see, it has brought us together as brothers and sisters. I'm sure Great Grandfather is pleased with us today."

The people weren't paying attention to him, so he stopped talking. Some of them even walked away from him. At first, Chief Salamander found it quite rude, but then he worried if he might have offended them. He then saw members of the Eagle Clan joining the others. They were all hugging and laughing. Everyone appeared so happy and excited. Chief Salamander quietly gave thanks to Great Grandfather and then hurried over to greet his neighbors. "Friend-of-eagle, as you can see, we, all of us, are so happy to see you."

"Chief, we're honored to join you, but I apologize for being so late. It took a long time for all of us to climb down those ladders, especially the older ones."

Chief Salamander couldn't believe it. "You mean to tell me everyone climbed down all those steps?"

"Not all of us, we had to leave four or five behind, the old ones who have to be supervised, for their own protection. They acted like they were being held captive up there. I guess they are, but only because they will harm themselves if they ever do get out. I thought only a few of us would want to come and represent the rest of the clan, but they all wanted to attend. As a matter of fact, they demanded to be here. I hope Jopin is well enough to see everyone. They all want to visit with him. It was tough leaving old man Happy-song and Purple-lily-squaw behind. They're so sweet. I wish I could say the same thing about old man Sour-apple. Warrior Strong-hold is watching them. You know about these old ones, they're always trying to escape."

"Yes, we have similar ones, ourselves. I'm so honored all of you have come. I speak not only for myself, but for the entire village. Look at how happy and excited everyone is to see you. I attempted to start the meeting, but they all wanted to wait for the Eagle Clan. Their commotion kept me from proceeding with business."

"That makes me feel good. Thanks for the welcome, Chief. Perhaps you better start the meeting, since you've waited long enough. We can visit afterwards."

"Yes, let's begin." He motioned for the drummers to once again, announce the start of the meeting. They beat their drums very fast and then immediately stopped. Chief Salamander publicly expressed his gratitude for everyone attending and offered a prayer. "Great Grandfather, we thank you for creating the Great Migration, which is already wiping out pride and prejudice from our village and replacing our bad traits and habits with peace and harmony."

Wild-flower had a very big smile on her face, for she was so proud of her nephew, the chief. Chief Salamander then gave a short summary of the events that had led up to the decision to evacuate Tyuonyi and join the Great Migration.

Friend-of-eagle expressed his concerns about the old who require continual supervision. When asked about how they would get down those ladders, he told them he had thought about how he could wrap them in elk skins, and then carefully lower them to the bottom with leather slings.

Some of the villagers mentioned they were still not certain about joining the Great Migration, using the excuse they would remain behind to care for the very sick. They would join the villagers after their loved ones had passed on to live with their Almighty. The meeting remained friendly and informative. Even Thunder-head and his two friends refrained from making any negative remarks. Some discussed the criteria they had used to determine what they must carry out, such as seeds, dried food and hunting materials. Some discussed how they were building stretchers to carry the old and sick. Others described how they were constructing harnesses, so their dogs could carry some of their possessions on their backs.

The meeting could have continued on throughout the entire day, but Chief Salamander cut it off, so they could have time to visit. Some wanted to talk with Jopin and Bright-sunflower. Others just wanted to catch up on family affairs.

"Mother, are you home? I've come to visit. Father, I want to know how you're feeling."

Bright-sunflower cried out in joy as she pulled the door covering over to one side. "Double-eagle, is that you? I can't believe it. Great-grandfather must have listened to my prayers." She put her arms around his neck, tightly hung on to him, and then kissed him on both cheeks, cradling his face in her hands. With her tears rolling down, she cried out in disbelief, "What are you doing here? I thought we would never see you again."

He nervously looked around, searching the room. Not seeing Jopin, he gently returned his mother's hugs in an effort to console her. "I'm so happy to be here with you. Double-eagle cleared his throat and prepared to ask what he was afraid to hear. "I came to find out about my papa. Is he; uh, where is Papa?"

His words reminded Bright-sunflower of how it all started, just a few days ago, when Deer-tracker came looking for his grandfather. She remembered her comments. "Grandson, do you not care to know about how your grandma, Bright-sunflower, is doing? Why is your grandpa so much more important than your grandma? Do you love him more than me? Do you not have enough love for both of us? Well, perhaps I should turn myself into a little bird and fly away, so you won't have to share your love between your grandma and your grandpa anymore."

Her silence saddened Double-eagle, making him believe she must be in shock. He gently put his hands over hers. Are you okay? "Mama, what's wrong? Where is Papa? I came too late, didn't I? Is he gone? I came as fast as I could, but I guess it wasn't fast enough."

Bright-sunflower realized what Double-eagle had been asking. "No, no, your father is fine, as fine as can be expected. He should be back soon. There were so many people coming to visit with him, he finally got some time to himself. He's behind his favorite rock. I didn't answer you right away, because you reminded me about how this nightmare started, just a few days ago, when Deer-tracker came asking for his grandfather. I'm fine and your father is fine. Please sit here on the bear rug. You must be starving. Let me get you something to eat and drink. We need to talk. There are so many things I need to tell you. I don't know where to start. Why didn't you bring Painted-feather and the kids with you?"

"Mama, tell me about this nightmare. Does Papa need me to go help him? Where is this favorite rock of his, so I can go find him?"

Bright-sunflower looked surprised, and then started to giggle. "I don't think he needs your help. Your father has been constipated. He finally got some private time to himself, to take care of his personal business, if you know what I mean."

Double-eagle let out a big sigh of relief, and then started to laugh. She joined in on the laughter, but only for a short time, until she started telling him about how Deer-tracker had come looking for his grandfather, just a few days ago. She handed Jopin's canteen over to him, and motioned for him to have a drink, and to eat some jerky. She started talking, while Double-eagle drank water. Double-eagle had to stop her, because she was talking so fast. He couldn't understand what she is saying. It was as if she had to blurt out the whole ordeal, all in one breath.

Jopin heard voices as he approached his home, "Double-eagle, is that you? I can't believe it. We were wondering if we would ever see you again."

Double-eagle quickly stood up to greet his father. "Papa, I've been so worried about you." Looking at his father's new headdress, he carefully gave Jopin a giant hug. "Mother was just beginning to tell me about the things that have been happening around here. Are you all right? How's your head?"

Bright-sunflower looked surprised. "How's his head? I haven't told you anything about his head, yet. How do you know about his head?"

"Chief Salamander sent for me. He had Warrior Quick-foot come get me. Quick-foot refused to tell me why he was bringing me to see you, until after we left Tsankawi. Why is everything such a secret? He said Chief Salamander was very appreciative of your sacrifice. Father, I've been so worried and afraid you would be dead and buried by the time I got here. I feared I would never see you again."

"No, Son, I don't think I'm going to die, not for a while, anyway. Did Quick-foot tell you anything about your brothers? Will they also be coming to see us?"

"I don't think so. He made it clear there would only be enough time for me. Apparently, Chief Salamander thinks the others live too far away. Does he really believe everyone can get ready to leave in four days? I'm afraid I'm the only one who gets to see you. How is your head? Are you in a lot of pain?"

Jopin removed his headdress and showed Double-eagle what Medicine-maker had done to him. He tried to act strong in front of his son, by joking about the hole in his head and about his unique headdress. "Yes, Chief Salamander is serious about the very short time he has given us to get ready. We already used one of the four days, so we'll be leaving in three days. The chiefs decided that any more than four days would bring about a lot of confusion and chaos. Just look at you. You're here, when you should be preparing your family for the Great Migration. Tsankawi is evacuating, isn't it?"

"I've only heard rumors. I think they have been waiting to see what Tyuonyi is going to do."

Jopin realized this was the only time he had to talk to his son. "I have so much to tell you. Great Grandfather has spoken to me. It's important for me to tell you what he has said. I've already told the village. It's too bad your brothers aren't here, because it's so important." Jopin told him about his conversation with the god of darkness and then with Great Grandfather. He reminded Double-eagle about being the least of everyone. "It's of utmost importance. I believe this may very well be Great Grandfather's greatest commandment."

Double-eagle noticed Jopin was uneasy and introverted to the point of appearing guilty. "Father, you act as if you have done something wrong. What is it?"

"Son, I'm so ashamed of myself."

"Why, Papa? How can that be? Look at what you have just done for your people. You sacrificed yourself for everyone, just like Knee-nose. You're now a most sacred member of Tyuonyi."

"Knee-nose was sinless. I could never be as sacred as he. He sacrificed himself for me, so I could live. Knee-nose stood with me, as Medicine-maker started to cut into my scalp, letting me know everything would be all right. He was there with me throughout the time Medicine-maker worked on me. And then, when I started to wake from my visions, I could see him jumping with joy, because I was going to be all right. You know how deer jump up, with all four legs in the air? Knee-nose would jump over a star, stop to look at me, and then jump over other stars. The brightest star was the sun, the spinning sun. Knee-nose wanted to let me know he was jumping with joy, because I survived. He died so I could live. Most interesting, he wanted me to know the sun was indeed spinning. Knee-nose became my spiritual advisor. He will now help me become the person Great Grandfather wants me to become. I also know he'll be there when my time comes to greet Great Grandfather at the end of my life."

"You have proven that you are the least of your brothers, just like Knee-nose."

"No, Great Grandfather showed me how I've been just the opposite. I used to see the dirt on others' hands, but was blind to the filth on my own hands. That pure light revealed mud, so thick and dirty, that I couldn't recognize my own body under all that crud. And now, I just had the best visitors I could possibly have ever asked for. I mean, other than you. Our neighbors, the thieves and promiscuous women, all wanted to come and visit with me. That was so touching."

"Why, Father. What was so touching about that?"

"I'm the guiltiest of all. My sins are greater than all the others. You see, as the longest serving elder of the council, I've used pride in enforcing the laws set forth in the village, one of which was not to allow these people to live here alongside our children and respectful citizens. These people know I was responsible for keeping them out of Tyuonyi. Yet, they genuinely came to see me. This very act, in itself, proves they are the least of everyone. I, on the other hand, now know how my soul is stained with a lot of pride and prejudice. I explained to Deer-tracker that having more than his brethren, demonstrates one has not taken good enough care of his brothers and sisters. Yet the thieves and promiscuous women, whom apparently have more material possessions than the rest of us in the village, are truly the least of our brothers. They came to see me, their enemy. My prejudices have caused the entire village to sin against these people. When I proposed to ban these people from living in Tyuonyi, I not only portrayed myself, as being better than them, I caused everyone else to likewise judge themselves as being greater than these people."

"But Father, these people have committed grave sins. It's not right to steal, or to trade sex for favors. How can you say you're not better than these people, those sinners?"

"Son, you're correct about their sins being bad. I'm not saying it's acceptable to do what these people do. We know better than to commit such acts against Great Grandfather. However, these people will someday stand before Great Grandfather's pure light, just like the rest of us. I'm sure that, if they choose to go with Great Grandfather, they'll be welcomed with open arms. Of course, they'll have to walk through the light of purification, where Great Grandfather will purify them with the fire of his love."

"But you're acting as if your sins are worse than theirs. How can that be?"

"I'm not really comparing my sins to theirs. If Great Grandfather can accept us, just the way we are, then we should also accept these people. We don't have to accept their sins. They're our brothers and sisters, just like the other members of Tyuonyi."

"I'm getting confused."

Jopin had trouble figuring out how to respond, so Bright-sunflower tried to explain in a different way. "I think your father is trying to say that Great Grandfather wants us to live with him forever, in the after life. We, on the other hand, tend to think only of what is happening now in our lives, where we tend to compare our sins to others'. As you just noted, stealing and promiscuity are major sins. But from what I understand, Great Grandfather looks at our readiness to change, so we can successfully be purified for him. Our standards in the skies will be much stricter in comparison to here on Earth. Yes, Great Grandfather will forgive our sins, whether they are small or serious. I think your Papa is saying we must be willing to change our ways, our bad habits, and our negative traits, the very core of our nature, and become the least of our brothers. Jopin, is that what you were trying to say?"

Jopin was pleasantly surprised. "Well yes, you expressed it so clearly. How were you able to think of all of those things? I'm the one who just came back from seeing Great Grandfather."

"I, my dear husband, am the one who has always been tuned in to you. I'm tuned in to you too, Double-eagle. You're right about sins. However, Great Grandfather expects us to work towards becoming like him. He accepts the sinner, but not the sin."

Jopin chimed in. "That's exactly right. The one thing I learned from Great Grandfather is, he doesn't want us living with him if we believe ourselves to be greater or better than anyone else. We may think we have something better than our brother, be it possessions, personality, status, common sense, or intellect. It can be almost anything. These things are worthless in Great Grandfather's eyes. The problem starts when we think or believe we're better than someone else, because we have something they don't. That is very serious, especially in the afterlife. So, I learned two very important lessons from Great Grandfather. The first is, we can't think we're greater or better than anyone. The second is, it wasn't necessary for me to have a hole cut into my skull."

Jopin explained about how Great Grandfather sends his gods to teach his people religious ceremonies and prayers, so they can learn how to listen to his voice. "Great Grandfather wants us to silence our thoughts and open the ears of our minds. We can then learn how to identify his voice and listen to his messages."

Double-eagle and Bright-sunflower reached over to touch and hug Jopin, letting him know they loved him. They told him they were so proud of what he had done for his family and for his people.

Double-eagle told them he would spend the night. Bright-sunflower would now have enough time to tell her son about all of Jopin's experiences. Jopin and Bright-sunflower would also get a chance to catch up on the latest news about their grandchildren and relatives. They tried to make the most of every precious moment, because they knew this very well could be the last time they would ever be together.

Footsteps could be heard approaching the door. "Mama and Papa, we came to visit. Great-hawk just arrived. He brought you some elk meat. Papa, I know it's your favorite." Brilliant-pebbles continued to talk as she walked through the doorway. "Oh my goodness," she yelled out. "When did you get here?" She rushed in and gave her brother a giant hug. Great-hawk and Deer-tracker followed closely behind, carrying some choice pieces of meat. The room was very crowded. However, they all managed to fit in the small area.

Great-hawk hugged Bright-sunflower, handed her the meat, and then moved over to talk to Jopin. He approached his father-in-law, and carefully hugged him. "Papa, I've heard about everything that has happened to you. I feel so terrible, because I wasn't here to help. How are you feeling?"

"I have a little pain, but I'll soon be fine, especially now that my family is together. I'm especially happy that my daughter has her husband back. I bet Deer-tracker is happy. He has done so much to help me through this ordeal."

"He can't stop talking about his wonderful grandfather. You mean so much to him. He wanted to do something special for you, so he brought some heart, liver, and kidney meat to cook. He told me how much you love these meats, diced together and fried with onions."

I'll cook them up for you, right now, Grandpa, so you can regain your strength."

Great-hawk laughed. "You see, he's so excited about everything you did for him these past few days. We appreciate everything you and Mama have taught him."

Jopin held out his hand to stop Great-hawk. "Wait. You're thanking me? No. Deer-tracker is the one who deserves the thanks."

Great-hawk had that proud, parent look on his face. "Perhaps, I'm the one who should thank you. Deer-tracker has matured and grown so much, in just a few days, because of you."

"You're right about Deer-tracker. He's certainly very special and mature for his age."

"Deer-tracker and Brilliant-pebbles told me about your recent sacrifice and experiences. I don't even know what to say, other than to feel honored to be your son-in-law. I'm sorry I wasn't around, but I'm glad Deer-tracker helped. However,

I'm now here and ready to do whatever I can. The three of us are all very proud of you."

Great-hawk stopped talking to greet Double-eagle, who was walking towards him. "Double-eagle, what a pleasant surprise. You couldn't have picked a better time to come visit. Are Painted-feather and the kids with you?"

"No, they had to stay behind." He told them about how Chief Salamander had sent for him, and how he had rushed to see Jopin.

Deer-tracker decided to cook his dish outside, over a campfire, so as not to create more heat in the already tight living quarters.

Brilliant-pebbles reminisced about her childhood. "Do you remember the time when we got lost?"

"Just wait one moment, Sis. We were never lost. I knew exactly where we were going. You were the one who was scared, so you decided we were lost."

"That's not true. You were the one who took us in the wrong direction. We walked further and further away from Tyuonyi, but you just won't admit it. Like all men, even after all these years, you just don't want to admit we were lost. Please repeat after me, "Sister, I took you in the wrong direction. I'm sorry I got us lost." She had this big teasing smile on her face.

He burst out laughing. "Don't you ever give up? Every time I see you, you try to get me to admit I was lost. As I recall, you couldn't have your way, so you started to cry, and there was nothing I could do to quiet you down. We were almost at the bottom of the canyon near the big river. It's an easy walk from the river to Tyuonyi. But no, you wanted us to stop going down the canyon, insisting we retrace our footsteps and go back up the very steep canyon."

"Retracing our steps and walking up the canyon did get us back home, didn't it?"

"Kind of," Double-eagle answered with a big smile on his face. "We retraced our steps back up the canyon until it got dark. As a matter of fact, it was too dark. We couldn't see anything, and certainly, not our footsteps. So I guess, I can finally admit, thanks to you, at that time, in complete darkness, we were lost."

The never-ending feud between brother and sister had once again, become the main topic of discussion. It was interrupted when Deer-tracker appeared with the heart, liver, kidneys and onions dish. Bright-sunflower noted she had been lax in her duties. "I should have been making us some bread to eat with this delicious meal."

"No, Grandma, I brought some from home. Mama had made a pile of flatbread for when Papa would return. The meal is complete and ready now. I cooked enough for all of us, but I would like for Grandpa to have the first taste, so he can get his strength back. Mama said this combination of organ meat is very nourishing. It will make you feel better, Grandpa." The aroma of the freshly cooked meat filled the room.

"I already feel better. What would I do without my grandson, without any of you? I'm so lucky, because the best family in all of Mother Earth is right here. Great Grandfather has been so good to me, to all of us." Jopin raised his hands up to the skies, offered prayers of thanksgiving, and then signaled it was time to start eating.

Deer-tracker handed him a piece of bread. Jopin carefully folded it and then stuffed some meat into the fold. He took the first bite. "This is absolutely incredible. You all must have some of this delicious meat." They took turns filling their flatbreads.

Great-hawk managed to once again, move in close to Jopin. "Papa, I want to let you know I'm here to do whatever I can to help, especially getting us ready for the evacuation. Even with everything you had to go through, you made time to talk to Deer-tracker. Thanks for helping me and Brilliant-pebbles teach him in the ways of Great Grandfather."

Aware that Deer-tracker might have told his father about everything Jopin had taught him, Jopin decided to explain. "Double-eagle, I have an apology to make. I told Deer-tracker about the legend of Spirit-boy and about the Shrine of the Twin Lions. It was not my intention to tell him. It just happened. I know you had planned to talk to him at an appropriate time, but it just came out. I'm sorry."

"No, Papa, I don't mind at all. There's no reason for you to apologize. I'm very appreciative. That boy adores you, just like Brilliant-pebbles and I do. So thank you. The timing turned out to be perfect. I had planned to take him to the Shrine of the Twin Lions this summer. However, as we all know, we won't be here. Great Grandfather must have given you that special time together for a purpose. We're very thankful for everything you have done for our son."

"Papa," Brilliant-pebbles interrupted. "There's a rumor going around about Thunder-head. Do you know anything about what he's doing?"

"No. What is he doing this time? Nothing would surprise me about that man and his two friends. What have you heard?"

"The neighbors were saying that he wants to build a raft to carry the old and sick across the big river."

"That doesn't make any sense. Chief Salamander said we would be camping, a little ways north of here, along the Frijoles Creek. Does Thunder-head want to take them in the opposite direction? I had this hole cut into my head, because of all of the unrest they caused, and now he doesn't want to join the rest of us on the migration. Well, enough said."

"I heard he doesn't want to join the Great Migration, well not with the rest of the village, anyway. He will stay behind and help care for the sick, until the end of summer, when the river runs low. At that time, he will take them across the river. He knows of a place near the base of Black Mesa, where he intends to create a new village."

Jopin rubbed his chin. "If he doesn't believe in the Great Migration, then why doesn't he just stay here, in Tyuonyi, and take care of these people in their homes? He doesn't have to take the old and sick across the river, even when the water level decreases."

"Perhaps, he's afraid of the giant egg," Bright-sunflower said. "He would still have to go somewhere if he's afraid of the fire."

"You're probably right. I guess he's so anxious to become chief, he will do whatever it takes."

"That means he must first learn how to be the least of his brothers." Deer-tracker wanted Jopin to know what he had learned. "He'll have to care for the old and the sick."

Jopin was proud of his grandson. "Yes, but he may have ulterior motives. A person does not plan or work to become a chief. His people make him their chief."

Bright-sunflower looked disappointed. "My husband, you don't know if Thunder-head's motives are sincere or not. His intentions may be good and proper."

"I just wanted Deer-tracker to know that motives must be pure. You're right. Thunder-head might become the least of his brothers by helping these poor people."

"Are you going to tell Chief Salamander about this?"

"No. He will find out soon enough, and who knows, it might only be a rumor."

Jopin asked Double-eagle if he knew where Tsankawi might be going. Double-eagle didn't know. "Perhaps Father Sun will guide all tribes to one common area. I believe we'll go west, over the mountain. It would be nice if we would all meet somewhere along the path and be together again."

"Yes, that would be ideal for our families."

The meal was quickly consumed, but the conversation continued into the middle of the night. Great-hawk, Brilliant-pebbles, and Deer-tracker did not want to leave, but they decided to give Jopin and Bright-sunflower some private time with Double-eagle. They kissed and hugged Double-eagle, and walked out.

Double-eagle spent the night, and reluctantly left early in the morning. Jopin and Bright-sunflower tightly hugged each other, as they watched their son walk away. Double-eagle turned to look at them one more time and sadly, waved goodbye as he disappeared behind the Tyuonyi walls. Jopin and Bright-sunflower stared out into the direction where they could no longer see him. Would this be their last goodbye?

Bright-sunflower's tears ran down her cheeks. There were so many emotions, yet she managed to get some words out. "I'm so proud of our children."

Jopin positioned himself in front of Bright-sunflower, and looked directly into her eyes. "I'm so grateful for you, my little bird who has threatened to fly away. You were afraid I might no longer be here to take care of you, but you'll have me around a little longer, headdress and all. I love you very much. Great Grandfather has blessed me with such a good wife. Our children have grown to become so wonderful, because they had such a loving mother who took the time to care and teach them right from wrong. You taught them the meaning of love. They have so many of your traits."

"I'm so grateful for you too, even though I've been so hard on you these past few days. We'll have to go thank Chief Salamander for bringing our son back before we leave. He didn't have to do that. We have a good chief, don't we?"

This reminded Jopin about the same question his grandson had asked him just a few days ago, when they were up on the cliff. "Grandpa, we have a good chief, don't we? Is Chief Salamander a servant to his people?" Jopin then realized that most of what had happened to him was because he did not want to trust and support his chief. Jopin had become too comfortable in his beautiful homeland. He had credited himself for making Tyuonyi into such a good place to live. After all, he was the most experienced elder of the council. This in turn, led to his pride and prejudice. He now knew that much of what he had done throughout his life was wrong. And now, all of these events had occurred. If only he had voted on the fourth day, as Chief Salamander had requested. Instead, he got himself stuck, halfway up that cliff. He had Knee-nose sacrificed, and he now had a hole cut into his head. This would certainly continue to bring him pain for who knows how long. All of this happened because he was not willing to obey Great Grandfather, as proposed by Chief Salamander. Jopin stopped thinking and finally acknowledged, "Yes, we have a very good chief. He is a true servant to his people."

"Jopin, I know this evacuation and migration will be very hard on us. Our sacrifices will be many, but I support you. I'm now ready to leave Tyuonyi."

"Jopin found it interesting that Bright-sunflower used the word, support. He gently grabbed hold of her hand. "Let's go visit our chief. We have to thank him for the many things he has done for us and for all of his people. I want to thank him for teaching me a very important lesson."

"What lesson?"

"I should have been supporting him and following his example. Instead, I challenged him, refusing to accept it was time for us to pack up and join the Great Migration. I wanted proof that the sun was indeed spinning."

"So, how did Chief Salamander teach you a lesson?"

"He came back from Chaco in full support of his chief. But I, the oldest and proudest of Chief Salamander's elders, wanted proof. Chief Salamander didn't get the support he deserved from me. Instead, I caused delays by not voting, wanting Great Grandfather to give me the answer I wanted. I'm very ashamed of my actions. I intentionally lied and disobeyed Chief Salamander, and even became judgmental of him. I had heard he was visiting one of the promiscuous women. I was so determined to prove him wrong, I became blind to the fact that Wild-flower was his aunt. He was right, and I was wrong. He was trying to pass on Great Grandfather's commands, but I refused to listen. Instead, I had Knee-nose sacrificed, and then I had this hole cut into my thick skull. It was not until Knee-nose showed me the spinning sun, that I finally believed it was time to evacuate and follow Father Sun. I was then ready to support Chief Salamander and finally ready to join the Great Migration, in accordance to Great Grandfather's commands. Come, let's go see our chief. It's time for me to support Chief Salamander, to obey Great Grandfather, and to continue on with the Great Migration."

"But what about me, your wife? When will you start obeying me?"

Jopin gave her a big smile, put his arm around her, and then quickly became serious. "I specifically disobeyed you, my good-intentioned wife. You knew what would be in my best interests, when I did not. My record of obeying you has not been very good, but I will try harder. I promise."

"I know your intentions were good, but let's see if you have learned your lesson. I know of something you must do, other than go visit Chief Salamander."

"What is it?"

"Follow the spinning sun. I hope you won't want more holes cut in your head, just so you can be assured the sun is still spinning. It would be nice if all of us could see the sun spinning. I don't want you to be the one who is responsible for everything that will happen during our migration."

"Neither do I. Doesn't legend say our ancestors followed the sun until it stopped spinning? I assume we will all be able to see it spinning. Let's pray that Great Grandfather will order Father Sun to start spinning on the first day of our evacuation. We certainly need his guidance."

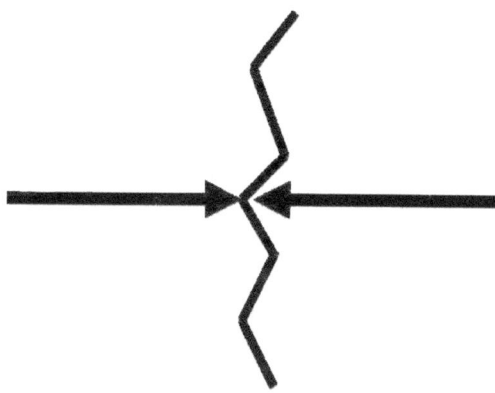

Second Thoughts

Deer-tracker couldn't stop thinking about the things that had happened. His grandpa had a hole cut into his head, and the entire tribe would now be leaving Tyuoni for good. He picked up his bow and arrows, and headed for his favorite hunting area. Several rabbits ran ahead of him, from bush to bush, but Deer-tracker didn't dare aim an arrow at them. He knew he might never walk these grounds again, nor would he ever get to accompany his father to the Shrine of the Twin Lions. No wonder why Grandpa had to go on his prayer quest.

The time and attention his grandfather had given him, while up on top, had been so special. He walked under the shadows of the tall cliff. A large rock protruded out of the ground, right ahead of him. Deer-tracker laid down his bow and arrows, climbed up the rock, and sat on a narrow, flat area on top. Instead of enjoying the beauty around him, he looked with sadness at the surroundings he would be leaving behind: the clear-water stream, the challenging cliffs and canyons, the village, and of course, his fond memories of hunting, fishing, and playing in his favorite places.

It sure would have been nice if Jopin could sit there, right next to him. He wondered if his grandfather would ever fully recover. There were so many other questions Deer-tracker would like to ask him. Although it had only happened once, Deer-tracker already missed the time he sat with his grandfather, just the two of them, in front of that campfire. No one could tell a legend with such feelings and emotions, like his grandpa.

Deer-tracker lay down on the rock, stretched out his arms and legs, and pretended to be Spirit-boy, like in the legend. With his eyes closed, he imagined Great Grandfather reaching down from the skies to lift him up. That must have been a most wonderful feeling. Deer-tracker soon fell asleep.

Brilliant-pebbles happened to be walking in the same area. She saw the bow and arrows on the ground and immediately knew something had happened. She looked up and saw Deer-tracker's arms and legs overhanging out the top of the huge rock. The cliff stood much higher than the rock, so Deer-tracker must have fallen off the cliff and landed on the rock.

Brilliant-pebbles climbed as fast as she could, and was taken aback by the look on Deer-tracker's face. It was so calm and peaceful. She was jolted with his appearance as he lay there motionless. Brilliant-pebbles reached over to straighten his hair.

Still half asleep, Deer-tracker tried to open his eyes, but the sun was too bright. "What's a happening, Mama?"

"Deer-tracker, don't move. You're going to be all right. I'm so happy that you're alive. Don't move. I'll get some help."

"No, Mom."

"Don't say that, and don't move. I better go for your papa."

"No, Mama."

"I can't go for help, if you're going to move."

"No, Mama. I'm not going to die. I was just talking a nap."

"Way up here? Why?"

Deer-tracker got up and made room for his mother to sit next to him. "I miss Grandpa, so I was imagining some of the things he told me, when we were up on top of the cliff."

By now she had her arms tightly wrapped around him. "You can't believe how happy I am, right now." She leaned away from him and gently lifted his chin. "Why do you miss him? He's not gone. Medicine-maker said your grandpa should have a complete recovery."

"I know. It's just that I climbed up here and started to think about everything we will miss when we're gone."

"Tell me what you will miss the most."

"Everything. I'm afraid of what we may never see again, like our home, and also of the things I still haven't seen, like the Shrine of the Twin Lions. Papa said he would take me there, this summer."

"Your father told me the very same thing. He so much, looked forward to taking you there. I guess Great Grandfather had other plans for us. You do want to please him, don't you?"

"Yes, more than anything. That's why I was lying on this rock. I wanted to hear his voice."

"There are many more, safer places, where you can listen for his voice, other than up here."

Deer-tracker laughed, and then Brilliant-pebbles started to tickle him.

"No Mama. It's too dangerous up here."

"Do you hear what you just said?" She squeezed one of his shoulders. "Can you promise me never to take a nap on top of this rock, or any other dangerous rock, again? You could've fallen off."

Deer-tracker smiled. "It's that I miss being with Grandpa. I wish he could teach me how to talk to the gods, like he does."

"Then why don't you get off this rock and go ask him to teach you. You know where to find him."

Deer-tracker nodded. "I'm sorry I scared you."

"It's fine now. Don't ever do that again." She slowly looked around to see why he would even want to climb such a treacherous rock. "This is a special place. It's not only peaceful, but the views are beautiful."

"I wanted to visit some of my favorite places, before we leave."

Bright-sunflower grinned. "That's what I was doing, when I saw your bow and arrows lying there on the ground." She wanted to tell him again about how she had reacted to seeing him there, but she decided not to. "Your uncles and I used to play here when we were growing up. I also wanted to visit some of my favorite places, one last time."

Chief Salamander had worked hard to get the villagers to follow him out of Tyuoni. Although they had finally agreed to evacuate, he knew Jopin would be the person credited for convincing them to do so. It had been important for Salamander to be viewed as a sound, confident chief, but most of his recent actions had exposed his weaknesses, which included his dishonesty and lack of integrity.

The elders had seen him panic under pressure. He even lied about Jopin's resignation. Then, the people had rebelled against him. He tried to regain their loyalty by leading them in a prayer-dance, when Jopin's head was being cut open, but it didn't seem to make much difference.

Rumors had already started to spread about Thunder-head and his followers. They would not join Chief Salamander on the migration, but rather, cross the river to a place near the base of Black Mesa. This was especially troubling, because Chief Salamander would once again, be portrayed as a weak chief. The task of leading his people to the unknown would be impossible, without their complete trust.

Chief Salamander needed more time, so he had to make up a reason to delay the evacuation, just long enough to regain control of his people. He could give Jopin a little more time to heal, and it would be proper for Little-acorn to have her baby in her home, before having to climb out of the treacherous canyon. His people would certainly find favor with such a compassionate chief, and perhaps consider his excuses as proper and humane.

Bright-sunflower could hardly wait to hear about the pregnancy. "Little-acorn and Chief Salamander, may we come in?" She always got excited with the arrival of a new baby.

The two women immediately started discussing the pregnancy, so Chief Salamander used the opportunity to talk business. "Jopin, I need your opinion."

"You must have hundreds of thoughts going through your head about tomorrow. But Bright-sunflower and I are ready to support you. We'll be right there, walking alongside you and your people."

"I've been thinking. Little-acorn will be having her baby any day now, and you still need more time to heal. What if we delay the evacuation by a few days?"

"Absolutely not." Little-acorn stood up straight, as if she had grown taller, and faced Salamander. "I don't know about Jopin, but I refuse to be your excuse for a delay. Tyuoni has lots of other people in worse condition than me. Why aren't you concerned about them?"

"I am, but Jopin just taught us how family must come first."

Jopin moved up to agree with Little-acorn. "Family must come first, but as chief, your family includes your entire tribe, not just Little-acorn and certainly, not me. Yes, I still have pain, and we are old, but both of us are ready to support you."

Chief Salamander looked nervous. "You once asked why I was in such a hurry to join the Great Migration, especially since the sun hadn't even started to spin. I was thinking about that. We don't really have to leave at this time. I'm sure you can better recover right here, and we should have our baby with us by then."

Jopin had seen his chief act like this before. What might Salamander be up to this time? "You're acting like you've changed your mind. So you're thinking of delaying the move? As Little-acorn just mentioned, I also, won't allow you to use me as an excuse for any delay, not even for a short time."

Chief Salamander picked up a stick to stoke the fire, even though nothing was burning. "I don't think I'm ready to lead us out of here."

Bright-sunflower nudged Jopin to say something.

"Of course you are. I almost forgot. That's why we're here. How can we ever thank you for everything you have done for us? It was so nice of you to send for Double-eagle. We got to see him one more time, before we leave this place. Also, I've heard nothing but praise about how you led everyone in prayer for me, as Medicine-maker cut into my skull. I can't think of a better chief than you."

"That was the least I could do for you and Bright-sunflower. The villagers and I are very grateful for what you did. You sacrificed yourself for your tribe."

"We're very grateful and especially moved by your thoughtfulness, but you shouldn't treat us any different than anyone else in your tribe."

"I'm sure everyone would approve. They're all thankful for what you have done for them, for us. You're very special and sacred. The people would expect nothing less of me, than to do everything to make you as comfortable as possible."

"I want to be comfortable, but not special. The only thing I now wish for is to serve my wife and family. Chief, the time has come for me to devote the rest of my life to Bright-sunflower and the kids. You'll need to find someone else to replace me. That's how I can be comfortable."

"But I need you now, more than ever. This will be the most challenging part of—"He stopped talking, because of the look both Bright-sunflower and Little-acorn were giving him. Realizing they didn't agree with what he was about to say, he approached Jopin and gave him a giant hug. "Thanks for everything you have done for me and the tribe. You're the only person who has spent your entire life in village government. We're all indebted to you. You'll certainly be missed."

"Thanks. I will also miss you, as well as the rest of the elders. I'll no longer be part of the council, but I'm still part of the tribe."

Jopin's lifetime of service had finally come to an end. Chief Salamander would have wanted Jopin to have retired before now, but the timing couldn't have been better. Chief Salamander's lie about Jopin wanting to retire would no longer be untrue, so perhaps he could get Thunder-head and his followers to believe he had finally removed Jopin from office. Such information might convince them to support Chief Salamander, after all. "Have you heard that Thunder-head, Fat-man, and Little-boy are planning to take some of our people across the river, to an area near Black Mesa?"

"What would they do over there?"

"Spite me. They're not happy with me as their chief, so they believe they can do better than I."

"About the migration?"

"Yes. They supposedly have promised some of the old and sick ones that, unlike me, they will care for them, and even carry them out of here."

"You also offered to carry the old and infirm out of here."

"I told them to decide whether to carry their loved ones out of here, or leave them behind."

"Is that why you're thinking about delaying the evacuation?"

"That's part of it. It would give me time to get to the bottom of what they're scheming. They—"

"What? I can't believe you. You're not concerned about me and the baby, you're worried about you. I'm tired of getting hurt by your insensitive actions." Little-acorn started to sob. "Maybe I should walk out of here with the rest of the tribe. You can remain behind to take care of those enemies of yours. I don't need you. No one does. Who needs a selfish chief?"

Jopin grabbed Bright-sunflower by the arm. "We have to go. Just wanted to thank you for bringing Double-eagle to see us. Thanks for everything."

Bright-sunflower pulled her arm away from Jopin. "Could the two of you go outside for a while? I need to talk to Little-acorn."

The two men uncomfortably walked out.

Bright-sunflower started to tell Little-acorn about some of the things she had gone through with Jopin.

"Why are you telling me about Jopin? He's not at all like Salamander."

"Because of the humungous pressure the move has put on him. He even had a hole cut into his skull. I think Salamander must be under the same kind of pressure, even more so, because he's responsible for everyone. I'm just asking you to consider what the migration has done to our men."

"The migration has been tough on him, but the things he has done lately, are inexcusable. I should never have married him."

Jopin didn't want to get involved in his chief's personal life, so he used the opportunity to continue the conversation they were having before the blowup. "You specifically told the people that no one would force them to join the Great Migration. The choice belonged to each individual, and not to you or the elders. Stand by your ruling. Let whoever desires to remain behind, remain behind."

Chief Salamander said he was worried about how to handle the unforeseen hardships they may encounter on the migration. The unrest of the village had made him question the timing of the move.

"Isn't this why we have to join the Great Migration, to rely more on Great Grandfather and less on ourselves?"

Jopin and Bright-sunflower left Chief Salamander and Little-acorn's house. "Did you get to tell her about—"

"Shh." She grabbed hold of his arm and hurried him along, to keep him from saying anything. Jopin thought they were going back home, but Bright-sunflower motioned for him to head towards the village exit.

"Where are we going?"

"I want to see the old house one more time, before we leave this place, that is, if you can make the trip up there."

"Looks like Chief Salamander might be delaying the evacuation, so we'll have other opportunities to go see your old house, or anything else you might want to see."

Bright-sunflower stopped walking. "You don't understand, do you? Little-acorn was really hurt by his remarks. There's no way she will allow him to use her pregnancy as an excuse to delay the evacuation, not after that comment. You don't treat a woman like that, especially a pregnant one. No, we'll be leaving tomorrow."

"I'm glad you were there to comfort her. She has been good for Salamander and for Tyuoni."

"Talking about Tyuoni, you surprised me when you told Chief Salamander he would have to find someone else. You have made me a happy woman, many moons later, but still, very happy."

They slowly walked up the steep path, and climbed up to enter the old place. The top of the opening knocked Jopin's headdress off his head. Bright-sunflower picked it up and helped him put it back on. "Did it hurt?"

"No. Medicine-maker must have known something like this would happen. We'll have to tell him it has already protected me."

They sat on the floor and looked at the canyon below, through an opening. The dust had accumulated so thick, the cave appeared to have a natural dirt floor, instead of plaster. Bright-sunflower remained quiet for a while, and then started to tell him about the good times she had experienced growing up. "That's where mom would hold me, when I would cry. She taught me how to cook on those flat stones. Papa gave me a scolding here in this spot. They slept against that wall, and I slept on this side."

Jopin allowed her to continue talking. He always wondered why they lived in a cliff dwelling, instead of in Tyuoni. Her father had, for some reason, felt more comfortable in the cliff dwelling, than in the village, even if they were one of the few families left, living up there.

"Didn't your father think his family was alone and unprotected?"

"No. He would say no one knew they were up there, so the village was in more danger of an invasion than we were. He was a proud man, not needing the village for anything."

"He sure brought up a wonderful daughter."

"I've heard that one before. What do you want from me?"

"You've given me everything, and even more than I could have ever dreamed of. I meant what I said back there. I want to take care of you."

They continued sitting on that dusty floor, holding hands and admiring the canyon below. Jopin finally broke the silence. "Weren't you going to show me the area where you used to play?"

They climbed down the ladder to a path below the cliff houses. She pointed out the various cave dwellings she would climb in and out of, with her friends. She then mentioned how she would like to visit another area.

They followed the path along the base of the cliff, where they met up with Brilliant-pebbles and Deer-tracker. They had all gone there for the same purpose.

The drums started to beat. "Looks like Chief Salamander is calling everyone to assemble for the last meeting, before tomorrow. We better get going."

A large crowd had already gathered around Chief Salamander. Jopin started to work his way towards the front, but Bright-sunflower stopped him. "Have you already forgotten? You no longer have to join him as the senior elder."

Chief Salamander usually had to call the people to order, but something was very different this time. They were ready for the meeting to start. Thunder-head and his friends stood close to the front, as if in full support of their chief. Not only had Thunder-head remained silent, he appeared to be obedient and respectful of Chief Salamander. Jopin wondered if Salamander had talked to him. Little-acorn couldn't be seen.

Chief Salamander thanked everyone for attending, and then announced that, as hard as it was to believe, the evacuation would take place in the morning. They would follow the path along the creek, to the top. Once on top, they would follow the spinning sun to their new homeland. Because this was a religious event, they would walk in prayer to the beat of the drums. He then raised his hands and prayed for Divine guidance. They certainly needed prayer. There was very little time left to make their final preparations for their journey.

Chief Salamander acknowledged everyone's efforts in helping to assure all would be assisted and cared for. The warriors had been preparing slings and stretchers to help carry those unable to walk on their own. He then asked if they knew of anyone who had been overlooked. "We don't want to leave anyone behind that wants to go."

It was almost as if no one dared to speak up.

Being that this would be the last day to prepare for the evacuation, Jopin had expected a lot of discussion, even rebellion, especially from Thunder-head and his followers. Everyone remained quiet and subdued.

There could've been countless reasons for their lack of participation. Thunder-head and his followers could have finally chosen to join Chief Salamander or perhaps, most of the people were planning to abandon Chief Salamander and join Thunder-head.

Bright-sunflower whispered into Jopin's ear. "Do you think they're letting Chief Salamander know they won't be joining him tomorrow? Look at how everyone appears so sad, even the chief."

Jopin raised his shoulders.

Chief Salamander also wondered why they remained so quiet, but he dared not ask. Instead, he reviewed what would be happening in the morning. "My warriors have already set up camp for us, just a little ways past the path leading to the Eagle Clan. You can wait here for everyone, or you can go ahead and find yourself a special spot on the camp. We have plenty of stretchers to carry all who can't walk out on their own. If possible, I would like us to be out of here by the time Father Sun is directly over our heads. Are there any questions?"

The people remained quiet.

"Very well, then. See you here, tomorrow morning."

Chief Salamander slowly walked home, not knowing who would be joining him in the morning.

Grandma's Bowl

Great-hawk, Brilliant-pebbles, and Deer-tracker had been packing since early in the morning. Brilliant-pebbles noticed how Deer-tracker had remained so quiet and serious. "Are you already missing this place?"

Deer-tracker couldn't stop worrying about his grandfather. There was no way the hole in Jopin's skull could have healed enough for him to make this journey. Instead of getting the proper rest required, his grandfather would be pushed to exhaustion. What if he got worse?

"No. I'll be fine."

"You're worried about your grandpa, aren't you?"

"Grandpa's in no position to be traveling. The journey will wear him out. How will he keep his wound from getting dirty and infected? I'll have to help him through all of this."

Great-hawk came in closer and stood in front of Deer-tracker. "It makes me happy that you have so much love for your grandpa, and it's good for you to want to take care of him. Your mother and I will also do whatever we can. We'll look out for each other and help Grandpa and Grandma, because we love them. A lot of things can happen as we travel out of this canyon. We don't know what awaits us. Accidents can happen." Great-hawk paused for a moment. "Don't blame yourself if something does go wrong."

"The path out of the canyon is treacherous. That's why I'm worried about him. Grandma too, but she's not hurting and trying to heal."

"Why don't you go over and help him. Don't worry about us. I've carried game, a lot bigger and heavier than this. He needs your help more than we do. I should've sent you over there earlier. Besides, we'll all be traveling together. Once we're out of here, we can all help each other."

Deer-tracker hurried out across the plaza, and entered his grandparents' home. "What's a happening?"

Bright-sunflower put her hands on her hips, and slightly rotated them to one side. "You know what's a happening. Everyone in the village must have everything packed and be ready to go by mid-morning. You're empty handed, so aren't you helping your papa and mama carry something?"

"That's why I'm here, to help. How do you feel Grandpa?"

"Fine, thank you. You better go back home and help your Mama and Papa. Everyone will have to carry something, especially the stronger ones, like you."

"They told me to come here and carry things for you."

"That's very thoughtful of them, but your mama needs your muscles. Doesn't she know Chief Salamander will send two of his warriors to carry our stuff? She needs you more than we do."

"She already knows about the warriors, but she still wants me to carry some of your things."

Bright-sunflower moved closer to Deer-tracker. "You're her only child. I'm sure she needs your help. Your family has belongings for three people. There are only the two of us, and we don't plan on taking much."

Deer-tracker thought about how he had been their only child, the only one who had lived past childbirth. He hadn't thought about how most of his friends had four or five siblings, until now. Grandma was right. His parents would have to carry everything themselves, but they were also younger and stronger than his grandparents. Perhaps he could share his time between his grandparents and parents. "I already helped them pack. Almost everything is ready. She said she was strong and healthy enough to help Papa carry everything. I will not only help you pack, but also carry some of your things. Grandpa's in no condition to carry anything."

"I'm already feeling better. Tell your mother not to worry. The warriors will carry our stuff. All I have to do is walk out of here on my own two feet."

"Doesn't that hole in your head hurt?"

"Not like it used to. Your papa was gone for a while. I'm sure you both have a lot of catching up to do."

"Grandpa, I want to be with you. They want me to be here. Papa said we would probably be doing everything together from now on, anyway. You see, my wish is coming true."

"What wish?"

"To be with you as much as possible. Mama understands, but she said I should make sure you don't mind."

"Aren't you taking any personal belongings?"

Deer-tracker smiled. The Great Migration would give him the opportunity to spend a lot of time with his grandparents. "I'm only taking my bow and arrows, and my canteen. They're outside, leaning against the wall."

Jopin ruffled Deer-tracker's hair. He then walked over to get a better look at outside activities. Almost everyone could be seen either checking their loads, or carrying possessions down ladders to the ground level. Chief Salamander walked around, greeting his supporters. "There are a lot of people out there, all ready to join him. I can't believe how much they're carrying. He seems to be doing everything right, but I still worry about his motives."

"Who are you talking about?"

"It's nothing. Didn't realize I was thinking aloud."

Deer-tracker, always being tuned into his grandpa, knew about these comments and remarks. Could his grandfather still be worried about Chief Salamander, even after everything the gods had revealed to him in his vision? "Grandpa, the people have been out there all morning. Let's go join them?"

"Chief Salamander said it would be better if we waited here. He already has a place set up for us at the campsite, so there's no hurry. If you're not going to help your parents, you might want to go out there and play with some of your friends."

"No, Grandpa." Deer-tracker couldn't even imagine being anywhere else. He looked around. All of their possessions were still in their proper place, hanging on the walls or properly placed throughout the dwelling. Bright-sunflower held a small bowl, with a lid on it, up against her belly. It had been made from a gourd. She would protect whatever was in it, wherever they went. He wanted to ask her about it, but he decided not to. "You're leaving everything behind. Don't you need any of these?"

"We plan to travel light," Jopin said. "That way, we won't be a burden to anyone. Those people out there, will start leaving things behind once they realize how heavy everything is. We don't need any of those things. Great Grandfather will take care of us. Isn't that the purpose of the Great Migration, to rely less on ourselves and more on him?"

"I don't know." Opportunities to discuss things like this were what Deer-tracker had been anticipating. He wanted to know about the true purpose of the Great Migration, but his grandpa's mood was more important at the time. "Is anything wrong?"

"No, not at all. You're here with me. What else could I possibly want?"

"You look so sad."

Jopin started telling him about how he had fought the evacuation because of Chief Salamander, but Bright-sunflower interrupted.

"Everyone looks sad. We're in our first day of our exodus."

"Grandpa's still worried about Chief Salamander." Deer-tracker turned to face his grandfather. "Aren't you, Grandpa?"

"Don't want to talk about it." Jopin turned towards Bright-sunflower, afraid she was ready to scold him.

Bright-Sunflower addressed Jopin. "You're no longer an elder, so it's not your concern. Let's enjoy the little time we have left, together."

This had been the second time Jopin had refused to talk about Chief Salamander. Bright-sunflower clearly didn't like for Jopin to talk about the chief. If it worried his grandpa, it worried him, as well. Deer-tracker would get to the bottom of this and find out if he could do anything to help. Why would Grandpa still be worried about Chief Salamander?

Families continued to assemble in front of the main kiva. The men had made stretcherlike platforms consisting of two long poles, with short logs tied crosswise, inbetween the poles. They had placed their possessions on top of the cross logs. A person, usually the husband, would hold up one end of the poles, and someone else, an older son or even his wife, would walk behind, holding up the other end. If she couldn't help him because she carried a baby or small child in her arms, he would hold up his end and drag the other end behind. Some of the men or older boys carried a pole across their shoulders, with pouches tied to each end of the pole. Smaller bundles had been attached to the backs of their dogs.

Leashes tied around their dogs' necks, ensured they wouldn't run off.

Chief Salamander met each family as they approached the meeting area. They carried large piles of possessions wrapped in heavy animal skins. The skins would be used for warmth and shelter. Also carried were pots full of dried food, seeds, medicinal plants, and other necessities. Only a few of the old or infirm had been carried out. Many of the sick men and women, even the younger ones, used crutches made from tree branches, with leather tied around the areas where their armpits would rest.

The women cried as they greeted each other. The dogs whined, not understanding their situations and certainly, not approving of how they were tied down. The crying made Chief Salamander uneasy, so he had his warriors escort them to the campsite. "Give them something to eat or drink, and try to keep them distracted." He also asked the drummers to get started. "Have them join you in prayer."

He didn't want them to change their minds. Chief Salamander wished they could've camped further away from Tyuoni, but it was the only area along the creek wide enough to occupy the entire tribe. It would be too tempting for them to walk back home, but there wasn't much he could do about the location.

However, he could turn the campsite into a place of song, prayer, brotherhood, and sharing. The warriors had already started to roast some deer and turkey. They also had a generous amount of corn brew, strategically offered at Chief Salamander's request. He wanted to make this first day an occasion of happiness and celebration. This would probably be the last time they would be drinking corn brew, at least until they would settle into their new homeland.

Father Sun had traveled halfway across the sky. The steady flow of families had finally stopped. Chief Salamander stood by himself, looking at a big, empty plaza. He hadn't expected this moment to bring him such mixed feelings. A big knot gnawed at his insides. The day had finally come, and everything had worked out as planned.

Chief Salamander looked up, wondering if he would ever see Father Sun start to spin. He had told the elders about his vision at Chaco. His story about the eagle and all the other winged creatures following the spinning sun, was not true. He had made it up to get the elders to support him with a positive vote. Great Grandfather might now punish him and never allow him to see Father Sun spin.

How would Chief Salamander ever get the people to follow him if he didn't know where to lead them?

Thunder-head approached him from behind. "Chief, I want to thank you for everything and also, to wish you luck on your journey."

Surprised, Chief Salamander jerked to one side, and then started to laugh nervously. "Didn't see you there." After regaining his composure, he blurted out, "It's sad that we all aren't leaving together. Take care of yourself, and of the others. I really appreciate your coming to talk to me."

"Even though I've given you a hard time, I will miss you."

"Same here. So you'll be taking the rest of the tribe across the river?"

"I like the area where the Tesuque creek joins the river. Our elderly probably can't travel any further than that."

"I'm actually relieved they will be with you. They're lucky to have you."

"And you're lucky to have Jopin. He's the only one in the whole tribe who got to meet Great Grandfather face-to-face. I should've never teased you about him."

"Don't worry about it. There's been a lot of truth to the things you've told me." Chief Salamander decided not to tell him about Jopin no longer being a member of the tribal council. He took one more look around. "Everyone who's joining me has already gone to the campsite. I better go join them. Tell everyone that I wish them the best."

They hugged each other. Thunder-head walked away. Chief Salamander took one last look around. Two of his warriors had arrived to pick up Jopin and Bright-sunflower's possessions. Great-hawk, Brilliant-pebbles, and Deer-tracker were also there. Chief Salamander waved at them and then walked over to check on Little-acorn.

"Hi. How are you feeling?"

"I'm fine. You were gone a long time."

"The people finally stopped coming. Even Thunder-head came to say good-bye."

"I saw the two of you hugging. Let bygones be bygones."

He gave her a big smile. "That sure was nice of him. How about you? Have you started to have any contractions?"

"I wanted to have the baby while you were out there socializing."

"Are you trying to tell me something?"

"Your people are more important than your wife."

"Like I just mentioned, they never left me alone."

"You sure left me alone. You could've had one of your elders take your place, at least for a while. You don't care about me, and you certainly don't care about the baby."

"I've been under a lot of stress, didn't think—"

"You? I'm the one who's about to go into labor, the one who doesn't have a husband who cares enough to even check on her. But don't worry. It won't happen for a few more days. Wouldn't want the baby to interfere with any of your plans."

"This ordeal has been very—"

"You're selfish. This evacuation has taken over your life. I predict you will no longer be chief by the time we finally reach our destination."

"What?" He hadn't expected those words to come out of her mouth.

"You don't deserve to be chief, much less a husband or father. Something is truly wrong with your behavior. Your actions will ruin you. I so much hope the baby will be born dead."

"What a terrible thing to say."

"You're the one who's acting terrible. I don't want my baby to come into a home where he's not wanted."

"That's not true." He tried to put his arms around her.

"Go hug Thunder-head. You care more about him than about me or your baby."

"We better go. Where are the guards? They were supposed to have been here by now."

"Go ahead and ignore what I'm telling you. I'm used to it. They already took my stuff, while you were busy trying to impress your wonderful people. They helped your wife more than you did."

He grabbed the few remaining things and helped her put the papoose carrier on her back. "This is heavy."

Glaring at him, she snapped, "It has everything the baby should need, everything except a father."

They begrudgingly walked out of their home, past the village wall, and then followed the path upstream, past the place where the thieves and promiscuous women live.

"Are you looking for her?"

"For whom?"

"The one who spent the night with you, up on the rock."

He abruptly stopped, faced her, and started to grab her by the shoulders, but then quickly pulled away. "There was no woman there. I told you the truth. Just looking to see who will be going with us and who will remain behind."

"So you're wondering if she will be going with you?"

He shook his head in disappointment, and started to walk away from her. She quietly waddled behind. They approached the area where members of the Eagle Clan were still lowering the last of the old and infirm down the long series of ladders. Several of the young men were there to help. Others watched from a distance, observing how they lowered those less capable. They were wrapped in heavy elk skins, being carefully lowered with ropes from above. A man would balance their bodies from below, guiding them as they were carried down the ladders.

Several women rushed to offer their assistance to Little-acorn. One of them took the heavy papoose carrier from her back. The others pampered her as they held her by her arms. Wild-flower approached, saying she would be honored to take care of her and the baby when it arrived. She mentioned that thanks to Chief Salamander, she would no longer practice her old ways. Instead, she planned to become the best aunt that little baby would ever want.

Chief Salamander remained behind until the last member of the Eagle Clan had been lowered. He then escorted them to the campsite, where most things appeared to be happening as planned. Plenty of food and drink had been made available for everyone. The drummers and prayer dancers had successfully kept the people focused on the purpose of the exodus. The men had been helping set up shelters for the night. Most importantly, many communicated to him how they believed they would be obeying Great Grandfather by going through this phase of the Great Migration.

Little-acorn had captured the attention of most of the women. They fussed over her and offered assistance in their own ways. Jopin also had a steady flow of people coming to see him, wanting to once again hear more about Great Grandfather and the gods. Chief Salamander didn't mind the women coming to see his wife, as it allowed him to take care of other matters. However, he was becoming jealous of all the attention the villagers were giving Jopin.

Almost everything had gone as well as could be expected, but Chief

Salamander still worried about the unknown. They would make the steep climb up the canyon in the morning. He dreaded any problems they might encounter. The narrow path would be steep and treacherous, especially in the area where the loose gravel would make it difficult to keep both feet firmly on the ground.

He complimented everyone for joining the Great Migration, and then attempted to prepare them for the challenge ahead. "Tomorrow will be a tough portion of our journey. If you can make it up this canyon, you can probably make it through anything."

He then took the elders and some of the warriors aside to assess what had happened, and to discuss how to assure success on the following day. They soon started to talk about the hundred and twenty people who had remained behind with Thunder-head.

Chief Salamander should have been happy, because over six hundred had chosen to join him. He still became upset upon hearing some of the names who had not joined him. He wanted to believe they had stayed to care for their loved ones and not necessarily to support Thunder-head, but he knew he had given them more then enough reason not to trust him. "Forget about them, they're traitors and besides—" He realized how easily these people could turn on him as well, if they began to see his true feelings towards Thunder-head and Jopin. They may side with him regarding Thunder-head's past actions, but to be jealous of Jopin? No. After everything Jopin had done, the people would never side with Salamander. He'd better control his behavior if he wanted to win them back.

Exodus

Deer-tracker awoke at sunrise, ready to partner with his grandparents. Today, he planned to carry the load of one of the warriors and walk alongside his grandfather. He would then have plenty of time to ask Jopin about the secret of communicating with Great Grandfather and the gods.

Brilliant-pebbles heard him walking around. "What are you doing up so early. Couldn't you sleep last night?"

"Sure did. What about you?" Deer-tracker gave his mother a long gentle hug. "Where's Papa?"

"Chief Salamander had him leave early, way before daybreak. He wants us to have enough to eat when we get to the top. Your father left a long time ago, in the dark."

Deer-tracker quickly looked around. "Did they get someone to carry Papa's things?"

"No. That's why I asked if you got a good night's sleep. You'll have to help me carry our things."

"Mama, you shouldn't have to carry anything heavy. I'll drag our possessions behind me, like Papa did, yesterday."

"He only had to pull it over flat ground. The climb out of here will be too steep for that. It'll take both of us to get this heavy load all the way to the top. Don't worry. We'll do it together."

"Mama, you should probably walk with Grandpa and Grandma. I'm sure they'll need your help."

"Chief Salamander's taking care of them. I'll help you. I mean, you will be helping me by taking your papa's place."

Lean-to shelters had been set up wherever space allowed. People started crawling out of them as the morning grew brighter and the people started talking. Some had lit campfires. Others were getting water from the stream. "Grandma's at the stream by herself. Grandpa's usually the first one up. He's probably hurting."

Brilliant-pebbles studied Jopin's body as she spoke. "He'll need to rest a little longer if he is hurting. I'll go see if Mama can use some help. She'll know about Papa. Don't bother your Grandpa." Brilliant-pebbles hurried over to join Bright-sunflower. Deer-tracker stayed behind. His eyes continued to study the shelter where his grandfather lay.

Jopin finally did sit up, giving a little moan.

"Grandpa, are you alright?"

"Yes, of course. Where's your grandma?"

"She's at the stream with Mama. They're washing up."

"Have you already had something to eat?"

"No, but I did save some food from last night. Mama told me to save it for today."

"We didn't raise no dummy for a daughter. I'm very proud of her and also, of you."

"Thank you. Grandpa, now that we'll be spending a lot of time together, could you teach me how to communicate with the gods? You're the only one who has ever heard Great Grandfather's voice."

"We both know that's not true. But, I'll tell you about the things I do know." Jopin looked up for a while. "We'll have to look for an opportunity for you to go on your vision quest. That's when you might get to hear his voice."

"I may never get that opportunity. Papa left early this morning to go on a hunt. I'll have to carry Papa's things."

"Good."

"Good? I'll never have any time with you."

"Sacrifice is good. That's exactly what Great Grandfather expects of us. Do you think your father enjoys being away from his family, especially now? We will all be eating because of him. He, like you, will find favor with Great Grandfather."

"Did you wake up your Grandpa?" Brilliant-pebbles gave Deer-tracker a questioning look.

"No Mama, he woke up on his own."

Jopin held up his hand. "Deer-tracker's not bothering me. He's not only my grandson, he's my best friend."

Deer-tracker moved closer to Jopin and hugged him, keeping his eyes fixed on his mother.

Chief Salamander wanted them to start climbing as soon as possible, so he encouraged those who had risen early to get going. He suggested that the old and weak members of each family walk directly in front of the younger, stronger ones. Thus, those requiring help would get it from their loved ones.

Quite a few of the people had already left when the warriors arrived to help Jopin and Bright-sunflower. They walked over to the path, and got in line. Jopin insisted that Bright-sunflower walk in front of him. The two warriors stood behind Jopin. Deer-tracker and Brilliant pebbles got in line, behind the warriors.

They had only walked a short distance when the line stopped moving. And, it took a long time before the line started to move again. The loose sand and gravel had presented a barrier for the old and weak.

A good portion of the morning had passed, and most of the villagers were still standing around at the campsite, waiting. Chief Salamander worried that some of them would get discouraged. They were camped so close to home. He had done all he could do, so he went back to check on Little-Acorn.

"What's the problem? No one's moving."

"It's too treacherous, especially for the old ones, exactly what I feared."

"Can't you do anything?"

"I sent two warriors to go help, but the path may be too narrow to let them by. They probably had to climb the mountain to get past them, and then climb back down to the path in front of them."

People kept showing up to ask Chief Salamander if he knew what the problem could be. The conversation kept repeating itself.

"Do you know what the problem might be?"

"The path is too steep and treacherous for our old ones."

"How do you know?"

"I went up there the other evening to check it out, and even I had difficulty."

"So why are we going up this way?"

"Do you know of a better way?"

Little-acorn had heard the same story over and over again. She soon started to believe his explanation about the other night and even felt badly about her accusations. But she knew better than to tell him anything.

She saw him looking at her. "What are you looking at?"

"I'm worried about you. The strain might cause you to have the baby. This is no place to have a baby."

Raising her brow, she said, "I'll be all right."

It took the entire day for all of them to make it to the top. The women flocked to Little-acorn's side, asking if she had started to feel any contractions. Jopin and Bright-sunflower appeared worn out, but quite satisfied with their accomplishment. The people showed signs of satisfaction, accomplishment and relief.

The campsite had been set up among tall ponderosa pine trees, on flat ground. Like the previous day, the warriors and hunters had prepared a campsite to welcome everyone to the smell of game roasting over a cooking fire. They even had containers full of water awaiting them.

Chief Salamander had been too busy to see if Father Sun had started to spin. He looked up, but it was too late. The stars would soon be appearing. Father Sun always traveled across the sky from east to west, so Chief Salamander figured he couldn't go wrong by taking them west. He knew of a spring, not too far away. He planned to make it there on the next day.

With their bodies exhausted but their belly's full, the conversations died down. The campsite soon became quiet. The fires slowly burned themselves out.

Father Sun welcomed them the following morning. Chief Salamander didn't rush them, for the trip to the spring wouldn't take more than half a day. The ascent would still be steep, but the path would be wide and not as treacherous. Once again, he sent the hunters ahead to prepare a new campsite with food. Water would be plentiful at the spring.

The entire tribe slowly climbed the mountainside. Deer-tracker remained optimistic, walking alongside his grandparents. Jopin gave out a faint moan.

"Grandpa, what's wrong. Are you hurting?"

"I'm fine." He smiled. "Just thinking aloud."

Deer-tracker didn't find it so funny. "About what?"

He pointed to the top of the mountain. "I asked myself if I really wanted to climb to the top."

The warriors looked up, moaned, and then started to laugh. "That is a big mountain."

Bright-sunflower leaned close to Jopin. "You can't fool me. What's wrong?"

"That's a long ways up there. That's what's wrong."

"I never saw you look up. Why won't you tell the truth?"

Jopin whispered, "My head hurts every time I take a solid step. I don't want the kids to worry."

"I'll ask Medicine-maker to take a look at you."

The entire tribe continued to slowly make its way up the mountain. All of a sudden, Little-acorn bent over hugging her stomach.

Chief Salamander rushed to hold her up. "Take a deep breath. I'll find a place for you to rest. Is the baby coming?"

"Yes. You will be a daddy soon."

"We can camp right here. I'll ask the warriors to bring us some water."

"No. Let's continue. The walk helps me to think of something else, other than having the baby right here."

Chief Salamander put his left hand under her elbow, and hugged her with his other arm supporting her back. "What will you need, so I can have it ready?" He looked around as if he were lost. Sweat started to bead down his forehead.

She smiled. "I've never seen you so nervous. I packed the things I'll need. Don't let the warriors carry them away from me. Can you ask Honey-bee and Wild-flower to walk with us? The baby might decide to come before we get there."

Chief Salamander whispered her wishes to one of the warriors.

Wild-flower pushed Chief Salamander aside. "I'm taking over. You have a tribe to lead."

He went to the other side of Little-acorn and grabbed her by the arm. Looking over at Wild-flower, he said, "The tribe is doing a good job taking care of itself right now."

Honey-bee rushed in also, pushing Chief Salamander aside. "Don't worry Chief. We'll take care of Little-acorn."

Chief Salamander walked alongside Honey-bee. He tried to tell them what to do, but they let him know he wasn't needed.

At times, Little-acorn would stop, bend forward hugging her belly, but she always insisted they continue walking. They could finally see the campsite.

Honey-bee told Chief Salamander to stop. "Tell the rest of the tribe to go on to the campsite. We'll stay here, behind these bushes, away from everyone. I'll need a fire, water, and some privacy from all those people."

Chief Salamander ran off with the color drained out of his face. He quickly returned with a burning log, placed it on the ground, and started to break every dead branch around him.

"Salamander, slow down. The baby's not here yet. Take a deep breath. We'll take care of the fire. Now you can bring us a solid flat rock to place the water bowl on it?"

He looked bewildered, but he did manage to take a deep breath. He laughed nervously. Little-acorn called him over. "I can't believe you're acting like this." She gave him a big loving smile.

Chief Salamander gently kissed her on the forehead. "I love you so much. I'll be the best papa ever." He hoped she finally believed him.

"I love you too. You'll be a papa soon."

He finally prepared all the things Honey-bee had asked of him. Little-acorn's contractions continued thru sunset. Her water bag broke, and she soon delivered a baby girl. Honey-bee handed Chief Salamander his daughter. He gently kissed his baby as if she would break, lifted her up to the sky, and offered her up to Great-Grandfather. He then laid his daughter on Little-acorn's belly. "You have made me the happiest father on Mother Earth."

The people had expected to lose one or two of the weaker ones throughout this most difficult canyon. Instead, they now felt blessed with the newest addition to their tribe. This birth gave them an element of excitement, as well as hope for their future. Nothing but good had come to them since leaving their homes. They would probably remain there for at least another day, until Little-acorn got stronger. The extra time would help them to relax, give thanks, and pray for continued success, before resuming their trip up the mountain.

Deer-tracker finally had his first opportunity to ask his grandfather a few questions. But first, he wanted to see what Medicine-maker would be telling Jopin.

Medicine-maker removed Jopin's headgear. "Your wound is red and inflamed. Have you been using the salve?"

"It wasn't convenient to apply the salve while climbing up the canyon yesterday."

"You seem to have gotten some dirt in your hair."

"The dirt and sand kept falling on all of us, from above."

"I remember." Medicine-maker patted the top of his own head to demonstrate how Jopin should gently wash the dirt off. "Then put some salve on the clean wound."

Bright-sunflower said she would get some water and wash Jopin's wound.

"I'll get the water, Grandma." Deer-tracker ran off to the spring and then quickly returned with it.

Bright-sunflower took the water jug from Deer-tracker, started to pour some of the water on Jopin's head, and then applied the salve.

Jopin said he needed to talk to Deer-tracker.

"Here I am, Grandpa."

"Could you do something for me?"

"I'd be happy to do whatever you need."

"I want you to go play with your friends."

This statement shocked Deer-tracker. "OK." He then sadly started to walk away.

Bright-sunflower gave Jopin a questioning look.

"Wait. Let me explain. I'm worried about you. You're spending too much time with me and not enough with your friends. I've already told you everything you need to know. Sacrifice, but not for selfish reasons. Don't want you to end up like Chief Salamander. Fasting helps one to stop concentrating on our own needs and more on what Great Grandfather wants. Now, go find your friends."

"Sure Grandpa." Deer-tracker reluctantly walked away.

"Why did you do that? That boy thinks the world of you." She looked disappointed.

"That's why. He shouldn't."

Jopin didn't want to tell Bright-sunflower about his concerns. The pain and suffering had been worse than what he had led her to believe. His death would be too much for Deer-tracker to handle. Bright-sunflower would also miss him, but he felt she would be better prepared to handle such a loss, compared to Deer-tracker.

Salamander couldn't stop talking about their beautiful daughter. He told Little-acorn he would be the best father his daughter could ever have, which included being a good husband. Little-acorn had remained quiet and reserved, not even reacting to anything he had to say.

"What's wrong?"

It wasn't so much that she didn't believe what he had been telling her. The new baby had brought her more joy than what she could ever possibly imagine. She feared for her daughter's safety. Little-acorn had protected her baby, while inside her belly, but now, she felt helpless. "How can I protect her through this journey to who knows where?"

"What do you mean? I'll protect her."

"You can't. We're supposed to keep our baby inside until her skull has hardened. How can we keep all those evil spirits away from her?"

Salamander realized what she meant. "I'll be right back. Medicine-maker might be able to help."

Medicine-maker had been expecting a visit from his chief. "Congratulations, big Chief Daddy. I hear you have a beautiful daughter. Are both mother and daughter doing fine? I won't ask about you, because I know you're not."

"What do you mean?"

"Your face says it all. What are you so worried about?"

"We're worried about protecting our baby from evil spirits. A mother usually keeps the newborn inside a home until the skull hardens up, but we don't have such a place."

"I expected you to come visit me. Take this and put it on your daughter's head. She must wear it at all times." Medicine-maker handed him a small cap made from skunk fur.

Chief Salamander knew exactly how it would work. Skunk fur was known to repel evil spirits. He held it up to get a better look. "How did you get it to be so soft?"

"It took a lot of work. I had some skunk skins at home, but they weren't soft. We really don't need them to be soft, when we cover our moccasins with them, for ceremonial dances. I knew Little-acorn would be delivering soon, so I've been working on this piece since before we left Tyuoni. Oh, and here's a tiny medicine bag for her. Both of these items should be enough to protect her."

"This was so thoughtful of you. Please come with me to give them to Little-acorn, yourself. She's so worried."

"I'd be happy to do that, and I also want to give your baby a special blessing."

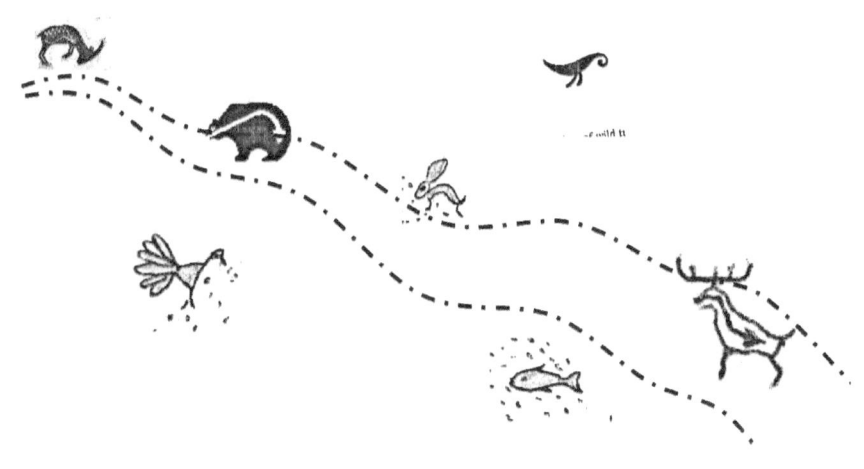

The Abundant Way

Their two-day rest came to an end when Little-acorn decided she could walk and carry her baby in the papoose carrier. Chief Salamander and Little-acorn had seen a white dove drink from the spring, so they decided to name their baby after the dove. Chief Salamander joked about how his daughter should have been named Little-skunk, because of her little cap. Little-acorn thought it would be a cute name, but inappropriate because the cap would only be worn for the first forty days of their child's life. The skunk cap would someday be handed down to the next baby born into the tribe.

They climbed the ridge to the Lake of the Mountain Gods, a beautiful pond fed by a spring. The wind sent ripples through the water, causing reflections of the tall aspen and fir trees to appear like gods dancing on the surface. Chief Salamander had wanted his baby to be born in this sacred place. They now approached the area with their newborn infant.

The Lake of the Mountain Gods blessed the entire tribe by giving them the opportunity to reflect on how Great Grandfather had cared for them so far. Not only had he protected them, he had supplied everyone with good health, pleasant weather, and plenty of food.

Chief Salamander felt especially proud about how he had successfully led his tribe out of Tyuoni. Having a baby on the trail helped him to be portrayed as a lovable, caring husband and father, making him the center of attention, instead of Jopin. Allowing Jopin to retire had turned out to be one of the best decisions he had ever made. He no longer had Jopin or Thunder-head to contradict him.

Life got progressively better. They descended the grassy slopes to the Land of Bubbling Springs, a huge volcanic crater, rich in water, wildlife, and vegetation. They became like children, enjoying the gifts Great Grandfather had given them. Instead of heading west, as Chief Salamander had planned, he led them from one watering hole or stream, to another, regardless of the direction. He wanted them to think of him as their most popular chief, ever. They spent the entire summer exploring the land, eating, and enjoying their good fortune.

The fish there were much larger than those in Tyuoni, so Deer-tracker and his friends enjoyed fishing the numerous streams and springs. Likewise, an abundance of grass had allowed them to grind the seed into flour. They had to do without corn, but Great Grandfather had supplied them with plenty of grass seed, which was just as good and nourishing.

Jopin wondered about Chief Salamander's lack of direction, but he wasn't quite ready to climb the western ridge. Any little motion would cause him extreme pain. His wound had become so infected, he kept his headgear on as much as possible to hide the swollen, painful bump.

Medicine-maker walked over to visit Jopin. "I've come to check on your wound. Have you been able to keep it clean?"

"I sure have. How are you doing?" Jopin did not want Medicine maker to see his wound.

"Fine, but I'm here to see how you're doing. Let's look at your head."

"I'm doing really well." Jopin directed the conversation to Bright-sunflower. "Have you seen Deer-tracker? He hasn't come here in a while. Could you get him for me?"

"No I can't. You've been acting kind of strange lately. I also want to see your head."

Jopin slowly removed his headgear.

Both of their mouths dropped open. The swelling was about the size of a small fist. The skin had stretched out so much, it had turned red, shiny, and appeared ready to burst like a large cyst.

Medicine-maker crossed his arms in front of his chest. "Why haven't you said anything? This should have been dealt with a long time ago."

"I didn't want to worry anyone."

"We're a lot more worried now. I'll have to do something to relieve the pressure."

He reached into his bag and pulled out a thin, pointed bone. "This will hurt, but I have to do this."

Jopin bowed his head. Shifting his weight made him moan.

"Just hold your head up straight."

Medicine-maker got a small woven cloth and gently placed it over the wound. He then slowly pushed the point into the wound. The pus shot out in between his fingers and past the cloth.

Jopin closed his eyes from the pain.

Medicine-maker applied pressure to the wound in an attempt to force out the pus. He had to poke the wound in a few more places to get the rest of the pus out. "I think that will do it. That should make you feel better."

Jopin didn't say anything at first, but continued to squeeze his eyes shut. Tears ran down his cheeks. "I feel better now. What a relief."

Medicine-maker addressed Bright-sunflower. "I'm really concerned that this may happen again."

"I'll wash it every day myself, especially now that there's no dirt flying around."

Looking at Jopin, "That's not the problem. The plug I made out of clay and bone hasn't grown into your skull. You'll have a big hole in your head, if I remove it."

"And if you don't?"

"It can become inflamed again." He scratched the top of his head. "Don't know which will be worse. You don't want to get hit there, so wear your headgear at all times."

The three of them sat quietly, looking at each other. Medicine-maker and Bright-sunflower had blank expressions on their faces. The pain had left Jopin. However, Bright-sunflower appeared to have now taken over his worries.

Medicine-maker asked Bright-sunflower to wash the pus off of Jopin's wound and apply salve on it. He then addressed Jopin. "I'll be coming back to check on you."

Word spread quickly about Jopin's condition. Chief Salamander announced they would not leave the campsite until Jopin had a full recovery.

Deer-tracker overheard Bright-sunflower and Jopin discussing Chief Salamander.

"Don't be so judgmental. He's only trying to help you."

"He's not," Jopin snapped back. "When has he come to check on me? Our fake chief wants everyone to see how sympathetic he is. We're supposed to be on a migration. Am I the only one who sees Father Sun spinning?"

"What? Why haven't you said anything?"

"Because I'm trying to stay out of his business. Besides, I don't want to be the only one who sees it. Don't say anything. That's the worse that could happen. I'm too old and in no condition to do Chief Salamander's job for him."

"You have definitely changed. I'm so proud of you. The only thing important to me is for you to get well."

"I want to get well for you and the kids."

Deer-tracker continued to observe his grandparents from a distance. Although old, the two of them portrayed quite a bit of affection for each other. Following the path set forth by Great Grandfather had blessed them with a long and satisfying life, the kind Deer-tracker would someday want for himself. His parents had hinted about a certain girl, the daughter of a distant friend of theirs. But that would never happen, not now that Tyuoni no longer existed. She would probably be traveling with her tribe to who knows where.

He couldn't stop thinking about the spinning sun. How could it be that his grandfather was the only one who could see it spinning? Deer-tracker would look up into Father Sun, but the intense brightness blinded him. He remembered how his grandpa had been blinded by Father Sun on the day Knee-nose appeared.

Jopin noticed Deer-tracker rubbing his eyes. "Your eyes look terrible. What's wrong? Did you get dirt in them?"

"I've been looking at Father Sun. Aren't we supposed to be following the spinning sun?"

Jopin couldn't believe what his grandson had just asked. There were a few hundred grownups, all of them, supposedly on the Great Migration, but not one of them had shown any interest in following the spinning sun, not even Chief Salamander. White-dove had brought Salamander a lot of joy. Everyone liked to hear the baby's chuckling laughter. However, the tribe had been wandering around in circles, enjoying the beautiful, abundant valley for the entire summer.

"The sun has burned your eyes. Cut a yucca root in half and hold each half against each eye. They will soon feel better." Jopin wondered if he should tell him about the spinning sun. "Wait until sunset, and then look at Father Sun after he goes down behind the mountain."

Deer-tracker had a big smile on his face. He now knew the secret.

Deer-tracker did see Father Sun spin at the end of every day when Father Sun started to go into Mother Earth. Was it because Father Sun was too bright to see during the day, or because Father Sun wanted them to follow him to the west, to an area behind the mountain?

Others soon noticed how Deer-tracker kept looking up at the sky. His friends asked him what he saw.

"Just looking to see if Father Sun has started to spin."

They also started to search the skies themselves and soon, many of the adults could be seen looking up at the sky. Chief Salamander became aware of the activity, so he gave Jopin a visit.

"What brings you to my camp, Chief?"

"I've come to see if you're ready to travel. Looks like you've got your entire family with you today."

"Not exactly, don't know where my married sons and their families might be."

Chief Salamander looked up to the sky. "As you can see, Father Sun has started to spin. It's time for us to go."

"I'm ready. Do you know where Father Sun wants us to go?"

"Well, right now, he's right above our heads, so I'm not sure. We'll go west, because that's where he goes."

"Sounds good. You follow Father Sun, and the rest of us will follow you."

Jopin surprised Chief Salamander by telling him exactly what he wanted to hear. Confident that all would go well, Chief Salamander announced the continuation of the migration. They would be leaving in the morning.

They didn't leave until the afternoon.

Some of the older ones, especially those from the Eagle Clan, delayed the process. They had been given the opportunity to bathe and thus, soothe their old bones in the steaming warm, spring water. They hadn't felt this good in years, so they weren't in any hurry to leave.

Chief Salamander proclaimed they would leave. "These old people don't realize they are delaying us. My warriors will pick them up and carry them out of here. We must continue on our migration."

Some of the people spoke up on behalf of the old ones and demanded empathy, just like Thunder-head and the others had been given the right to remain behind.

Chief Salamander tried to convince them that leaving would be for their own good. But it didn't take much for them to be mad at him. The more he argued, the greater the number of people who opposed him. They didn't want to hear about the snow that would soon be covering the area. He finally backed down, realizing he lacked the ability to persuade them.

Seventy seven people, consisting of the old, their families, and those who stood up against Chief Salamander, remained behind at the Land of Bubbling Springs. He was losing his influence.

The tribe slowly walked away from the Land of Bubbling Springs. They worked their way up the steep slope, and started to travel west, to unfamiliar territory. Chief Salamander feared he would no longer be able to guide his people through the wilderness. Father Sun should have started to show his intentions to Chief Salamander by now, but there were no signs. Chief Salamander would continue to read the faces of those whom he believed could see Father Sun, and act accordingly. But, he knew it would only be a matter of time before his people would figure out the truth about him.

However, luck continued to be on Chief Salamander's side. The mountain range continued to supply them with plenty of wildlife, water and vegetation.

Jopin carefully stepped over the rocks and debris to minimize the pain felt from each little bump on the path. They walked down a long steep canyon and set up camp near a clear running stream. Jopin started to walk off to explore the area.

Deer-tracker hurried to catch up to his grandpa.

"Are you following me?"

"I want to make sure you're safe."

"You're not responsible for this old man."

"Grandpa, I learn so much just by being with you. Please stop pushing me away."

The wound had been throbbing, so he knew his time would soon be coming. "Let's walk to this side. There's something very interesting here."

"What?"

"This."

"That's nothing but a hill with a lot of weeds on it. Let me go get my bow. This looks like a good place for rabbit."

"Not right now. Let's walk through here." Jopin approached a large rock. He closed his eyes and started to take deep breaths,

"Grandpa, are you feeling sick?"

"No. Come sit here next to me. This used to be an old village, the home of our ancient ones."

"How do you know?"

Jopin didn't answer. "Put your hand on this rock and do as I tell you. Close your eyes, take a deep breath, and then slowly let it out. Now as you let it out, I want you to imagine yourself going down into the first level of Mother Earth. So, take your time as you let out your breath to thank Mother Earth for allowing you into her first chamber. You must let all of the air out of your lungs. Are you in the first chamber?"

Deer-tracker nodded his head.

"Good. Now take another deep breath, and then slowly let it out. You will now enter thru the next level of Mother Earth. Once again, you must expel all of the air out of your lungs. Remember to thank Mother Earth for allowing you into the second chamber."

Jopin guided Deer-tracker down into the third and then, into the fourth level. "The fourth chamber is where everything is remembered, everything that has ever happened on Mother Earth. Are you in Chamber four?"

Deer-tracker nodded.

"Good." Jopin had him repeat a special, sacred prayer. "Now ask Mother Earth to give you knowledge about the rock."

Deer-tracker saw the rock protruding high above the ground level, about waist high. Noticing a vertical groove on the rock, he touched it with his fingers and followed it up to the top. A beautiful young girl, dressed in a white buckskin tunic, lay on top. A medicine man prayed over her. He stood at her head, held up a knife high above his head, closed his eyes, and then stabbed her on the chest. She had been sacrificed to the gods.

"Ouch, ouch, ouch!" Deer-tracker held on to his chest.

"It's all right." Jopin gently talked to Deer-tracker, trying not to disturb his vision. "Tell me what you learned."

Deer-tracker shouted out, "I died right here, in a previous life. I was a beautiful young girl, eight years old. The medicine man sacrificed me to the gods."

"Are you sure that's what happened?"

"Yes, Grandpa. I not only saw it, I felt it. I died right here."

Jopin closed his eyes, as if praying. He opened them, spotted some smaller stones, and started to turn them over.

"What are you doing Grandpa? Let me help you."

"I want to see what's under this flat rock."

Deer-tracker helped his grandpa move the rock aside. Jopin scratched the area underneath the rock, and exposed the blade of a large knife.

"Grandpa, how did you know that was there?"

Once again, Jopin never answered. "Here take this blade in your hand. Do what you did before and ask Mother Earth about the knife."

Deer-tracker closed his eyes and started to take deep breaths. He started to cry, threw the knife aside, and then took it and hid it under a rock.

"What are you doing?"

"I don't know. I may have sacrificed the girl."

"You can't be both the girl and the medicine man."

"Grandpa, I'm confused. I know I can't be both, but I felt as if I was sacrificed, and also, as if I'm the medicine man who killed her. I was her father! I killed my daughter!" Deer-tracker couldn't stop sobbing.

"I need to explain a few things to you. Mother Earth holds all memories in the fourth chamber. Emotions are the strongest memories. You picked up very strong emotions, those of the girl dying, and those of her father killing her. I picked up the memory of where the knife was buried."

"I picked up memories of a groove on the rock. Where is it?"

"You had your fingers here. Did you see blood running down the groove?"

"Grandpa, that girl could've been me, in a previous life."

"No she couldn't. We only live once. In the end, we must decide whether to go with Great Grandfather, or with the god of darkness, but not back to be born again."

Deer-tracker looked confused.

"Other people will tell you about their previous lives. But you now know the truth. You couldn't be both the father and the daughter, because both emotions happened at exactly the same time. But, you did experience both of their very strong emotions."

"I understand, Grandpa."

The experience had been more than Deer-tracker could ever have expected. Jopin hugged Deer-tracker as they walked back to the campsite.

"Thank you, Grandpa."

"You're welcome. Please don't tell anyone what we did today."

Deer-tracker nodded.

"What you learned today will help you on your vision quest."

"I don't know if I'll ever get to go on a quest, now that we're no longer at Tyuoni."

"You have to make it happen. Look for an opportunity, like when we stayed in the Land of Bubbling Waters for so many days. There'll be days when your papa's not hunting. You can even start fasting ahead of time. Get away and make it happen."

Deer-tracker couldn't believe his luck. Everything he had been hoping for had just happened.

Jopin felt satisfied, having had a good start in preparing one of his loved ones for his death.

Little-acorn had begun to feel uneasy around one of the promiscuous women. Sweet-peach had been nice enough to Little-acorn. She and Wild-flower would help Little-acorn with chores. Sweet-peach had even offered to babysit White-dove. However, Little-acorn didn't trust her. She decided to talk to Chief Salamander about her.

"I'm worried about Sweet-peach."

"Why? What has she done?"

"Nothing, really. It's the way she looks at you?"

"What do you mean?"

"She can't keep her eyes off of you. She follows you around, seeing every thing you do. She's interested in knowing who you talk to and what you're saying."

"What do you tell her?"

"We haven't talked about you. It's just a feeling I have." She became very quiet, wondering how to ask him. "Was Sweet-peach the woman with you at the top of the mountain that night?"

Chief Salamander moved in closer and covered her hands with his. "You saw how much trouble we had climbing up that canyon. I went up there, because I was worried about whether the disabled would make it to the top. But, an extreme sadness hit me when I made it to the top. I realized we would never see our beautiful canyon again. Everyone would abandon their homeland because of me. I sat on top of that rock at the edge of the canyon, questioning if I had made the right decision. It had nothing to do with Sweet-peach."

"Then why can't she keep her eyes off of you?"

"They all have their eyes on me. I'm their chief. Besides, haven't you noticed? I'm very handsome."

"That's not funny. To be honest, it's more about how you look at her."

"Now, that's not funny. I don't look at her."

"I know. You always turn away when you see her looking at you."

"I do? I hadn't been aware of it, but I don't need her or any other woman. You, White-dove, and my mother are the only females I need and love. I'm not worried about her, so you needn't worry about her either."

Special Purpose Bowls

Chief Salamander had planned to make it to lower ground before winter, but a snowstorm caught them by surprise. They had to stop walking and take cover under the trees. The men walked out into falling snow and started to set up camp. The day would soon be coming to an end, so they intended to handle the cold night under warm covers. Some of the children ran out to play in the snow. The older boys were sent to gather firewood.

But the clouds soon opened up, revealing a beautiful, blue sky. The people came out to see what the storm had brought them. The white snow had covered everything in the highlands. An infinite band of yellow grass could be seen at the lower elevations. Vast, grassy lowlands, which seemed to extend as far as the eyes could see, lay before them. Father Sun could be seen a little above a band of clouds on the horizon.

The view brought despair to Chief Salamander. He had successfully fooled his people into thinking they had been following the spinning sun. The mountains had given him the opportunity to lead them to an abundance of food and water. He had even fooled himself into believing he was their hero, a true, loving leader to the tribe.

The view made his people think of something else. For them, this moment marked the end of their trek through the mountains. The cold of the approaching winter had surprised them, but the reality of an unknown adventure across wide, open plains awaited them. It even shook their confidence. Sparsely populated shrubs and trees meant little water, and perhaps, no wildlife. Some of them questioned if Father Sun would lead them across the vast grasslands. They wondered why Chief Salamander had been the only one who could see Father Sun spinning.

The sunset turned out to be especially spectacular. Father Sun lowered himself behind the clouds, turning the sky into beautiful shades of orange. Rays of light streamed across the sky from different holes in the clouds. They stopped and then shot out from different areas of the clouds, as if the clouds were moving. But they weren't. Father Sun was the one moving, causing his rays to shine across the sky, at different times, and from many different areas of the clouds.

"Look, Father Sun is spinning." The people were in awe, excitedly telling each other to look at Father Sun.

Deer-tracker looked back to get a reaction from his grandpa. Jopin slowly bowed his head, giving Deer-tracker an affirming smile.

The entire tribe stood motionless and speechless, seeing the rays amazingly change color and position in a circular fashion. This event continued until darkness.

Chief Salamander felt relieved and took advantage of the situation. He would no longer have to live a lie about seeing Father Sun spin. His people would now be more willing to follow him, because they saw it with their very own eyes. From now on, finding food and water would be his biggest concern. Recognizing the opportunity to use the event to his advantage, he announced, "Father Sun spins when he's about to go behind the mountains, so that area, those mountains, must be where our new homeland awaits us."

They made it down the mountain and started to walk across the grassland. The open area allowed Deer-tracker to finally walk alongside Jopin.

"What's a happening, Grandpa?"

"You've been walking with us since we left Tyuoni. You know what's a happening. What's on your mind?"

Deer-tracker lowered his voice. "I need to talk to you."

Jopin motioned for them to walk away from the group. "What's wrong?" He motioned his intentions to Bright-sunflower.

"I've seen nothing but sadness since I saw that girl sacrificed."

"Of course you would. She had a very emotional death, and you felt all of it, as if you were the one being sacrificed. It'll take some time before you get over it."

"I'm not talking about the girl." Deer-tracker looked around to make sure no one could hear him. "I now see a lot of things in people, things they wouldn't want me to know. There is so much sadness. I even know what happened to Wild-flower when she was a little girl."

Jopin took a deep breath before deciding what to say. "You've been given the gift of knowledge. That's what's happening. I should've thought about how it would affect you before I led you into the depths of Mother Earth."

"I'm glad you did. My eyes have been opened to memories saved inside Mother Earth, memories that will be there forever. But I don't want to know about my friends' secrets."

"Believe me; I know exactly how you feel. Secrets are memories we don't want anyone else to know. Mother Earth keeps them in the fourth chamber, like all other secrets. I felt you were ready to be taken there, since you needed your questions answered. Perhaps I was wrong."

"No, Grandpa. I kept asking you to teach me."

"I knew there could be serious consequences. It will take a lot of maturity on your part, to carefully handle the gift you've been given. Your friends wouldn't want to be around you, if you knew about their secrets. I do understand. Sometimes, I consider it to be a curse, rather than a gift."

"What should I do?"

"You have to make the right decision, each and every time you receive knowledge about someone. Everything you do, everything you say, can have serious results. You must listen to what I have to tell you." Jopin put his hands on Deer-tracker's shoulders. "You must handle the information very wisely and cautiously. Most of the times, it may be better to say and do nothing. You must always understand that you cannot use any information you receive for your own selfish reasons."

"Like what?"

"Some men, who have been given the gift of knowledge, have used it to convince girls to have sex with them. A man with a gift will know what's important to a certain girl, so he will fool her into thinking he really cares for her."

"Some of the older boys talk about how they tell girls what they want to hear. Do they have the gift of knowledge?"

"They might just be too smart for their own good. You do understand that their behavior is bad?"

Deer-tracker nodded. "That's terrible. Don't they know sex outside of marriage is bad."

"This is much worse. Someone who uses the gift of knowledge to get his way with sex, or anything selfish, is evil. Great Grandfather hates evil." Jopin paused to get his thoughts together. He wanted to make sure Deer-tracker understood. "You already turned twelve, the age when most boys start to think about sex. Great Grandfather might never let you join him, if you use this new knowledge of yours for selfishness."

"I think I understand."

Jopin ruffled Deer-tracker's hair.

The grasslands hadn't turned out to be as flat as they had appeared from the top of the mountain. At first, the terrain consisted of rolling hills. Water tended to flow or settle at the bottom, where two or more hills met. Wildlife would assemble around the water, so all continued to be good. They did encounter some human footprints every now and then, so they knew they were not alone.

Jopin's headgear began to feel uncomfortable, applying pressure on his wound. He didn't want people staring at the swollen bump on top of his head, so he got into the habit of setting up camp away from the rest of the tribe. He could then remove his headgear and enjoy the convenience of not having that extra weight on his head.

Bright-sunflower likewise, could reminisce about the contents of her bowl without having to explain what was in it.

Deer-tracker discovered some hard, glossy rocks at their campsite, so he settled under a tree and started to chip away, replenishing his supply of arrowheads. He also planned to continue working on a pipe he had been making. His intent was to use it for ceremonial purposes, just like Jopin had used his at the Shrine of the Soaring Eagles.

His grandparents appeared to be enjoying themselves, eating freshly cooked venison, and talking about their latest experiences.

Deer-tracker thought about how, as old as his grandparents were, they had managed to successfully keep up with the rest of the tribe, even with his grandfather's health issue. They had climbed the steep path coming out of Tyuoni, walked over the mountain range, and now, had traveled across vast grasslands. Deer-tracker had been ready to help carry them, if necessary, but instead, his grandparents had been teaching him about dealing with life, mostly by example.

Bright-sunflower had been sitting on a large rock, running her hands over the coveted bowl. A stranger snuck up and grabbed hold of the bowl.

"Don't! That's mine. What are you doing?"

Deer-tracker heard his grandma screaming. He turned around to see a stranger pull it away from her. She reached to take it back, but he pushed her away. She fell backwards on the ground, hitting her head on some rocks which encircled the edge of the campfire.

Jopin stood up and grabbed the stranger from behind. A second man appeared. One side of his head had been shaved off. Long hair reached down past his shoulder on the other side. He grabbed Jopin with one arm, and struck him over his head with a club, with his other arm. Jopin's knees buckled as his body was thrust down to the ground.

"No," Deer-tracker yelled.

The man picked up his club and approached Deer-tracker.

Deer-tracker quickly raised his bow and shot an arrow, hitting the man in the throat. The man dropped his club, using both hands to grab the arrow, and yanked it out. Blood spurted from the wound, creating a red, spray-like pattern in the air. Deer-tracker grabbed another arrow, took aim, and shot again. The arrow sank deep into the man's chest. This time, the man fell backwards, on top of Jopin.

Great-hawk came running in disbelief.

"Papa, he's got Grandma's bowl."

Great-hawk ran after the thief.

The man hid behind a bush, and waited.

Great-hawk saw the club coming at his face. He ducked, and raised his arms up, just enough to stop the blow. The thief came closer, positioning himself to deliver the next blow, but Great-hawk rolled over. He picked up a stone, and threw it, hitting the thief between his eyes. The stranger reached for his knife. But Great-hawk already had his knife out. He grabbed the thief's head, pushed it over to one side, and slit his neck.

Deer-tracker knelt next to his grandpa. Jopin's head had been split open. His grandpa was dead. Deer-tracker stood up, pushed the dead man off his grandpa, and then started to kick him. "Why? I hate you. You killed my grandpa. I hate you."

Bright-sunflower gave off a faint moan. Deer-tracker stopped kicking the man, and rushed to help her. He moved her away from the fire, and then gently placed her head on his lap. He whispered in her ear. "Grandma, don't worry. I'll take care of you. Grandma, can you hear me?"

Brilliant-pebbles came running, and froze. "Deer-tracker, what happened?"

Deer-tracker started to cry.

Brilliant-pebbles saw her father's body on the ground. His head had been crushed open. She also saw the dead man with an arrow sticking out of him, and then, she saw her mother's limp body on Deer-tracker's lap. "Here, let me hold her," she said. "Wait." She walked over to the dead man and kicked him on the side of his ribs. She then sat next to Deer-tracker.

Deer-tracker gently placed his grandma in his mother's arms. Blood had covered Deer-tracker's lap.

"Go get Medicine-maker, hurry."

Great-hawk hurried back to return the bowl to Bright-sunflower. He stopped when he saw what had happened. Jopin was dead, and Bright-sunflower lay there, lifeless on Brilliant-pebble's lap. Brilliant-pebbles was sobbing.

Great-hawk fell to his knees. He gently pushed Bright-sunflower's hair aside, and kissed her forehead. He then put his arms around Brilliant-pebbles. They cried for Jopin and Bright-sunflower.

The tribe had gone through many challenges, but protecting from intruders hadn't even crossed their minds. But now, one of their own had been murdered, and another close to death. Chief Salamander sent his warriors to search the area around the camp. "Hunt down whoever else might still be out there."

The warriors later returned, reporting only two sets of footsteps had been found. The tribe would be safe for now. Chief Salamander still ordered the guards to watch over the tribe, especially during the night. He asked them to hide the two bodies and their belongings, in case their friends would come looking for them. The guards couldn't find the club, which had been used to kill Jopin. Deer-tracker told them he had thrown it in the fire. They retrieved the stone part of the maul, and then buried it.

People approached the area, but out of respect, kept their distance. Seeing Jopin and Bright-sunflower laying on the ground, saddened their hearts. It also made them fear for their own safety. How could something like this have happened? Jopin, the most respected man of the tribe, the living legend of Tyuoni who always had the right solution for them, had been murdered. Brilliant-pebbles, Great-hawk, and Deer-tracker sat there, devastated, waiting for Bright-sunflower to take her last breath. She was not going to make it.

The devastation overwhelmed them. Brilliant-pebbles asked Deer-tracker to bring her some water to wash and prepare Jopin's body for burial. Deer-tracker soon returned with a large bowlful. He placed it on a flat rock, next to the campfire.

Great-hawk and Brilliant-pebbles had already removed Jopin's tunic and placed his body on top of an elk skin. They used the water to cleanse away the dirt and dried blood.

Deer-tracker went to visit Flower-bird, the bowl maker. Her hands were coiling long, thin rods of clay into the shape of a large bowl. "I didn't know you worked at night," he said.

"I usually don't. This will be for your Grandpa." She stopped working long enough to look into his face. "I'm so sorry. A terrible thing has happened. Your grandpa will be missed by everyone. The whole tribe is in shock."

"Thank you. Could you paint the sign of the spinning sun on the bowl? Grandpa even had a hole cut on top of his head to ask the gods about the migration."

"I would be happy to do that. Your grandpa willingly took a chance with his life for the tribe. That's the least I could do. Anything else?"

"Not for Grandpa. For Grandma, can you paint a flowerbird on her bowl?"

"What? "Oh no, I'm so sorry. Your family must be devastated."

"Grandma's still alive, but who knows for how long. Medicine-maker said her brain has been punctured. She's not responding to anything."

"I know how to draw a flower bird, since I was named after them. Would that be OK?"

"Yes. She used to say she wanted to be a little bird, so she could fly away."

Deer-tracker had trouble swallowing the lump in his throat. "She will soon be flying away like that little bird."

"I can make her, her very own special bowl when the time comes. She might surprise all of us and recover."

"Her breathing is very shallow. Wouldn't it be easier to make two of them at the same time? I would gladly carry it with me, especially if she gets up and walks away from here."

"I don't think so. She wouldn't appreciate your carrying her burial bowl on the trip. I will make a bowl, but not break a hole in the bottom of it. We can always use it for something else."

"Thank you. We'll bury Grandpa tomorrow."

"His bowl will be ready tonight."

The campfires burned all night long. The people lined up to offer their condolences to Brilliant-pebbles, Great-hawk, and Deer-tracker. They prayed over Jopin and offered blessings to Bright-sunflower. They then returned to their campsites, where they sat around the fires, talking about the many things Jopin and Bright-sunflower had done for all of them. Jopin would certainly be missed. Many stories were shared about the good times they had with Jopin. Some of the stories were funny. Even Chief Salamander gave Jopin credit on how he had taught him everything he knew about being a good chief. They all recalled how Jopin and Knee-nose had sacrificed themselves for them. Their living legend now would become like all other legends, something that happened in the past.

Deer-tracker and his parents looked with dismay at the onset of dawn. The emergence of Father Sun would mark the beginning of Jopin's funeral. Great-hawk and Brilliant-pebbles had put a clean tunic on Jopin. They bent his body into the fetal position. Elders Pine-needle and Little-raccoon had worked through the night, digging the grave, mostly with their bare hands.

Father Sun rose. Chief Salamander appeared with four warrior guards to take Jopin's body. Brilliant-pebbles asked if they could have the service right there, near Bright-sunflower.

"Of course." Chief Salamander motioned for the guards to go call the people.

The entire tribe gathered around. Chief Salamander lit the sacred pipe, offered it up to Great Grandfather, and then blessed Jopin's body by blowing smoke on it. "Great Grandfather, we offer you your most precious and sacred son, Jopin. You will be pleased to welcome him back into your home. This most beautiful and sacred brother of ours has taught us so many things, especially how to sacrifice ourselves for each other. We now offer him back to you. The tribe of Tyuoni releases Jopin's soul, so he can go live with you and become a most gracious and loyal servant of yours."

People couldn't help but wonder if Bright-sunflower knew what had happened to Jopin. She had remained motionless and expressionless. It appeared she would soon be next.

Chief Salamander motioned for the warrior guards to take Jopin to the burial site.

"No. Please wait." Brilliant-pebbles hadn't realized it would be so difficult.

Great-hawk and Deer-tracker held her. "Mama, it will be all right. Grandpa will continue to live with Great Grandfather. We will see him again."

"I know, but it's so hard. I need a little more time with him."

Two warrior guards picked up Jopin by his arms. His body had become stiff, so he remained in the fetal position as they walked with him. Flower-bird met them at the graveside. She handed the bowl to Deer-tracker. Deer-tracker looked at the painting of the spinning sun at the bottom. Flower-bird had broken a small hole in the middle. Deer-tracker hugged her and then took the bowl to show it to Brilliant-pebbles and Great-hawk. "Grandpa sacrificed himself to determine if Father Sun would spin or not. Father Sun can now lead Grandpa's spirit through this hole, up into the skies, where Great Grandfather waits for him."

A deerskin had been laid at the bottom of the grave. The warrior guards placed Jopin's body on it, as if he were sitting up. Brilliant-pebbles handed Jopin's sacred pipe to Great-hawk. "This belongs to Papa."

Great-hawk jumped into the grave and placed the pipe across Jopin's lap. Deer-tracker then handed him the special bowl. Great-hawk carefully covered Jopin's head with it, making sure to line up the hole with the top of Jopin's skull. They then covered the body with the elk skin Jopin had layed on throughout the night.

The members of the tribe lined up for their moment of prayer at the grave. They each threw a handful of dirt on top of the body.

A feast followed. The women had started to cook early in the morning, so the meal would be ready immediately after the funeral. Deer-tracker was too sad to eat. Instead, he sat next to Bright-sunflower, gently touching her and whispering into her ear.

Chief Salamander announced they would continue to camp there for as long as needed. The warrior guards would continue to watch for any signs of intruders.

Bright-sunflower died in Deer-tracker's arms.

They washed and prepared her body. Campfires burned all night, and Bright-sunflower was buried next to Jopin on the following morning. Deer-tracker explained about the special bowl. "Grandma would joke about how she wanted to be a little bird, so she could fly away. Her spirit can now fly up through this hole to meet Great Grandfather and my grandpa."

Another feast was held in honor of Bright-sunflower. Brilliant-pebbles handed Deer-tracker a piece of meat. "Eat this. You must not get weak. I'm worried about you."

"I'm not hungry. I'll eat later."

Spotted Owl

Chief Salamander announced they would leave in the morning. The tribe had stayed four days at the campsite without any further encounters with strangers. However, it would only be a matter of time before friends of the two dead men would come looking for them.

Deer-tracker walked down to the creek to wash his hair. The water slowly moved over a layer of sand. He missed the stream at Tyuoni, especially the sound of the clear, cool water trickling over stones and pebbles.

Great-hawk had been looking for him, worried, because Deer-tracker hadn't eaten or drunk anything. "There you are. You're mother's worried about you."

Deer-tracker turned his face away from Great-hawk, and continued to wash his hair.

Great-hawk noticed tears running down Deer-tracker's cheeks. He put his hand on Deer-tracker's shoulder. "I also miss them. Life will never be the same."

Deer-tracker faced his father. "I miss them so much, but that's not why I'm crying."

Great-hawk remained quiet to allow Deer-tracker to talk.

"I killed a brother of mine." His upper lip started to tremble. "I tell myself I didn't mean to, but I wanted him dead, after what he had done to Grandpa."

"You had no choice. He would have killed you otherwise, just like he killed Grandpa."

"I know, but I also kicked him, even after he was already dead. I hated him for what he did, and now, I hate myself for what I did." Deer-tracker started to cry. "I'm doing a cleansing of the hair ceremony. I need to ask forgiveness for killing that brother of mine. I must release his spirit to Great Grandfather."

Great-hawk looked surprised. Deer-tracker had not only expressed sympathy for his enemy, he had also been deeply saddened for offending Great Grandfather. Deer-tracker had inherited so many good traits and qualities from Jopin. "I'm so proud of you, not only because of what you're doing, but because you have once again, taught me something." He looked up to the sky, as if in prayer, and then continued. "You know, I also killed a brother of mine for the first time, just like you, and for the same reasons, just like you."

Great-hawk knelt next to Deer-tracker and started to wash his own hair. "Great-grandfather, I come to you as a murderer. Please forgive me for taking the life of one of my brothers."

They both remained there for a good part of the afternoon. "Your mother says you haven't eaten for a few days. Let's go make her happy."

Deer-tracker froze. "Papa, I haven't eaten anything for four days, and I haven't drunk anything, not even water."

"Why?" Great-hawk stood back and waited for a response.

"Grandpa told me to look for an opportunity to go on my vision quest. I hadn't planned to not eat, but now would be an ideal time. I just cleansed myself, and I've denied myself of all food and water for four days, so I think I'm ready."

"It's very dangerous right now. Other strangers might be out there looking for their friends. You know what these men can do."

"I know. You and Mama would worry about lions or other wild animals, if I were to do it near Tyuoni. This place might also have lions."

"I don't know. Let's go talk to your mother."

"She won't let me go, not after what happened to Grandpa and Grandma. This is something I must do on my own."

"But you haven't had any training from your clan leader. When I did it, I knew exactly what prayers to say, what ceremonies to perform, and what to ask Great Grandfather. You're not ready."

"I am ready, Papa. Grandpa taught me. I've already killed a man. I must go on my vision quest, and I must go, now."

Great-hawk knew Deer-tracker had every right to demand this, yet there would probably be more men out there. Deer-tracker would be an easy target. They had just lost Jopin and Bright-sunflower to these people. How could he possibly allow Deer-tracker to go out to be slaughtered, as well? "No. Let's go see your mother."

Deer-tracker walked back with his father. Going on his vision quest had been part of his plans since before they left Tyuoni. He had never disobeyed his parents before, but he had no choice. Things could go wrong without his parents' blessings. Perhaps he could somehow convince his mother.

Brilliant-pebbles had just lost her father and mother. Her son now wanted to go out, unprotected and vulnerable to pray at the mountaintop. "Absolutely not."

"But Grandpa wanted me to do this. Don't you want me to please him?"

"That's not fair. He didn't know there would be people out there who want to kill you."

"Why would anyone want to kill me?"

"You killed one of them."

"They don't know he's dead. I think you're worried about nothing. Every boy goes on a vision quest. I've already prepared by fasting and purification. The only thing left is the vision quest. Papa can go and protect me from a distance, if that makes you feel better."

"What if they sneak up on your papa and kill him?"

This thought left Deer-tracker dumbfounded. He would never forgive himself if something were to happen to his papa. Yet, he had waited too long for this moment. "I won't stop fasting, even if you forbid me from going." He looked around in desperation. "I have no choice but to go on my vision quest, right here."

"What do you mean?"

"Here, on the hill behind our camp. Papa can help me get started, and then give me some time alone. The warrior guards protect that area. Don't they?"

Brilliant-pebbles raised her eyebrows at Great-hawk, seeking his opinion.

Great-hawk raised his head, smiled, and started to talk. "I can help Deer-tracker create a proper sacred area. The place must be properly marked, and offering poles set up."

Deer-tracker didn't know about offering poles. He had planned to walk up the highest hill, and then mark the place, as his grandpa had done at the Shrine of the Soaring Eagles. Realizing that his father could actually help and guide him through the process, Deer-tracker said, "I need you, Papa."

The camp had an overabundance of firewood, so Great-hawk decided to use some of the longer logs for offering poles. Great-hawk and Deer-tracker walked along the valley to collect sage and other cuttings. "We will carry all of these to the top of the hill, but first, we must have a blessing of the sacred pipe." They put all of the offering poles, sage, tobacco, and other objects in a pile.

Deer-tracker had already cleansed himself at the stream, but Great-hawk worried about what could go wrong. If performed incorrectly, Deer-tracker could become vulnerable to evil spirits. Serpents had been known to attack during ill prepared ceremonies.

"We must smoke the sacred tobacco and ask for protection. You will ask Great Grandfather and his gods for a gift, which must benefit all of your relatives, all living creatures. Your gift will be for everything on Mother Earth, not for you. Do you understand this?"

"Yes, Papa. Grandpa taught me about sacrificing for each other. Selfishness is bad."

Great-hawk filled the pipe with sacred tobacco and placed it on the ground in front of Deer-tracker. He raised his hands up to Great Grandfather and then to the four directions. "So you wish to gain knowledge from Great Grandfather?"

"Yes, Papa. I need your help and guidance. Please send your voice up to Great Spirit."

Great-hawk stood up and prayed to the skies. "You are so great and mighty. Everything on Mother Earth, everything above, and everything below exists because of your creation. To you, we are sending a voice. Deer-tracker will soon step on sacred ground. Please bless this young man, your son."

He then looked around and started to beg the gods. "Deer-tracker will be asking for a sacred relationship with all of you. Please help him, so he can live his life in a holy way. " He also asked all creatures to join Deer-tracker in offering the sacred pipe to Great Grandfather.

Great-hawk took the sacred pipe and lit it. He took four deep puffs and blew smoke on the pile of offering poles, sage, tobacco leaves, and a bear skin. He then handed the sacred pipe to Deer-tracker. "You must bless these items by blowing all of the smoke from this pipe on them. We don't want any bad spirits to hide in here."

It was time to carry everything up the hill. The smoke had made Deer-tracker dizzy. He carefully balanced himself as he carefully stepped into the cold creek. A serpent stuck his head out of the water. "Doesn't this water feel good on your feet? It would feel better in your belly."

A drink of water would be so refreshing, but Deer-tracker knew about temptations. "Get away from me. I will not drink or eat anything, until I hear from Great Grandfather." Deer-tracker looked at his father, who continued to walk alongside. He must not have noticed the serpent.

They reached the top, chose a spot, dug a hole for the center offering pole, and put a bed of sage down next to the pole. Great-hawk walked five spaces to the north and dug another hole. Deer-tracker walked ten spaces south and dug a hole for the south offering pole. The east and west offering poles would each be erected ten spaces away from the center. Tobacco leaves and sage cuttings were tied to the top of each offering pole.

Great-hawk lit a smudge stick and used the smoke of the sacred sage to bless each offering pole. "This will keep all evil spirits away." He then explained how to walk the sacred area.

Deer-tracker would start by offering a special prayer to Great Grandfather at the center pole. Holding his sacred pipe in front of him, he would walk west and offer the same prayer at the west offering pole. He would return to the center and offer the same prayer again, before continuing to the east offering pole, where he would offer up another prayer. He would walk in the form of a cross, north, south, east, or west, always stopping at the center.

"Great Grandfather exists at the center of everything. Every time you walk the cross, you will return to the center, to Great Grandfather. You will be asking Great Grandfather to be merciful to you and to your people. Ask him to give you a voice. Remember to also ask your winged brothers of the sky to help you, as well as from everything that grows on Mother Earth. Remember all of your relatives."

Deer-tracker walked his father back down the hill. "Thank you, Papa."

Great-hawk gave him some last minute instructions. "You must be poor in the things of the world, so remove everything, your moccasins and even your loincloth. Put the bear skin over your shoulders if it gets cold."

Deer-tracker left his clothes behind, and then slowly headed up the hill. Exhausted and dizzy, he could barely hold up the sacred pipe in front of him and walk at the same time. "Great Spirit, be merciful to me and to my people." He entered the sacred area, walked directly to the center pole, said a prayer, and then slowly walked west, holding his pipe in front of him. A spotted owl swooped down and started to land on the west offering pole. Two mice ran past his feet and hid under some rocks that held up the center pole.

Deer-tracker remembered what his grandfather had said about how witches could be owls. He waved his arms and scared the owl away. "Get away from me. I know what you are."

Deer-tracker prayed at the west pole, and then started to walk back to the center pole. "Great Spirit, I come to you begging for a voice." He stopped to look at the rocks where the two mice had hidden from the owl. Perhaps the owl had only been interested in chasing the mice.

Deer-tracker walked around the center pole, and then continued his walk towards the east. The owl returned and landed on the east offering pole.

"I told you to leave me alone."

"But I have a message for you. Let me talk."

"Go away. You're evil."

The owl flew up and then circled around Deer-tracker's head.

"What are you doing? Get away from here."

"Showing you how I'm not evil. Look at what I can do." The owl flew away and then back into the sacred area. "Can you see what I'm doing?"

"So what? Get away from me. You can't be in here."

"Why not? Look." The owl, once again flew away and then returned to the sacred area, encircling Deer-tracker's head. "Can you see what I'm doing?"

The sage and tobacco offerings had been tied to the poles to keep all evil away. "The blessing didn't work."

"It did work. I'm not evil. May I stop and talk to you?"

Deer-tracker didn't answer at first, rather he just stayed thinking. "Brother-owl, please stop and talk to me."

The owl landed on top of the east offering pole. "I'm not evil, just an old wise owl. Great Grandfather has a message for you. You will be given the gift of wisdom to help you handle the gift of knowledge which you have already been given. Use it wisely. Ha, ha." The owl flew away.

"Brother-owl, please come back. I have other questions."

Brother-owl continued to fly away. "Use your gift of wisdom."

Deer-tracker continued walking the path of the cross late into the night, begging Great Grandfather to give him a vision. Four days of fasting had taken a toll on him. Exhausted, he laid down on the bed of sage, and covered himself with the bear skin. Deer-tracker fell asleep, asking Great Grandfather to present him with his vision. His last words were, "What about my spiritual advisor?"

He did have a vision, one as real as life.

Knee-nose kept pushing on Deer-tracker's ribs, disturbing his sleep. Knee-nose ran around each offering pole, and then around the center pole, jumping over Deer-tracker each time. Deer-tracker grabbed hold of Knee-nose and kissed him on top of his head. There was no hole there. "Knee-nose, you're OK."

"Of course he's OK. So am I. See?" Jopin lowered his head to show Deer-tracker the top of his head. "It's me. What's a happening, Deer-tracker?"

"Grandpa, I didn't think I'd ever see you again." Deer-tracker held on to his grandpa, crying and sobbing. "I miss you so much."

Jopin put his arms around Deer-tracker, and kept running his hands through Deer-tracker's hair, putting Deer-tracker back to sleep. Deer-tracker couldn't have had a better vision.

Father Sun caused Deer-tracker to cover his eyes.

"Why is it so bright?" Deer-tracker looked around for Jopin and Knee-nose. "Grandpa, where are you? Grandpa."

"They went away with your vision." The spotted owl had returned to the center pole. "But don't worry. Jopin and Knee-nose have now become your spiritual advisors. So from now on, all you have to do is call on them. They will help you get through the various trials and challenges of your life. You now have them to walk with you along the path of life set forth by Great Grandfather."

"What about you? Will you also be my spiritual advisor?"

The owl flew up and circled around Deer-tracker. "Call me. I'll come running, I mean, flying."

Deer-tracker got up on his feet. He didn't want his experience to be over, so he once again, started walking the path of the cross, begging Great Grandfather to take him back into his vision.

But his mind had been filled with too many emotions. He couldn't calm down enough to receive a vision from Great Grandfather.

Deer-tracker walked down the hill, got dressed, and headed for his parents' campsite.

Chief Salamander had called for everyone to get ready to leave. Brilliant-pebbles started to pack their possessions. She picked up Bright-sunflower's special bowl and put it on her lap, wondering if she should open it. Her mother had been killed for this. There must be something very valuable in there.

She opened the lid and looked inside. Seeds. She spread its contents on her lap. Three peach pits, a few beans, some kernels of corn, squash seeds, etc. These might have been valuable, but surely, others would have packed seeds as well.

Brilliant-pebbles saw some things that looked like little white seeds. They weren't seeds, but baby teeth, probably those which came from Brilliant-pebbles and her brothers. That brought tears to her eyes. Her mother had been killed for these. "She couldn't give up her babies' teeth."

Deer-tracker and Great-hawk walked up. "What's a happening, Mama?" He noticed the tears. "What's wrong? Were you worried about me? I'm fine. No one bothered me."

"Come here. I have something to show you, Look. Grandma's bowl."

"What are those, seeds?"

"Yes, seeds and teeth."

"Teeth? Are those your teeth?"

"I believe so, mine and your uncles."

Great-hawk hugged Brilliant-pebbles. You were very important to her."

"I understand how she felt. I was really worried about both of you. Someone could have sneaked up on you."

"Papa didn't see anyone, not even me."

"What about you. Did you receive a vision?"

"Mama, I saw grandpa and Knee-nose. They are now my spiritual advisors. Grandpa held me and put me to sleep."

Great-hawk looked worried. "Are you sure you didn't have a dream, and not a vision?"

"Brother-owl appeared to me first. He told me Great Grandfather had given me the gift of wisdom. I then fell asleep. Knee-nose woke me up, and then Grandpa appeared."

"Son, that sure seems like a dream."

"But Papa, Brother-owl came to me again in the morning, after I had stood up. He told me Grandpa would now be my people spiritual advisor, and Knee-nose, my animal spiritual advisor."

"What about Brother-owl?"

"I asked him. He told me all I had to do was call him, and he would come." Great-hawk asked him if anything else had happened.

"I fell asleep, because I was so tired. Nothing else happened."

"It's obvious. Great Grandfather has given you the gift of wisdom. You will become a counselor to your people." He looked at the pot of food Brilliant-pebbles had prepared. "That smells really good. Let's hurry and thank Great Grandfather, so we can eat."

Great-hawk took the sacred pipe from Deer-tracker and lit it. He took four puffs, and then asked Deer-tracker to smoke the rest of the tobacco.

"Great Grandfather, you have been merciful to Deer-tracker by giving him the gift of wisdom. He is now ready to walk the sacred path of life which you have created. Please accept this pipe as appreciation and thankfulness for sending a voice to your people. You have set up a relationship with Deer-tracker. He can now bring new strength and wisdom to your people. Thank you for answering our prayers."

Chief Salamander sent word for everyone to get ready. Hungry, the two of them started to eat. Deer-tracker asked his parents not to tell anyone about his vision quest, especially the chief.

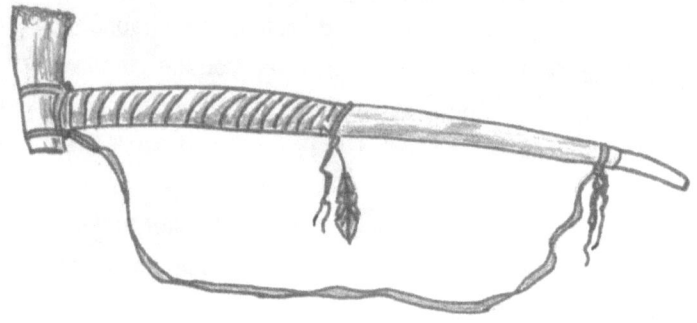

Peace Pipe

They finally left the area. The bodies of the two murderers had been well hidden, so Chief Salamander felt relieved and confident no one would come seeking revenge. His fears would be left behind. Even Jopin could no longer judge him. Chief Salamander always hated the way Jopin's eyes appeared to penetrate deep into his soul. The chief hadn't sought the advice of his elders since leaving Tyuoni. He, singlehandedly, made all decisions, shouting out orders. His tribesmen always obeyed, without complaining. He enjoyed the power it gave him. Jopin would not have approved of such behavior, but Chief Salamander liked it that way. He thought about what he had to go through, just to get Jopin and his friends to agree to the evacuation. All of his problems and concerns had been taken care of, but why was he still uneasy?

Life was good. Mother Earth continued to supply them with enough food and water to keep them traveling from day to day. They had been walking down a long canyon, headed towards a wooded area. Chief Salamander had learned to camp at, or near these low areas, where water could usually be found.

Each person had a specific duty. The men set up camp. The boys collected firewood, and the women would grind grass into flour in preparation for the meal. Chief Salamander no longer had the hunters go out ahead of the rest of the tribe to scout the area. The game usually came down to them, to the water, late in the evening, or early in the morning.

Deer-tracker and his friends explored the area, while collecting firewood. He found it interesting that the canyon seemed to end at a low point, where high grassy hills stood in front of them to their right, and to their left. They had picked a good place to spend the night. Everything would be directed to their campsite.

They had walked through quite a few fallen trees, so Deer-tracker decided to go back there for firewood. He spotted some men, quite a distance away, walking towards them. Deer-tracker climbed a tree to get a better look at them.

One of Deer-tracker's friends saw him peeking out of a limb. "What are you doing? Do you see a deer?"

"Be quiet. We're being followed."

The friend climbed up a fallen log to see for himself. "Who are they?"

One of the younger boys heard what they were talking about. The boy screamed and started to run back to camp. Deer-tracker and his friend had no choice but to also run back.

The strangers saw the boys running. They yelled and started to run after the boys, even though they were still far away.

The boys' parents started to scold them, telling them to be quiet.

"We're being attacked. A bunch of men are coming."

"Where?"

"Back there."

Chief Salamander looked around, wondering what to do. "Let's go up to the top of the hill, where we can better defend ourselves. We can throw rocks at them from above."

They started to run towards the hill in front of them, but then a line of men approached them from the crest above.

Chief Salamander ordered his tribe to change direction up the hill to their right, but strangers came rushing down that hill to intercept them. They would soon be surrounded.

"We must go back to the trees. Form a circle around the women and children! Pick up whatever you can use for a weapon, but wait for them to come close enough, before you throw anything at them." Chief Salamander had no choice. The men would soon be upon them.

The men stopped to study Chief Salamander and his people, to determine what they were going to do next.

This gave Chief Salamander a little more time to prepare his men for battle. His men were hunters and farmers, not warriors. Even in Tyuoni, his warrior guards just controlled visitors, coming in and out of the village. The only two men, who had ever engaged in battle, were probably Great-hawk and Deer-tracker, not more than ten days ago. They were not prepared for battle. "Form piles of rocks behind the trees. You can use the trees as shields, and throw rocks, spears, and arrows at them from behind the trees."

Deer-tracker was scared. Great Grandfather had given him the gift of wisdom, but a battle didn't seem like the place to use it. He wondered if these men could be seeking revenge for the two men they had murdered. Deer-tracker closed his eyes. "Great Grandfather, please help."

"Deer-tracker, Great Grandfather gave you two gifts, first the gift of knowledge, and then the gift of wisdom. Now is the time to use them."

Deer-tracker recognized that voice. It belonged to his grandfather, although it sounded muffled. "Grandpa, is that you? How do I use my gifts?"

"Knee-nose is also here. You should start by offering up prayers with your sacred pipe, the pipe of truth. The truth will set you free. Ask Mother Earth for knowledge."

Deer-tracker grabbed his sacred pipe, and started to count backwards, from four to one. "Mother Earth, please help me."

He expected to hear something, but nothing happened.

Jopin finally spoke again. "Deer-tracker, use your gift of knowledge."

"Where are you, Grandpa? I need you."

"You don't need me. Hold up your pipe, close your eyes, and ask for knowledge."

A vision of a big, black rock appeared. Deer-tracker asked for an answer, for knowledge, not for a rock. Frustrated, he opened his eyes, and looked around, wondering how to get Mother Earth to talk to him. That's when he spotted the rock he had seen in his vision. The huge rock stood out, almost at the top of the hill, beyond the area where Chief Salamander stood.

Chief Salamander saw him looking up. "Deer-tracker, stop standing around. Get your bow and arrows ready. I need your help."

The strangers started to come down again. Chief Salamander started to yell at everyone. "Get ready. They're coming."

Deer-tracker noticed something rubbing against his knee. Knee-nose jumped out ahead of him, as if asking Deer-tracker to follow him. Knee-nose walked around Chief Salamander and started to climb the hill. Deer-tracker snuck behind Chief Salamander, and then proceeded to follow Knee-nose.

Chief Salamander saw Deer-tracker walking towards the enemy. "Get back here. What are you doing? I order you to come back and fight."

Deer-tracker didn't care what his chief had to say.

However, he did hear his mother scream out. "Deer-tracker, come back. Great-hawk, go get him."

Deer-tracker turned to face his father. He held up his sacred pipe in front of him, letting Great-hawk know he had a plan.

Great-hawk wondered what Deer-tracker might be up to, but Deer-tracker seemed focused. It must have had something to do with the gift of wisdom Great Grandfather had just given him.

Deer-tracker then turned around, and continued to climb the hill, towards the enemy.

Chief Salamander jumped in front of Great-hawk. "Let him go."

"Get your hands off of me. I'll go after my son if I want to."

It's too late to save Deer-tracker. I need you."

"Get your hands off of me. I don't care what you need."

By that time, several of the men had circled Deer-tracker. They carried heavy clubs like the one used to murder his grandfather. The men escorted him up the hill towards the black rock. Deer-tracker continued to hold the sacred pipe in front of him.

The rest of the men continued to walk towards Chief Salamander and his tribe, completely surrounding them.

An old man stood on top of the big, black rock, waving for Deer-tracker to join him. Deer-tracker and his escorts walked behind the rock, and disappeared.

The old man came down from the rock. He stood with his legs spread apart, arms crossed in front of his chest.

Deer-tracker noticed the old man's long silvery hair. It hung down, almost to his waist, just like Jopin's.

The old man had his men search Deer-tracker. No weapons. He then motioned for Deer-tracker to join him at the campfire.

Not knowing what to say or do, Deer-tracker decided to introduce himself. "What's a happening? I'm Deer-tracker."

The old man smiled. "What do we have here? Are you the chief?"

"No. Chief Salamander is down there."

"Why would your chief send a boy to do his job?"

"He didn't send me. He wanted me to stay behind and fight."

"What kind of a chief is he? You're too young to fight."

"I've come to offer you the sacred pipe, the pipe of truth."

"How do you know about the pipe of truth?"

"Great Grandfather told me to bring it to the rock."

The old man looked long and hard at Deer-tracker, wondering what to do. What could this young boy have to do with him? "We better smoke the sacred pipe. I wouldn't want to disobey Great Grandfather."

Deer-tracker lifted the pipe up to the skies. "Great Grandfather, we will soon offer up this sacred pipe for all of the peoples of the world, the two legged, the four legged, for those living underground, and for the winged who fly above. Its sacred smoke will rise up and fill the skies, bringing peace to everything living on earth, below the earth, and also to those living in the skies above."

The old man wondered how this young boy could possibly know how to properly smoke the sacred pipe. He picked up a burning stick and handed it to Deer-tracker.

Deer-tracker took the burning stick in one hand, and handed the sacred pipe to the old man with the other. "It would be disrespectful for me to smoke from the sacred pipe before you."

The old man bowed his head in appreciation. Deer-tracker held up the flame for the old man.

The old man raised his eyes up to the skies. "I now light the sacred pipe of truth, which Great Grandfather sent us by way of White-buffalo-woman. Its sacred smoke will rise up and fill the skies, bringing peace to everything living on earth, below the earth, and also to those living in the skies above. All these creatures, plus the rocks, the trees, everything around us, will hear us, so we must tell the truth. Please guide us in this most important event." He took four puffs and then handed the pipe to Deer-tracker.

Deer-tracker took the pipe, repeated the prayer, took four puffs, and then handed the pipe back to the old man.

The old man asked Deer-tracker why he specifically asked Great Grandfather for the truth.

"My grandfather told me to do this."

"Why didn't he come here, instead of you?"

"My grandpa died, but Great Grandfather made him my spiritual advisor, just a few days ago, during my vision quest. I closed my eyes and asked Grandpa what to do when your men surrounded us. He told me to use the gift of knowledge and wisdom, which Great Grandfather had just given me at my vision quest. Grandpa told me that no matter what, to tell the truth." Deer-tracker stopped to think before continuing. "You look and act a lot like Grandpa. Can I ask you a question?"

The old man nodded.

"What's your name?"

"My name is Spotted-owl. I'm the chief."

Deer-tracker's mouth opened, showing his surprise.

"What's wrong? Was that also your grandpa's name?"

"No. My grandpa's name was Jopin."

"Jopin? That's a strange name."

"It was just a nickname."

"So why were you surprised when you heard my name?"

"Great Grandfather spoke to me in my vision, through a spotted owl. The spotted owl told me I would be wise like him."

Chief Spotted-owl smiled. He took four more puffs and handed the pipe back to Deer-tracker.

Deer-tracker took four puffs and then became serious. "Chief Spotted-owl, why did you have your men surround us? Are you going to kill us?" He then passed the pipe back to Chief Spotted-owl.

"It depends. I'm looking for my son. We followed his footsteps, but they ended at your camp, his and his friend's. Perhaps you saw him. He used to shave his head, but only on one side."

Deer-tracker quickly turned his face away. He had killed this man's son.

Chief Spotted-owl could tell Deer-tracker knew something about his son. He handed Deer-tracker the pipe. "Smoke from the pipe of truth, and then tell me what happened to my son."

Deer-tracker inhaled a large amount of smoke, deep into his lungs. Tears filled his eyes. Pretty soon, he couldn't stop from sobbing "I'm so sorry. I didn't mean to. I killed him. I killed your son."

This time, Chief Spotted-owl was the one who looked shocked. How could this boy have killed his son? His son had been trained to kill, to die in combat if necessary. This boy didn't appear to be the kind who could hurt anyone, much less kill. He studied Deer-tracker for a long time. Perhaps the chief had sent the boy to offer himself, like a human sacrifice, so that the tribe could be spared.

"It looks like your grandfather was correct about the truth. You will have to die, and in doing so, you spirit will be released." He studied Deer-tracker's face as he continued. "Your guilt will be erased from your soul."

Deer-tracker didn't show any expression.

"Did you also kill the other man?"

"No, my father killed him."

The response surprised Chief Spotted-owl. This boy didn't know how to lie. "Why would you turn in your father? Do you want me to kill him also?"

"No. My Papa is a good man. He led me on my vision quest. Papa will someday take me to visit the shrine of the twin lions. I don't want you to hurt him."

"Then why are you telling on your father?"

"We have smoked from the pipe of truth."

"Even if it means you have to die?"

Deer-tracker lowered his head. His heart was pounding. "Grandpa told me to be sure and tell the truth. I agree with you. I must pay for my sins."

Since you're so agreeable, can you tell me what happened? How did my son die? Remember, you have smoked from the pipe of truth."

Deer-tracker told about how they had just settled down, when the two men tried to take the special bowl away from his grandmother. Tears came to his eyes when he told about how Chief Spotted-owl's son split his grandfather's head open, killing him with one blow of the club. He cried again when he told about how he had shot two arrows into Chief Spotted-owl's son, and then sobbed uncontrollably, when he told about kicking his dead son.

This confession released the guilt he had been carrying. Deer-tracker would now be ready to die. However, seeing tears in Chief Spotted-owl's eyes brought back a different kind of guilt. Not only had he killed a man, he had deeply hurt Chief Spotted-owl as well. "I'm so sorry for all of the hurt I caused you and your family. My death will release my soul of my sin."

Chief Spotted-owl's bottom lip began to tremble. I must take my son's place, and ask forgiveness for killing your grandfather and grandmother. Please forgive him."

Deer-tracker stood up and hugged the chief. They both cried and comforted each other.

"What was your son's name?"

"Quick-raven. He used to be such a happy boy, chasing rabbits with his bow and arrows. He grew up to be a good hunter, and later, one of the best warriors of the tribe."

"That's why I had my bow with me. I was hunting rabbits for my grandpa and grandma, when your son and his friend jumped them."

Deer-tracker stopped talking, and looked up to the top of the rock. "Is that where you will sacrifice me?"

"That would be a good place. We can offer up your soul to the gods."

"What about my father? Will you also kill him?"

"I never liked my son's friend. Quick-raven became a different person, a trouble maker, when he was with this man, no longer the son I had raised." Chief Spotted-owl caught himself. He hadn't intended to let his true feelings be known. "However, your father did kill a man."

"Can't you let my sacrifice pay for Papa's sin, as well?"

Chief Spotted-owl approached Deer-tracker and shook his head. "It's time."

Deer-tracked looked up at the rock, wondering how it would feel to be sacrificed. He remembered his vision, when Mother Earth had given him the knowledge of what the young girl must have felt when sacrificed by the medicine man, on top of the ancient rock. Would Chief Spotted-owl also stab a knife into his chest?

Chief Spotted-owl put his hand on Deer-tracker's shoulder and looked into his eyes. "I've decided to let you go. My son had to be stopped from doing evil. You have brought me the truth. Your grandpa was right. The truth has set you free."

"What about my Papa?"

"We won't harm him, either. But I do have one more question. We saw the two graves, but I guess they belong to your grandpa and grandma. What happened to my son's body?"

Deer-tracker told him about how Chief Salamander had the bodies hidden.

Chief Spotted-owl remained quiet for some time. "I'll have to decide what to do about your chief. He hid my son's body and—" Chief Spotted-owl stopped talking. "Your chief is not a good man."

"That's what Grandpa used to say. Well, he didn't exactly say that, but I could tell from his actions. He didn't trust Chief Salamander."

Chief Spotted-owl held his chin between his thumb and forefinger. Deep in thought, he spoke softly but forcibly. "Go back and tell your chief I'm very upset with him. He must come and offer himself to me, here at the rock, before sunrise. We will not harm anyone, if he sacrifices himself for his people. My men will continue to surround the camp through the night until your chief comes up here. No one will be allowed to escape."

"Why will you punish our chief?"

"Can I trust you?"

"Yes."

"Your people deserve a better chief. I want them to know what kind of a person he is." He patted Deer-tracker's head as he sent him back. "Go. Don't tell him what I just said about him."

Follow the Spinning Sun

Chief Salamander grabbed Deer-tracker's arm and took him aside. "What did you see?"

"They wanted to know what happened to two of their men, the men who killed Grandpa and Grandma."

"That means they haven't found them. I hope you told him we didn't see them."

"They know we did. Their footprints were tracked to our camp, where they disappeared."

"I knew I should've gone up there myself, instead of allowing you to go."

Deer-tracker didn't know how to respond. Chief Spotted-owl didn't even know Chief Salamander personally, yet he knew him by his actions. Deer-tracker decided to tell him about Chief Spotted-owl's demands.

Chief Salamander raised his voice. "Why would that chief want to sacrifice me? You and your father are the ones who killed his son and friend. Didn't you tell him the truth? What exactly did you tell him about me? You blamed me for those murders, didn't you? You're just like your grandfather, always getting me into trouble."

The comment surprised Deer-tracker. "I told the truth. I would never lie."

Chief Salamander pointed his finger at Deer-tracker. "I want you to listen to what I have to say. You are not the chief, so you had no right to walk up there. We'll soon have a meeting to discuss what to do. If you disagree with anything I say, I will tell them how you lied to save your own neck. The entire tribe is now in danger because of you."

Chief Salamander called a meeting. "Deer-tracker has met with Chief Spotted-owl. Thanks to Deer-tracker, Chief Spotted-owl agreed to give us until tomorrow morning to prepare for battle. They will attack us at sunrise, so we must all work together to get ready."

They worked all night building barricades from fallen trees, making arrows and spears, collecting rocks, and positioning themselves for battle.

In the meantime, Deer-tracker talked to his parents about what really happened up on the hill. He then told about how Chief Salamander had threatened to call him a liar. "He even called me a troublemaker like Grandpa."

This angered Great-hawk. "The people are beginning to learn the truth about Salamander. Don't worry. He will meet with Chief Spotted-owl, even if we have to carry him up there." Great-hawk wasn't about to have the entire tribe killed, just because of their cowardly chief. Besides, if Chief Spotted-owl let Deer-tracker go, he probably would spare Chief Salamander's life, as well.

Morning came. Tired, hungry, and ill-prepared for battle, they fixed their eyes on the hills around them, looking for the first indication of an attack.

The men, with clubs, had moved in closer.

Chief Salamander ordered everyone to grab their weapons and take their positions. "We must defend ourselves and protect our families."

Great-hawk and another hunter approached Chief Salamander. "Chief, we're here to escort you up the hill."

"I'm not walking into any trap." Chief Salamander motioned for his warrior guards to help.

Seeing that the guards had grabbed hold of his father, Deer-tracker started to run up towards the huge rock.

Chief Salamander became furious. "Deer-tracker, come back. You and your father are traitors."

Deer-tracker looked back at Chief Salamander and motioned with his hand. "Come with me."

Chief Salamander froze.

Deer-tracker turned away and continued up the hill, walking right through the enemy line. Chief Spotted-owl signaled for Deer-tracker to join him on top of the huge rock. "I want you to see this."

"Our chief won't come. My father tried to bring Chief Salamander up here, but the warriors grabbed him.

"Look at this." Chief Spotted-owl pointed below to the camp. "They have tied your father and his friend to a tree. There's no way that your tribe can win. Your people are even fighting amongst themselves."

"Why are you going to hurt my family?"

No answer. "Watch." Chief Spotted-owl raised a long spear, with feathers tied to its tip, up towards the sky, and then slowly lowered it. His men started to holler and shout as they ran towards the camp."

Deer-tracker looked in shock. Chief Spotted-owl could not only keep an eye on Chief Salamander's every move, he controlled the battle from that very location. The weak points of Chief Salamander's defenses were obvious.

Deer-tracker grabbed Chief Spotted-owl's arm. "Why are you doing this?"

"What?"

"Hurting my family."

Chief Spotted-owl raised his spear back up to the sky. His men stopped, awaiting their next signal. "I'm not going to hurt anyone, well, not yet. I wanted to talk to your chief, but he's a coward. He doesn't know how foolish he is." Chief Spotted-owl pointed to one of the weak areas. "Look. My warriors are ready to enter your camp through there, and there, and there. I'll let your people go, because they are not to blame for what happened to my son. However, tell your chief what you have seen here. Tell him he must answer for what he has done. I will soon deal with him."

Although Deer-tracker felt relieved, he swallowed hard.

Chief Spotted-owl then grabbed Deer-tracker by the shoulder and swung him around to face him. "There's something I forgot to do yesterday." He looked up to the sky for a rather long moment, wiped the tears from his eyes, and then took a deep breath. "I forgive you for what you did to my son."

Deer-tracker fell to his knees. "I'm so sorry for the pain I have caused you and your family. Both my father and I conducted a washing of the hair ceremony, where we asked Great Grandfather for forgiveness, and to release your son's and his friend's spirits. Your forgiveness helps to release me of my guilt."

Chief Spotted-owl raised his spear up to the sky and turned it sideways. His men turned away from the camp and started to march away, back to where they had come from.

Chief Salamander's voice could be heard, proclaiming victory. "Congratulations men. You scared them away. They knew they wouldn't be able to break through our barriers."

The people shouted with joy. Some of them started to sing and dance.

Chief Spotted-owl hugged Deer-tracker. "Do you see how foolish your people are?"

"Yes."

"Please remain here for a while, so that you can observe and think about the things we have discussed. You have a very stupid and selfish chief. Don't forget to give your chief my message."

"I'll tell him."

Deer-tracker saw the warriors release his father. He stayed there until Chief Spotted-owl and his men were far away. A deer herd appeared over the crest, so he sneaked down to tell his father.

Great-hawk and the other hunters grabbed their spears and bows, and took off to hunt the herd.

Deer-tracker told Chief Salamander about what he had seen and about Chief Spotted-owl's message.

"Our people believe they scared the invaders away," Chief Salamander said matter of factly. "A positive attitude, such as this, will help your fellow tribesmen survive the rest of the journey. The truth will only hurt them. You can help them by keeping your mouth shut."

Chief Salamander had wanted them to get out of Chief Spotted-owl's territory as soon as possible, but they hadn't eaten for two days.

The hunters soon returned with enough meat for the tribe to feast on. They celebrated, ate, and relaxed before heading out of the area.

Chief Salamander never liked the way Jopin used to look at him. But now, Deer-tracker's eyes were the ones following him around. Chief Salamander couldn't stand to be around Deer-tracker's accusatory looks.

It wasn't too long before the grasslands dried out. Although winter had come, the desert presented them with very little water, not even in the form of rain or snow. Chief Salamander pressured his hunters, especially Great-hawk, to go find the deer. Sometimes they were lucky enough to kill a javelina or two, but no deer. The teenage boys caught a few rabbits now and then, so Chief Salamander started to demand more from them, as well.

Father Sun would travel across the sky, spin over a distant mountain, and then stop spinning as it traveled the rest of the way to the western horizon. But Chief Salamander no longer cared where Father Sun wanted them to go. He led the tribe all over the desert in a random fashion, searching for food and water, always looking behind his back to see if Chief Spotted-owl would sneak up on him. This behavior of his would obviously continue for who knows how long.

Deer-tracker, now responsible for having to help his father feed the tribe, walked away to be alone. He closed his eyes and started to pray. "Great Grandfather, I need your help. We don't have any water, much less, food. Even the rabbits are hard to find. What should I do?"

Jopin's muffled voice called out to him. "Go to Mother Earth. She will show you."

Deer-tracker yelled out, "Grandpa, is that you?"

No answer, but Deer-tracker knew it was.

Deer-tracker started to count backwards, from four to one. "Mother Earth, I need some information." His mind soon entered the lowest chamber, where he recited the sacred prayer Jopin had taught him.

Deer-tracker started to receive a vision. Knee-nose ran up a steep canyon near Tyuoni, jumped over two large, peculiar-looking stones, and then turned around to show Deer-tracker something. He put his nose to one of the stones, and then to the other. Each stone had been carved in the image of a lion.

Two lions jumped out of the stones. They ran, played, and chased each other. One of them found a small hole in the ground, where he quietly, but patiently, waited opposite a trail leading away from the small opening. A prairie dog stuck his head out of the hole. The lion quickly grabbed it with one of its paws. The other lion waited at another hole. He caught a snake coming out of that hole. Both lions proceeded to eat their meals.

Deer-tracker remembered what Jopin had told him about hunters. "They make the trip to the Shrine of the Stone Lions, at least once in their lifetimes, to ask the twin lions for help and advice."

Deer-tracker thanked the lions for the lesson. He now knew how to hunt in the desert.

He opened his eyes, saw the scorched land, and then looked up to the sky. "Great Grandfather, how do I find water in this place?"

Deer-tracker was given another vision. Jopin pointed at some birds flying, and then at animal trails. "Your animal brothers also need water. Follow them to their watering holes." Jopin then pointed to the area where a dry creek made a sharp turn. "Dig there. If the water's too deep, do this." Jopin cut a cactus in half, and then put his lips under the juices dripping out of it.

Deer-tracker took a moment to look up to the skies. He thanked Great Grandfather, Mother Earth, his grandpa, and Knee-nose for the knowledge they had given him.

Deer-tracker then walked to an area where prairie dogs made their homes. He patiently waited next to one of the holes. Deer-tracker grabbed a prairie dog by its neck, when it stuck his head out.

The prairie dog turned his neck around and bit Deer-tracker on his hand between his thumb and forefinger.

"Ouch! Ouch!"

"There you are. What are you doing with that prairie dog?" Great-hawk had been looking for Deer-tracker.

"I tried to grab him as he came out of his home, but he bit me and refused to let go."

"Why did you grab him?"

Deer-tracker told his father about his visions. "Knee-nose took me to the Shrine of the Twin Lions. Grandpa taught me how to hunt and find water in this place."

Great-hawk became excited. "We might get Chief Salamander off our backs if every man learns how to survive on small animals and cactus."

"Yeah, but we'll have everyone going around with bites on their hands."

Great-hawk laughed. He looked around, picked up a small branch, and broke pieces off of it to form a fork. "Not if they use this." He stabbed the ground to show Deer-tracker how they could use the fork instead of their hands.

Deer-tracker and Great-hawk taught their friends how to catch small animals and cut cactus to quench their thirst, as well as for food. "Great Grandfather supplies us with our needs. That's the purpose of the Great Migration, to depend more on Great Grandfather, and less on our own abilities." The entire tribe learned to eat whatever Mother Earth gave them at the time, such as prairie dogs, rats, birds, lizards, snakes, and certain insects.

Chief Salamander should have been grateful, since he was no longer pressured by the almost impossible task of finding enough food for his entire tribe. Instead, he became suspicious of Deer-tracker, not trusting anything about the twelve year-old boy.

Chief Salamander insisted the tribe must continue to search for water, regardless of its ability to survive by drinking from cactus. Father Sun could be seen spinning above a mountain to the west; but Chief Salamander led them to the north, where they would find plenty of water. After several days of traveling, they approached a large array of rugged hills. But unlike the past, these hills were barren of grass and water, as were the valleys.

The people complained, telling Chief Salamander they would no longer allow themselves to be led to nowhere.

Chief Salamander gave Deer-tracker another visit. "I want you to stay out of my business. What are you telling them?"

"Chief, I don't tell them anything about you."

Chief Salamander pointed his finger in front of Deer-tracker's face. "You little liar. You promised not to tell them what Chief Spotted-owl told you. Do you enjoy making me look bad?"

"You have to worry about Chief Spotted-owl, not me. I didn't tell them anything. But I also told you I would not lie. Why are you so insecure? Papa and Mama asked me what happened up there, so I told them." Deer-tracker suddenly stopped talking, as if something in Chief Salamander's face caught his attention.

"What are you looking at?"

Deer-tracker bit his lower lip, and then spoke up. "You and Sweet-peach on the bank of the big river."

Chief Salamander jerked back. His nostrils flared opened. The color of his skin darkened in anger. "What are you? Do you practice black magic?"

"No. Grandpa prayed for Mother Earth to grant me the gift of knowledge. She gives me such information when necessary. Mother Earth must have thought I had to see you and Sweet-peach. The rocks, the trees, and the grass saw and heard everything that happened. Mother Earth allowed me to see and hear what you have done. I don't enjoy knowing these things about you. Why would I wish you wrong?" Deer-tracker stopped talking long enough to gather his thoughts together, and then smiled. "I used my gift to stop Chief Spotted-owl from killing us."

Chief Salamander lowered his head and ran his fingers through his hair. This boy had the power to ruin him. All these years, he felt that being chief gave him the right to do anything he wanted. And, what his people didn't know wouldn't hurt them. He had successfully fooled them into thinking he was great, all of them, except for Jopin and Deer-tracker.

He now knew why Jopin always made him feel so uncomfortable. Jopin liked to offer advice, but Chief Salamander never wanted his opinions. Chief Salamander had welcomed Jopin's advice on how to become a good leader, at the beginning when he first took on the job of chief. But as time went by, Jopin's penetrating eyes did nothing more than make Chief Salamander feel guilty and inferior. He no longer liked to be around Jopin, nor did he want his advice.

Jopin knew exactly what kind of person Chief Salamander had become. Yet, Jopin still sacrificed himself by allowing a hole to be cut into his skull, saving Chief Salamander from the rebellious crowd. Chief Salamander took a deep breath, realizing he had intentionally betrayed the one person who had loved him like a son.

Chief Salamander needed to figure out what to do about Deer-tracker. Jopin knew about Chief Salamander's dirty little secrets. And now, Deer-tracker knows. All this time, Chief Salamander believed he had fooled his people. But if Jopin and Deer-tracker knew, others probably knew, as well. Worse, if ordinary men can find out what he has done, Great Grandfather surely must know everything. Great Grandfather and the gods would know his thoughts, emotions, and every desire. He couldn't hide anything from them. Chief Salamander began to feel so guilty and ashamed, simply useless and worthless.

"Please don't tell Little-acorn."

Deer-tracker remembered about using wisdom with his information. "I don't wish you any harm."

Chief Salamander slowly walked away as if he had been completely exposed.

Great-hawk had been watching from a distance, wondering if he should go help his son. "What did Chief Salamander want?"

"He wants me to get out of his business."

"Should I talk to him?"

"You don't have to. He'll never bother me again."

Great-hawk gave his son a proud smile. "In that case, I'll talk to my friends. It's time for us to get ourselves a new chief. Chief Salamander sure looked defeated."

But Great-hawk didn't have to talk to anyone.

Chief Salamander went straight to Little-acorn. "I have worried more about being a good chief to the tribe than being a good husband to you, and a good father to White-dove. It's time for me to tell them they will have to pick another chief. I know you won't mind. I must now concentrate on being what you and White-dove need me to be." The thought that Little-acorn would someday discover his infidelity, and that Chief Spotted-owl would be just one step behind him, would haunt him from now on.

Surprised, Little-acorn stood up to get a better look at him. "I don't mind at all." She decided not to ask him any questions. "You will make me very happy by doing that." She picked up White-dove and put her on his lap. "Your Papa loves you very much."

White-dove put her little fingers on his face.

Chief Salamander gently took White-dove's hands and put them on his lips as he kissed them. "Yes. Your Papa loves you very much." He turned to face Little-acorn. "I have made many mistakes. Please let me make it up to you. I intend to love and take care of both of you the way a good man should."

Although Little-acorn welcomed her husband's new attitude, she still appeared a little confused. "What will you do?"

"Take care of you and White-dove. Being chief is no longer my priority." Chief Salamander remembered the prediction Little-acorn had made about him not being the chief by the time they finished the migration. He didn't mind giving up his position as chief, but he certainly intended to work hard, even fight if necessary, to keep his family together.

"Who will take your place?"

"Any of the elders, I suppose. There are a lot of good men who could do the job well."

"What about someone like Great-hawk or even, Deer-tracker?"

He cringed at the thought of being replaced by a boy, especially that boy. "Deer-tracker is a special person, but he's still very young. However, Great-hawk might make a good chief."

"I don't really care who replaces you. I'm just happy you will be here with your family."

Chief Salamander called a meeting and announced his resignation.

Sure enough, the people started to talk about the possibility of Deer-tracker becoming their new chief. This boy had done more for them than any other person in the tribe, other than Jopin.

Great-hawk and Bright-sunflower decided to talk to Deer-tracker. "We hear that you're being considered for our new chief." Great-hawk put his hand on Deer-tracker's shoulder, and then continued. "This would make your mother and me very proud. They wouldn't be talking about our son becoming chief, if they didn't think of you as being very capable."

Deer-tracker took a while before responding. "Grandpa finally concluded that Tyuoni made a mistake when they asked Salamander to be their chief. It had something to do with a chief having to be the least of everyone. I believe Chief Salamander was only nineteen. Although the tribe thought he was ready, he wasn't. I'm much younger and certainly less ready than what he was." Deer-tracker looked at Great-hawk and smiled. "I was hoping they would ask you, Papa. You would be a good chief."

"Thanks, but they're talking about you. We just want to prepare you, in case they do ask you."

A group of elders approached them as they were still talking. "Great-hawk, may we have a few words with you?"

They had come to a decision. Although Great-hawk had never served as elder, they wanted him to be their new chief. Elder Pine-needle did the talking. "We want you to know how impressed we are with you and your family, especially the way you brought up Deer-tracker. You should know, many in the tribe wanted Deer-tracker to be the new chief. And the elders agree. Deer-tracker would be a good chief, but we decided he may still be too young."

"I disagree. Deer-tracker is more mature than many of us, including me. He saved us from Chief Spotted-owl's warriors, and he taught us how to survive in the desert."

"Believe me; we have already discussed Deer-tracker's traits. Some of the men worry he might become another Salamander, being that he is still so young. If you reject our offer, we will have to find another man."

"Let me talk to Brilliant-pebbles and Deer-tracker." Great-hawk looked worried. "I hope you didn't pick me, just because Deer-tracker may be too young. Deer-tracker spent a lot of time with Jopin. So, I'm sure Jopin had a lot to do with influencing Deer-tracker into the person he has become, maybe even more than I, because I was always away on a hunt. "

They talked to Great-hawk about how they wanted to, once again, make decisions as a council, in accordance to the ways set forth by Great Grandfather. "You, Great-hawk, have proven to be the least of your brothers."

Great-hawk agreed that they needed to work as a group, especially now, as they traveled across unknown and dangerous territory. "Great Grandfather must once again, be at the center of the decisions and actions made by the elders of the tribe. Father Sun will lead us to our new homeland, where we will have to build a new village."

Deer-tracker and Brilliant-pebbles watched from a distance, wondering if they were asking Great-hawk to be their new chief. Sure enough, Great-hawk announced what the meeting had been about. "They wanted Deer-tracker, but I think they decided to settle for second best because of Deer-tracker's age. I told them I had to check with the two of you."

Deer-tracker hugged Great-hawk. "It would be nice to be the son of the chief. I'm sure Grandpa is also excited." Brilliant-pebbles agreed.

Later in the day, Brilliant-pebbles looked up. "Father Sun only spins when he's above that mountain. Do you think Great Grandfather wants us to make that place our new home?"

"I might be chief, but I'll first have to check with Deer-tracker. I will then tell the elders and the rest of the tribe what my son thinks." Great-hawk laughed. "Great Grandfather and Mother Earth talk to him about such things. Deer-tracker will have to be my special advisor."

Brilliant-pebbles ruffled Deer-tracker's hair.

Deer-tracker became sentimental. "I was so sad when Knee-nose died, and then again, when Grandpa and Grandma were murdered. Grandpa had talked about how Great Grandfather will sometimes allow the souls of our ancestors to come back and help us. I'm so lucky that Great Grandfather made both Knee-nose and Grandpa my spiritual advisors. They will continue to help me whenever I need them. I wish Grandma could also be one of my spiritual advisors."

Jopin's spirit spoke to Deer-tracker. "Your grandma has become someone else's spiritual advisor, a woman from another tribe. But she wants you to do something for her. The north sides of the mountains remain damp for a longer part of the year than the other sides of the mountains. Plant your grandma's seeds, especially the peach seeds, on the north side of the mountain that Brilliant-pebbles just asked about. Plant them there, in honor of Bright-sunflower. This would make her very happy. And tell your new chief that your mama is right. You will soon arrive at your new homeland."

www.ingramcontent.com/pod-product-compliance
Lightning Source LLC
Chambersburg PA
CBHW020435030726
47495CB00006B/1821